The Sea Child

Linda Wilgus

SIMON & SCHUSTER

London · New York · Amsterdam/Antwerp · Sydney/Melbourne · Toronto · New Delhi

First published in the United States by Ballantine Books, an imprint of Random House,
a division of Penguin Random House LLC, New York, 2026

First published in Great Britain by Simon & Schuster UK Ltd, 2026
This paperback edition, 2026

1 3 5 7 9 10 8 6 4 2

Simon & Schuster UK Ltd,
7th Floor, 199 Bishopsgate, London EC2M 3TY

Simon & Schuster Australia, Sydney
Simon & Schuster India, New Delhi

www.simonandschuster.co.uk
www.simonandschuster.com.au
www.simonandschuster.co.in

The authorised representative in the EEA is Simon & Schuster Netherlands BV,
Herculesplein 96, 3584 AA Utrecht, Netherlands. info@simonandschuster.nl

Simon & Schuster strongly believes in freedom of expression and stands against
censorship in all its forms. For more information, visit BooksBelong.com

A CIP catalogue record for this book is available from the British Library

Paperback ISBN: 978-1-3985-3828-3
eBook ISBN: 978-1-3985-3826-9
Audio ISBN: 978-1-3985-3827-6

Typeset in the UK by M Rules
Printed and Bound in the UK using 100% Renewable Electricity
at CPI Group (UK) Ltd

Linda Wilgus grew up in the Netherlands in a house full of books and has lived in Italy, Belgium and the United States before settling in the UK. A graduate of the University of Amsterdam, she worked as a bookseller and a knitting pattern designer before becoming a full-time writer. Her short stories have been published in various literary magazines. Linda shares her home with her husband, three children and dog.

Praise for *The Sea Child*

'A stunning debut deliciously laced with
folklore, mystery and romance. I loved it'
Liz Fenwick, author of *The Cornish House*

'*The Sea Child* is an enchanting love story: the tension
between Isabel and Jack keeps me turning the pages, and
Linda's lyrical prose conjures an equally spellbinding setting'
Jane Yang, author of *The Lotus Shoes*

'Passion and adventure combine to make this
breathtaking debut a completely gripping read. The
freedom of the sea and the wild, mysterious beauty
of the Cornish coast provide a captivating backdrop,
as romantic as the story itself. Unputdownable!'
Fiona Valpy, author of *The Dark of the Moon*

'I absolutely LOVED it. Linda is such a wonderful
writer – the lush descriptions of Cornwall made me want
to be there. Her turn of phrase is so pitch perfect'
**Tracey Rees, author of *Amy Snow* and
*The House at Silvermoor***

'Steeped in pistols, smugglers and Cornish
myth, it is a wonderfully romantic story, and
I thoroughly enjoyed escaping into it'
Joanna Miller, author of *The Eights*

'Gentle and lyrical, yet laced with danger and adventure,
this captivating love story took my breath away'
Bex Hogan, author of *Nettle*

To Brandon, Noortje, Emma and Sebastian

CHAPTER ONE

Her arrival in the village is made of whispers. They start the moment she descends the two steps from the coach onto the dirt road. Two women stand in front of one of the thatched cottages built against the side of the cliff, their black, knitted shawls drawn tightly about their shoulders. The women aren't pointing, but their looks are. Isabel cannot hear them with the wind blowing, but she can tell that they're talking about her. Behind the window of the next cottage, a dirty strip of curtain moves against the breeze.

Her velvet pelisse isn't made for the sort of wind they have out here, but the chill she feels consists of more than that. *They know.* The thought comes into her head, or maybe it was there all along, muttering behind all the other thoughts she's had today, about the landscape, which is rough and beautiful, and the dreadful springs in the coach and the disapproval in the lean coachman's face when he stopped

1

to change horses in Helston. Despite drinking hardly anything during the ride she couldn't hold it any longer and the coachman said she took too long; he had letters to deliver.

They snaked their way up the cliff, the coachman, the Royal Mail guard and her, the road narrowing until she felt she was passing through the gut of the village. The high walls on either side of the road, covered in ivy, squeezed the coach until, suddenly, a gap opened up and through it she glimpsed the river, all dark diamonds, and the boats bobbing up and down on the swell. Flowers bordered the wall, hundreds of them.

The river isn't truly a river but rather a tongue of the Atlantic pressing deeply inland, fringed by piles of seaweed on the riverbank. There haven't been any other passengers since Truro. She has come to the end of the world.

The coachman moves fast now, unbuckling the straps around her case and heaving it from the coach. With a grunt, he places it on the road beside her, while the guard carries the box with letters into the inn. *The Shipwrights Arms*, it says on a sign dangling from a post by the door. The women are still whispering. A third woman comes walking up the road, some years younger. She's carrying a basket on her back, suspended from a leather strap around her hat, and an infant wrapped in a shawl on her front. This woman greets the other two and then she's staring, too. Even the infant, tucked so deep in the folds of the knitted cloth Isabel can only see its eyes and nose, appears to examine her, her case, the coach. *They know*, she thinks again. *They have had word.*

She closes her eyes, breathing deeply. The ribbon of her bonnet flits against her face, straining to loosen in the wind. She feels the weight of the women's stares press on her arms and burrow under her dress, under her chemise and her stays. The inn's walls used to be white. The building stoops, with a narrow doorway to the side the only apparent entrance. To the left of it is a flat, rocky expanse and across this she can see the river. The sight of it hits her, almost like a blow, every time she looks at it. The ocean is just around the corner. If the road made her doubt her reasons for coming, the river reassures her, in cool, glittering tones: *this is why you've come.* Her fears ebb away, replaced by a sense of calm. The sea has that effect on her – it always has. Losing George hasn't changed that.

She's being unreasonable, of course. These women – what are they, fishwives? – could not possibly know why she has left London. They won't have heard the rumours; they never will. She has left all that behind. They're only looking because she's a stranger.

The coachman tips his hat to her and mounts the box; the guard takes his seat at the back of the coach. A click of the tongue, a flick of the reins, and the coach turns effortlessly in the small space. Isabel watches it roll down the hill, feeling unaccountably alone. She waits until she can no longer hear the sound of hooves on the road, then she turns back to the inn.

Sensing the eyes of the women on her back, she goes to the door. The dark blue paint on it peels. Before she can go in, it opens inwards and a balding man ducks through the doorframe. When he unfolds himself, he's even taller than Isabel expected. Thin and as sharp-looking as the blade of a letter opener, he's taking her in with sage-green eyes tinged with the same curiosity as the staring women.

'Got yourself in a bit of a pickle with that case, haven't you?' the man says. The fingers of his left hand play with his apron, a rough-spun affair in a surprising shade of peach-pink. Isabel has to strain to understand the man; the intonation of the words is off and some of the vowels sound different.

'I beg your pardon?'

'Aren't you the lady come to live in the old pilchard shed?'

Now it's her turn to stare. 'I've come to take Trevernan Cottage. Not a ... a shed.'

The man laughs. 'It's the cottage by the shed. We call it the old pilchard shed – but what am I saying? I forget my manners.' He lifts his cap and, bowing, says, 'Allow me to introduce myself. Tom Holder, keeper of the Shipwrights Arms here.'

Isabel inclines her head. 'Mrs Isabel Henley.'

He looks around as if he expects George to pop up from behind one of the low walls around the houses. 'Of course. You're married. "Née Farnworth", it said on the paperwork, so Mrs Dowling said. We've had word of your coming. Mrs Dowling has talked of nothing else since she had confirmation of you taking the cottage.'

Isabel inspects her travel case. She shouldn't have brought

it. It's too unwieldy and far too heavy, yet it only holds a fraction of all the things she wanted to bring. The air has trouble going down her throat. It's difficult to swallow, too. This doesn't happen often, not anymore. 'Not married,' she says. 'Widowed.'

'I'm sorry to hear it.'

'It's fine. There are rather a few of us these days.' Her laugh is as light as it is hollow. She hates the pity that flashes across Tom Holder's face, the prick of the fishwives' eyes on her back.

'Don't mind them,' Tom Holder says. 'They like to talk.'

'It's because I'm a stranger here, isn't it?' she says.

He shakes his head. 'It's because you're not.' Glancing at the travel case, he says, gently, 'This is all you've brought?'

She meets his eyes and the understanding in them is like the tide, swelling high inside her. One more look like that and it's going to spill over. She swallows and swallows. 'My husband had some debts. The prize money . . . after his death, it wasn't forthcoming. Being mentioned in dispatches doesn't come with any monetary rewards, unfortunately.'

'Your husband was a sailor?' Tom Holder says.

'He was a midshipman on board HMS *Neptune*.' Her throat is so tight the words she pushes through it come out squeaky. Tom Holder looks like he's having trouble hearing them over the wind. He's leaning into her and she can smell his breath, which is sour. Her hand moves to her chest, where George's Trafalgar medal sits under the velvet of her pelisse, suspended from a black ribbon around her neck. Already, the ribbon is starting to fray at the edges. She'll have to save up to replace it. She has never had to save up for anything before.

She pushes her hand between the buttons of her pelisse. The silver of the medal is comfortingly unbending in her hand. This, at least, is something that will never change. She'll always have George's medal. If the silver tarnishes, she'll shine it, the way the maids used to. Glancing at the women by the house, Tom Holder says, 'It's all they can gossip about, you coming back here. All of the village has been talking since we heard the old pilchard shed – that is to say, Trevernan Cottage – was let to an Isabel, née Farnworth. But now you're here, the talk will die soon enough.'

One of the women has fetched a broom, but she isn't sweeping. Her dark eyes rest on Isabel while she says something to her companion.

Tom Holder says, 'You won't get far with that.' He indicates her travel case. 'Trevernan is about a mile outside the village, along the coastal path. I'll send my boy, Richard, to carry the case for you and show you the way. I'll send word to Mrs Dowling, too; she'll want to come meet you.'

'I don't wish to trouble you,' Isabel says. 'I did not realise – I assumed the cottage was here in the village. I'd be much obliged for your son's help.'

'It's no trouble, Mrs Henley. The boy's twelve and sturdy as they come.'

She's glad to leave the shawled women behind as she follows Richard around the end of the inlet, where the coastal path veers away from the road. The path is like a tunnel, green on every side. Above, too; the boughs of the trees touch in the middle. They remind Isabel of the arched roof of a church. It smells like spring, sweet and forest-like. The path is high enough she can't smell the seaweed, but she can hear the water and when she licks her lips, she can taste the salt.

Tom Holder's son, who looks closer to sixteen than twelve, doesn't say a word as he carries her case to Trevernan Cottage. Sweat drips down his forehead and after a while he stops and puts the case down to remove his jacket, which Isabel offers to carry.

The path climbs for a while and then, narrowing, moves down to the water. The river has swallowed up all the seaweed here. The water laps at the rocks. She wants to walk out to where the land turns away and the river becomes the ocean. She wants to see if the pebbly little waves are higher there. The desire is so strong, so sudden, it makes her suck in her breath and hold it. She doesn't just want to see the ocean; she wants to feel it, the way she used to long for George's arms around her – the way she still does, sometimes.

She drags her gaze away from the water. There's nobody about but her and Richard, the innkeeper's son. The green tunnel seems to be closing in on her. When she pictured the cottage, far, far away at the southern tip of Cornwall, she imagined it would be remote and isolated, but she never envisioned anywhere as lonely as this.

After some fifteen minutes, the dirt path opens onto a wider gravel path, which leads to a squat, stone cottage on one side and down to the water on the other. The sound of the river washes away her worries about taking the cottage sight unseen. She has to resist the urge to go right down to it and wade in. Growing up in Norfolk, she felt similar and even in town, she sensed a hint of the feeling whenever she was near the Thames. Only she has never felt the tug of the ocean as strongly as here, today.

'This here is the cottage.' Richard points superfluously, dragging her from her thoughts.

She turns away from the river. A small oak, still a sapling, grows by the side of the house, not far from the door. The grey of the slate roof is a shade darker than the walls, which are made of stones roughly cut into misshapen bricks. To the left of the cottage is a lower building with a roof made of thatch. Moss grows in the mortar between the stones.

'That's the old pilchard shed,' says Richard. 'It hasn't been used since old Nance died.'

The gravel path leads to the low front door. Richard says, 'The coastal path is used by the revenue men. You'll see them going by on patrol, looking for smugglers.'

'Are there many smugglers in these parts?'

Richard doesn't answer. The door makes a scraping noise on the doorstep when he pushes it open. Behind it lies a small, grey kitchen. Apart from a wooden table, two spindle-back chairs and the low wooden beams across the ceiling, everything in it is made of stone: the flagged floor, stone counter, stone sink, stone fireplace, with only a blackened metal rack for cooking. There isn't an open range like they had in the kitchen in Greenwich. It's like living in a cave, she thinks. Cold and dark like one, too.

A high step leads into the room. The single window is small and set far back in the wall, which is about a foot thick. The glass in the window is poor, painting everything the purply-grey of dusk. Richard sets her case down and she gives him a shilling, which, judging by the unguarded pleasure on his face, must be a lot. She chides herself inwardly: she must be better about these things. She has nothing to spare now.

'Mrs Dowling will come soon,' Richard says. He sounds as if he wishes to go but feels bad about leaving her. 'Will you manage until then, Mrs Henley?'

His father must have told him about her situation. She's not a child. Poor, yes, and that will take some getting used to, but she's not helpless – not entirely.

'Thank you,' she says. 'I believe I shall manage just fine. Please convey my gratitude to your father for his assistance.'

The boy says he will and bolts. The small kitchen sighs empty behind him. It smells musty and damp. Isabel tries to open the window, but it's stuck fast, so she opens the door again and then sits down on top of her case, her face in her hands. She knows she must get up and look at the rest of the cottage. She must unpack and learn how to do things, simple things, such as make a fire and cook food. But she's so weary from the journey she cannot contemplate anything other than sitting here. She feels as if she's in a trance, as if the events of the past months are a dream. As if she could look up and see George coming towards her, arms out, the years in-between erased by the sound of the river.

The wind has picked up and there are proper waves now; she can hear them. The rushing makes the longing in her rise again. If only it were a dream, if only she could wake up and start a new day at home in Greenwich.

At the crunch of steps on the gravel, she looks up. Mrs Dowling curtsies awkwardly and says, 'I received word from Mr Holder. It's an honour, Mrs Henley.'

She says, 'It's a pleasure,' though right now, nothing is.

'I shall show you the cottage,' Mrs Dowling says. She's not wearing a black shawl like the women in the village, but a navy blue one with a delicate knitted lace pattern. The wool looks fine and soft with wear. She has grey curls that try to get away from the handfuls of pins stuck in her hair. Conscious of it, Mrs Dowling keeps pushing the hair back from her face. The wind doesn't help, Isabel thinks.

Mrs Dowling is looking at her – *inspecting her*, Isabel thinks. Is she saying those things to herself that people used to say when they heard how she ended up the daughter of Admiral and Mrs Farnworth of Woodbury House? That with hair the colour of wet sand and eyes the grey of the Atlantic in winter, with freckles that congregate in such numbers on her arms and legs in summer they blend together to form an almost orange canvas, she looks like a child of the sea and not of the fair-skinned, dark-haired Mrs Farnworth?

Isabel's features are the opposite of her late mother's: her nose and mouth large, her eyes somewhat small, but still in proportion so that most consider her handsome, though it's generally accepted she doesn't possess anywhere near the level of beauty of Alice Farnworth.

Of course, Mrs Dowling cannot know these things. She didn't know Isabel's father; she can't compare her to him, nor did she know Isabel's mother, unless they met that one time, nineteen years ago. As far as she's aware, Mrs Dowling doesn't have any connections in London, nor in nearby Greenwich. She may be inspecting Isabel, but she cannot have heard the rumours – cannot find her *wanting*. Like the fishwives in the village, Mrs Dowling cannot possibly know the other reason Isabel has moved to Cornwall, besides her evident poverty.

Downstairs, there are only two rooms in the cottage: the small kitchen and a larger sitting room with a second stone fireplace, this one with a chimneypiece to match the wall, and two more spindle-back chairs. A stack of logs is piled on either side of the fireplace. The doors are so low even Isabel has to lower her head. A narrow set of open, wooden stairs leads from the sitting room to a small bedroom upstairs, under the rafters. 'It has a staircase,' Mrs Dowling says, as if this is some choice piece of fruit in a pie. 'You don't often see that in a cottage like this. Mostly, it's ladders, you see, if there's an upper floor at all. You'll find bed linens in the chest.'

'The privy is out the back. Just two steps into the garden,' Mrs Dowling says. Isabel expects cobwebs, dust, grime – Mrs Dowling says the cottage hasn't been lived in for three years – but the rough stone surfaces are spotless. She tries to picture going out to the privy at night. She wants to ask if there's a chamber pot or if she shall have to purchase one, but it seems a private sort of thing to enquire about, so instead she asks to be shown the garden. Mrs Dowling makes her way down the stairs and through the back door. There is a small shed which turns out to be the privy. A patch of grass, some shrubs, and a path which leads through them. 'Where does that go?' she asks.

'I'll show you.'

Mrs Dowling goes ahead on the path. It's shaded and overgrown. At the sunlit end of it, they step into something very different from the simple, dark cottage – something akin to paradise. Another patch of grass pushes up against a low wall of mossy grey flags, piled on top of one another in what seems to be a haphazard sort of fashion. The stones are covered in ivy and white and magenta-pink flowers. Bees flit among them. There are flat grey stones on the ground, too, forming a small terrace, with a wooden bench on it that's painted white and a square wooden table, also whitewashed. The paint is old and dry from the sun. In some places it's flaking, but something about this bench, about the fact that someone has taken the time to paint it, makes her ache with sudden feeling. She turns away from Mrs Dowling lest the landlady sees it in her face – raw, rising tears.

The terrace looks out across the river, which by now has turned a powdery blue in the sun. A plump apple tree spreads its branches across the bench. On a hot day there will be shade in the afternoon. The wind sweeps the water into tufts, like cream on a pudding, swaying the boats at anchor, and in the distance the headland on the other side lies in a green, still haze. Again she feels the sudden, heavy tug of desire, to go across the water and see the land on the other side; to find the open ocean, to swim in it. It flusters her and she's glad she's looking away from Mrs Dowling.

To the left of the patch of grass, half-hidden by an overgrown bush is a stone well. 'This here is the well,' Mrs Dowling says, following her gaze. 'It's deep enough that the water isn't brackish. You may want to clear some of this hawthorn.' A pause, then, a little uncertainly: 'I hope it's to your liking.'

Isabel is looking at the boats. They're painted black and green and white; some have white sails, others red. Gulls circle above them, squealing – they must be fishing boats, she thinks. Two of the boats fly a black flag with a white cross on it. She takes a deep breath, tasting the sea, salt and water, fish and seaweed. 'It's perfect,' she says.

Mrs Dowling says she's pleased to hear it. 'I'm on my own, too,' she says. 'My Harry died two years ago.'

There's something distasteful about the way she says, 'my Harry', Isabel thinks. She could never imagine calling George 'my George', as if he belonged to her. As if anybody could belong to another person. Mrs Dowling is older than her father would've been, had he still been alive. Does she think that because they are both widows, they have something in common?

'Should you like to come visit sometime?' Mrs Dowling says, as if this is a logical conclusion following the declaration that she, too, is on her own. Isabel suppresses a sigh – there's a difference in rank. Then she catches herself: there isn't any difference anymore. She's as poor as Mrs Dowling. Poorer, because Mrs Dowling owns Trevernan Cottage and on her widow's pension, Isabel can only afford to rent it.

She finds herself saying she'd be much obliged. It isn't what she wanted to say. Not because of any lingering difference in standing between them, but because she intends to keep to herself. She hasn't come here to make friends. She has come to get away from Greenwich, from the shame of her reduction in station and the turning of the rumour mill. From George, too – from her memories of him. Because staying right on top of them cuts into her a hundred times a day, still.

Three years have passed since the great Battle of Trafalgar and it has hardly got any better. Their marriage lasted three years, too, before a bullet from a French musket ended it. She was only seventeen, George eighteen, when they wed, and he was always at sea. In the years that followed, she felt the absence of him all the more sharply for the knowledge that this time, he would not return to her. In Greenwich, taking her tea alone in the breakfast room left her feeling hollow. So did every walk in the park without him and the Sunday mornings in church, the place in the pew beside her empty. Evenings grew long knowing he would not come in after a summoning to the Admiralty or a meeting with a friend;

knowing her bed would be cold and that there would be no more letters. In the three years of their marriage, they spent only five weeks and one day together. That's why it still hurts now, more than anything, because George was taken from her before any of it became real.

Mrs Dowling goes ahead down the path. Back in the sitting room, she says, 'I've laid a fire for you.' There are several logs stacked in the hearth, with twigs underneath. 'I was surprised you instructed me not to arrange for any servants. Not even a cook or a scullery maid. Will you be looking to hire anyone now that you're here?'

The heat swarms in her cheeks. 'I'm afraid my current situation requires that I do without the assistance I'm accustomed to. I can only hope I'm a quick study when it comes to household tasks.'

She feels the older woman's gaze on her. Then, to her relief, Mrs Dowling says only, 'It's not usually this cold in April. Shall I show you how to light the fire?'

Isabel says she'd be very grateful and Mrs Dowling gets the tinderbox from the chimneypiece and shows her how to strike the steel on the flint, how to light the char-cloth and with it, the match to light the fire. 'You'll want to close the box quickly or you'll lose half your tinder,' Mrs Dowling says. 'Here, you try it.'

Isabel removes her gloves and takes the box. It takes her five attempts to light the fire. At last, the twigs catch flame and the logs begin to smoulder. Isabel cups her hands and blows, carefully, the way Mrs Dowling tells her to, and watches the glow spread. She only just stops herself crying out in triumph.

Mrs Dowling says, 'There are some candles in the larder as well as butter, eggs, bread, a jug of milk and a little tea.' She adds in a meaningful tone, 'We get tea at very good prices here. I shall tell you about it when you're ready to purchase some yourself. The nearest shop is in Manaccan, but then you know that; you wrote to Mr Griggs.'

Isabel found Mr Griggs' name in a local newspaper, especially brought to her for the purpose, and wrote him to enquire if he knew anyone letting a cottage in the area, preferably in the village of Helford. If she had to go somewhere to disappear, she figured she may as well go to the place she was found and perhaps learn what happened that day. Mr Griggs wrote back within the week; less than two weeks later, she boarded the mail coach.

Mrs Dowling continues, 'There's a market twice a week outside the Shipwright Arms, on the Tuesday and Saturday morning, which will have most everything you might need. Bread's to be got from John Lanyon, the baker, if you don't make it yourself; fish every day when the catch is brought in, and for meats you'll want to speak to Josh Angove at Elm Farm.'

'Thank you very much. How much do I owe you for the food and candles?'

'Nothing at all, Mrs Henley. You'll find we take care of our own here. If you need help with anything, you know where to find me. Please knock whenever you like.'

'Thank you,' she says again. 'I'm sure I'll be fine.'

Mrs Dowling adjusts a hairpin. She's on the doorstep, but she's not going, not yet. Her eyes glide over Isabel's face, up over her hairline, and come to rest on some indeterminable point above her. 'I saw you that day,' Mrs Dowling says. 'I saw you when you first came out. I was standing at the window and I saw you come up the road. You were barefoot and very small. Small for your age – that's what we all said later; the girl was small for her age. You wore only a shift, though they say it was of the finest cotton. Your hair was darker than it is now.'

She reaches out, almost reverently, and Isabel takes a step back too late: Mrs Dowling's dry finger runs along her forehead. 'It must've been darker because it was wet. Mind you, I couldn't see you were wet from where I stood. I thought about going out to you, but I told myself you had to be someone's child. You must've wandered into the garden at Hardwick soon after.' A pause. 'Maybe if I'd known you were soaked to the bone, I would've gone out to meet you.'

There's a strange undercurrent to the woman's words, Isabel thinks. All of a sudden, she feels as if it's not widowhood that binds the two of them together in Mrs Dowling's mind, but this: the possibility that she might have been Mrs Dowling's daughter, if only Mrs Dowling had gone out to her that day, nineteen years ago. Preposterous idea, of course. She can't imagine being anybody but her mother and father's child.

She cannot remember anything from before that moment,

when her mother swept her up into her arms, not caring that she was cold and wet through, and she, Isabel, buried her face into the silk of her mother's dress. It's as if the start of her life never happened; she was always meant to be theirs.

Isabel's tongue takes a cough to pry loose. 'Came out of what?' she says.

'I beg your pardon, Mrs Henley?'

'You said you saw me when I first came out.'

'Why, out of the sea, of course. Mind you, not everybody believes it, that the Sea Bucca brought you.'

'Sea Bucca?' Her voice does an odd thing, rising and falling on the words as if she's singing. There's a whooshing in her ears. She can tell Mrs Dowling is serious, deadly so. She must be mad. 'What—'

Sensing her consternation, Mrs Dowling pats her arm. 'You didn't speak a word of English, did you?'

'That can't be right. My parents never mentioned it.'

Mrs Dowling says, 'You didn't speak at all, that's what they say. Of course you wouldn't have, what with the Bucca.' Sounding exasperated, she adds, 'You don't know about the Sea Bucca, do you? He's a merman about this high,' she holds up her hand just below her waist, 'with the skin of a conger eel and seaweed for hair. Well, that's what some say; I myself prefer a more romantic picture.' Her smile has something of a little girl's, the way her laughter did earlier, but she vanquishes the effect with her next words. Fixing her milky blue eyes on Isabel, Mrs Dowling says, 'Some say you are his daughter.'

Tersely, she says, 'My mother told me there must've been a wreck. Or perhaps I'd wandered off; perhaps somebody didn't pay attention when they should have.' An accusation lay in her mother's words. Alice Farnworth knew she would never have let her attention slip from her child, if the Good Lord had seen fit to bless her with one of her own. She called Isabel a gift so often that Isabel felt her shortcomings all the more.

Mrs Dowling says, 'Perhaps your mother tried to protect you from the truth. Word has it she couldn't leave Helford fast enough once she found you.'

Ice, sliding down her spine. People have been talking about her here, too, just as they have in Greenwich, albeit for different reasons. They've been talking about her for almost twenty years. She staggers back into the cottage. She wants to say, *that's outrageous* and, *how dare you speak of my mother like that*. But in the end she only says, 'If you'll excuse me, I really must unpack.'

'Of course. Please let me know if there's anything else you need.' Mrs Dowling says it in the most normal of tones, as if they haven't just been discussing mermaids.

When she shuts the door behind her, Isabel sees there's a gap under it on one side while the other is so flush with the doorstep it scrapes whenever the door moves. She waits a few minutes and opens the door again. The gravel path is empty. The fresh sea-river air pushes in, inhabiting the rooms, forcing out the musty old house smell. She's on her own and it doesn't hurt – yet. Maybe it's the newness of the situation that's keeping her. Maybe it's the sea. She can hear it through the open window, not the rush of the surf breaking on rocks or the crash of waves, but a constant quiet lapping. There's a comfort in it, she thinks. And a promise, maybe, though of what she doesn't know.

She finds a knife in a wooden box on the counter and a plate in one of the cupboards and, sitting by the fire, she eats a slice of bread with butter for an early supper. The bread is coarse, but it has a good, strong flavour, as if some herbs were used in the baking. The glow of the fire spreads inside her. She lit it herself – that's something, isn't it?

Halfway through the meal, she realises she shouldn't have used as much butter. When she has finished, she puts the plate on the stone counter. She should wash it, but she's too tired to get water from the well. Instead, she opens her travel case and gets out her worn copy of *Robinson Crusoe*. The book falls open on the page she keeps the newspaper clipping from *The London Chronicle*, 20 October 1789. Her mother kept the entire paper, most of which was filled with news from France, where the Revolution had begun three months before, but Isabel cut out the one small article which read:

Falmouth, Cornwall. **A CHILD APPROXIMATELY FOUR YEARS OF AGE WAS FOUND** on the wild and beauteous Coast of Cornwall late last month without any Family to claim it. The populace believes the Child to have Risen from the Sea after a Wreck, although there has been no report of such. Unless a Relation comes forward the Child shall be adopted by Admiral and Mrs Farnworth of Woodbury House, Norfolk and raised as their Daughter. If anyone has any information regarding this Child, please write to Messrs Enright and Pickering, Solicitors, Mayfair, London.

The unease grows in her again until it roars. Mrs Dowling's story about the merman fuels it, as does the knowledge that even here people have been talking about her. Why was Mrs Dowling so interested in her past? Does she suspect something? *Impossible*, she tells herself.

Her nerves disagree, jittering under her skin. Clipping in hand, she goes to the door and opens it wide. It's growing dark outside. The wind pushes against the door, the young tree next to it sways. Down the gravel path, the river dances in the last of the sun. A reminder that she's close to the sea – so close. Breathing deeply, she tastes it: salt, water, the tang of wet seaweed. Gradually, a quietude envelops her, made of waves and foam, ebb and flow, the current steadying her. By the time she closes the door again, a renewed sense of purpose courses through her. She's going to make this her home, come what may.

CHAPTER TWO

In bed that night, she listens to the river and the wind crashing about the cottage. She's all alone. She cannot think of it. She's not alone – the wind is made of voices. They're calling, *come home.* The sea lies just around the bend in the river. She's dreaming, of course. Or half-dreaming, hovering in the fuzzy state between sleep and waking, in which her mind jumps from one thing to another, forging connections that cannot be real.

A creaking sound rouses her. The house groans in unexpected places; there is a sound like feet on the roof. The bed is hard and built for two. The mattress is filled with straw that pricks her back, but the sheets are clean. Who lived here before her? Mrs Dowling said the cottage was empty for three years. It must've been an old man and his wife, she thinks. Did they die in the bed?

The sea–river is louder at night, the waves from earlier

grown into maturity. The sound soothes her and eventually her mind wanders, the way it does when she balances on the edge of sleep: the house in Greenwich, her parents, George and her after the wedding, during the two days they had before he went back to sea. They were too young, George's older brother said. There would be plenty of time after the war. Only there wasn't.

The morning comes with heavy rain. The tide is out; the inlet has turned into a swathe of seaweed and rocks. The wind sweeps the rain against the windows in sheets. The sky is low over the river. They're both grey, the water a stony grey and the sky the grey of overly washed cotton. Braving the rain, she puts on her pelisse and stands in the paradise garden, watching the water rise and fall in the wind. She isn't sure what she is meant to be doing. *Is this how people live?* she thinks. *Is this what it's like when you're well and truly on your own?*

Back in the cottage, she puts some kindling in the fireplace. She goes through the motions Mrs Dowling showed her; striking the flint, using the cloth for tinder, but the fire won't catch. Half the tinder gone, she's nearly crying with frustration, when suddenly the flame jumps. Now she could cry with relief. There's too much feeling in her since she arrived; everything makes her want to weep.

Around noon, there's a knock on the door. Could it be Mrs Dowling again? She doesn't know anyone else in the village, apart from the innkeeper and his son and they have no reason to call on her. When she opens the door, she's surprised to see the red shirt and blue pantaloons of an officer of the Revenue Service. Above the stiff cotton necktie, the man's face reminds her of the moon; it's pale and round, and there's something mournful about the way his eyes droop at the corners. He looks perhaps ten years older than her.

The man removes his hat, bows deeply and says, 'Lieutenant Arthur Sowerby, Riding Officer of the Revenue Service, at your service, madam,' as if he cannot see the squalid cottage, as if it's entirely usual for her to answer the door herself.

'Mrs Henley. Most charmed.' She curtseys, and, to her shock, he reaches for her hand and presses his lips to it. The touch of them is cold. Rain drips from his reddish–blond curls, trailing down his cheeks and into the collar of his shirt. Somewhere outside, a horse snorts. She says, 'But you must step out of this rain, lieutenant.'

She moves aside and he folds himself through the door, saying, 'Thank you, madam. I'm most obliged.' His size belies the gracefulness of his movements: he walks as if he's dancing. By the kitchen table, he stops and turns. 'I've come to call on you, madam, to warn you.'

'Warn me? Whatever for?' Her voice is oddly loud. It doesn't belong in the cottage; it needs more space.

'I understand you live here alone?'

'My, how news travels.'

'I'm based in St Keverne. It's only five miles from here.

We've had word of your coming. I believe the wife of my most particular friend the Deputy Lord Lieutenant, Sir Hugh Darby, intends to call on you soon. Lady Darby is keen to make your acquaintance, as am I. As you may be aware, there aren't many people of our standing in the area.'

She'd like to offer him tea but isn't sure how to make it. She has no other drinks to offer, either. Heat rising, she reaches for the medal around her neck. The length of the ribbon she wears it on places it close to her heart. 'As you can see, I'm much reduced in circumstance, Lieutenant.'

Lieutenant Sowerby has the decency to pretend he only now notices. 'I see. Even so. I feel it is my duty to warn you, madam, that these parts are rife with smugglers. As a woman living alone, you're particularly vulnerable. I would advise you to lock your doors and windows at night.'

Isabel glances at the door behind her. There's no lock.

'Or have a lock fitted,' Lieutenant Sowerby says. 'For the safety of your person and your possessions. If anything is ever amiss, please let me know at once. I'd be honoured to come to your aid, should you need it.'

He sounds terribly officious. Looks it, too, with his shoulders squared and his chin sticking up like that. The kitchen is too small; he's towering over her. She takes a step back, but he follows her, dance-stepping closer. His voice drops when he says, 'You are a widow, are you not?'

'I am.' Her hand clasps the Trafalgar medal. The ridges of Admiral Nelson's profile dig into her hand. On the reverse is a view of the battle in which George died, with above it the words of Nelson's signal, *England Expects That Every Man Will Do His Duty.*

Lieutenant Sowerby says, 'So you are in need of protection. As a woman, not perhaps of means, but of rank, living alone in what is a rough and dangerous land.'

She thinks of the loveliness of the paradise garden, the flowers, the river. 'I've only seen very little of it so far, but it doesn't strike me as rough,' she says. 'It looks to me quite lovely.'

'That's because you're a woman. You have a romantic heart. But I have seen what this land is truly like. I've had to fight its sons upon the waves and cliffs. Lawless, these people are. They're all in on the smuggling. Fishermen, miners, shopkeepers, farmers. Their wives and children too! They're all involved.'

The anger rises in her as if he's drawing it out with a hook. She thinks of Tom Holder and his son, Richard, and Mrs Dowling. She has only just arrived in Cornwall, but it seems unfair to accuse the entire population like this. She has no love for smugglers – she imagines they are dangerous. But the farmers and fishermen? Their children, even? She lets go off George's medal, balls her hands into fists. 'Surely it cannot be that bad?'

'It's worse, madam. I used to think I could bring the men I captured to justice. I had them imprisoned and tried for their crimes. Smuggling, piracy. But nearly all were acquitted. Even the juries are on their side.'

He's looming over her, his moon-face too close. She can

smell his breath, which is oddly sweet, as if he's been drinking spirits; she can sense the anger pulsing under the polite exterior. He hates it here, she thinks. He hates Cornwall; hates its people.

She thinks of his cold lips pressed against the skin covering her knuckles. For the first time, she wishes the rules governing her limited interactions with men before she married still applied. In widowhood, she has far more freedom, but now she wishes this freedom revoked, if only for today. Lieutenant Sowerby would never dream of standing here, alone with her, if she were unwed.

Lieutenant Sowerby says, 'These days, I don't risk a trial.'

'How do you mean?'

'How do you think I mean, madam?' The edge in his voice grows sharper. 'I ensure justice takes its course. I have them hanged, as traitors should be.'

'Traitors?' she squeaks, willing away the picture he's drawn before her eyes. He hangs them? Boys, like Richard Holder?

'You don't believe smugglers are traitors?' There's a fury in him, but it's controlled, simmering under the surface of a polite smile. 'Their smuggling aids the French. We're at war, madam.' His eye falls on George's medal. His tone, his entire bearing, changes to one of suspicion. 'Where did you get that?'

Taken aback, her hand goes to the medal again. 'My husband, George Henley, was a midshipman on His Majesty's Ship *Neptune* at Trafalgar. He died of a bullet fired from the top of the *Bucentaure*.' She has spoken these words so many times they have almost become meaningless. They cannot convey how the world turned black when she received word of his death; of the cutting of everyday things, of how much she still misses him and how much she wishes she had known him better.

'Well. A proper hero,' Lieutenant Sowerby says. There's a hint of sarcasm in his tone and she wants him out, suddenly, with a vehemence that makes her desire to be alone when Mrs Dowling lingered on her doorstep pale in comparison. Before she has the chance to say anything, Lieutenant Sowerby returns to his officiousness and, placing his hand on the hilt of his sword, says, 'I hereby offer you my protection, madam.'

She swallows her sigh. 'I'm terribly grateful, sir, but I don't believe I need it.'

The way his expression crushes – had he really believed she would accept him, then and there, as her protector, whatever he thought the role entailed? 'Madam, I must insist. A woman, such as yourself, with your . . .' He shakes his head as if searching for words. 'Your virtue and such purity of character. Do you have any idea, madam, what a band of smugglers would do to a woman like you if they found you here alone?'

He lifts his hand, reaching for her as if he's about to illustrate his point. A wetness has appeared in the corners of his mouth. 'What would your late husband say?'

'My dear sir!' The words fly out in a gasp. She backs up all the way to the door, wrenches it open. 'I'm afraid I'm going to have to . . . tend to the fire. Thank you for calling on me, sir. I shall bear your warning in mind.'

He looks at her for a creeping moment, his jaw working as if he's chewing down a protest. His breath is coming too fast; the sweetness of the liquor on it surrounds her like a cloud. She's nearly pinned to the door, he's that close. She watches in horror as his hand goes up again, reaching for her. His eyes are fixed on a point below her chin – her chest, she realises. A cry escapes her. The lieutenant blinks. Stepping back, he wipes beads of sweat from his forehead and makes a stiff bow. 'Very well,' he says. 'I have done my duty.'

'So you have, and I thank you for it.' *Now go, please. Leave me be.*

'If it doesn't inconvenience you, I shall call on you from time to time as I pass by on patrol, to ensure you are safe.'

'I'd be much obliged to you, sir,' she says, her voice wavering.

He nods, as if her answer is satisfactory, though barely so. She waits in the doorway as he gets on his horse, a strong-looking brown mare. The rain has slackened a little. She thinks of the smugglers he likes to hang. The sensation of his cold lips lingers on her hand. It's only when the greenery of the coastal path swallows Lieutenant Sowerby's over-large shape and she turns to the swirling river that she can breathe freely again. The shudder in her limbs subsides as she watches the rain pelt the surface.

Back inside, she sits down at the table, her fingers around George's medal. Perhaps she should call on Mrs Dowling and ask her how to make tea. *The wife of my friend, the Deputy Lord Lieutenant, will call on you soon,* Lieutenant Sowerby said. She wants to both laugh and cry at the thought of the wife of the Deputy Lord Lieutenant of Cornwall knocking on the door of her cottage. She wouldn't know what to serve the woman. Not tea, that's for certain. She lives in a different world now.

The hours ahead seem as long as those she used to spend waiting for a letter from George. She glances at her travel case on the floor in the nook by the door of the sitting room. It looks as if it's yawning. Inside its mouth are cottons and linens, and the silk chemise she bought for when George would come home. At the time, she pictured the scene over and over, how she'd come into the room wearing only the chemise, the look on his face; how it would be when they weren't nervous because it was the first time or because he had to go back to sea the next day. She doesn't know why she has brought the chemise. It doesn't belong in a place like this. She has never worn it and now she never shall. The familiar sting inside at the thought; the screwing shut of her throat.

She pushes the chemise back into the case and, shutting the lid, replaces the memory with a happier one: the two of them, walking in Hyde Park, arm in arm. How he'd say something funny and laugh at his own joke. She wants to reach out and pull him to her, to smell the mix of cologne and after-dinner brandy on him and the wool of his jacket as she pushes her face in the crook of his neck.

Then she's crying, as if it happened that week, as if she's

only just had the news. She gives into the tears, crossing her arms on the table and putting her face on them, letting the sobs run through her. She loved him, but sometimes she worries she did not love him enough.

After a few minutes, she wipes her face. She needs to get out. She looks out of the door to make sure Lieutenant Sowerby really has gone and goes to inspect the shed. The door to it is latched but unlocked. Light filters through two narrow windows at the back and along the wall runs a single shelf, waist high, with a wooden work chest on it. Closer inspection of the chest reveals a hammer, a handful of nails and a tool with a flat end that she thinks may be a chisel. She imagines the shed still smells of fish, but that's impossible. The innkeeper's son told her it's not in use anymore; it hasn't been for years.

She turns back to the door and in the light falling in through the opening, she catches a glint on the wall. A padlock, almost the size of the palm of her hand, hangs from a hook in the wood. It's locked and there isn't a key. She wonders who put it there. The padlock isn't rusted.

Upon leaving the shed, the coastal path beckons. The rain has stopped and the sun tries to escape the clouds as she walks. Everything smells new. After a few minutes, the path starts to hug the cliff. In some places it's so narrow she has to step into the grass on the hillside so as not to get too close to the edge. God knows how the Riding Officers of the Revenue Service negotiate the path on horseback.

She passes a small cove filled with splashing foam. Looking

down at it from the top of the cliff, it's as if an invisible rope runs from the water to a point inside her chest and every wave breaking on the rocks pulls on it. The sea has always drawn her, but never like this, with such restiveness. She wants nothing more than to get in, to feel the water rush around her, but the thought of Lieutenant Sowerby and his men patrolling on the path holds her back.

She's about to go home when she catches sight of a ship, a mile or two out from shore. It's a cutter, she thinks, shielding her eyes from the sun, or perhaps a sloop. George would've been able to tell her. The wood of the hull has been painted black and the sun hitting the sails turns them almost too bright to look at. The ship is sailing away, out to where the ocean is so deep no one knows the end of it.

She thinks of her father, who spent so many years at sea. Did he feel it too, this tugging and longing? Did George? She wishes she could've spoken with George about it, how the sight of the sea moves her. She almost told him once, but the moment flitted away before she found the words. And what would he have thought? In the nine years since he became a midshipman, he grew to love the sea, but unlike her, he didn't feel the need to be near it in order to breathe freely. Which was ironic, because he spent most of his short life at sea and in the end it took him.

Since his death, the desire to go where he went, to see what he saw, has only grown stronger. George rests at sea; she hasn't got a grave to visit. She has only the ocean. She'd never envy George, but it's deeply unfair she'll never be able to go sailing like him. The deck of a ship is as closed to her as the doors of Parliament.

She watches the ship until it's a white dot hovering on the horizon. The walk home to the cottage seems longer, somehow.

The next two days pass as slow and empty as the first. To fill the hours, she walks the coastal path, learning where it leads, where she can climb down the rocks and stick her feet in the water. On the morning of her fourth day in Helford, a Friday, her breakfast consists of a rock-hard piece of bread. After some debate, she calls on a gratified Mrs Dowling and in the course of the next few days, she learns how to make tea, bread, stew, how to clean and prepare fish. Everything she does takes four times as long as it should. Peeling her first potato, she ends up with half of it stuck to the peel. The second one is the same, as is the third. Gulping down a cry of frustration, she attacks the fourth, which comes out better but takes even longer. No matter. She'll get faster – so Mrs Dowling says. When she's an expert, she'll be able to do the whole thing without breaking the peel.

She carries a small notebook and copies Mrs Dowling's neatly written recipes in it. Mrs Dowling is as proud of the fact that she can read and write as she is of the handful of cottages she owns in the area, which used to be her late husband's and which she lets mainly to tradesmen and fishermen.

One afternoon, Mrs Dowling shows her where to go for the day's catch and how to negotiate the best price. 'The biggest one is for the Bucca,' she says, indicating the display of fish.

The owner of the boat, a grizzled-looking fisherman, overhears. 'An offering, for a flat sea and a decent catch,' he says, nodding. 'I heard him calling today, Mrs Dowling.'

Mrs Dowling looks up. 'Do you think there's a storm coming, Mr Penrose?'

'Could be.' He turns to Isabel. 'When it blows from the south-west, that's the Sea Bucca calling.' Lowering his voice, he adds, 'But then you know all about that, don't you, Mrs Henley?' His eyes are dark, nearly black, and he gives her a look that seems to imply some shared secret.

A chill tiptoes up her spine. She isn't sure what unnerves her more: Mrs Dowling and the fisherman speaking matter-of-factly, the way one might discuss the weather, or Mr Penrose's words, *you know all about that*. But underneath the apprehension lies an odd, insistent sense of recognition. Could she have heard about the Bucca when she was here as a child? She glances at the river and the feeling grows stronger, mixing with the lure of the water and reducing Mr Penrose's conversation with Mrs Dowling to a murmur.

By the time their words grow into separate entities again, Mrs Dowling is talking about a storm in which one of her cottages lost its roof. Isabel feels bad she initially thought to refuse the woman's friendship. Without asking for anything in return, Mrs Dowling is teaching her all of the things her mother would have taught her if she'd been born a cottager's daughter. She wonders if perhaps she *was* born a cottager's daughter. She studies the face of every person she meets. Could this woman with the fish basket be her mother? Does that man there share the colour of her eyes? The people in Helford treat her as if she has come home.

The storm doesn't materialise, though the south-westerly stirs up the water. The sea is a constant presence, beseeching, coaxing, consoling. Whenever her frustrations mount, whenever the night is too long in the empty cottage, she has but to step outside and listen to the waves to feel a sense of calm.

Sometimes she watches the men of the Revenue Service pass by on patrol on the coastal path, the Riding Officers, alone or in pairs, and others on foot. She should be glad they're patrolling so frequently, but whenever she thinks of it, she can't help but remember the way Lieutenant Sowerby towered over her, his sweet, liquor-tinged breath in her face; the look in his eyes when he reached for her. She remembers the anger in him as he espoused the virtue of hanging smugglers, the way he wetted his lips as he envisioned the torments he claimed they'd put her through.

When she asks Mrs Dowling about the patrols, the landlady tells her smuggling has become so widespread, the revenue men are growing more and more ruthless. Just last month they caught hold of a farmer in Coverack who stored contraband on his farm and they shot him – no investigation, no trial, nothing. Mrs Dowling's indignation is as hot as the tea she purchases at what she calls 'a particularly good price'.

On Tuesday, Isabel goes to the market and buys cheese,

flour, carrots and a side of ham. Fish, too: mackerel, brought in with the catch. Mr Penrose gives her the same meaningful look as before, but he doesn't say anything.

Mrs Dowling has told her the market is always busy, but she didn't expect it to be this crowded. On her way back to the cottage the narrow road heaves with men, women and children, all moving in the direction of nearby Manaccan. An excited chatter rises from them like heat from a freshly baked loaf. Curious, she turns away from the coastal path and follows the throng.

As they approach the crossroads, the voices fall silent. Some people point, but Isabel can only see an ocean of hats, bonnets, caps and scarves. Somewhere to the left, a blackbird chafes at the quiet in a long, drawn-out trill. It's cool out this morning, but the road is dappled with sun. She has a soup to make – her first-ever soup. She ought to turn away and go home, but curiosity tethers her. She pushes ahead, slipping between sweat-scented bodies, past the hard–soft shapes of other women. An elbow pokes her side and then she sees it.

At first, she thinks it's a construction to help lift something, such as you might see in a shipyard. Or perhaps it's a ship's mast, taken from its hull and incongruously put down here, by the side of the road to Manaccan. But then her gaze falls on the row of revenue men, armed with pistols and swords, and the prisoner, arms tied behind his back, being led to the low scaffold.

And she sees the man leading the prisoner. One hand gripping the prisoner's arm, the other the butt of his pistol, is none other than Lieutenant Sowerby. 'Oh!' she gasps, nearly dropping her basket.

As if he has heard her, Lieutenant Sowerby looks up. A grin appears on his blushing moon-face; there's no hint of the anger she saw in him before. If anything, he looks gratified, the way a man might when he's about to cut the meat of the stag he's shot.

Lieutenant Sowerby gives her a nod as he shoves the prisoner onto the scaffold, pushing him towards the waiting noose with such force the man stumbles and drops to his knees. Grabbing him by his shirt, Lieutenant Sowerby hauls him back to his feet. 'Trying to get away, Ferries? I'm afraid it's a little late for that. The noose awaits – and hell beyond it!'

His voice drips malice above the hum of the crowd. The prisoner's gaze swerves over the people before he turns to his captor and says something inaudible. Lieutenant Sowerby laughs and, raising his voice, says, '*I'll* burn for this? You must be confounded, man! That pretty fate is all yours.'

At the sight of the noose, the prisoner's knees buckle and Lieutenant Sowerby snaps at the nearest of the revenue men, 'Help me hold him up.' Then, to the prisoner, 'Try not to make a spectacle of yourself. Your wife's watching, I'm sure.' He utters another short laugh. 'You wouldn't want to soil yourself in front of her, would you?'

As if the moment isn't wretched enough, Lieutenant Sowerby looks over again and finds her in the crowd, giving her a flushed smile. Voices rear up, hard-edged and raw. 'He deserves a trial, damn you!' one man shouts and, 'You monster!' This from the woman next to Isabel, a slender, ageless figure encased in stiff black cotton with her hair tied under a matching black bonnet. The woman has balled her hands into fists, pressing one to each side of her face. Turning to Isabel, she cries, 'Poor Agnes! It's unspeakable!'

To the left of the row of revenue men, a young woman stands supported by two older women. The blue cloth of her dress is stained as if she's been kneeling in dirt; her hair is loose and uncovered. She looks around with unseeing eyes until she catches sight of the prisoner and a thin, horrible wail escapes her.

Lieutenant Sowerby appears not to hear, or if he does, he gives no sign. Standing beside the prisoner on the scaffold, he calls above the noise: 'Jed Ferries, you are condemned to death for treason in a time of war! You shall be hanged from the neck until pronounced dead.'

'All he did was smuggle some tea!' A boy this time, maybe fourteen years old. Voices around him chime in and Lieutenant Sowerby searches the crowd, but not for the boy who called out, she thinks; for her. She flinches back into the throng. The smell of sweat and dirt mixes with that of the mackerel she bought at the market and she nearly gags.

She begins to make her way back to Helford, wiping her hand on her gown over and over. He was in her cottage. He kissed her hand, right there by the knuckles. Behind her, the crowd has quieted again. Glancing back over her shoulder, she sees the onlookers have removed their hats. There isn't any birdsong now; the air has grown still as stone. Then there's a crunch and a snapping, clear even from this distance, followed by a woman's scream so full of despair it could split the marrow in one's bones.

Back at the cottage, she goes through the motions of cooking the mackerel and carrot into a pasty-looking soup. She opens the door a crack to let out the smells. Gradually, the shakiness inside her drains away. The sound of the river sloshes in through the open door. It doesn't calm her as much as it normally does, because through it she keeps hearing the crunch and the desperate cry that followed.

At night, the house creaks and moans around her. When she sleeps, she dreams of footsteps. The servants, up at all hours. They are calling in subdued voices. Did something happen? Is somebody ill; is there a fire?

She sits up with a jolt. She's not dreaming. The footsteps are real. They're downstairs and there are voices trailing them, climbing over them: male voices, low against the sound of the wind.

Her heart drums in her throat. She's certain they can hear it. She places her hand on her throat and feels it pulsing against her palm. A scraping noise downstairs – a chair being moved or the door? She looks around the room for something to defend herself with. The fire poker. It's made of wrought iron with a pommel at the end. The iron is cold in her hand, the poker reassuringly heavy. The air swishes when she gives it a swing.

She stands behind the bedroom door, clutching the poker.

Footsteps start to come up the stairs and stop. 'It's narrow, but I think we can haul him up,' a voice says and there's a groan from somewhere down below.

'There's a bed. It'll be worth your while, Captain.' The first voice again and then the speaker's feet resume their climbing.

Other feet follow. They're moving more slowly than she expected. There's another groan, loud enough to be heard above the wind. A man in pain, she thinks. A man who is being carried up the stairs. A glow appears in the doorway.

Then the doorway fills – there are five of them, but in the light of the lantern, she sees only him. Sweat pastes a shock of black hair to his forehead and even in the faint light, she sees his face is so pale it has an almost grey hue, laid over the evidence of suntan like a veil. He's clean-shaven and his shirt is unlaced and partly torn, revealing a bleeding wound some-where in the middle of his torso. The white shirt has turned mostly red. The man's eyes are closed and for a moment she believes him dead, but then he opens them and fixes them on her. And, extraordinarily, he smiles. Quietly, he says, 'Look what the wind has blown in.'

Three men carry him; a fourth follows behind with a wad of bloodied cloth and a lantern, a tin and glass one he holds up high. They turn to her and the one at the back reaches for something at his waist, fumbling with the cloth as he does it – a pistol, she realises, and she lifts the poker, but the wounded man says, 'Oppy!' sharply, the muscles in his face pulling taut, and when the man called Oppy looks at him, the wounded one shakes his head, before closing his eyes as they lower him onto the bed.

When he opens them again, she's still standing there, transfixed, the poker halfway to her shoulder. One of the other men, a bearded, bull-necked fellow with black teeth, says, 'You can lower the poker, miss. We're no threat to you, if you aren't one to us.'

CHAPTER THREE

The room is crowded with the five of them in it. There's very little space to stand around the bed. The smell of blood mixes with the damp old smell of the house. 'What happened to him?' Her voice isn't her own. Tremulous, high.

The wounded man himself answers. 'I got shot.' Then the man called Oppy bends his thin-as-a-reed body over the bed and places his lantern on the windowsill. With two hands he presses the bloodied cloth to the man's stomach. The wounded man swears loudly, using words she's never heard before, though it's clear what they mean and Oppy grimaces as if he feels the pain himself. He runs a hand through his thick brown hair and some of the blood from his fingers sticks to it.

'He needs a doctor,' she says, less shrilly.

'We're well aware.' The man who says this is mostly bald like the innkeeper of the Shipwrights Arms, but he's young to be so, only a few years older than her, she thinks. The wounded man, too, is fairly young, maybe twenty-nine or thirty, though possibly the pain makes him look older. The other two she thinks are in their mid-thirties. The shorter of these, who's strong-looking in a wiry sort of way, is holding two pistols, one in each hand.

Her heart still beats in her throat. Sweat runs down her back, underneath the cotton of her chemise. There are five strange men in her room and she's in a state of undress. Her hair is in a long plait down her back. It's coming loose. She isn't wearing her stays. *How's that for rumours?* She feels sick, her legs pudding-like.

A low moan from the wounded man drags her out of her thoughts. Oppy is still pressing the cloth to the wound, but it isn't doing much good. The cloth is too drenched with blood. She thinks of George, of when he was shot on board HMS *Neptune*, how there wasn't a bed for him to lie in or a woman to help care for him. She goes to the stairs and when the taller of the two older men moves to stop her, she snaps, 'I'm going to get water from the well.'

The man says, 'Captain?'

'Let her go, Moyle,' the man on the bed says tiredly.

She walks down the stairs as if in a dream, her hand on the wall for support. She's shaking inside, rattling with it. Any moment now, she thinks, her teeth are going to chatter, but they don't and she feels her way along the wall to the back door. Trembling, she takes her pelisse from where it hangs on a nail in the wall and shrugs it on. In the garden, too, everything is dreamlike. There's no moon and she wishes she'd brought a candle, but after a moment her eyes adjust. The sea appears to emit a faint light as she walks down the path to the paradise garden.

The well is dark and bottomless. She has trouble gripping the pulley crank, at first; she's shaking so. As she begins to turn it, she thinks she shouldn't be doing it. She shouldn't be fetching water for these men. She should run. She should make her way to the village and call for help. They are smugglers, she's sure of it – smugglers or perhaps pirates. They wouldn't come in the dead of night carrying pistols if their business was respectable. She should try to go to St Keverne and find the Customs House and ... and watch these men get hanged just like that smuggler, Jed Ferries, this morning? Condemned without a trial, on her testimony alone, for ... what, exactly? Bringing a wounded man into her house? She has no proof of their smuggling, and – she almost jerks with the realisation – even if she did, she'd be loath to hand them over to a man such as Lieutenant Sowerby.

The thought steadies her. So does that of George, dying on *Neptune*. James, who'd been a member of one of the gun crews, told Isabel afterwards that he'd watched as they brought George below. He told her of George's last moments, of his bravery. James said he lay there, waiting for the surgeon to pass judgement, James himself with a leg wound beside him. When it was George's turn the surgeon said there was nothing he could do for him and there were others he might save, so George lay there, breath frothing because of the hole in his chest. 'He said to tell you he loves you,' James told her. She'd pictured it: George, choking on blood, saying, *tell her I love her.* The image never left her.

Tears slip down her face as she turns the crank of the well. She brushes at them angrily. Her grip slackens; the bucket drops, but she grasps the crank hard and, using both hands, hauls the bucket all the way up.

She returns to the bedroom carrying the bucket and her chemise from the travel case, the silk one with the lace she'd bought for George's homecoming. The man called Moyle and the balding man are about to leave. The other two regard her warily as she approaches the wounded captain on the bed, bucket in one hand, the silk chemise bunched in the other. She considered taking one of her other chemises, not wanting to spoil the silk, but she has only three others, all functional, strong cotton ones, which are more useful for wearing here.

'There you are,' the captain says, as if he's been waiting for her, or perhaps he guessed she might run and tell somebody. He says, 'I apologise for disturbing you. We believed the cottage empty.'

'You shouldn't talk.' She's still wearing the pelisse. Pushing up a sleeve, she dips the garment in the bucket and wipes the sweat from the captain's brow. His eyes, dark blue by the light of the lantern, stay on hers as she does it. After a moment, she hands the cloth to Oppy and says, 'That cloth is soaked through. Use this instead.'

He lifts it up, fingering the material as if he's a buyer in a shop. 'This fine stuff?'

'It'll do the job the same as cotton.'

She takes the sullied cloth from him and places it on the floor by her feet. There's the sound of footsteps on the stairs, going down, then the scrape of the front door as Moyle and the bald man leave.

Oppy says, 'I'm going to fetch the doctor, Captain. Dick will stay here. I'll be back as quick as I can.' When he lifts the silk, a fresh trickle of blood flows from the wound. Isabel takes it from him and presses it to the captain's stomach again. The skin around the wound is coloured by the sun, too, and there are ripples where the muscles have arranged themselves in a pattern of squares. A thin line of black hair runs down the centre to the right of the wound. She feels strangely moved by it, by the vulnerability of him. George was fair-haired and had some hair on his chest, but not down here, down his stomach.

The blood is still flowing. She presses down harder and the captain swears, before saying to Oppy, 'Take Dick with you, in case you run into trouble.'

Oppy looks doubtful, but the captain glances up at her, and there's that smile again, very faint, despite everything, despite her hurting him with the cloth and the fact that he's bleeding all over her mattress and he may be dying, just like George. He says, 'I believe I'm in good hands.'

'Are you sure, Captain?' says the wiry man called Dick.

'Go. The sooner Rowell gets here, the better. Be sure to steer clear of the path.'

'Aye.' Dick takes one of the two pistols he's been holding

and puts it on the bed by the captain's right hand, which lies limply on the blanket.

'You won't need that,' she says shakily.

'It's not for you.'

When the door shuts behind the two men, the captain closes his eyes again. He keeps them closed for so long she worries he has fallen asleep or perhaps he's dying. He has lost an awful lot of blood, but he doesn't talk like a dying man. He has too many things to say, still, to be dying. That doesn't mean it couldn't happen. She hopes the two men, Dick and the other one, will be back soon with the doctor. She doesn't know what she'll do if the stranger in her bed dies. The thought is too dreadful to contemplate.

Just as she thinks he isn't going to wake up until the men get back, the captain opens his eyes and says, 'You're the Bucca's child. They said you were coming.'

She looks around for another clean cloth and when she doesn't see one, dips her hand in the pink water in the bucket and rubs some onto his brow. His skin is cool under her touch and she thinks maybe she's doing the wrong thing, maybe she should be making sure he's warm. She hasn't felt the cold herself since she woke up. Meeting his eyes, she says, 'I'm not a child.'

His gaze moves up from her knees, leisurely and squinting a little, as if she's made of glass and she's catching the sun. When it reaches her face, he says, 'I can see that.'

She grows hot under his look. She's conscious of the way the pelisse falls open at the front and the chemise under it clings to her, outlining the shape of her hips and legs. A rivulet of sweat runs down her back. She wishes she was wearing her stays, at least. Maybe she should do up the buttons of the coat. But she'll get blood on the pelisse and it's her only one, her favourite of the four she used to have, thick, luscious green velvet and with the way things are, she'll never have another. She leaves the coat unbuttoned. The captain is still looking at her. To hide her confusion, she says, 'Are you cold? Shall I make a fire?'

'There's no need. I'm perfectly warm. But thank you.'

'I'll remove your boots for you.' She moves to the foot of the bed and takes hold of the left one. They're black leather Hessian boots, similar to those worn by the men in town, coming up to a pair of buckskin breeches that is entirely unlike the fashion for knit pantaloons in London. The breeches have bloodstains at the top. She wonders if it'd be possible to wipe them clean, since they're leather, or if the stains are permanent. The boots are tight-fitting; she has to pull hard to remove them. She worries she's hurting the man, but if she is, he doesn't let on. 'That's better. Thank you,' he says as she places the boots on the floor.

'Would you like some water?'

'Have you got anything stronger?'

She likes the sound of his voice. Even when it's strained and a little raspy on account of the pain, it's deep and, she thinks, full of feeling. Shaking her head, she says, 'I've only just moved here. And I've no money.'

'Haven't you? Your manner of speech says otherwise.'

She dips the silk chemise in the bucket, rinses it, squeezes out the water. The trickle of blood has stopped. The edges of the wound are ragged-raw. She presses the cloth to it again. 'My manner of speech doesn't tell of my husband's debts.'

Just thinking about it, she feels it: the chill when she discovered George's disastrous investments after his death, the series of failed and non-existent crops overseas. His uniform, purchased on credit. For years, she held off their creditors with the promise of prize money – money which never came. To flee the subject, she says, 'What's your name?'

'Jack.'

'Jack what?'

A smile tugs on his lips. 'Nothing you need to know. What's yours?'

She's going to say Mrs Isabel Henley or maybe just Mrs Henley or maybe that's nothing you need to know, but she finds herself saying, 'Isabel.'

He raises his eyebrows. 'Just Isabel?'

'For now, yes.' For you, she thinks, yes, I can be just Isabel. It's a strange thought. She hasn't been *just Isabel* since she was found in Helford nineteen years before.

'Very well, just Isabel. And where is your husband now? May we expect him soon? Shall I be able to count on his discretion as I count on yours?' His hand moves around the butt of the pistol, the tips of his fingers grazing the flintlock.

'You may not,' Isabel says. 'My husband is dead.' After a moment, she adds, 'He caught a bullet at Trafalgar.'

Jack is quiet for some time. She wonders if he's thinking

of his own gunshot wound. She wants to ask, *Are you dying?* She wants to say, *Don't. Don't die. Don't you dare.* She doesn't know if she would be saying it to him or to George. Eventually, Jack says, 'Do you miss him very much?'

She hesitates a beat too long. 'I miss what we could have had. Yes, I miss him, very much indeed. But in three years we only had five weeks together, so I miss perhaps more that which should have been, but wasn't.' The hair coming loose from her plait falls in front of her face as she looks down at her hands. Is it true, she wonders, or is she merely telling herself this? Is she really missing George's arms around her, the way his voice dipped when he spoke her name, the clear, unadulterated affection in it? She believed she'd have a lifetime's worth of those things. Through her painfully constricted throat, she says, 'If that doesn't sound like nonsense to you.'

'Isabel.' When she doesn't react, he says it again, 'Isabel.' He's trying to make her look up, she thinks. After a moment, she does it. She's not going to weep – not yet. Jack says, 'It isn't nonsense. It makes perfect sense. It's why I refuse to wed. In my line of work, one never sees much of one's wife and one may die tomorrow, leaving too many things unsaid, undone.'

Before she can stop herself, she says, 'Or today.'

Incongruously, this makes him laugh, which makes him wince. It's like watching him curl up inside himself, away from the room as the pain washes over him. Then he comes back out of it and says, 'I should hope not. I'm only twenty-nine. But I won't subject a wife to that sort of thing . . . or,

God forbid, any children. It's too dangerous, like it was for your husband.'

She says, 'Don't compare yourself to my husband.'

'Why shouldn't I? He was a sailor, same as me.'

'He fought for his country. You're a . . . a smuggler.' It's an insult, the way she says it.

He doesn't deny it. Instead he says mildly, 'I prefer the term free trader. And prize money, I am sure, never featured into the equation where your husband was concerned. Or did it? I don't believe your husband and I are all that different.'

'My husband wasn't too cowardly to marry.' She wishes she hadn't said it: it makes him laugh again. 'Stop that,' she says, 'You're hurting yourself.'

'The revenue men's bullet did that. But you've got me there, madam. Still, there's a fine line between bravery and foolishness. I should know – I've crossed it one too many times myself.'

'You shouldn't talk so much.' She dips the cloth again. The water runs pink from her fingers. Outside, beyond the yellow glow of the lantern, the sky is greying at the edges. She says, 'It'll be morning soon.'

'Good.' He closes his eyes, his face nearly as pale as the sheet. 'I should like to see the morning.'

He sleeps for a while, or perhaps he only rests. His eyes are closed and she studies his face, the faint lines around his eyes, the way his hair curls at the edges, the shape of his mouth, which is quite small for his face but suits it all the same and which has a perfect Cupid's bow. Every ten minutes or so, she checks the wound. It isn't bleeding now, but it is looking awfully raw and deep. She has to turn her head away and not look at it too long or a queasiness rises in her stomach.

The air in the room has grown close. It smells of blood and the wick of the lantern. Whale oil, she thinks. She wants to open the window, but she doesn't want Jack to get cold, so she merely keeps sitting there on the edge of the bed, rinsing the cloth while she waits. Time passes like treacle. Where is the doctor? Why haven't they brought him yet? The captain thinks the same. When he wakes, he says, 'Where is that damned doctor?' And then, 'I beg your forgiveness, madam.'

'You have it,' she says, and she goes into the kitchen and pours him a cup of milk, of which he manages three sips before falling back into a slumber.

Dawn lifts itself up from the river. She watches the sky turn grey and then a faint pink through the window-glass, which is of better quality than that of the kitchen window, but still somewhat opaque. She pictures the sea, around the bend of the river, turning into the sweeping, turquoise-blue field it'll be in an hour or two, when the sun has fully risen.

Watching the river calms her, but only a little. The captain's face is as pale as the milk in the cup on the sill. She hesitates, then puts her hand by his mouth. He's still breathing.

Time slows further. Just as she's beginning to truly fear for the captain's life, there's a noise on the gravel path. A late owl hoots outside. Then the front door scrapes and Jack is fully awake at once, the pistol in his hand, hammer cocked, muzzle pointing at the bedroom door. Isabel draws in her breath sharply. Her heart's pounding hard again. Footsteps and then a voice . . . 'Captain, it's us. I've got Rowell here.'

She lets out her breath slowly. Her legs are pudding, but this time it's from relief. She draws back into the corner as they enter: Oppy, Dick and the doctor, ducking through the door one by one. The doctor looks more like a farmer than a doctor, with an unlaced shirt under a brown wool coat and knee-breeches in the old style. He takes off his coat and places it on the side of the bed. The mattress sags under the weight of his leather bag.

'*Myttin da*, Jack,' the doctor says, sitting on the edge of the bed near the window, where Isabel spent the past slow hours. Under the linen of his shirt, his arms bulge with muscles. 'Got yourself in a stew again, have you?'

Jack says, 'There's one aboard the *Swallow* that aims a little too well for my liking.'

'Did you manage to unload?'

Isabel watches the doctor closely when he lifts the silk from the wound. The look on his face doesn't assuage her fears.

Jack says, 'Not yet.'

'They're blocking the way into Nelly's cove,' says Oppy. 'We pulled in here after the captain was shot, so we could get you as fast as we could. Didn't expect this one to be living here.' He jerks his thumb in Isabel's direction.

The doctor looks up. 'Are you the woman of the house?'

'I am.'

'Could you get me some fresh water, please?'

She lifts the bucket and carries it to the door. Before going through, she looks back at the captain. He's watching her as the doctor examines the wound. She tries to give him an encouraging smile, but her mouth does a funny thing, sort of drawing down as if she's about to weep, and then she's through the door and almost runs down the steps and into the garden.

The light is fully flowing now, pink and purple and early-morning grey vying for dominion of the sky. The wind has largely died down, the river laps at the roots of the stone wall around the garden. After the closeness of the room, the scent of sea, grass and flowers is as fresh as the new day. She pulls the air into her, mouth open, breathing deeply, and throws the reddish water from the bucket over the wall. The light hits the stream and everything turns soft pink; the water, the sky, the river. Isabel feels soft with it, as if the edges of her have worn away.

The moment lasts maybe a minute, then she jogs to the well. Her arms ache from how fast she turns the pulley crank. Some of the water spills from the bucket as she lifts it over the stone edge. She has filled it to the brim and makes a trail of drops on the floor as she carries it in.

The doctor says, 'Oh, thank you,' distractedly as she places the bucket on the floor beside him. A selection of metal instruments sits on a clean cloth on top of the bed. If the sight of them inspires a fright in her, she wonders how the captain feels. He doesn't look afraid, but maybe that's just for the benefit of his men. Mainly, he looks desperately weary.

'Is he going to live, doctor?' She surprises herself. The doctor, too; she can tell by the tinge of irritation in his voice when he says, 'I have good hope of his full recovery. It doesn't appear that anything vital was hit, which is a piece of mighty luck with a shot in these regions. I shall, however, have to remove the bullet as it's still in the wound, possibly along with some of the cloth of his shirt. Do you have any brandy or rum perhaps?'

Her tongue has gone dry. 'I'm afraid not.'

'We've got plenty on the ship,' Oppy says and the captain smiles, again very lightly.

'Pity,' the doctor says. 'Looks like you'll have to bear it sober, Jack.'

Jack says, 'No matter. I've lost enough blood I feel drunk.'

The doctor turns to Isabel. 'Madam, if you'd be so good as to leave us, I shall get on with the operation.'

At the door, the captain's voice calls her back. 'I should like her to stay, if it's all the same to you, doctor. I reckon I'll swear less in the presence of a woman.'

She turns and just looking at him she feels the edges of her softening as they did in the garden. 'You may swear all you like,' she says, going over to kneel next to the bed. She's terribly close to him now; she can smell the sweat on him and wipes it from his brow with her sleeve. When she reaches for his hand, there's a faint smell of something else, something sharp and metallic – gunpowder, she thinks, though she has never smelled it before.

She lifts his hand from the bed. It's clammy, but any

limpness leaves it as he grips hers, hard, when the doctor begins to apply his trade. Jack doesn't make a sound all through the surgery. He just looks at her, his eyes glued to hers, not once looking away, his grip at times so strong she has to fight not to show it hurts. The only sounds in the room are those of their breath, mingling in the stale, sweet air, the click of the doctor's instruments as he replaces one with another, the odd mutter as the doctor works and the sharp intake of air from Dick or Oppy or maybe both when the doctor pulls out the bullet, saying, 'I've got it. Thank Jesus, it's out, both the cloth and the bullet.'

Only then does Jack's gaze leave her. His hand slips from hers and she thinks he's going to faint, with his eyes turning away like that and his expression going slack, but then he's back and he sighs so deeply his entire body seems to sigh. He says, 'Thank you, Rowell,' and then he looks up at her and smiles, saying, 'And you. I'm much obliged.'

'It's nothing.' Her knees ache from kneeling on the bare wooden boards and her hand aches from how hard he squeezed it and she knows it's not nothing. What she did, yes, that was nothing, and she only wishes someone could've done it for George; she wishes someone could've held his hand as he lay dying and the thought cuts and cuts. But this man now, the smuggler, Jack, he's alive, he's going to be all right and she got to do it for him.

All through the operation, she didn't once think of George.

The doctor is getting out strips of bandaging, needle and

thread and suddenly Jack is reaching up with the hand with which he held hers, saying, 'Don't cry,' but he cannot quite reach her face, so she wipes it herself and says, 'I'm reminded of my husband, is all.'

The sun is by now pushing above the horizon. Puddles of light fall on the bed, the wall and the doctor as he bends over the patient and finishes bandaging the wound. 'I'll come see you two days from now to check on the wound and change the bandaging,' he says, washing his hands again in the bucket.

'Can I get back to the *Rapide*?' Jack asks.

'Not if you don't wish to die,' the doctor says. 'You'll want to stay put for a couple of days. At the very least until I've been to check on you. Longer would be better, but I appreciate you'll have to be moved before the moon is grown too fat.'

Jack says, 'I'm afraid I must impose on your hospitality a little longer, Isabel. Will you permit me to stay until the good doctor releases me from his care?'

'I don't see what choice I have.'

'I'll compensate you for it, and well.'

'I don't want any compensation.'

'Why not? You could use it, with your husband's debts.'

'I don't want it,' she says angrily. 'And I don't want any trouble, either. You leave as soon as you are able. You don't get to stay a minute longer.'

He closes his eyes. 'Of course.'

The two men, Dick and Oppy, go back to the *Rapide*,

which must be the name of the ship, she thinks. The captain tells them they'll have to unload the cargo as soon as they can arrange for a new landing place. Then he closes his eyes again, looking beyond exhausted. The doctor speaks to Isabel in hushed tones, telling her what signs of infection to look for, what to do in case of fever. 'Try to get him to eat something,' he says, and then he's out the door, too, and she's alone with the smuggler. His mouth is open and his breathing is very heavy, bordering on snoring.

She sits on the floor beside the bed, close to him. If she draws her legs up and places her arms around them, she just fits. Leaning her head against the wall, she watches the morning sun move along the wall opposite, shifting and sliding, making patterns. One looks like a hand, reaching for her and there's a man's face, bearded and strange, and a fish's tail . . . the room grows comfortable, then warm. Maybe she's dreaming.

Later – much later, judging by the sun – she goes down and returns with bread and cheese, of which the captain eats only a little, as well as water and more milk. She's standing by the side of the bed, waiting for him to hand back the cup. He drinks eagerly, which pleases her. He has the most singularly blue eyes, she notices now the room is full of sun. They're not sea-blue or sky-blue or cornflower-blue, they're simply blue-blue. She can't imagine anything bluer.

'Thank you,' he says. 'For allowing me to stay, too. It was never my intention.'

'To get shot? I should hope not,' she says.

'To cause you any trouble.'

Her feeling darkens and he reads it in her face, she can tell by the way he's looking at her. He says, 'It's why you left London, isn't it? Because of trouble.'

Now the fear creeps in. Does he know something? But how could he? He's a smuggler, a captain of a ship that tries to outrun the cutters of the Revenue Service all the way at the tip of England. How could he possibly know about the rumours?

'I told you,' she says. 'My husband left a lot of debts. He was a good officer, but I'm afraid he had no talent for business. He was advised badly and lost all of our wealth in a series of investments overseas.' It feels disloyal to George to say even this much. She adds, 'He was going to take his lieutenant's examination as soon as he got home. His captain recommended it.'

'I don't doubt it,' Jack says. 'Is that why you wear his medal?'

Her hand goes up to the ribbon, feeling the silver. 'Yes.' Then: 'You don't really believe that, do you? That I'm the child of this creature, the Sea Bucca?'

'I don't know. You look like you could be the daughter of merfolk.'

'I've been told the Sea Bucca has the skin of an eel and seaweed for hair.'

He says, 'You're as pretty as a mermaid's daughter. You could be one of the sirens, calling to the sailors, luring their ships onto the rocks.'

She looks down to hide the blaze in her cheeks. 'Now you're jesting.'

Glancing up, she catches his smile, light and quick. 'Perhaps. In any case, I cannot fully discount the tale. Didn't you arrive dripping wet as if you'd come out of the sea? And at such a young age. It's strange, you'll have to admit that, at least. Don't you wonder where you came from?'

'My parents – the ones I was born to – are either dead or they did not want me. So no, I do not wonder about them.'

'Yet of all places, you moved here, to Helford.'

She has no answer to that. 'The fact that I was found in this manner is strange, I do agree,' she says, 'But that doesn't mean there was anything . . . *unnatural* to it.'

'There's nothing unnatural about the Bucca. He's nature itself; he's a part of the sea.'

She cannot tell if he's serious. It irks her and she bursts out, 'But to believe in such a thing!'

'I don't, necessarily. I merely keep an open mind. I always leave a fish as an offering in the cove before a cruise and upon our return, it's always gone. Did the gulls eat it or was it the Bucca, accepting my offer and sending fair winds? Who knows . . . but though I've sailed in many a storm, I haven't yet lost a ship.' A pause, unexpectedly heavy, then he says, 'The men reckon it's the Bucca's doing. Who am I to contradict them and set their nerves a-fraying?'

'That's very calculating. It sounds like you don't know what you believe.'

'Is it? I like to think of it as insurance.'

Part of the blanket hangs off the side of the bed. She pushes at it with her foot and watches it sway. 'Why do you do it?'

'Do what?'

'Smuggling.' She thinks of Lieutenant Sowerby's words, of how smugglers aid the French, and how he hanged Jed Ferries for treason. 'It's not just breaking the law; it's aiding the French.'

With obvious effort, he tries to push himself up on his elbows. She says, 'No, don't, it's not good for the wound'. Jack says, 'Do you know what the tax is on brandy?'

'Does it matter? People can do without brandy very well if they can't afford it.'

'Tea, then, and salt? The tax on tea alone is over one-hundred per cent.' Studying her, he adds, 'I'll wager you didn't know that.'

Of course she didn't – she has never had to buy her own tea before. And if it's taxed at 100 percent, she won't be buying it as often as she had hoped on her widow's pension. She tries not to show her disappointment as Jack continues, 'Or what of sugar, tobacco, dried fruit, coal even?'

'You never smuggle coal,' she says, thinking, *sugar, too?*

He laughs, softly this time, so it doesn't pull on the wound. 'True. There's no profit in it.'

'So don't make out as if you're smuggling out of the good of your heart, for the people to have their goods cheaply.'

'Not cheaply – affordably,' he says. 'And I don't make any such pretence. Of course I'm doing it for profit. I've just had a new ship built. She's fifty tonnes and I intend to make thousands in her.' A pause as he shifts on the mattress. 'We had several poor harvests in a row, starting in '99. That's what got me to consider smuggling. I needed the money.'

She looks at him sharply: she hadn't taken him for a farmer. But with the tan — yes, she could see him working on the land. Jack continues, 'Now I've got a taste for it. The profit comes first, but my men and I wouldn't be able to get those profits if the system of taxation wasn't inherently unfair. And so, by smuggling and augmenting my wealth, I do help those that could not otherwise afford such things.' He looks as if he's about to say more but then stops himself.

'And you help the French,' she says, grasping George's medal.

'I suppose I do.'

'That does not bother you?'

'Not very much. I get the feeling it bothers you far more, as a widow of Nelson's campaign against the French Navy.'

'Of course it does. It should bother everyone.'

'Why? Because the French believe every man should be equal? Because they decree *liberté, égalité, fraternité*?'

He pronounces the French effortlessly, with the correct accent. It's not what she expected. She says, 'Because they cut off the heads of their superiors and those who disagree with them.'

'I don't much like the way they've gone about things, I'll admit. But the principle of the thing doesn't upset me. Though one does wonder how they manage to run a ship, being each other's equals.'

'They're not,' she says, thinking of her father's absolute authority aboard his ships. 'They couldn't run a ship if they were. Or perhaps that's why they keep losing.'

'Only at sea. Boney did all right at Austerlitz.'

She pushes the blanket with her foot again. 'I'm certain nobody truly believed they were Napoleon's equal in that battle or any other.'

'You're probably correct. Still, the taxes levied to keep the war going are what's fuelling the smuggling. Show me one Cornishman who believes the tax is fair and I'll gladly give it up.'

She holds his gaze and says, 'You would never.'

He laughs again and she watches the pain move across his face. 'You've got the measure of me, madam.'

'Not madam,' she says. 'Isabel.'

'Isabel,' he says, more soberly. 'Are you as weary as I am?'

'Wearier.'

'Shall we rest awhile?'

She leans back against the wall. The light patterns are turning to shadows. 'You rest.'

He lifts his head and says, 'I've been here before . . . to the cottage. The place has been empty for years. I'd heard you were come into the area, but I didn't realise you'd be living in the old pilchard shed.' He shuts his eyes a moment as if gathering his thoughts. 'I know this is the only bed in the cottage and I'm afraid I'm in no state to leave it at present. However, you're welcome to share it with me. There's enough space for two and, though I may not look it, I am a gentleman—'

he stops and says quickly, 'at heart, that is. I wouldn't lay a finger on you, even if I were fit to do so.'

He looks terribly earnest. Sounds it, too. The bed is calling her, even with the hard mattress and the straw pricking her back. She's so, so tired. 'People would talk,' she says.

'Not if they don't know.'

She holds her top lip between her teeth as she thinks.

Jack says, 'I'm trusting you with my life at the moment. I think you can trust me with this.'

She gets up, smoothing down her chemise as if she's fully dressed. 'Very well.'

He pats the space next to him with his left hand and she walks to the other side of the bed. Lifting the hem of her chemise, she climbs on top of it. It's warm in the room and after a moment's consideration, she shrugs off the pelisse and places it at the foot end. Then she lies on her side, leaving as much space between her and the smuggler as she can find and pushes her hand under her cheek.

CHAPTER FOUR

The bed has shrunk. It was small before, but now that she's lying in it with Jack, facing him, it is not at all the size a bed for two should be. When he turns his head to look at her, she feels his breath on her skin. The room smells of blood and sweat. Maybe she should roll over. Then again, it may be better to keep an eye on him.

What did he mean when he said he was a gentleman at heart? He's a smuggler. A criminal, albeit a wounded one. She'd be able to get the better of him if she needed to, wouldn't she? She's too conscious of the man lying next to her for sleep to come easily, but listening to the muted swish of the river, it eventually crawls up and she drifts off, riding the waves of the Atlantic, a fishtail at her back.

When she wakes, Jack is looking at her. He's still on his back, but his face is turned towards her and he's awake and smiling at her. Has he been smiling the whole time or did the smile appear when she opened her eyes?

'Good morning,' he says. 'Or rather, good evening.'

The room is dark, shadows huddling in the corners. The lantern burned out long ago. She says, 'Good evening,' and gets up to light the candle. When the flame springs to life, she sits back on the bed and draws her legs under her. The room is still warm. She doesn't put the pelisse back on; the smuggler has already seen all there is to see. 'I never got dressed today,' she says, a little surprised, and he smiles and says, 'I never got undressed.'

'Doesn't it seem unfair to you that women aren't allowed to go to sea?' She has longed to go ever since she set foot on her father's ship at the age of five, the desire fuelled by the incessant tug of the ocean, but it has changed into something more essential since she lost George. As if by feeling a ship's deck move under her feet and chasing the wide horizon she'll be able to touch some part of him and draw him close.

Jack frowns. 'Where does this come from?'

'I was dreaming of the Atlantic Ocean.'

'Ah. I see. And no, I don't consider it unfair. Why? Do you feel it is?'

'George got to go to sea and so did my father, but I never will. It seems unjust, that's all.' She has always felt the injustice of it. Watching her father sail from Portsmouth as a little girl made her deeply sad, not only because she'd miss him, but because she couldn't go with him. How she misses him now. The sea did not take him – he would've much preferred that, she's sure – but illness did, six years after she lost her mother. His stories planted the seed of her yearning for seafaring – a yearning which her governess called unnatural in a girl. Isabel's longing for the ocean was her own, but that for shipboard life was her father's, transferred onto her like a stamp on a wax seal.

Jack says, 'Unjust, is it now? The sea is a dangerous place. People like to talk about how beautiful it is or how treacherous its moods. Both are correct to a point, but mainly it's dangerous. It's not a place for women.'

'But who's to say women aren't able to face danger? Don't we face it every time one of us births a child?' Another unnatural thought, according to her governess, but true. How well she remembers her stepmother's screams when each of her stepbrothers was born. The second birth almost killed the new Mrs Farnworth. How was that any different than facing the enemy's guns or the whims of the weather aboard a ship?

'You have very singular ideas, Isabel.'

With some satisfaction she says, 'So do you, Jack.'

She checks her stores – there's enough food for them both for another day or two – and she checks Jack. There's no sign of infection or fever. She heats up the soup she made the day before and watches him eat with something resembling relish. It tastes better on the second day, she thinks as she swallows a mouthful herself.

She returns to the bed and they talk until the night has deepened to the point it's flat, it's so dark. With the candle out she cannot see Jack, but she can hear him, his breath between words, his voice, low and deep; she can feel the shape of him, close by, without touching him. This time, when she sleeps, she doesn't dream.

In the morning, she's awake before him. She dresses with the same effort as always, fumbling with the ties at the back of her gown – her last clean one. The air is fresh and cool with drizzle when she steps outside to get water; the sun hides behind a deck of clouds. The tide is going out and for the first time since the smuggler arrived, she longs to follow it to where the river becomes the ocean. The desire is as strong as the need to draw air into her lungs. Only when she turns away from the water does the feeling abate. It is unfair, she thinks walking back to the cottage; no matter what Jack says about the danger of the sea.

In the kitchen, she cuts the leftover bread in thick slices. The bread has grown hard, but not so hard you cannot eat it. She makes a tray with cheese, the bread, two cups of water and, for lack of any other decent offering, a sliced carrot. She's about to take it upstairs when there's a knock on the door.

The tray wobbles; the water lurches in the cups, nearly spilling. Placing the tray on the floor behind the stairs, she goes to the door and takes a breath so deep it hurts the bottom of her chest. She smooths first the skirt of her dress, then her expression, and opens the door.

'Lieutenant Sowerby!' Too high; too loud. She shouldn't have said it like that. Can he tell? She drags up a smile. Her ears fill with the sound of the crunch she heard at the hanging; the ripped, agonizing scream. 'To what do I owe the pleasure?'

He bows. 'Mrs Henley. Please, may I come in? It's raining again.'

She glances past him: it's barely a drizzle. 'Naturally, please, do come in.'

She steps aside and he takes up the same spot as the first time he called on her, one hand on the table, filling the space. His face gleams; he has sweated his way up the path, she thinks.

'My dear Mrs Henley,' he begins. She tries to hide her shudder. 'I must impress upon you once more the danger in which you may find yourself, living in remote quarters such as these, all alone.'

Breathe, she tells herself. Slowly, naturally. 'I thank you for your concern, Lieutenant, but I assure you I am perfectly fine.'

'You may have heard there was an engagement at sea two nights ago, between a cutter of the Revenue Service, *Swallow*, and the smuggler vessel *Rapide*, not far from here.'

What should she say? Is it suspicious if she has heard of the event or if she hasn't? 'I hadn't heard that,' she guesses. 'Were you involved yourself?'

'I wasn't, but my most particular friend and esteemed fellow Riding Officer Lieutenant Sullivan was.'

'I hope your friend hasn't come to harm?'

'He's perfectly fine, I assure you.'

Is he making fun of her, saying it like that, using her own words, *perfectly fine* and *I assure you*? She wants to stand in the doorway to the sitting room to block his way to the stairs. Her fingers pluck at the lace edging on her cuff.

'However,' Lieutenant Sowerby continues, 'I have it on good authority that one of the smugglers was wounded during the action. The captain, if reports are correct.'

The shock runs through her so violently she sways on her feet. Putting a hand against the wall to steady herself, she blurts, 'Your friend – Lieutenant Sullivan – saw the man?'

Lieutenant Sowerby cocks his head, studying her. 'Not quite as such. Lieutenant Sullivan managed to shoot him from the deck of the *Swallow* at the range of some one-hundred yards – he's a crack shot with a musket – and with the smoke from the guns, he couldn't quite make out ...' He runs the tip of his index finger along his nose. 'The smuggler in question appeared to be giving commands in the stern of the ship and he wore a hat such as one would expect of a young officer. I believe we may conclude he was in fact the captain of the vessel. In any case, we believed him killed at first. It would've given me great pleasure to avail you of the news, had this indeed been the case, but it appears he lives and has made his escape. You don't happen to have heard of anyone looking for a place to hide or trying to contract the services of a doctor, have you?' As he talks, his eyes roam the small space.

The tray, she thinks. It's under the stairs and there are two cups of water on it. Keeping her voice soft, she says, 'I haven't heard any such thing. But if I do, I shall send word to you at once.'

What is the punishment for aiding smugglers? she wonders. Is it the same as for the crime of smuggling itself ...

death? Or something slightly less terrible; transportation, maybe? Her fingers are cold. She has found a thread sticking up from her sleeve and tugs on it, again and again.

'Just so,' says Lieutenant Sowerby, lips pursed. A drop of sweat rolls down his cheek and, with a look of irritation, he brushes it away. A fly zooms against the window. After a moment, he says, 'I saw you the day before yesterday. At the hanging of that traitor. You looked . . . troubled.' He tilts his head. 'Did the proceedings make you uneasy, Mrs Henley?'

Breathe, for God's sake! 'I . . . I had not witnessed an execution before. It did make me uneasy, but . . .' A tremor. Has he heard? She pressed ahead. 'I understand smuggling is a terrible crime.'

'Just so,' the lieutenant says again. 'It's intolerable to watch these criminals have free reign of the land. That's why I don't wait for them to be acquitted at trial. I ensure justice takes place. You see this, surely?'

'But of course.'

'I do wish you'd accept my offer of protection, Mrs Henley. They're cutthroats, the lot of them. I can't bear to think what they would do to a woman of such refined qualities as yourself.'

As on his previous visit, he looks as if he can not only bear to think of it easily, but rather enjoys the image. A trail of red spots creeps up his neck and into his face until he is blushing, his eyes grown dark, his mouth half-open. She doesn't mean to take a step back; isn't even aware she has done it until she feels the rough planks of the door against her shoulder blades.

'I entirely agree,' she says. At the sound of a light thud, she jumps; Lieutenant Sowerby has heard it, too. He's listening carefully, but there's no other noise.

'A bird, I suppose,' he says. 'Slamming into the window there, perhaps, the poor, useless creature. If you permit my saying, I noticed your reaction of fear, just now. It's clear to me you are ill at ease and you are right to feel so, living in this Godforsaken place all alone. I could protect you, madam, if you would but let me.' He pats the hilt of the sword at his side. When she doesn't say anything, he adds, 'I hope I may have the pleasure of your company again soon, at the dinner organised by my most particular friend, the Deputy Lord Lieutenant of Cornwall, at Weatherston Hall.'

'Dinner?'

'Oh dear, we do seem to have a knack for misunderstanding one another this morning. Has Lady Harriet Darby not come to see you?'

'She has not.'

Lieutenant Sowerby says, 'I hope you'll forgive me, but I made mention of your circumstances to Lady Darby, in case it might influence her desire to make your acquaintance. However, she assured me it did not; I believe she said – in her own words, which tend to be quite remarkable – she should not care a jot however much you were reduced in circumstance, for she was in dire need of decent company.'

The thread comes loose from her sleeve and she rolls it between her fingers. 'Perhaps something has prevented her coming.' She doesn't really believe this. Most probably, Lady

Darby took one look at the old pilchard shed and high-tailed it back to Weatherston Hall.

'Perhaps, indeed.' He purses his lips again, which would make him look comical if it wasn't for the odd, lingering blush in his cheeks. He raises his hand to his brow, wiping. Two days ago, that same hand put a noose around a man's neck. 'Well, an invitation may yet be forthcoming,' he says. 'The dinner is not for another fortnight. I shall look forward to your presence, if it may be procured.'

'So shall I,' she says. 'To your presence.'

'Much as I should like to linger, I'd best go. There are smugglers to catch, after all.'

His eyes fasten on her chest and he steps closer until, as before, she's trapped between his hulking body and the door. The sweat on him is pungent, sour-smelling. Leaning in so closely his breath grazes her cheek, he murmurs, 'You are an extraordinary woman, Mrs Henley.'

Her heart nearly beats its way through her skin. With the back of his hand, he moves as if to caress the left side of her face, but before he can touch her, she drops low and dodges his arm. Spinning around to face him, she says, 'I wish you Godspeed, sir.'

Lieutenant Sowerby stands very still, breathing hard. He's still red in the face when he says, 'Do let me know if you find yourself in need of aid at any time, Mrs Henley. Upon my honour, it vexes me that you should choose to live here like this.'

It's hardly a choice, she thinks, but she doesn't say it. 'I shall, sir.' *Go! Please go!* The wish is so strong she worries he'll see it on her face, so she looks down at his boots as he opens the door and crosses the doorstep. The boots are knee-length and made of brown leather. They're too clean for patrolling the coastal path. He must have them shined often.

The rushing of the waves reaches her over the lieutenant's steps. She draws strength from the sound as one might from a draught of water when thirsty. Would that leaving a fish for the sea spirit the Cornish people believe in gained one not protection from inclement weather but from noxious men, she thinks. She'd buy a fish just for the purpose every day in that case. If she weren't so deeply shaken, this thought would've made her smile.

She watches the boots make their way up the gravel path, watches the lieutenant mount his horse, then lifts her eyes to catch him raising his hand. 'Good day, Mrs Henley!'

Then he's gone. At once, she starts to tremble as badly as she did when Jack and his men entered her bedroom. She waits behind the door; she doesn't dare go up yet. Upstairs, all is quiet. After what feels like years, she opens the front door a crack and looks out. What she can see of the coastal path is empty. It has stopped raining but the air still smells of rain, a wet, leafy scent more suited to autumn than early spring. The river is swollen with the tide. She pushes the door open wider and takes a step outside, wanting to dip her fingers in the water and watch the waves move over them, but Jack waits upstairs. Deep breaths, then, tasting the sea air – the next-best thing for allaying her fears.

'Isabel,' Jack calls under his breath as she trembles her way up the stairs. He lowers the pistol when she steps into the room. 'Who was it?'

'Lieutenant Sowerby.' She sinks down on the bed, her head in her hands. 'Oh dear God.'

'What? What did you say to him?'

'Nothing! That's the problem. He's an officer of the Revenue Service and I lied to his face.' *It wasn't just what she didn't say to him; it was the way he looked at her.*

Jack says, 'I'm terribly grateful.'

'Oh, do hold your tongue,' she says. 'You knew I'd never say anything.' A sob rises in her throat. 'He hanged a man two days ago.'

'Jed Ferries from Penzance. I heard.' Jack pushes himself up before she can tell him not to and reaches for her hand. 'Your hand is very cold.'

'It's often so.'

He wraps his own around it and says gently, 'I didn't know that you wouldn't say anything. I hoped you wouldn't—' he stops himself and, letting go off her hand, says, 'I shall leave at the earliest opportunity. Rowell will be back tomorrow. I'm feeling better already.'

He does look a little better. There is some colour in his cheeks. 'I'm glad,' she says.

'You're still determined not to take any money for your hospitality? You're taking a considerable risk hiding a fugitive.'

'Don't remind me. And yes, I'm determined.'

'Then would you consider a business proposition instead?'

'What sort of business proposition?'

'We've used the shed – your shed – in the past for the storing of goods, until they could be moved further inland. A couple of days at most. It's a convenient spot, out of the way, down the inlet.'

That explains the padlock, she thinks. Jack says, 'I should like the use of it in the future, if you'll allow me.'

'No. Absolutely not.'

'It would only be a few times a year. You'd never see us – we'd come in with the new moon and leave before you even realise there's contraband stored on your property. I would pay you as well as any of our accomplices. Better, when we have some good runs of it with the new ship.'

She's going to say 'no' again but the word has got stuck on her tongue. She thinks of the farmer Mrs Dowling told her about, who was shot by revenue men for storing contraband on his property. It'd be madness to say yes.

Jack says, 'It would be a way to augment your income. And it wouldn't be charity. You'd be doing us a service.'

She will say it now. *No.* Simple, short, and *why* in Heaven's name is it so difficult to get the word out? 'I shall think about it,' she says.

'Please do.'

'How will I get word to you when I've made my decision?'

'Speak to Tom Holder, the keeper of the Shipwrights Arms. Tell him you've got news for his friend from the cove – say it exactly like that, not "my friend" or "a friend", but "your friend from the cove". Then tell him your news, in this case a simple "yes" or "no" will suffice.'

'Very well.' She feels stupidly pleased. She worried that once Jack left, she wouldn't see him again. The feeling annoys her. She should not see him again. He's a smuggler. She has done her Christian duty, helping him, and that's enough. She cannot get involved with smuggling. 'How much?' she says, feeling more foolish still.

'The compensation? Two percent of the profits. On a good run that can easily amount to,' he taps his fingers, thinking, 'ten pounds.'

'*Ten pounds*?' Her widow's pension is two shillings a day. Her mind whirls with the numbers. Ten pounds, that'd be a hundred days' worth of income. For a couple of nights' work. No, not even work – she wouldn't have to do anything but turn a blind eye to the cargo being stored in the shed.

Jack says, 'Does that change things?'

'I have to think about it.'

'Let me know when you've decided. I could use another friend along the river.'

'I shall.' She looks at his hand on the bed. She wishes it was still wrapped around hers. He was awfully forward taking her hand in his, but she cannot deny she liked the feeling. 'Shall I see you again after you leave?'

The smile appears as it did the day before, when she first saw him. He's quick to smile. He seems glad even though he's laid up here with a gunshot wound in his side and a Riding

Officer knocked on the door not thirty minutes ago. 'Should you wish to?'

'Yes. No. Maybe.'

The smile widens. 'Well, which is it?'

'I shall have to think about that, too.'

'You know how to reach me.'

'Yes,' she says. 'Yes, I do.'

When the doctor returns the next afternoon, he pronounces Jack a miracle, he's recovering that fast. 'You must rest another three weeks at home, at least,' he says. 'And nothing strenuous for four weeks thereafter. However, it's probably best if you move tonight, under cover of darkness, before the moon waxes too bright. Shall I send word to Dick Pascoe to come get you with the boat?'

'I'd be much obliged,' Jack says.

'You haven't had any trouble since I last saw you . . . of the lawful kind, I mean?'

'Sowerby showed up, but Isabel saw him off. She's a fiery one.'

She says, 'You should see me wield my tinderbox,' which makes Jack laugh.

The doctor looks from him to her. 'There hasn't been any sign of infection? No fever?'

He speaks to her as if she's Jack's nurse. 'None,' she says.

'Good. Has he eaten anything?'

She details the bread, the cheese, the soup and milk.

The doctor says, 'I heard about the hanging. He's a right bastard, that Sowerby, isn't he?'

'He's worse than most,' Jack says.

The doctor puts his coat back on, the fabric taut over his bulging arms. After he takes his leave, Isabel says, 'He doesn't much look like a doctor, does he? Is he a surgeon?'

'He's a veterinarian.'

'You're not serious?'

'He was a ship's surgeon at one time, but he couldn't bear watching the press gang at work. Said he didn't like having men under his knife who never chose to join His Majesty's Navy in the first place. He's very good. And he can be trusted.'

The hours until nightfall flow by like water. Before she knows it — before she wants it — there's the call of an owl outside, hooting four times in a row. 'That'll be Dick,' Jack says, pushing himself up.

'How will they move you?'

'I'll walk.'

'It's bad for the wound.'

'It's only down to the boat. Can't be more than five steps from the house.'

She likes how he says 'house', as if it's more than a two-room cottage. It makes her think of her old house in Greenwich. Aside from George's debts, she left it to escape the rumours that had begun to swirl about her and James. And now she finds herself here with a smuggler. How has it come to this, in only a week?

Jack's voice pulls her out of her thoughts. 'Thank you again, Isabel.'

'It's nothing,' she says, at a loss for words.

Dick and Oppy come up. Even by the light of the candle and the lantern Oppy carries, she can tell they're both paler than they were two nights before. Oppy has blue half-moons under his eyes and a stubble flecked with red; Dick's eyes are red-rimmed, as if he hasn't slept for the past two days.

Jack says, 'All well?' and Oppy tells him yes, they've unloaded the cargo, it's stored and will be taken inland in two days. They have brought him a clean shirt and Isabel begins to turn away so he can change out of the bloodstained one he's wearing over the bandaging, but then she catches the look of pain on his face as he struggles with the cloth.

'Here, let me do it,' she says. The heat from her face runs down her arms, down her stomach, making her feel as if every inch of her is blushing as she helps him pull the shirt over his head. He's smiling at her. There's the thin line of black hair down his stomach again, only the top of it visible, the rest is under the bandage. The hair on his chest matches it, dark against his tanned skin, and he's broad-shouldered, but not as much as Dick or the doctor; he's leaner, as if not everything about him is hard, as if she could discover some softness in him if she had the chance. This makes her blush worse and he sees it and now he's not smiling, but openly grinning as she fumbles with the clean shirt and, finally, manages to slip it on and fasten the laces.

She has only ever seen George like this. That takes care of the blush; it seeps away from her cheeks, from her stomach. Now she does turn away and says, 'I don't think you should walk.'

No answer. He's too stubborn, she thinks. Oppy hands her the lantern and he and Dick move to carry their captain, but Jack tells them to support him under the arms instead. As they hoist him up, the pain digs into his features and she says, 'No, don't. You shouldn't,' but then he's on his feet and takes a tentative step towards the door. It's the first time she has seen him upright and not on the bed or being carried. He's stooping and leaning heavily on his friends, but she can tell he's taller than she had thought, almost as tall as Tom Holder, who is the tallest man she knows.

She goes ahead, holding up the lantern to light the way, counting Jack's steps. Every one of them takes a long time. Two to the door, because he got off the bed on the side closest to it, then ten down the stairs. These are the worst and take the longest. Then four more to go through the kitchen. The scrape of the door and then they're outside. The moon is a sliver in the sky. The gravel crunches under the soles of the men's boots. At the bottom of the garden, close to the wall, a small rowboat is pulled up on the rocks. The night is black as coal, but on the river, it's a little less so, as if the water makes its own light.

Dick and Oppy get in first, then they help Jack into the boat. When he's safely seated in the stern, Oppy takes back the lantern and puts it next to Jack, while Dick gets out to push the boat into the water. The two men each take a set of oars. Jack looks up at her and half-bows, which is difficult sitting down and, she worries, must hurt his stomach even more. 'Fair winds, Isabel!' he calls softly and she lifts her hand, calling, 'Goodbye!' almost in a whisper, and then the oars slide into the water and quietly, smoothly, the boat pulls away from the shore.

She stands by the water, watching the three figures in the boat until the night swallows them. She shivers in her dress; she should've worn her pelisse. Perhaps she should learn how to knit herself a shawl like the ones the Cornish women wear. It'd be another thing with which to occupy herself, now that she no longer has to care for a wounded smuggler. There are many such things. She has more cooking to learn and much in the way of cleaning, washing and other tasks. Her life is full enough as it is and she doesn't want any trouble. Most of all, she doesn't want any whispers to trail her like they did the past months, before she came to Cornwall. No one can know about Jack's two-day stay at the cottage. The mere thought of what people might say if they knew is unbearable.

It's why you left London, isn't it? Because of trouble, he said, far too astute for her liking. The thought of Jack learning of the rumours about her and James is upsetting in its own right. Why, she isn't sure. Jack's a smuggler; he breaks the law for a living, yet the possibility that she might lose his good opinion makes her feel queasy. She resolves never to tell – if she sees him again, which isn't at all certain.

Making her way back up the path, she casts a glance at the shed. It's so dark she can only see its outline, black against the sky. She couldn't very well allow smugglers to store their contraband in there. She'd be committing a crime.

The cottage's window glows yellow. She goes in, drawing

the door shut behind her and, taking up the candle, goes upstairs. The room still smells of Jack. Of blood, too. She lifts the bloodied shirt from where he dropped it on the bed. She'll have to wash all these blankets and sheets and scrub down the mattress. Tomorrow, she'll figure out how to use the tub and clean her clothes. It can't be hard, can it? She'll use water from the river; it'll be easier than getting water from the well.

Practical things. She has a new life to learn, to live. It doesn't have smugglers in it. It shouldn't have.

She strips the blankets and sheets from the bed and drops them in the corner on the floor. Taking her cloak from the travel case, she drapes it over her as a makeshift blanket and lies on top of the mattress. She never took her dress off, the second night she slept next to Jack. She doesn't take it off now. The room is colder without him in it. Darker, too. She didn't think she could feel any more alone than she did during her first night in the cottage. It takes a long time for sleep to find her, for the sea to draw her to it.

When she does sleep, she's back in the water. The fish-tail behind her swishes and she's propelled forward, the sea moving around her like the wind. Far below her are shapes, dark ones, like moving shadows. Large fish – only not quite. The tail swishes. There's a power in it, a force of sorts. It runs through her veins; it shapes her muscles.

Upon waking, the sense of power lingers. Next time Lieutenant Sowerby comes too close, she'll tell him to desist, she thinks. She has no use for his attentions and while he may have the authority of the law behind him when it comes to smugglers, he has no such control over her.

Richard Holder knocks on her door that morning, just before noon. He's clutching a letter. It looks small in his hand. He says, 'My father said I'd best bring it to you straight away.'

For a split second, she thinks the letter is from James, then she recognises her stepmother's slanted, jabbing script. Of course it isn't from James. 'I'll write,' she told him before she left, but he told her not to. He was to go back to sea and if she wrote to him, it'd only cause more trouble.

She nearly fainted the first time he came to see her, when he told her of George's last moments. Maybe that breached the distance in rank between them – him grabbing hold of her and guiding her to an armchair. Or maybe it was the way they talked, about seafaring and ships, about her father, under whom James had served when the Admiral was still Captain Farnworth, and about George. He was a good officer, James said. The men liked him.

James's stories forced the sharp teeth of time to recede. That's why she invited him to tea, why they took walks along the Thames together, James still limping from his leg wound. That was not the only injury he sustained in the battle. Underneath an exterior hardened by over two decades at sea lay a dented spirit. He had trouble sleeping, he said; was startled by the slightest noise. When he did sleep he dreamt of the cannon shot that killed half the gun crew.

She, too, spent her nights in the past. In the dark, empty

bedroom, memories whispered to her until they took on the colour of the sea, fading to a misty grey-blue in sleep; during the day, they followed in the wake of James's voice. Her friend Louisa later called him a 'common sailor'. There was nothing common about James, but Isabel knew his lack of rank meant their friendship might raise eyebrows, and soon, gossip swirled around Greenwich. After losing George, it was a small thing – it was nothing. And it stayed nothing until Louisa saw them that day, three months ago.

James had George's Trafalgar medal, which she'd kept in its case for a year, put on a black ribbon for her and she allowed him to fasten it around her neck. In that moment, it felt as if the silver disc was all she had left of George. Eyes streaming, she turned to James and embraced him. His arms locked around her shoulders and he was just telling her she was going to be fine when the footman showed in Louisa. *I found her in the arms of a common sailor.* That was the story Louisa, not much of a friend after all, told their acquaintances. *The one she goes walking with. What would her husband have said?*

Her protests were in vain. It wasn't just their difference in standing that lent wings to the story, it was her widowhood, too. The fact that James had served under George made it worse: soon, it seemed as if all of Greenwich was talking. As the months passed, the stares and whispers became un-bearable. Already she knew she wouldn't be able to keep the house, not with their money gone. The rumours were the final straw. She had enough, of Greenwich, of London, of the whole of society.

The cottage Mr Griggs wrote to her about sounded like a sanctuary. And now that she's here, it is, in a manner. She has never before felt so alone, but neither, she realises as she cuts open her stepmother's letter, has she ever felt so free.

The letter contains a summons to Woodbury, her late father's house in Norfolk. Her stepmother's willingness to risk her reputation by association surprises her, but she couldn't live under one roof with the new Mrs Farnworth. Not even now. She much prefers the cottage and the village with its sea-river and people full of strange beliefs and stories — stories which stir a feeling in her not unlike the memories trailing James's voice. As if the past is closer.

CHAPTER FIVE

During the days that follow she keeps up a flurry of activity. She washes clothes, sheets and blankets until her hands are raw and hangs everything out to dry. She washes Jack's shirt, too, but the blood doesn't come out. The cotton is very fine. No wonder, she thinks, with the kind of profits he's making. Mrs Dowling tells her for stains on white, you want to put the garment out to dry flat on the grass in the bright sun. 'That'll bleach it good and proper,' she says. Isabel doesn't tell her what kind of stains they are.

She starts to mend the tear in the shirt. This is something she can do, at least; and can do well. It's a long rip, right across the bottom half, with a small part missing where the bullet took part of the cloth. She used to mend things for George sometimes. He could do it himself, they were taught how as midshipmen and of course any of the servants could do it, but she liked to do it for him.

Every afternoon, she sits on the white bench in the garden and sews. The river fans out before her like a length of blue silk-satin under a partly cloudy sky. She watches the gulls dip and rise as she stitches. They make her think of the creatures George saw on his journeys: all manner of sharks and dolphins, strange fish with spiky bodies and giant white birds in South America, and once, a whale nearly the length of the ship. Nobody believed that one, but he swore it was true. She thinks of the villagers' belief in the sea spirit shaped like a merman. Could it be that there are things in the ocean of which they have no knowledge? Almost as if in response, the sun appears, lifting the blue into bright iridescence as it hits the water, and the longing to get in and follow the current briefly takes her breath away.

The nights are quiet, apart from one. It's the evening before the next market day, late enough only the moon differentiates between the black of the river and that of the sky. She's working her way through a leather-bound volume titled *The Experienced English Housekeeper* which Mrs Dowling has lent her. She has just started on Chapter Fourteen, *Possets, Gruel &c.* when she hears footsteps on the gravel path. Putting the book down, she listens closely. In response, the gravel crunches again, nearer to the cottage. She blows out the candle and, heart racing, feels her way to the fireplace in the sitting room.

Gripping the fire poker, she tiptoes to the front door, cursing herself for not getting a lock, cursing, too, the scrape across the flagstones as she opens it. Slivers of cloud drift past the moon, high above the river. The trees lining the coastal path stand silhouetted like frozen spectators. She feels as if something in the trees has its ancient eyes on her. There isn't a shred of wind, nor the sound of footsteps. She's lifting the poker, about to call out when—

'Mrs Henley! But you are awake!'

The poker hits the gravel as she clutches her chest, finding her breath. 'Lieutenant Sowerby – sir. You gave me such a fright! What in Heaven's name are you doing here?'

'Forgive me, madam, I believed you abed.' Lieutenant Sowerby's garments are in a state of disarray, the red shirt partly unbuttoned, necktie loose, hat askew. Snatching it from his curls, he bows and exhorts, 'There's a threat, madam. Smugglers lurking about. I wanted to ensure you're safe.'

Her breath slows. She catches a whiff of drink on him, mixed with aniseed or caraway, as if he's been chewing comfits. She hides her uneasiness by bending down and lifting the poker. Somewhere in the dark, the lieutenant's horse drags its hoof across the ground. 'The only person I see lurking about, sir, is you.' The words come out more sharply than she intended. She remembers the dream she had after Jack left, of the power of the sea running through her. She cannot afford to alienate the lieutenant – besides a Riding Officer, he's the only member of society in the area with whom she's acquainted – but she can try to make sure he doesn't come too close again.

'All I have in mind is your wellbeing, madam,' Lieutenant

Sowerby says, retying his necktie. 'As you're still up, could I come in and keep watch for a while? It would greatly allay my concerns for the safety of your person.'

'I was about to go to bed. I've already put out the candle.'

'It wouldn't be long. I expect they'll pass by in the next hour.' He's already making his way to the door.

She casts a glance at the river before she lets him in, drawing a measure of fortitude from it. She has but to look at Lieutenant Sowerby to hear the echo of Agnes Ferries' scream as she watched him hang her husband. The kitchen thrums with the sound as he perches on one of the chairs by the window, looking out at the dark.

He stays the full hour and then some, sipping from the cup of milk she's offered him and largely filling the time with a monologue about the evils of smuggling and the necessity to stamp it out. He delivers this in a breathless sort of voice that makes the hair on her arms stand on end. She keeps hold of the fire poker, underneath the table, the whole time. What she'd do with it, she isn't sure, but it feels good in her hand.

When at last, the lieutenant gets up to leave, she steps aside so as not to get cornered again, but he follows her until she's with her back against the stone counter, only a foot of space between them. His eyes are glazed, his face turned a blotchy red as if he's in a fever. He begins to say something in praise of her person again, something to do with purity, but she barely hears as she raises the fire poker until it sits resolutely between them.

'I should like you to leave now, sir,' she says. She remembers the feeling of the fishtail in her dream, the strength she possessed. 'Now,' she repeats, gripping the poker harder.

He rakes his eyes across her and then steps back, saying, 'Yes, indeed. I bid you goodnight, madam.'

After he goes out, she takes the fire poker up to the bedroom. She falls asleep with her hand around the handle and dreams of a whale the size of the cottage, which swallows Lieutenant Sowerby whole.

The weather turns to full spring. Even the mornings are pleasant now. Walking on the coastal path in the sun six days after the smuggler left, she marinates in sweat under the tight stays and layers of chemise, skirts and gown. The climb down to the cove she selects for her purpose is steep along black rocks, but when she gets to the bottom, she cannot be seen from the path. She's out of sight of the inlet where the fishing boats anchor and cannot see any vessel from where she stands. She's tired of resisting; the possibility of revenue men passing by on the path can no longer stop her.

The outgoing tide has pushed the beach into wet ripples, as if the sand, too, is a live thing, full of motion like the sea. Indecision grips her another moment, then she kicks it to the side and strips down to her chemise as fast as she can. The breeze pulls at the fabric, caressing her skin and she looks at it, at the crisp white cotton which took so long to wash and dry and then she takes this off, too, as well as her stays. The river bites her flesh when she enters the water, it's that cold — like dropping through ice.

She kicks her legs hard and moves her arms, puffing with the effort, and then she's through the worst of it. The cold recedes and she kicks off properly, away from the rocks, and swims. She's quite warm now. The water glints around her. With the sun on it like this it's no longer black, but a hundred shades of green and blue, like the turquoise stone George brought her back from Naples. She glides through the water, revelling in the way her arms and legs are free from the constraint of her clothes and the weight of gravity. She has always been a good swimmer, though she doesn't remember the first time she swam. Her parents swore they didn't teach her; it's simply something she has always been able to do.

She swims for maybe half an hour. She could go longer, but she has supper to prepare. She wishes she could swim the whole day and all through the night, going and going, right out to sea and then across the ocean. She wonders what the ocean feels like at night, when it's so dark you cannot imagine there being an end to it. Perhaps it's like that if you go deep enough under the surface; perhaps it's always night.

The swimming is more than just refreshing. For the first time since she came to Helford she doesn't feel alone. No, that's not right – for the first time since the smuggler left the cottage. Every time she walks by the shed, she wonders if she should go to the innkeeper, Tom Holder, and tell him she has news for his friend from the cove.

As she steps back onto the beach, she hears a voice. Only, it's not truly a voice . . . it's the breeze, she thinks, or maybe it's the seagulls squawking or the water softly reaching for her. *Swim*, the voice says. *Come home.* She looks back at the river, squinting against the light. A shadow moves along the edge of the inlet. A fish, only the shadow is too long, like the shapes she saw in her dream. She looks at it until it has moved out of sight. A cloud passes before the sun, making her shiver. She thinks of Jack's words, *There's nothing unnatural about the Bucca. He's nature itself; he's a part of the sea.* The landscape is playing tricks on her; the villagers' notions about the merman are making her see things.

Taking up her clothes, she finds a spot in the sun and lets the warmth of the day dry her. An hour later, she's walking down the gravel path, her eyes fixed on the shed again, when a loud snort nearly makes her shriek.

A black stallion rears its head and snorts again, stomping its right foot. The horse is tied to the oak sapling by the door. It's a magnificent animal, tall on its legs, its black coat in places almost silver in the sun, with a thick, smooth mane. The horse couldn't look more out of place next to the cottage. Stomping again, the stallion shakes its head, as if it knows it.

At the sound of a woman's voice, she spins around. 'Buttons! You impatient thing. We've only just got here.'

Buttons? Isabel thinks. The woman, too, doesn't belong. She's standing on the path that leads to the water and she's as young as Isabel – younger, perhaps – with blonde curls as shiny as the horse's mane, a heart-shaped face and eyes that could vie with Jack's for bluest. Despite the weather, she's in a full riding habit of the finest green wool, with gold-thread embroidery along the front and a matching silk ribbon wound into her elaborately pinned hair. Isabel used to see women dressed like this in London – she used to be one of them.

This must be Lady Harriet Darby, she thinks, whom Lieutenant Sowerby said wanted to visit and who, she's sure, must be regretting her decision to come. She glances at the cottage, seeing again how small and dark and simple it is. How squalid. Not to mention, she looks more than a little shabby herself. Certainly, her second-best gowns still far outshine those of the women around the village, but her hair is wet from her swim, her shoes have dried mud stuck to them and she isn't wearing any gloves.

The woman walks up and caresses the horse's nose. Her hands are slender, encased in kidskin. White, not cream. The contrast between the white of the leather and the black of the horse's coat is as startling as the woman's presence in front of the old pilchard shed. Isabel opens her mouth to say something, but the woman is quicker. Turning away from the horse, she says, 'Mrs Isabel Henley. May I present myself? My name is Lady Harriet Darby, of Weatherston Hall. I was told of your coming into the area and I hope very much you don't consider it presumptuous of me to introduce myself.' The words tumble out like marbles. Lady Darby's fingers flutter to her face. Giggling, she adds, 'The truth is, I've been desperate to meet you.'

Isabel curtsies and to her surprise, Lady Darby does the same. Isabel says, 'I'm honoured to make your acquaintance, Lady Darby.'

'I'm ever so pleased,' Lady Darby twitters. 'I had meant to come sooner, do you know, but I was laid up with the most horrid cold. My nose is still red, can you see?' She turns her head to show her profile.

Isabel says, 'I cannot tell, Lady Darby. You look lovely.'

'Oh, thank you. I don't believe I do, but it's kind of you to say.' Behind Lady Darby, the horse snorts again and she turns to him. 'We'll go riding again later. I'm much too glad to have made a new friend.' To Isabel, she says, 'I do hope you don't mind me calling you my friend. I know we've only just met ... oh, minutes ago, but I am sure we shall be the best of friends. Do you know, this is such empty country? I could ride for a day and not meet a friend. Except now you've come. Weatherston is only three miles from here.'

Isabel smiles. Just listening to Lady Darby makes her feel more like herself again. She's about to say, *would you like to come in*, but then remembers the cottage. She looks away, her hand moving to George's medal, her eyes on the sparkling river, and then she has it. 'Should you like to take tea in the garden with me, Lady Darby? It's particularly lovely this time of year.'

'Oh! I should like it of all things. And please, call me Harriet. I don't stand on ceremony, not with friends. May I call you Isabel, Isabel?' She giggles again. 'Isabel, Isabel. I'm such a dooby, aren't I?'

'Will your horse be all right here?'

'Buttons? Yes, he's fine. He's an impatient fellow, but I shan't be more than an hour, I'm sure. My husband expects me home by five. Oh,' she adds, suddenly, 'do you mean on account of the smugglers? My friend Lieutenant Sowerby told me there has been an engagement at sea recently, shots fired and so on. They seem to be growing more impudent by the day.'

Isabel glances at the shed, saying, 'It would appear so.'

Harriet says, 'You don't think they would try to steal Buttons?'

'I'm sure they wouldn't dare; not when we're right here. But perhaps it's best to put him in the shed. I can't lock it, but he'll be out of sight.'

Ten minutes later, Harriet is sitting on the white bench in the garden, the colour moving in her face as she drinks in the view of the river. Isabel has taken her around the cottage rather than through it. It's not much of a path, more of a strip of grass, that wraps around to the back, but it meant she didn't have to show Harriet the kitchen and sitting room.

Harriet says, 'It's ever so pretty, isn't it? Just as I think I cannot love this country any less, I'm presented with a view like this, which turns my entire judgement upside down again.'

'I'll fetch the tea,' Isabel says. 'It will take me a little while, I'm afraid.'

If Harriet wonders about her getting it herself, she doesn't say. In the kitchen, she flies through the motions: the fire, the pot, the tea leaves, floating like so many paper-thin boats, the strainer. She's glad she has saved the tea for any potential guests.

The cups are earthenware, but she has milk and a little

sugar. Thank heavens she went to the baker that morning; the bread has barely had time to cool. She cuts the slices far thicker than she would if she were on her own. She has butter, too, and a pot of strawberry jam from Mrs Winters who lives down the road, where the inlet peters out into mud, and who wouldn't take any money for it.

She feels foolish for thinking she did not want any friends when she came to the village. She has been here only just over a fortnight and the people in Helford treat her like one of their own. Mrs Dowling even calls her that, *one of our own*. 'It's because you were born here,' she says and Isabel is inordinately grateful she says it like that, *born here* and not, *found here* or worse, *brought here by the Sea Bucca*.

Balancing everything on the tray isn't easy as she walks down the uneven path, through the tunnel of greenery into the paradise garden. A part of her worries she has taken too long and Harriet will have left. But no: she's still sitting on the bench, gazing at the river, her gloved hands folded in her lap. Isabel didn't realise how much she missed having a friend like Harriet until she saw her standing in front of the cottage when she returned from her swim. She didn't realise how much she missed feeling like herself.

Harriet smiles when Isabel brings the tea. Her speech is fast and punctuated with giggles. From time to time, her fingers move across her face and throat, as if she's brushing away a fly or a tear. She proclaims the tea delicious, the garden utterly delightful, the bread and jam the best she has tasted south of the Tamar. She tells Isabel a little of her life in the west country, of the lack of society, of how much she misses London and her parents' ancestral home in Kent. More than anything, she wants to hear what she calls 'the latest gossip' and Isabel says, 'It's not really the latest. I came into Cornwall a fortnight ago. And I lived in Greenwich.'

As she says it, the fear claws inside her. Harriet has friends in London. Family, too. Could she have heard the rumours? But if she did, Harriet wouldn't have come to call on her, would she?

Harriet says, 'Greenwich is nearly London though, isn't it? And a fortnight still far more recent than anything I've heard. My friends are too busy calling on each other and attending balls to send more than a few lines every couple of weeks. I've no idea what I'm missing out on and have only my imagination to paint the picture for me.' Harriet's hand dangles by her side. She plucks a daisy from the wall – Erigeron, or Fleabane, Isabel's mind supplies after a lesson from Mrs Dowling – and begins to remove its petals one by one.

The fear ebbs away. As they drink their tea, she feeds Harriet bits and pieces of the life she has left behind in Greenwich. Harriet doesn't ask about George. She does say, 'Aren't you lonely, living here by yourself?'

'I am, a little,' she says after a moment. 'But I suppose one gets used to it.' Her voice wavers, belying the sentiment. She thinks of George, of how she used to pass the months waiting for him. She was on her own then, too, although there were the servants, of course. But it was different, because she knew he'd be coming back. Until he didn't.

The tears rise in her so suddenly she makes a choking noise in her attempt to hold them back. She tries to turn it into a cough, but it's useless: Harriet has seen her distress and reaches for her hand, patting it lightly. With effort, she manages a smile. 'It's not that bad, truly. And . . .' she hesitates, unsure if she could make Harriet understand.

'And what, Isabel?'

'This may sound strange, but there's something appealing in being on one's own. I've never really had the chance to do things for myself or make my own decisions. It was always father or George who decided for me and after I lost George, the house was always bustling with people, friends and servants and so on. It's quiet here. I feel I'm able to think more easily. And while I still have much to learn and sometimes barely manage, I do feel as if for the first time I'm . . . well, truly independent.'

'Oh.' Harriet breathes the word, like a sigh, her mouth round with it.

Isabel looks down at her cup. 'That must sound awfully strange to you.'

'Oh, but it doesn't. On the contrary.' Harriet colours; she brings up her hand, pushing unseen hairs from her face. 'I think it sounds heavenly, my dear Isabel. To be in control of one's decisions, why, it must be so very freeing. I only wish . . . oh!' She clasps her hand to her mouth. 'Oh no, I did not mean for it to sound as though – I love Sir Hugh dearly and I could never . . .'

'Of course.' She places her hand on Harriet's kidskin-clad

wrist. 'I do understand you. Marriage, even under the best of circumstances, can make one feel hemmed in, can it not?'

She had never put it in those words before, not even in her own mind, but now that she says it, she feels it's true. There's value in her new independence, she sees suddenly – she's poor, yes, but she's free. She hadn't considered remarrying the past three years, despite two offers by well-respected, if slightly older gentlemen, because the pain of losing George was still too raw. Her stepmother urged her to accept the second offer, but she didn't see how she could be another man's wife if the motions of everyday life still cut inside her. Of course, at the time, she still believed the prize money forthcoming; she did not realise what George's debts meant.

Now she feels there may be another reason not to remarry, if she were given the chance. Maybe her independence is too valuable a dowry to pay.

Sounding relieved, Harriet says, 'Yes, that's what I meant. 'Hemmed in' is a good way to describe it. Not like a gilded cage, nothing so dire as that, but perhaps a garden, free to grow and flower as it will as long as it stays within its walls and hedges. I suppose you have moved beyond your hedges, Isabel. Mine are rather prickly, I'm afraid. Sir Hugh can be *very* exacting. Which is why I should probably ...'

She lifts the small gold watch dangling from her waist and gasps. 'Is that the time? Oh, but I'm afraid I must dash. I've overstayed, it's been an hour and ten already – I must go at once.' She jumps up, the alarm wild in her, pushing her features into a shocked frown. 'I do apologise, Isabel. I've spent such a marvellous while with you in your lovely garden, I lost track of the time. Sir Hugh detests it when I'm late. He dines early, as they do in the service – well, you being an officer's wife, you understand, I'm sure.'

Isabel rises and Harriet embraces her as if they're sisters. She smells of sunshine and roses – some perfume, Isabel thinks. Harriet says, 'I do hope I shall see you again soon, Isabel. Please call on me at Weatherston any time. Oh! I almost forgot the purpose of my visit, besides making your acquaintance. I do hope you haven't found me presumptuous coming like this. I couldn't think who to ask to make the introduction besides Lieutenant Sowerby, who has been rather busy as of late. Besides, I understand he has not been formally introduced to you himself.'

'He came to warn me about smugglers,' Isabel says, willing any trace of disgust from her voice. 'So I believe the lack of a formal introduction may be forgiven.'

'Yes, yes, most certainly. And he is a man of unblemished character, I can assure you.'

'Isn't he – don't you find him – a little ruthless?'

'Ruthless?' Harriet's eyes widen. 'My dear Isabel, it's the smugglers who are ruthless!'

'He hanged a man the other day,' she says, unwilling to let it go.

'So I heard. A hardened criminal from the sound of it. I'm grateful Lieutenant Sowerby is so zealous in his pursuit; Cornwall shall be safer for it. Do you know, he's from London too? Born and bred, I believe.'

'Is he?' Her heart thumps. If Lieutenant Sowerby learned about the rumours about her and James — it doesn't bear thinking about.

'Well, I must dash. Dear Isabel, I shall see you soon, I hope.' Harriet darts up the path, around the house.

Isabel hurries after her. 'Harriet. The purpose of your visit, you said?'

'Oh, yes, of course. Sir Hugh and I are having a small dinner party Tuesday next week. Just a few of our friends in the area. Lieutenant Sowerby will be there, as well as another officer, Lieutenant Sullivan. Then there's Mr and Mrs William Tredinnick, who own several mines, including the largest copper one — I forget what it's called — and Mr John Carlyon, owner of an estate at Roskorwell, and lastly, Mr Frederick Pickford of Pickford House. And you, I hope, dear Isabel. As you see there will only be one other lady in attendance and she's past fifty. Do say you'll come.'

Isabel's stomach clenches at the thought of seeing Lieutenant Sowerby again. But then she thinks of the blue muslin gown she wore to the ball at Blakemore where she first met George and which she didn't expect to ever wear again. Besides this, the thought of the food alone is enough — she can almost taste the meats, the cheeses, the puddings they'll serve. She'd like to see Harriet again, too. And the other guests may prove decent company. Surely they won't all be like Lieutenant Sowerby?

She glances at the cottage again. It couldn't be more unlike anything the other guests will have for a house, but she has only just come down from Greenwich, which, as Harriet says, is nearly London. This carried enough weight, apparently, for Harriet to disregard her reduced circumstances in favour of making her acquaintance. Most of the guests at the dinner won't know of the way she's forced to live now – not unless Lieutenant Sowerby or Harriet tells them. 'I'd love to come,' she says. 'Thank you.'

'It won't be anything grand, mind you,' says Harriet, getting into the saddle.

Isabel bites back a laugh, thinking, *It'll be grander than a supper of fish and carrot soup.* Smiling, she says, 'It sounds like just the thing.'

She gives Harriet a wave and turns to close the door of the shed, the question of the storing of contraband back in her mind. As much as ten pounds on a good run, Jack said. It'd be wrong, but with ten pounds she could buy another gown like the blue muslin. Or, more practically, she could buy better sheets, a new mattress, an armchair. She could buy all manner of things that would make life in the cottage more comfortable.

And then, suddenly, she cannot do it any longer. All through the past week, she has occupied her mind with practical things, filling her days with necessary but oftentimes mindless tasks; all to keep Jack out of her head. But now he's in it again and he's taking up all of the space and she misses him the way you shouldn't miss someone you've only known for two days – someone you will likely not see again. She misses the way they talked and the sound of his laughter and how he made her not think about George so much.

Storing contraband in the shed was never about getting ten pounds with which to buy gowns or sheets.

She gets her change purse from the kitchen – she may pick up some fresh fish on the way home, mackerel or maybe pollock if there is any. Along the way people greet her. They're people she knows from introductions made by Mrs Dowling, who knows the entire village, and some only from moments like this, when she walks up the road and sees the same faces day after day. So what if half of them – maybe all of them – believe she is the Sea Bucca's daughter. They're friendly; they've taken her in. She isn't sure it will be the same at Weatherston Hall. Although, if Harriet's enthusiasm is anything to go by, she'll be fine.

When she reaches the Shipwrights Arms, she spots two women on the doorstep of one of the cottages. One watched her arrive in Helford, the other is younger and wears a shawl that's similar to her companion's, but in bright green and blue instead of black. The women watch her approach the inn and she feels the weight of their stares as she did before. They can't know about Greenwich. Do they, like Mrs Dowling, believe in the Sea Bucca story?

She turns back to the women and lifts her hand in greeting. A moment, the length of a swing from the inn's sign, then both women wave back. The older one smiles a dark gap of a smile.

The Shipwrights Arms is shadowy and empty but for two

craggy men sharing a jug of ale at a table by the window. Everything inside the inn's common room is brown: the wooden planked floor and wall panelling, the tables, the chairs, the cabinet where the spirits are kept. It smells brown, too: tobacco smoke and ale. The only thing not brown are the stumps of candles mounted on the walls and the black residue left on the panelling where they've burned for a hundred years or more.

The glass in the windows is better than that at the cottage. The river lies behind it like a torpid, silver snake and beyond that waits the sea, beckoning.

'Mrs Henley!' Tom Holder exclaims when he comes out of the backroom. Bowing, he says, 'To what do I owe the honour?'

'Good afternoon, Mr Holder.' She enquires after his family; Richard, doing well, he says, and the little 'uns — there are four of them, between three and eight, and his wife Mary. Then he offers her what he calls 'a sip of something', saying he's got ale and various spirits.

'No, thank you,' she says. 'I've come to . . .'

The two men at the window have stopped talking. She lowers her voice: 'I've got a message for your friend from the cove.' She has gone over it in her mind countless of times, yet it still comes out wrong. 'News,' she says quickly. 'I've got news for your friend from the cove.'

'Do you now, Mrs Henley?' he says, with a smile that seems equal parts amused and astonished. 'I dare say you've come to know my friend very quickly. You must feel at home here in Helford.' The way he says it – he's enjoying this, she thinks. He feels it's part and parcel of living here. A sign she belongs. She remembers Lieutenant Sowerby's words, *they're all in on it*. Maybe they are. It's wrong, but maybe a tax of 100 percent on tea is wrong, too.

Just a month ago, she couldn't have fathomed doing what she's about to do. She remembers Lieutenant Sowerby's other assertion, too: *they're aiding the French*. She doesn't want to aid the French, but she does want to help Jack and she likes the idea that people may be able to buy sugar and tea, things they couldn't otherwise afford. She herself, too.

Most of all, she wants the war to end, and with it, the high taxes.

George and his friends, his fellow officers, used to jest about it. They dreaded the moment when, in their words, 'peace would break out', taking with it all chance of promotion and prize money – Jack wasn't wrong about the latter. In the midshipmen's mess, they'd toast 'a bloody war and a sickly season.' When George told her, she merely smiled, but she felt cold at the thought. All she wanted was for the war to end and George to stay home with her. It hurt to know he wished for the opposite.

Perhaps, she thinks, Jack is right not to marry.

'So what's the news?' Tom Holder says.

'Yes,' she says. 'Just that … yes.' *Yes, I will let you use the shed for storing contraband. Yes, you have corrupted me into aiding smugglers like you, Jack. Yes, I want to see you again – yes, yes, yes.*

Tom Holder nods. 'My friend will know your meaning?'

'He will.' She hesitates, then says, 'Mr Holder, do you remember the day I arrived in Helford?'

'I certainly do. It was only a fortnight ago, wasn't it, you got down from the coach?'

'I meant the day I first arrived, as a little girl.'

'Ah, then.'

One of the men at the table asks the innkeeper for another jug of ale. Tom Holder pours the brown liquid, then says, 'I do remember it. I didn't see you that day, but the story spread around the village like a fire in a haybarn. I wondered about it for a long time – we all did. Not just about how you were found, wet through, but also about the luck of you running into Mrs Farnworth that day. You could've been any of our daughters instead.'

She has thought of this, too. How different her life would have been, for its first twenty-three years, at least. 'Did anyone ever come forward to say they were missing a child? Years later, I mean?'

'No, madam. You would have heard if they did.'

'Of course.' She nods. 'Thank you, Mr Holder.'

'You know what they say about you, don't you? About you being the Bucca's child?'

'Yes. I can't understand why anyone would think it.'

The innkeeper scratches his chin. 'It's hard to say. Strange things happen in the country, Mrs Henley.'

'Strange things happen everywhere. That doesn't mean there are mermaids.'

Tom Holder says, 'I understand why you'd say that,

madam, but we here know differently. My brother Gerens is a fisherman, he could tell you some things. And Jori Penrose's boat would've sunk in a gale two years ago, if it weren't for the Bucca, who lifted the thing clear off the cliffs when it was about to be smashed to pieces.'

'Did Mr Penrose see the Sea Bucca?' she asks.

Tom Holder holds her gaze. 'It was too dark,' he says eventually. 'But the boat was lifted free *against* both wind and tide. Jori owes his life to the Sea Bucca and he knows it.'

She's looking at him, not saying anything. Would she have believed him, had he said that, *yes, Mr Penrose saw the Sea Bucca*? Most probably not, she decides. Still. There could be other explanations for such an event, reasonable ones, but something about the story touches some place inside her, as if it's rooting around for memories to latch onto. Of course she's not the Sea Bucca's daughter. How could she be, when there's no such thing? Only, it would explain the way the sea calls to her. Her dreams, too.

Tom Holder says, 'Well. I'll let my friend from the cove know your news. Do be careful, Mrs Henley. There are people who do not like my friend and they take against his friends also.'

'I shall. Thank you, Mr Holder.'

Outside the inn, she purchases the fish, a small pollock, enough for two suppers. She looks around for Jori Penrose, who was saved by the Sea Bucca, but doesn't see him. She walks home wondering how long it will be before she hears anything about the shed. Will Jack himself contact her? He'll still be resting, recovering from his wound. Three weeks' rest, the doctor said. Still, he may send word. Or will the smugglers come at night when she's asleep and she'll never even know they were there? She hopes it won't be long.

CHAPTER SIX

Nothing happens for a fortnight; nothing that isn't practical, in any case, nothing to do with smuggling. She cooks and cleans and washes. She takes her daily walk, she longs to swim and on some days, she risks it. On one such occasion, she watches the strange shadow flit along the edge of her sight again. Her dreams are filled with waves and currents; she wakes from them feeling oddly wistful, as if she dreamt about George. On Sunday morning, she attends the service in the little church at the end of the inlet together with most of the village.

The fleabane on the garden wall explodes in a carpet of flowers. The days alternate between heavy rain with shoving winds and those as warm and soft as summer. On the fair days, the garden is the most pleasant place she's ever been.

The pulley on the well breaks and she has to wait for her widow's pension to come in the post before she can get someone to fix it. Hauling up the water without the mechanism makes her muscles burn to the point she feels even the smallest motion, such as pushing a sewing needle through cloth. She finishes mending Jack's shirt and places it folded on the kitchen table. Now that she has spoken to Tom Holder, she may be able to return it to its owner.

She's about to go back into the garden when there's a knock on the door. A wiry boy with thick black hair, perhaps nine or ten years old, hands her a note. Lieutenant Sowerby's hand is so full of loops and dashes the words nearly blend together. 'My dear Mrs Henley', he writes. 'Please may I have the honour of accompanying you to Sir Hugh and Lady Darby's dinner, this coming Tuesday at three o'clock? There is a matter of some urgency I should like to discuss with you. I await your response <u>most ardently</u>. I am, your most obedient and humble servant, Lieutenant A. W. Sowerby.'

She balls her hands into fists, crumpling the paper, then smooths it out again to jot down her response. *NO! Not in a million years* – that's what she wishes to write. But Lieutenant Sowerby is Harriet's friend and the twin corsets of propriety and custom dictate her polite acceptance. *I should be delighted,* she writes. She hesitates, feeling as if she should say more, but not finding anything, she folds the note and hands the boy two pennies for his trouble.

In the garden, she stands watching the river, the point where it shifts into the sea, her hands at her back. She takes in the choppy waves, the smell of seaweed and the white flashes of gulls circling the boats and holds them, the way one holds one's breath, until she exhales, pushing away all thoughts of Lieutenant Sowerby and what he may wish to discuss with her.

The morning of Harriet's dinner party dawns in a ruffle of sudden nerves. She belongs at Weatherston Hall, she tells herself as she struggles with the hooks on the back of the muslin gown. One of them slips for the second time and she groans. Who is she trying to fool? She doesn't belong in a place like that, not anymore.

Lieutenant Sowerby arrives a few minutes before three and they set out along the coastal path together, him leading his horse, her trying to hide the swirl of nerves and distaste inside her. 'I'm so very pleased to accompany you,' he says after a while. 'I've given much thought to your situation since our last meeting.'

When you snuck around my house at night, she thinks. She says, 'Have you?'

'Indeed I have. It grieves me that you are forced to live as you do. I ask you, madam, would your late husband not wish to see you protected ... provided for; cared for, even, by one capable of defending your person?' He pauses to wipe his face with his sleeve, then adds, fervently: 'And by one who holds the deepest admiration for your character, your virtue and rank?'

Her gaze falls on his hand, holding the horse's rein; the same hand that put the noose around Jed Ferries' neck. She says, 'Forgive me, I cannot – I could not consider—'

'I beg your pardon, my dear lady. I understand you're still

filled with grief for your husband, a hero of Trafalgar; indeed, if I may say so, one of Lord Nelson's band of brothers. I shall not encumber you with a formal offer at present — would not wish to presume ... but if I might see more of you, I am sure that—'

'Look, a ship!' she blurts. They're at the point where the land falls back and the wide, blue-grey expanse of the ocean stretches to the horizon. Far in the distance, a small fishing boat with a single mast tacks its way back to the mouth of the river. Watching it, the yearning rises in her, overtaking her — if only she could sail away on that boat, on any boat, or swim and feel the water's tranquillity settle under her skin as she escapes.

Tearing her gaze away, she starts up a mindless chatter — anything to keep Lieutenant Sowerby from revisiting the subject he has just broached. She doesn't stop until they reach the gate of Weatherston. The wall around the grounds is of old stone, but it's well kept and there's hardly any moss on it. The guardhouse stands empty, two stories tall. They walk up the long drive, which loops around a terraced rose garden and comes to rest in front of the house's façade.

Four stories of blind windows and admonishing chimneys stare at her from the same grey stone as her cottage, but it's all so well-arranged the effect is one of light rather than darkness. The house is as large as Woodbury. The windows are tall and grouped together in the Elizabethan style and behind one of them there's a movement, a flicker of something, a looking-glass, perhaps, or a piece of silverware catching the light.

A black carriage stands in front of the steps leading to the double-fronted entrance. A man in livery opens the door and helps out first a stocky, grey-haired lady in a maroon velvet gown too hot for the weather and then a be-whiskered man holding a wooden box, whom Lieutenant Sowerby greets enthusiastically. Isabel hangs back, battling the desire to turn around and run home.

But then Harriet, resplendent in peach-pink silk, steps out saying, 'I thought that was you, Isabel, I'm so pleased you're here,' and 'let me introduce you to our friends,' as she throws her arm about Isabel's shoulders and ushers her through the doors.

Inside, one of the footmen takes her bonnet and the silk gloves she was so glad she kept. There's a flurry of introductions, first in the cavernous, black and white tiled entrance hall to Mr and Mrs William Tredinnick of the Lanart mine, then in the light, open space of the drawing room to Mr Frederick Pickford, a portly man in his early forties who looks as though he's carrying twins under his waistcoat.

'Mr Pickford owns Tregowran mine, six miles from here,' Harriet says. She takes Isabel by the arm as she sweeps through what she calls 'the green room', suggesting a rainbow of other drawing rooms elsewhere in the house.

Harriet's husband, Sir Hugh Darby, proves a bit of a shock. Isabel expected a young man, perhaps a few years Harriet's senior, as handsome as Harriet is lovely, but Sir Hugh is at least thirty years older than his wife, with a face as lined as a shelf of ash wood and a manner as austere as his unadorned black coat. He could be her father. Grandfather, almost.

Isabel glances at Harriet and her new friend gives her a small smile, as if to say, *now you know why I didn't want to be late for dinner.* She remembers Harriet's comparison of her marriage to a walled garden and feels all the bitter luck of her own freedom.

The silk wallpaper shines in the late afternoon sun dipping through the windows. It's a vivid, grass green, with furnishings to match: green silk brocade seat coverings, a settee of cream and green satin. A marble fireplace reigns over one side of the room, the other holds a selection of paintings, spread across the wall like butter: ancestors of Sir Hugh in doublets and codpieces, in a variety of uniforms, in long coats and tall, powdered wigs. The room smells of tulips arranged in large vases on various tables and sideboards and of the sweaty perfume of the guests. The servants are in a dark blue livery so similar to what they used to wear at home in Greenwich, she half expects to look up and see a familiar face filling her wine glass. But no, it's a different servant, with a different smile, polite, detached. She feels like an imposter standing here with her glass; she had her arms up to her elbows in dirty washing not four hours ago.

The sinking feeling in her stomach deepens when she spots Lieutenant Sowerby making his way across the room with another officer of the Revenue Service at his side. They each carry a gold-coloured drink in a small, crystal glass. She looks for an escape – perhaps she could go stand by the window and admire the view of the garden, but before she can move, Harriet takes her elbow and turns her in the direction of the two men. 'May I present Lieutenant Charles Sullivan?' she says. 'Lieutenant Sullivan, this is Mrs Isabel Henley, come to grace us with her presence all the way from London.'

'I'm pleased to make your acquaintance, sir,' she murmurs, scanning the room as she curtsies.

Harriet says, 'Isabel, I believe you've met Lieutenant Arthur Sowerby.'

Lieutenant Sowerby pops a comfit into his mouth and chews. Drops of perspiration stick to his hairline. 'Mrs Henley and I came together, my dear Lady Darby.'

'Did you?' Harriet says, raising her eyebrows.

'You look awfully becoming tonight, Mrs Henley,' Lieutenant Sowerby says, chewing. 'Pray, is that true Indian muslin?'

'I . . . yes. Thank you.'

She half-turns away, looking for something, someone, and Harriet is saying, 'That's everyone, my dear Isabel, apart from . . . oh, there you are, Mr Carlyon. May I present my dear friend, Mrs Isabel Henley. Isabel, this is Mr John Carlyon.'

Isabel pivots, steps, stumbles, and there is Jack, saying, 'Mrs Henley, it's an honour.'

He has caught her by the shoulder and lets go the moment she steadies herself. She searches his face – he is as surprised as her, she thinks, but has recovered quicker. There's a flicker of pain, too, as he straightens up, but he masks it instantly.

What is he doing here? Should he even be out of bed? Three weeks' rest, the doctor said. It has only been two. His eyes are bluer than she remembers, his face both more angular and more deeply tanned, and standing like this, he's taller, too. It's as if in the bright light of the late afternoon sun pouring through the windows everything about him has become intensified – so, too, the way he's looking at her. She feels it in her stomach, a low, liquid-like fluttering. The room spins. Two worlds have collided and she's reeling from the impact.

Her mind reaches for his name – his full name, she realises with a second jolt. She knew it'd be John, as Jack is the usual diminutive, but there are so many Johns, she never expected … 'Mr Carlyon,' she says, curtsying. 'I'm pleased to make your acquaintance. I …' Again her thoughts stretch and reach. 'Have you had the pleasure of visiting Weatherston Hall often, sir?'

Eyes on her, questioning, Jack says, 'I have on numerous occasions had the pleasure.'

She's absurdly pleased she's in her best dress. Then she remembers he has seen her in her underdress. Heat rises between her shoulders, tripping up her neck. 'In that case, may you be prevailed upon to take a short turn about the garden with me, sir? I should very much like to see it.'

He catches on, smile breaking free. 'I should be delighted. If there's time before dinner, that is. Lady Darby?'

Harriet looks bemused, but the boom of her husband's voice distracts her. 'Harriet, come and have a look at Tredinnick's specimens. He's brought a box full.'

With a quick shake of her head, Harriet says, 'Duty calls, I'm afraid. Please do show her the gardens, Mr Carlyon; after dinner it will be dark. I believe we shall dine in half an hour, that should be enough for you to ramble about a little, perhaps down to the folly?'

Isabel's gown whispers across the parquet floor. In the entrance hall, she says, 'I can't believe—'

'Wait till we're outside.'

A footman opens the door and then they're among the rose bushes. The air is lightly scented by a few early roses. The path cuts through the flowerbeds, but Jack takes her arm as if they're a couple and steers her to the back of the house, saying, 'We won't be overlooked on this side.'

His maroon wool coat is buttoned all the way up, despite the weather, covering the top of his black kerseymere pantaloons and the bandage he must still wear underneath. The wool is of high quality and brushed to the point it's smooth like a fox's pelt. She imagines his shirt, under the coat, of the finest cotton or perhaps silk, and winces at the thought of the mended shirt sitting on the table in her cottage kitchen. What possessed her to presume he would occupy such a position in life that he'd want a stained, mended shirt?

The garden at the back of Weatherston is of the parkland variety, with flowerbeds close to the house and a more natural landscape beyond it. The path runs parallel to a woodland on the right and a small lake on the left. Past this, fields slowly climb to a point in the distance, where a whitewashed folly in the Palladian style straddles the view.

Jack slows down the moment they've rounded the corner of the house.

'You should sit down,' she says. 'The doctor said you ought to have three weeks' rest.' She draws a slow breath. 'You shouldn't have come.'

'This dinner is too important.'

She looks up at him – he appears serious. She can't help but scoff. Surely even smuggling wouldn't be important enough to risk his health for, but a dinner party? She says, 'If I've learned one thing since coming here, it's that a great many things take precedence over a dinner party in terms of importance, no matter how enjoyable the company or food.'

'Such as?' He sounds amused.

She kicks a pebble on the path and watches it skid into a cluster of daffodils. 'Getting the dough to rise correctly before baking the bread. Laying the fire so you don't waste half your tinder lighting it. Not thinking about the eyes when you put fish in the soup . . .' she stops and adds, 'I know it sounds silly, but I used to ask the cook to remove them.'

'What else?'

She hadn't realised she missed his voice, too. 'The right time of day to do the washing, so it has time to dry. Knowing what the sky looks like for rain.' Her hand goes to George's medal. Her voice drops. 'Not being alone.'

He looks as if he wants to reach for her hand, but instead he says, 'Are you certain you're not turning into a bit of a revolutionary, yourself?'

'I've turned into a pauper, that's what,' she says. 'But

strangely I find I don't despise doing all of those things half as much as I thought I would. I do very much look forward to dinner tonight, though. It's certain to be extensive, isn't it?'

'Sir Hugh lays a good table.'

'Still, there's something far more important than this dinner and it's the reason you shouldn't have come.'

'And what may that be?'

'Your health, sir.' She doesn't know why she says it like that. *Sir.* He's been Jack in her head all this time, but it comes out sounding both natural and distant.

'I'm "sir" again, Isabel?' he says mildly. 'You know I go by "Jack" to those who know me well.'

Is she one of those? she wonders. She says, 'I don't want to slip up in company.'

'Of course.'

'So why—'

But she doesn't get to ask him why the dinner is important or tell him she spoke to Tom Holder about hiding contraband in the shed. Nor does she get to tell him that he may well laugh and she doesn't dispute it's preposterous, but she has missed him – but then she wouldn't really tell him that, she would only do so in her mind. A voice cuts into their conversation, coming from up behind: 'Mrs Henley! Mr Carlyon, sir!'

Lieutenant Sowerby is jogging down the path towards them. He's red in the face and panting as if he has run the length of the coastal path. He addresses Isabel in puffs: 'Lady Darby told me Mr Carlyon is showing you the gardens. As I have often had the honour of visiting Weatherston myself, I should like to join you. I find the prospects from the back of the house among the best I've ever seen – though, naturally, I cannot have visited as many great houses as you, Mrs Henley. I understand your father was Admiral John Farnworth of Woodbury Hall?'

'Oh, I am sure you have, sir. But yes, Admiral Farnworth was my father.' So this is at the heart of it, she thinks; she must discourage him. 'Upon my father's death, the estate has gone to the eldest of my stepbrothers.' Jaw clenched, she adds, 'You're welcome to join us on our walk, of course, though I do believe we shall dine soon.'

She glances at Jack, but to her surprise, he doesn't seem irritated by the interruption and proceeds to engage Lieutenant Sowerby in conversation at once. For a few minutes, she feels the hurt of the slight and barely listens to the two men, but then she catches Jack saying, 'And do you have any sense, my dear sir, of where those dastardly criminals may be landing their cargo next?'

'I do not at present, but we keep a close patrol all along the east side of the Lizard, particularly on the night of the new moon when smugglers are bound to attempt a landing. We hope to catch them red-handed, but it's a difficult thing, as you might imagine.'

Jack puts his hands behind his back. He speaks casually, but Isabel hears the note of interest in his voice. 'You must find great satisfaction in thwarting their efforts. If I may ask, what are some of the difficulties you run into during this admirable pursuit?'

Lieutenant Sowerby glows with pride as well as perspiration. Pushing his fingers into the folds of his necktie, he loosens the cloth. 'Well, sir, there's the problem of their ships, which are fast, and they do not mind standing out to sea for days on end, while our men, wanting their beds, don't wish to stay aboard a small vessel for long. Do you know, they sometimes hide their cargo on the bottom of the ocean, fastened by long lines, and haul it up later? It makes it a difficult proposition to catch them and as you may be aware, the law demands we catch smugglers with their cargo or the crime cannot be proven in court. Of course, that's only if it comes to a trial – I have my own means of preventing such a travesty from taking place.'

'Do you indeed?' Jack says. He still speaks casually, but there's a tension in him, visible in the way he's squared his shoulders.

'I do, sir. They'd be acquitted at trial, but I see them hanged for treason. They are aiding the French, after all. In fact, that's the most difficult problem we run into – the level of complicity.'

Jack darts a glance at her. It lasts no more than a second, but it's enough: Tom Holder told him about the shed. 'Complicity?' Jack says, keeping Lieutenant Sowerby on the subject.

'Why, yes. The entire population is in on it, sir!' His voice rises. Taking a lace-edged handkerchief from his pocket, he dabs his forehead and utters a dry laugh. 'We in the Revenue Service say in order to stop the crime of smuggling entirely, we'd need to pay half the inhabitants to keep an eye on the other half!'

Isabel's nerves are taut like the skin of a drum. If the lieutenant learned of Jack's secret identity, he would see him hanged. She thinks of the woman in the stained dress at the crossroads to Manaccan; of the crunch, the scream. *You're playing with fire*, she wants to tell Jack. *Please, please be careful.*

They have reached the point at which the path ends and the field begins. Advancing into the meadow, Jack steps into the hollow between two clumps of grass. She sees the pain bloom in his face as he catches himself, then vanish with the brush of his hand across his forehead.

Lieutenant Sowerby has seen it, too. Sucking on his lip, he says, 'Are you ill, sir?'

Jack says, 'I pulled a muscle going after a deer. Got her in the end, though.'

Isabel's hands become fists, tight around the muslin of her gown as she lifts the hem over a tuft – as tight as her chest feels suddenly.

'Perhaps we should hunt together someday,' says Lieutenant Sowerby at last.

She lets out her breath slowly. Jack says, 'I should like that.'

When Lieutenant Sowerby takes out his pocket watch, she looks away, gazing at the low sun carving out the shape of the folly to hide her relief as he says, 'Is that the time? We are expected at dinner, my friends.'

The dinner is a long succession of delights. It is served *à la française*, with every dish on the table at once, and consists of no less than thirty different offerings. For a while, Isabel concentrates only on eating – it has been too long since she tasted food like this. The dinner talk wafts around her like a fine drizzle. Jack sits at the other end of the table from her, where he continues to wheedle information from Lieutenants Sowerby and Sullivan. Sir William Tredinnick, besides a mine owner, is also a naturalist and holds forth about his collection of specimens until Sir Hugh redirects the conversation to the rising copper prices and their effect on the market; a move that allows the quiet and apparently shy Mr Pickford to join in.

Harriet sits diagonally across the table from Isabel, far enough to make conversation difficult, which she doesn't mind at the moment as Harriet is talking over Mr Pickford's shoulders with Mrs Tredinnick on the subject of local shops and the meagre selection of fabrics in Cornwall as compared to that in London – or something to that effect. Isabel catches only shreds of their conversation until Mrs Tredinnick's voice rings out, the sound of it as large as her bosom: 'Mrs Henley, I have heard a positively astonishing rumour about you! You shall have to tell us if there's any truth to it.'

Isabel's spoon clatters onto her plate. All conversation stops; only Mr Pickford is still saying, 'depending on the situation in Bodmin,' and then he, too, falls silent.

She can hear the sea in her ears, the crash of the waves; she wishes she was underwater, untouchable, free. She wants to look at Jack but finds she cannot. She can't give away how, stupidly, he means too much to her; how it hurts to know she'll lose his good opinion. Harriet's, too – she's a friend, but she won't be any longer once Mrs Tredinnick tells them what they're saying about Isabel in London.

The food on her plate looked so appetising before. Now it's a swamp of meats, gravy, vegetables, pudding, potatoes – peeled to perfection by the cook, she thinks, and then: what an odd thing to think when she's about to be ruined for the second time, at the very moment of her re-entrance into society. 'I ... I'm sure I don't know what you mean,' she says. Sweat drifts under her dress. Her thighs stick together.

'Oh, I am sure you do, Mrs Henley. Everyone is talking about it.'

It's hard to hear Mrs Tredinnick through the crashing waves. The woman is laughing, her red-velveted body is shuddering with it. 'I ...'

Harriet says, 'What is this about, Isabel?'

'I shall tell you, if Mrs Henley won't,' says Mrs Tredinnick. 'Will you believe, my dear friends, that a story goes around that Mrs Henley here is a foundling, who is none other than the *daughter* of a *merman*.' She stresses the words *daughter* and *merman* as if they're sweetmeats she wishes to savour.

They're all laughing. Sir Hugh has lost some of his sternness as he slams his hand into the table, exclaiming, 'Do they say this, truly?'

The crashing in her ears continues. *Daughter. Merman.* The words filter through the waves. Mrs Tredinnick's rumour isn't about her and James. The swamp on her plate begins to take the shape of food again. She hears Jack say, 'Ah, that story. Indeed, I've heard it, too. They say Mrs Henley is the daughter of the Sea Bucca.'

'The Sea Bucca?' Harriet says. 'Pray, what is that?'

'It's a fabled creature, a sea spirit, whom many call a merman. It stands about two feet high and has the skin of a conger eel, with seaweed for hair – so the story goes,' Jack says.

'And my dear friend would be the creature's daughter? What stuff!' Harriet says.

Isabel gives her a grateful smile.

'My, the look on your face, Mrs Henley,' Mr Tredinnick says. 'You'd almost think there was something to it and my wife here had discovered your great secret.'

Lieutenant Sowerby swallows a mouthful of wine. 'What ridiculous notions the inhabitants of these parts hold. No wonder Mrs Henley looks startled. Skin of a conger eel? I declare, it's an insult! If I knew the man responsible for start-ing this absurd rumour—'

Jack says, 'There isn't a single man responsible. It's a local legend. A myth, if you will.'

But you believe it, she thinks. *Maybe.*

'But where would they get such a mad idea?' says Sir Hugh, pointing his wine glass in Isabel's direction. 'Do you know, Mrs Henley?'

'It's because there is *some* truth to it,' she says, forcing herself to look at them one by one. When she meets Jack's eyes, he gives her a nod. 'But only a very little. I am a foundling. I was found in the town of Helford, where I now reside, nineteen years ago, and I was adopted by my parents, Admiral and Mrs Farnworth of Woodbury House.'

Mr Tredinnick says, 'But that is remarkable! Have they never found your parents?'

'They have not. As far as I'm concerned, Admiral and Mrs Farnworth were my parents.'

'You have lost them both?' Harriet asks. 'I am ever so sorry to hear it.'

The cranberries look strange swimming in her pudding. How did she not notice it before? Quietly, she says, 'It happened many years ago.'

Sir Hugh says, 'That may be so, but it's tremendously difficult to lose one's parents. I know, as do my grown sons, who lost their mother, my first wife, when they were but small. But I've had the good fortune to marry again, a woman of great beauty and understanding: my dear Harriet.' He speaks with unexpected feeling and when Isabel looks up, he gives her a smile warmer than she imagined him capable of.

Her voice soft, yet carrying across the table, Harriet says, 'Thank you, Sir Hugh. I consider myself fortunate as well.'

After that, the conversation moves on. Jack resumes his assault on Lieutenant Sowerby's defences, prying from him what intelligence he can. Isabel eats quietly, sometimes adding a word here or there. Outside, the night grows dense. By the time the women rise to go to the drawing room, leaving the men to their port and snuff, it's past ten in the evening. Isabel casts a glance over her shoulder and catches

Jack looking at her. He mouths something – she thinks it's 'soon', but she cannot be certain.

In the drawing room the conversation moves along like a rusted wheel. Harriet and Isabel have much to talk about, but it isn't easy to find subjects that allow them to include Mrs Tredinnick. Despite this, as the evening wears on, Isabel feels more and more at ease. The house, the company of the two women in their silk dresses, the footmen in their livery offering brandy and port; all of it conspires to create such a copy of the life that was still hers just weeks ago that she begins to feel as if her time living in the cottage has been a dream and she has only just woken to reality.

The men seem to have no trouble with their conversation; they remain in the dining room for over an hour and only join the women for some twenty minutes before the party breaks up. Isabel hasn't found a moment to speak to Jack alone.

The Tredinnicks leave in their carriage and so does Mr Pickford. The two lieutenants have only a short ride to the Customs House at St Keverne and Jack, too, has come on horseback. When Isabel is putting on her gloves, ready to step out of the door, Jack moves to stand beside her and, leaning in, whispers, 'Can I continue to rely on your discretion now you know who I am?'

Before she has the chance to even so much as nod, Harriet has taken her arm. 'Oh, Isabel, you cannot mean to go out in the night like this! Not on your own, surely. You must stay.'

Jack says, 'I'm happy to accompany Mrs Henley back to her house.'

Her heart leaps, but then Lieutenant Sowerby says, 'As am I. I know where Mrs Henley lives; I've had the honour of visiting her several times, and unlike you, sir, I am well-positioned to deal with any bandits along the way.'

Harriet sees her consternation. 'Isabel? I'm afraid I must insist you stay the night. It's very kind of the two gentlemen to offer their services, but I would be glad of your company and it's awfully late and dark along the path.'

'I shall be glad to stay, dear Harriet,' she says. The regret sits heavy in her stomach; she wanted nothing more than the chance to ride back to Helford with Jack.

Harriet says, 'You shall have the best room in the house.'

'It's settled then,' says Lieutenant Sowerby, adjusting his neckerchief before going out. 'I promise I shall call on you before the week is out, my dear Mrs Henley. I look forward to conversing with you at length. It's my sincere hope the more mundane aspects of your current situation shall not deprive me of a few hours of your delightful company.'

Mundane aspects? she thinks. Does he mean the daily washing, cleaning, baking and cooking that now form the foundation of her existence? She tries not to grit her teeth when she makes her response: 'That will be lovely, lieutenant, thank you.'

CHAPTER SEVEN

Her bed that night almost makes up for the disappointment of not having Jack accompany her back to the old pilchard shed. One of the maidservants, a girl named Sally, helps her undress, just as Mary used to at home. Isabel luxuriates in the abandonment of her struggle with ties, hooks and laces.

The bed is a pudding made of silk and feathers, yet she lies awake for a long time. She keeps going over the events of the evening and the intense happiness as well as shock at seeing Jack again. *John Carlyon*, she says in her head, over and over, trying to get used to the name, but it's no good, he remains simply *Jack* to her.

Harriet knocks on her door in the morning to offer Isabel the use of one of her gowns. Isabel is touched but declines, saying she doesn't mind wearing the blue muslin another day, and doesn't Harriet agree the benefit of muslin cotton is that it so easily moves from day to night? Over a late breakfast of honey and plum cake, strawberries and fresh cream, brioche with jam, coffee, tea and hot chocolate, Isabel asks her friend, 'Pray, where is Mr Carlyon's estate? I don't believe he mentioned it last night.'

After eating steadily for half an hour, her stomach feels as if it's stuffed with wool, but she gets another slice of honey cake and nibbles on it. Now that the reality of the cottage hovers on the horizon again, she's determined to enjoy as much of the food at Weatherston as she can. If she eats enough, the meal may last her until the next morning. She has to resist the temptation to try to hide a fifth slice in the folds of her gown.

'Did he not?' Harriet says. She takes a delicate sip from her coffee. 'He did look at you often last night, Isabel.'

'Did he?' She keeps her voice neutral. The coffee tastes as if it was made for the gods of Mount Olympus; hot, bitter and strong. 'I had not noticed.'

'Do you know, he's still a bachelor?'

'Is he? And where, pray, is his estate?'

Harriet laughs. 'You needn't be coy with me, my dear. I could tell he caught your eye the moment I made the introduction. His estate is at Roskorwell, on the coast three miles from here. It's down the coastal path but in the opposite direction of Helford. It's mainly farmland, which he has tenanted, but the house is of a good size and the family name is an old one in these parts. I dare say you could do worse. But then, Lieutenant Sowerby speaks very highly of you, too.'

Roskorwell. On the coast. She repeats the name in her mind. 'I beg your pardon. What of Lieutenant Sowerby?'

'He speaks very highly of you and asked my opinion. I gave it freely, of course, and I assure you it included the highest praise of you. I shouldn't wonder if he's quite serious in his intentions.' Harriet sips her hot chocolate.

Isabel's cup clangs into her saucer. She hoped – in vain, she sees now – that she'd misinterpreted the lieutenant's words.

Harriet says, 'I hope I haven't offended you by speaking with Lieutenant Sowerby, Isabel.'

'Oh no, not at all,' she says, the cake heavy in her stomach.

Once they've finished breakfasting, Harriet asks her to take a walk in the garden, but Isabel says she really should get back, she has much to do, after which Harriet offers her the use of her carriage.

'Please do not trouble yourself,' Isabel says. 'The walk will do me good.' She embraces her friend and sets out at once. The moment she passes the gatehouse, she takes the coastal path in the direction away from Helford. The sea lies placid under a climbing sun, with only a little foam topping the waves that rush in and out of the coves. Watching them, it's as if the waves are rushing through her.

After about two-and-a-half miles she comes across a wooden sign pointing the way to Roskorwell. She's glad she's wearing such a light gown; it's hot for walking today. Taking off her gloves, she carefully tucks them into her change purse. She isn't sure what she's going to say to Jack; she only knows she must see him.

The path turns again and she crosses a small stream that runs down the cliff and then the woodland opens to a field and across it lies the house. It's far smaller than Weatherston and looks rather like an overgrown farmhouse, with wings added onto the original building, which is only two stories. Made of whitewashed clay, it possesses the same unevenness as many of the cottages in Helford. Ivy climbs the wall on one side and along the front grow swathes of bluebells and small white flowers. Clusters of hollyhock, not yet in bloom, push up against the many small windows, along with rose-bushes in need of a trim. The scent of flowers mixes with the sea air. The front of the house faces the fields and the back looks out across the sea.

A short gravel drive leads to a door with an ancient iron knocker. She lets it fall against the wood and listens to the boom of it inside the house. Her heart trips. She doesn't know what she's expecting – for Jack to come to the door himself or for a servant to take her to him. She doesn't know what she's going to say. A few minutes pass and nobody comes. From the front step she can see some buildings to the side of the house; a stable, she thinks, and what looks like a large shed, but there's nobody about. She bangs the knocker into the door again and waits. Gulls cry in the distance. The sea plays its endless melody, swoosh, crash, swoosh, crash upon the rocks.

At last, just as she's about to leave, the door swings open. A man with an impressive black moustache looks her up and down and, before she can say anything, he tells her that the master is not at home. She swallows down a new wave of disappointment and asks, 'When is Mr Carlyon expected back?'

'How would I know?'

'Is it today? Or has he gone to sea?'

The man narrows his eyes. 'It's today,' he says, sounding suspicious.

'In that case, could I wait for him, please? I must speak with him. It's important and I have come a long way.'

'From where?'

'Helford,' she says, even though she only walked from Weatherston this morning. When the man doesn't react, she adds, 'On foot.'

'On foot?' The man's gaze trails up and down her gown. He doesn't say it, but she can see him think it: *in a fine gown like that?*

'Please, may I wait for Mr Carlyon here?'

'It could take hours.'

'I don't mind in the least.'

The man steps aside to let her in and, without another word, takes her to a room crammed so full of books the bottom half of each of the three windows is obscured by stacks on the windowsill. A large desk with an in-laid wooden top stands in the centre of the room, piled high with papers, an inkwell and more books. It's part study, part library and smells of wood, leather, memories. She won't look at the papers, but once the man with the moustache leaves, she inspects the books on the shelf: Milton, Shakespeare, Hume, Voltaire, Rousseau. There are several volumes on the flora and fauna of the west coast, as well as on seafaring and navigation. Some are in French. Stuck on the wall are charts showing the coastline, the reefs, channels and shoals.

The man with the moustache brings her a glass of water and she drinks it standing by the window, looking out across the books on the sill. The blue horizon trembles in the sun. Seagulls tumble through the sky, dropping like shooting stars down to the water, and in the distance are two sets of sails, winking at her as they pitch on the waves. She watches the ships until they are out of sight and all of a sudden, she knows exactly what she's going to say to Jack.

He arrives two hours later in a flurry of heat, sweat and the smell of horse, his boots and the lower half of his buckskin breeches covered in dust. 'There you are!' he calls out the moment he enters the room. His words tug at something in her chest. They're the same words he spoke to her when he lay bleeding on her bed and she carried in the water from the well. How was that only two weeks ago?

A dog chases him – brown fur, ungainly on its legs, tongue dangling. When it reaches Isabel, it begins to dance around the velvet armchair she has occupied the past hour.

'Jib! Down girl!' Jack calls. The dog is wagging its tail so hard its entire body shakes. 'Down!' Jack calls again and then he has the dog by its collar and is pulling it away, out of the room.

A small whine sounds behind the door when he comes back in. 'Sorry about the dog. She's still a pup.'

Isabel rises, surreptitiously placing the book she's been

picking through on the seat of the chair behind her. 'Good morning,' she says and falters, casting about for a clock, then for the sky outside the window. The sun is high, set in a backdrop so pale it's nearly white. 'Good afternoon, I mean.'

Jack tosses his hat onto the books on the desk and crosses the space between the door and her chair in four strides and then he's bowing and holding out his hand to her and she slots her own into it as if it's the last piece to complete a puzzle. He presses his lips against the back of her hand where her fingers meet her knuckles and holds them there a few seconds. She feels every one of those seconds deep in her stomach. When he lets go, she looks at him a little dazed and he smiles and holds her gaze, long enough she feels she needs to sit down again.

'We had the same idea,' he says. 'I was at the old pilchard shed waiting for you. I wanted to talk to you. After a while, I realised I was on a fool's errand – Lady Darby might well have asked you to stay another day or you may have decided to linger long enough to secure a second dinner.'

She blushes at the insinuation; yes, she enjoyed the food immensely, because at home she only had her badly-peeled potatoes, bone-filled fish and mismatched soups.

Watching her expression, Jack says gently, 'I understand the fare you're accustomed to is not the fare you get in your present situation. It's nothing to be ashamed of.' He wipes his brow. 'By God, it's hot for May. In any case, I rode back and Tom told me there was a lady waiting for me. I knew it must be you. You've come straight from Weatherston, then?'

'I have,' she says. 'It pleases me that we each thought to meet the other. May I call you Jack again now?'

'You may call me that any time. Though you were right to take care last night. That Lieutenant Sowerby is a sharper knife than he appears.'

'You seemed to gain quite a lot of information speaking with him.'

He smiles ruefully. 'You see why the dinner was important.' He reaches behind her and lifts the book from the seat of the chair. *Voyage de La Pérouse autour du monde, publicé conformément au décret du 22 Avril 1791*, the title page reads. 'You read French?'

'I try.'

'He's been all over the world, La Pérouse. It's an interesting story.' He sounds wistful.

'Is that what you'd like to do?' she says. 'Sail across the world?'

'Only men sponsored by His Majesty's Navy get to do that, if they don't end up on blockade for years on end. Or ones who have the capital to finance such a voyage.'

'Is that why you're a smuggler, so you may raise the capital for a journey of exploration?'

He laughs. 'You've a too romantic picture of me, Isabel. I smuggle so that I may repair the roof and my tenants may put bread in their children's bellies with their share of the profits. Many of them are a part of my crew; they can use the extra income, especially if we have another poor harvest.' Still laughing, he hands her the book. 'You may borrow it, if you'd like to continue reading about La Pérouse's adventures.'

'Thank you. I should like that.' She runs her fingers over the leather cover, then looks up at him again. 'You really shouldn't be riding about the country. You should be resting.'

'I'm fine. I sail to France in five days.'

'So soon?' she says, ignoring the flutter of nerves. She's going to have to ask him. No, she thinks, not ask – *demand*. Secrets come at a price.

'We need to be back in time to land the cargo when the moon is new. Now, before we discuss business matters, let me ask you this. Has Tom offered you any refreshment?'

'He has, thank you.'

When she doesn't say anything else, he asks, 'Well, what did you have? Tea? Coffee? Brandy? I don't believe it's too early in the day. We've plenty of that, though most of our recent cargo has been watered down and sold.' At her look, he hastens to add, 'It's not what it sounds like. We ship it overproof so we can get more across in one run. It's too strong to drink – it'd burn your throat. So what did Tom get you and can I get you some more?'

'I enjoyed a glass of water.'

'You enjoyed it, did you? The scoundrel. Should you like a glass of coffee or port? We have some things to discuss. Chief among them the fact that you're now one of the few people not actively part of our operation who knows I'm the captain of the *Rapide*.'

Ten minutes later they're sitting in two brocade armchairs by the empty hearth in the drawing room, which like Jack's study looks out across the sea. The dog, Jib, lies at Jack's feet. The breeze wanders in through the window, accompanied by the crashing of the waves. The coffee smells a little burned. The weather is almost too hot for it today.

'Here's what I propose,' Jack is saying.

The way he keeps resting his gaze on her is distracting, as is the look in his eyes and how it makes her feel. There's something raw in it, as if something about her makes him hungry.

'Isabel?'

'I beg your pardon. You were saying?'

'I propose another two percent cut of the profits, on top of the two percent you'll get when we use the shed for storage. That's two percent for keeping mum about my name and two percent for the use of the shed. Tom Holder told me you're on board regarding the latter.'

She's shaking her head. Taking a deep breath, tasting the sea air, she says, 'I don't want another two percent cut.'

'You drive a hard bargain. Three percent, then, for your silence and two for the shed. That could add up to as much as twenty-five pounds for a single run.'

'I don't want money. I want something that will cost you far less.'

He leans forward, his elbows on his knees, curiosity alive in his face. 'Do you? And what would that be?'

'I want you to take me with you when you next go to

sea.' This is what she wants, what she *needs* — to go where George used to, and her father; to satisfy, at last, the unwieldy yearning she feels for a place so far from shore the horizon all around is made of ocean.

For perhaps ten seconds, he merely continues to look at her, the corner of his bottom lip caught between his teeth. And for that short moment she believes he's going to say yes. The intrigue in his face; the — dare she think it? — fondness. Hunger, too. Then he shakes his head and says, 'No.'

'No?' she echoes, stupidly.

'Under no circumstances will I do such a thing.' His fingers dance on his knee. 'Preposterous notion.'

She flinches as if slapped. 'But, Jack—'

'Do you have any idea how dangerous it is? How many ships are lost each year, gone down in storms or run aground where it shoals? That's nothing to say of the risk of an engagement with a ship of the Revenue Service.' He jumps up and begins to pace the room. 'I can't believe you would ask it of me, Isabel!'

Something in her bristles. 'You do it! You go to sea all the time! George and my father used to. Why shouldn't I? What makes you think I'm made of such weak stuff I couldn't withstand the danger the same as you?'

He stops and turns back to her. 'As if any man would want to have the death of a woman at sea on his conscience. Or anywhere.'

He sounds so bitter she shrinks deeper into the armchair.

'What of women who go abroad, to America, to India?' she says. 'Do they not board a ship?'

'Those sorts of voyages can't be avoided. You're mad if you think I'll take you on a smuggling run to France.' Seeing her expression, he sits down again and says, more calmly, 'I say this for your own sake. Why should you wish to go to sea, anyway?'

Looking down at her hands, clasped tightly around the coffee glass in her lap, she says, 'Why do you do it?'

'To trade. Evidently.'

Her glass has a smudge on it where her lips have touched it. She wipes it away. 'I'm sure that's not the only reason.'

'It's different for me. You're a woman. Why would you want to go sailing?'

Glancing up at him, she says softly, 'Maybe it's because I'm the Sea Bucca's daughter.' She doesn't mean it, of course. She's only trying to lighten the mood. Or is she? Listening to the distant crash of the waves, the desire is so strong, so undeniable, she must press ahead. She must make him see reason – at all cost.

'The sea is calling you, you mean,' Jack says, and there's a tinge of a smile now, chasing away the bitterness. 'Like a siren calls a mariner.'

She thinks of the first time she swam in the river; of the voice she heard in the shrieks of the gulls and the rustle of the breeze. 'That's what it feels like.' She says it very seriously and he smiles and says, 'But if the sea is a dangerous mistress, can you imagine what sort of parent she makes?'

The playfulness of his words emboldens her. She says, 'It would only be the one time. Please, Jack. I've always wanted to go to sea.'

He taps his coffee glass. 'This may come as a surprise to you, but I care not what you want.'

Her hands squeeze together in her lap. She hates herself for what she's about to say. The thought of Lieutenant Sowerby alone makes her cower under the weight of her guilt – just for saying it; for implying she would betray him. She would never do it. Still, Jack has got to believe she just may. It's the only way she can make him agree. She says, 'It's in your interest to care what I want, if you wish to prevent me speaking to the Revenue Service.'

Silence, apart from the waves. Then Jack says measuredly, 'You'll want to tread carefully, Isabel. There are other means by which I might prevent that.'

She thinks of the pistol in his hand when he lay wounded in her bed, at how quickly he woke and aimed it at the door at the slightest sound. For the first time, she thinks of him as a dangerous man. She hates this, too. Swallowing down something thick, she says, 'You wouldn't.'

He holds her gaze. Her heart runs, jumps. The carriage clock on the chimneypiece ticks away half a minute, then another. 'No,' he says, at last. 'I would not.'

She takes a shuddering breath. 'So you'll take me with you?'

'It appears I shall. God help me.' He locks eyes with her and there's something else in them besides resignation.

Concern, running deep, and that same affection she spied before. 'What happened to not wanting to aid the French?'

The sun pours in through the windows, into her skin, into her veins. Her mind throbs with it. She's going to sea. *She's going to sea. She's going!* 'Oh, thank you, Jack! I care not one jot about the French!' This isn't entirely true, but it's true right now, in this moment. She wants to embrace him; she wants to kiss him. She stays in the chair, clasping the glass so tightly she half expects it to shatter.

Jack says, 'It's worth it for the look on your face, I suppose. Though I must warn you, I don't like to be told what to do.'

Smiling, she says, 'I don't like to be told what I cannot do.'

He shrugs. 'That's your lot as a woman. But do not fear, I shan't tell you what not to do. Here's what you *will* do. You'll report to my house no later than six in the evening on Sunday. I will take you to the *Rapide;* I won't tell you where she's anchored. We finish loading the cargo and sail at nightfall. You may bring a small satchel with personal belongings, but nothing more. Every bit of space is reserved for the goods we pick up in France. Understood?'

'Yes,' she says.

Jack says, 'It's "aye, captain" aboard the ship.' A smile tugs at his mouth. 'I'll expect you to work. It's not a pleasure cruise.'

'Of course.' She'll do anything, she thinks, any task he'll set her. The *Rapide* – could there be a better name for a ship?

'I'm sure I don't need to tell you this, but not a word to anyone. Not to Lady Darby or anybody else. Make up some story in case Lieutenant Sowerby comes calling. I heard him threaten to do so. A visit to relations a fair distance away will do.'

'Very well.' She is smiling again – she's still smiling.

'As I said, it'll be dangerous,' Jack says, soberly. 'The *Swallow*'s prowling the coast and you've seen up close what a revenue musket does to a man. Not to mention her guns. I hope you know what you're getting yourself into.' A beat, then he adds, 'And I, as well.'

Over the edge of her glass, she says, 'Do you promise? You won't change your mind?'

'Upon my honour. I'll take you with me, but only for the one run.'

'That's all I ask.' A sip, then, 'I would never have betrayed you to the Revenue Service.'

'I knew it. But here's why your idea pleases me, now I've had a moment to think it over. See, you wouldn't have betrayed me, but aside from your character, which seems dependable enough, I had no assurance of the fact. Now I do. From now on, I can be certain you'll never talk, for you'll be one of us. If they start stringing up smugglers, you shall be one.'

He taps his glass again. The sound reminds her of a bell. Despite the sun pouring into the room, she has grown cold. She hadn't thought of this. *You shall be one.* She'll be a criminal. What would George have said? But he loved the sea; he loved the Navy. He would've understood, wouldn't he?

Jack says, 'Are you certain it's what you want?'

'Yes,' she says. 'Not the smuggling, but the sailing – yes. I've always wanted it. And as his Majesty's Navy won't take me, a cruise aboard a smuggling vessel seems just the thing.'

Jack says, 'You're a strange woman, Isabel Henley,' but he's smiling again and she thinks, *he doesn't mind that I am.*

When they finish their coffee, there's a pause long enough that Isabel says, merely to say something, 'I had best get home. I should like to try to get some mackerel when they bring in the catch.'

Jack says, 'I'll take you back to Helford. I'm meeting Tom Holder to discuss some arrangements.'

'What sort of arrangements?' she says.

'Is it your aim to make my business your own?'

'I believe it was you who made it mine when you decided to have your men carry you into my cottage so you could bleed all over my bed.'

'And a lucky decision it was,' he says warmly. 'I couldn't have wished for a better nurse.' Voice low, he adds, 'I couldn't believe my eyes when I saw you standing there across the room at Weatherston, looking for all the world like you'd never belonged anywhere else.'

'I used to belong,' she says, placing her glass on the small round table next to her chair. 'I don't anymore. If I looked as if I belonged, it's a testament to my skill at making pretence.'

Jack says, 'We're similar in that respect. I, too, once belonged in silk-clad drawing rooms and can pretend if I need to.'

'And where do you belong now?' she asks.

'In the back rooms of inns. In the coves at night, unloading goods and storing them in caves.' He chuckles. 'With my neck in a noose, if you ask Lieutenant Sowerby.'

'Don't joke about it. I can't bear the thought.'

'He has yet to catch any of us. Though he did hang poor Jed Ferries, the bastard.' He finishes his coffee and sets down his glass. 'I suppose most of all, I belong on the deck of the *Rapide*.'

'That's where I should like to belong, too,' she says softly.

Jack raises his eyebrows. 'There's a fine line between stubbornness and lunacy. I'd say you're on it.'

'Just as there is between bravery and foolishness?'

'Let's see how your stomach handles the waves of the Channel first, shall we?' Jack gets up from his chair and says, 'The horse will be up for another sortie. May I offer you a ride to the old pilchard shed, Isabel?'

She can't help but giggle. 'There's a contradiction in sentiments. So gallant the offer, so base the destination. Not even 'the pilchard shed', but the *old* pilchard shed. When do the pilchards come, anyway? I've heard much about them but have yet to encounter a single one.'

'You never encounter a single one,' says Jack, offering her his arm as they step out the front door. 'You encounter them by the thousands. Millions, sometimes. You'll know when they've arrived – the whole village helps get the catch in when they come.'

Jack shuts the dog in the house, saying, 'She's had enough exercise for a day; she's too young for another trot to Helford and back.' The stable hand, a boy of about sixteen, brings Jack's horse to him. She's a large, grey mare named Myra, one of four horses he owns, and looks strong enough to carry two. 'I don't have a saddle for two,' Jack says. 'Nor a side-saddle. Are you able to ride without?'

'I think so. I haven't tried it.'

'I'll hold on to you,' he says.

It's as if all the heat of her body pours into the bottom of her stomach. 'That's good,' she murmurs, and then he helps her up onto the horse's back and climbs into place behind her. He hasn't bothered with a coat in the heat of the day and through the cotton of his shirt, she can feel his chest rise and fall against her back, his thighs touching the back of her legs and his breath on her hair. She imagines she can feel the beating of his heart.

'Are you comfortable there?' he says, clicking his tongue to the horse.

She wonders if he's teasing her. 'Yes,' she says, but the word comes out chopped in half by a hitch in her voice, so she tries again, 'I am, thank you.'

He chuckles and they set out at a trot along the road to Manaccan, which presses inland for some time before turning back to the coast. For a while, neither of them speaks. Isabel wonders what he's thinking. Is he annoyed with her for having pushed him to agree to take her to sea? Or is he thinking about their physical proximity, just as she is; is it making him feel equally confused?

She thinks of what her mother would have said, had she

seen her ride like this, so close to a man, without a side saddle. As a widow, the constraints placed upon unmarried women don't apply to her, but riding like this with Jack is outside the bounds of propriety, as her mother would no doubt have pointed out.

After a while, they take the turn to Helford and Jack says, 'So how do you find your new life here? It must be very different from what you're used to.'

'It is. I confess I hated it at first. The difficulties I had doing the simplest things – it was infuriating. But then I found there's a certain satisfaction to be had in doing things oneself. I don't mind it much now, unless something goes dreadfully wrong. And Helford is a lovely village. The people are very friendly.'

'Have things gone wrong?' Jack says, sounding concerned.

'Not much,' she hastens to say. 'Apart from Lieutenant Sowerby calling several times, I suppose. Odious man. Other than that, the only thing has been the pulley breaking on the well. It needs to be reattached to the beam, but I can't reach it without risking a tumble. I dare not use it at the moment for fear the entire thing will come loose.'

'I'll take a look at it,' Jack says, as if it's the most normal thing. She revels in this sense of normality, as she does in the way his chest rises and falls against her back. Her stays are pasted onto her with sweat, her gown sticks to her thighs and it's riding up awfully high on one side with her sitting on the horse like this, but none of this matters; all that matters is the rising and falling, rising and falling.

'Oh, I didn't mean—' she begins, but he says, 'I know you didn't, but it sounds an easy fix and I can't have you risk a drop down the well now you're a part of my crew.'

She feels strangely floaty, as if the air around her is lifting her. Biting down on her lip to keep from smiling too much, she says, 'I am, aren't I? A part of your crew.'

'For the one voyage,' he says. And then, 'Tell me about your family. Your husband – what was he like? Would he approve of your desire for seafaring?'

Desire for seafaring. This, too, makes her smile, despite the *cut, cut, cut* inside at the memory of George. 'I believe he may have,' she says. The remainder of the ride passes quickly as she tells Jack about George, her parents, Greenwich, Woodbury House. It's only as the cottage comes into view, nestled between the tall grass and clouds of fleabane, that she realises she hasn't asked him about himself. He has told her only that his family has lived at Roskorwell for many generations, that his mother died of a fever when he was a boy of six and his father, who never remarried, when he was sixteen. He has three sisters, all married and living in different parts of Cornwall. Surely, she thinks, there's more to Jack Carlyon than this sliver of his family tree?

CHAPTER EIGHT

'Would you bring me a hammer and nails?' Jack is leaning over the well, inspecting the pulley. 'There should be some in the shed.'

'Do be careful,' she says, thinking of his wound. 'What about—' Then she breaks of, registering his words. 'How do you know there's a hammer?'

He smiles. 'How do you think?'

A split second, then she laughs. 'You're the one who left it there.'

'We used it with the crates we stored.' He pushes against the pulley.

When she hands him the hammer a few minutes later, she asks, 'How did you learn to do that?'

'Don't I have servants to do it for me, you mean?' He grunts as he twists sideways to hammer a nail into the beam. 'Hand me another nail, will you? We have to repair our own things on the ship. It's not as if I can afford to have a carpenter on board. Besides, I like to repair things around the estate when I'm not trading or sailing. I can't stand idleness.'

Ten minutes later, she gives the crank a turn: the pulley holds. 'Thank you, Jack.'

'It's nothing.' He hands her back the hammer and wipes his hands on his breeches.

'Could I offer you some refreshment? I could make tea. I don't know if you have time before you meet with Mr Holder?' Before he has the chance to answer, a thought hits her. 'Wait. If you're meeting Mr Holder this afternoon and you were waiting for me here this morning, why did you come all the way back to Roskorwell?'

Almost shyly, he says, 'I got cheated of the chance to accompany you home last night. I wished to claim the honour today.'

'You're not meeting Mr Holder?'

'I am, but not until seven this evening.' A smile; no, she thinks, a grin. 'You caught me.'

'Well, what were you going to do in the meantime? You've got the entire afternoon.'

'Besides fixing your well? I hadn't thought that far ahead. I suppose I could see if Tom has got time now.'

She picks at some of the moss growing between the stones of the well. It comes loose and crumbles in her hand.

'Isabel . . .'

Something about the way he says it, low and full of meaning. It gives her the courage to say, 'Should you like to spend the afternoon with me? We could take a walk.'

His smile settles in her chest. 'A walk would be splendid. If you don't mind a longer one, I could show you one of my favourite places on the coast.'

She says, 'I should like it very much, but what about Myra?'

'I'll stable her in the shed, if she could have a bucket of water.'

'Naturally. But as for the shed, I'm afraid there isn't a lock. Well, there is, but it isn't mine and I don't have the key to it.'

He laughs. 'And who do you think does?'

She stares at him, then she begins to laugh, too. 'Oh!'

She goes ahead of him into the house. Lifting a round tin off the shelf in the kitchen, she says, 'Shall I take some oat cakes? I baked them only two days ago. It'll be like having a picnic.'

'Is that my shirt?' Jack says, behind her.

She whirls around, skirt flying, hands fluttering. She says, 'No. I mean ...' She'd forgotten about the shirt. Why did he have to see it? She tries to take it from him, but he holds it high above his head.

'Why, I believe it is.' He shakes out the shirt and holds it up in front of him, inspecting the cloth. 'You've mended it.'

'I ... it was foolish. I thought you might have need of it, but that was before ... I did not realise you're a man of independent means and ... and I should've realised it, of course, because you did tell me of the profits you make smuggling, but quite apart from that, your estate ...' She runs her hand along her cheek. 'Suffice to say I was mistaken. I never got the stains out completely, you see, and the tear was very large. It's not good for wearing.' She forces a smile. 'It kept me busy. Like you, I don't enjoy being idle.'

'I hardly think you have time for idleness here,' Jack says, unexpectedly brusquely. He re-folds the shirt and she thinks he's going to hand it back to her, but he doesn't. 'Thank you for your efforts. It's mended very neatly.'

When he goes out, she quickly takes two oat cakes and wraps them in cheesecloth, before getting a bucket of water, which she places on the floor inside the shed. Jack has tied the horse to the shelf at the back. 'Don't forget this,' he says, taking the book about La Pérouse's voyage from his saddle bag and handing it to her.

The sun is still high in the sky when they set out. They follow the coastal path into the village, around the water's edge and the houses hugging the cliffside, past the Shipwrights Arms. To Isabel's surprise, they don't continue on the coastal path, nor do they wait for the ferry, but instead they strike out into the thick forest covering the banks of the river. Jack carries the bundle with the oat cakes as well as a bottle of something – wine, she thinks – which he took from Roskorwell in his saddle bag. 'It was meant for Tom,' he says, 'but I daresay we'll put it to good use.'

They walk single file and for about half a mile, Isabel cannot make out any sort of path, but Jack seems to know where he's going. After a while the grass drops back to reveal a trail, tucked among the brush. It's so narrow it could be an animal track. From time to time, Jack calls something over his shoulder about the land or the vegetation, but mostly they walk in silence. Just as she's beginning to wonder where he is taking her, the trail turns and then she sees it. In front of them lies a branch of the river, with tall, rocky banks covered in flowers and giant trees dipping their roots in the water, which is impossibly blue under the faded, sun-filled sky. 'Heavens!' she says, taking in the hushed beauty of the place.

Jack turns and gives her a smile. A canopy of leaves shields them as they follow the trail along the side of the creek, which cuts deep into the land. 'They call it Frenchman's Creek,' Jack says. 'We anchor here sometimes.'

After another half-mile, Jack stops and points at a rocky climb down to a small cove, with a strip of pebbles for a beach. The water babbles around the stones. 'Do you think you can get down?'

'I think so,' she says. 'If you'll go ahead of me.'

'It's easier to get here by boat.'

The black stone is warm under her hands; the way down steeper than she thought. Once, her foot slips and she catches herself by gripping a piece of rock jutting out, as Jack takes hold of her ankle and guides her to a better foothold. She still feels the pressure of his fingers by the time she reaches the bottom.

Jack puts the oat cakes and bottle on top of a flat stone and wipes first his forehead and then his neck. 'Absurd weather for the time of year.'

'Thank you for bringing me here,' she says.

'It's a handsome little cove, isn't it?' A grin, half-hidden behind his fingers. 'Handsome like you.'

'Jack, stop,' she says. She's laughing and blushing and her heart is soaring the way it used to around George when they first met. It shouldn't, but it is. How different Jack is, she thinks, from how he was in her bed, when he suffered through the operation to remove the bullet from his side, and how different too from how he was during the dinner at Weatherston. Even when he was in pain, he was quick to laugh, but now there's a constant smile playing on his lips, which turns into a grin readily. Most of all he appears freer.

To distract herself, she says, 'It's far too hot to be standing here.' Unbuttoning her shoes, she pulls them off and trips to the water. The pebbles burn the soles of her feet, but the river is mercifully cool. She wades in deeper, calling, 'It's wonderful!'

She watches Jack take off his riding boots and turns back to the river, squinting a little against the diamond-glimmer of the surface. The muslin of her dress fans out around her. How lovely it would be to go for a swim, she thinks, feeling the tug of the sea – but what would Jack say?

She splashes water on her face and neck and the impulse flies at her, too strong to resist. Flinging her arms out, she dives in, dress, chemise, stays and all. The water is biting cold, as it was before; it's biting her flesh and grabbing her breath and twisting it, but oh the feeling of it, the freedom.

'Isabel!' Jack calls and she turns belly-up in a swirl of cotton and waves at him.

'Come swim!'

'You're mad!' he shouts, but he's laughing and he's wading in deeper too and then he, too, dives in. He's a strong swimmer, she sees at once; he'll catch up with her in seconds, unless . . .

The river envelops her as she glides through the water, her arms and legs moving as if they've never done anything but swim and maybe, just maybe they haven't, because to swim in a cool sea-river on a day like today with Jack swimming alongside her must surely be the loveliest thing in the world.

The water swooshes, laps, sings; she's one with it, swimming like a fish. The ribbon with George's medal on it drags at her neck. Her gown flows around her like a second skin, like scales, and all of a sudden, she thinks: *I'm home.*

She doesn't know if she's thinking it because of the river or Jack or the village of Helford, in which she was found nineteen years ago. It's not even truly a thought. It's a feeling, a sense of homecoming.

'Isabel!'

She turns to look at him. To her surprise, she's some distance away, along the length of Frenchman's Creek. The arm of the river isn't very wide, but Jack is waving at her and calling to her as if it is.

She takes a deep breath and ducks under the surface, kicking her legs to gain depth. She begins to swim back to the cove underwater, but a sound makes her turn. Her dress follows in a slow, twisting billow. She strains to listen. Yes, there it is again, clearly: a voice, the voice from before, only this time it's not the breeze or the birds or any such thing. It's the river itself, calling: *Swim. Come home.* The voice is just ahead, towards the mouth of the creek. There's a seductiveness in it and, without quite deciding she's going to, she swims towards it.

Come home. Fainter, distant now. The river regains its usual sound of moving water mixed with the blood rushing in her ears. After another few strokes she gives up her pursuit. The river is a cool, green cocoon as she swims back to the cove, still underwater. She thought she felt more herself last night at Weatherston, but now she knows she was wrong: she has become herself here, at last, in the depths of Frenchman's Creek.

A hand clamps around her arm and yanks. The jolt is so sudden she opens her mouth to scream and it fills with water. The river has come for her, she thinks, panicking that the shadow has got her. Kicking, she tries to wrench herself free and then she's breaking through the surface, coughing and spluttering. Jack is holding her up, his feet on the bottom where she cannot stand, a stone's throw from the shore. 'My God, Isabel,' he says.

He's so close she can see every drop of water on his face and his lips, inches from her own. She'd only have to lean in to kiss him. He's still holding her, his arms around her waist now, their bodies as close as they were on the horse and she wants to kiss him, but instead she says, 'Why did you do that?'

His shirt sticks to his chest. She can feel every ridge under it. He says, 'I thought you were drowning. I've never seen anybody stay under that long.' He looks at her strangely. 'Are you certain you're not half mermaid?'

She laughs, ignoring the uneasiness spurred by the voice she heard in the water. 'That was never a part of the story. Half mermaid!'

'You swim like one,' he says, pushing a dripping strand of hair out of her face and tucking it behind her left ear. 'You're beautiful like one.'

'Jack,' she says quietly. *Now he's going to kiss me*, she thinks. They shouldn't kiss, but they will. It feels inevitable, like night falling at the end of each day, like the tide.

Only he doesn't. He lets go off her and swims back to shore, where he sits on one of the black rocks in the sun. As she swims back, she watches him pull his shirt over his head and begin to wring it out. Everything is sharp and distinct in the sun – the water gushing from where his hands tighten around the bunched-up shirt, the clattering sound the water makes as it lands on the rocks, the round shape of his tanned shoulders as he leans forward, a raised line on his left one, where the skin is lighter, the way his hair falls across his brow.

Her eyes fall on the bandage. *Oh no.*

She steps out of the water sheathed in wet muslin. The cloth clings to her legs, the outline of her hips, the swell under her stays. She sees it in the way he looks up at her; the way his smile appears and overtakes him. She's as visible to him as he is to her in his wet breeches and with his shirt removed. There's no embarrassment, neither on her part or his – or so she thinks. And there's the bandage.

'Your wound,' she says, sitting next to him on top of the rock. 'It's not meant to get wet, is it?'

'Rowell isn't going to be pleased with me. Doctor's orders were to stay out of the water. I do feel it still, with certain motions; it's sort of stiff. But just now, I clean forgot about it.' He chuckles. 'Watching you go for a swim rather pushed all other concerns out of my mind.'

'If you stay in the sun, it'll soon dry,' she says. Her eyes keep roving over the shape of him. She wants to touch him, to feel if his skin is hard and taut as it looks. 'What's this from?' She points at the line on his left shoulder, about six inches of raised, light scarring.

Jack glances at it as if he had forgotten it was there. 'That's from a Revenue Service cutlass. Three years ago, we were becalmed five miles from the coast. An unusual problem in these parts, but it was July and we had not a drop of wind. Twelve of them rowed over in the launch. We were like fish in a barrel when they boarded us.'

'What happened?'

'We fought them off. Most landed in the water and made it back to their boat. The *Red Kite* was as stuck as we were – this was before the *Swallow* came into these waters – and when the wind returned, we got away.'

'*Most* landed in the water?' she says, a feeling of trepidation creeping up.

Jack nods. 'You still want to go to sea, Bucca's daughter?'

She fights off the queasiness and says, 'I should like it of all things.'

He picks up a pebble and sends it sailing through the sky. It lands in the creek with a plop. 'Come, how did you really do it?'

'Do what?'

'Where did you learn to swim like that? To stay under-water for so long? Or do you have a set of gills concealed under those pretty locks of yours?'

She lifts the mass of wet hair drooping down the right side of her face. 'No gills. Nor flippers or the skin of an eel.'

'That I can tell. But how do you do it?'

'I don't know,' she says truthfully. 'I've always been able to do it. My parents swore they never taught me how to swim. Whoever did teach me taught me well.'

'And you've not a single memory from before your parents found you?'

'No. I've tried to remember, but . . .' she lifts her hands, palms up.

Jack throws another pebble. This one skips on the water twice before going under. 'I always considered myself un-fortunate to have lost my mother at such a young age, but at least I remember her.'

'But you see, I do remember my parents, for they're the ones I had since I was found.' How different her situation would've been now, had her parents still been alive. Years of command taught Admiral Farnworth to trust his own judgement and that judgement could be harsh, but he had loved her deeply and she feels certain he would've been able to look beyond the rumours about her and James. With her parents gone, she has nobody to fall back on.

Another pebble goes flying. Jack's voice brings her back to the present: the turquoise water, the tall trees rustling, the hot, rocky beach. 'And staying underwater that long, how do you do that?'

'You're all too interested in my swimming abilities,' she says.

'Naturally. Around here, people believe you're the Sea Bucca's daughter. I discounted it as nonsense for the most part, but now I've seen you swim.'

'Jack, you don't really believe there's anything to it? There's no such thing as mermen or mermaids. What of Voltaire and Rousseau on your bookshelves? Are you not a creature of reason like them?'

He laughs. 'You saw those, did you? I like to think I'm a man of reason, but one cannot grow up in Cornwall and not accept that there may be some truth in the old stories. Reason doesn't mean terribly much when your ship is caught in a November storm and makes it through by the grace of God or if you're far down a mine and something or someone protects you when there's a cave-in. There are too many stories of ghosts and piskies for me to discount every single one of them outright.' His gaze trails down her wet, clinging dress, coming to rest on her bosom. 'If there's no magic involved, you must have a prodigious set of lungs in there.'

'Jack!'

'What? I'm merely stating the facts.'

The sun burns a hole in the day. They eat oat cakes on the rocks and wash them down with wine from Jack's bottle, talking as their clothes dry. When, after several hours, they get up to leave, Isabel's face glows with sunburn. 'Thank you,' she says, as he helps her climb back up the cliff to the trail. 'I haven't spent such a lovely afternoon in a long time.'

'Neither have I.'

Back at the old pilchard shed, they part ways. Jack has Myra by the reins and leads her up the gravel path. 'The next time I see you, it'll be to board your ship,' Isabel says.

His expression clouds over. 'You haven't changed your mind?'

'Never in a hundred years. You're stuck with me, I'm afraid.' She feels her heart in her throat. *Please don't tell me you've changed yours.*

After a moment, the clouds clear. 'I wish you'd see sense, but as you're determined to persist in this folly, don't let this pleasant afternoon of ours stand in the way of you obeying my orders on board the *Rapide*.'

'Obeying your orders?' she says. 'You sound as if you mean it, Jack.'

He mounts the horse and, looking down at her from Myra's back, says, 'I wouldn't say it if I didn't. I told you, you're to work the same as the rest of the crew.'

'But doing what?'

He waves his hand dismissively. 'Hauling up the mainsail, reefing the stay, turning the capstan.' When he sees the look on her face, he laughs. 'I jest. These are a sailor's tasks, not a woman's.'

'I'll do them,' she says, jaw set. 'I'll learn.'

'I'm sure you would, too, but I've got a better job for you. I could use your help with the books – I'm too busy myself half the time. Do you know how to do arithmetic?'

'I had a governess.'

'Very well. You can be my bookkeeper for the run.' Lowering his voice, he adds, 'I'll give you the specifics on what we carry and where we plan to sell it when you present yourself for muster.'

'Aye, Captain,' she says and he laughs again and says, 'We'll make you a free trader yet.'

She wraps her hand around George's medal as she watches Jack disappear down the green gloom of the coastal path. Then she turns to the river and gazes at a late fishing boat pulling into the inlet. The low sun casts gold onto the water and a breeze has picked up, rustling the trees on the bank. To her relief, there are no voices in it and the water is clear of shadows.

Her gown dried long ago, but her hair is still a little wet. She has only to close her eyes to feel Jack's hands on her waist again, his chest pressed against hers. Apart from George, she was never this close to a man. The way Jack talks to her so freely, she feels almost as if they are closer. But that's a terrible thought, isn't it? A betrayal of George, of his memory.

She presses her fingers to her temples, willing herself to stop thinking like this. Jack is a friend, that's all. A friend who has vowed he'll never marry. She cannot be caught in a situation again where tongues begin to wag, as happened with James, forcing her from her home. Unlike James, Jack is her equal in terms of social rank and wealth — or was, before she lost everything — but that doesn't mean she can risk the sort of proximity that will cause rumours again. She has made a new home here in Helford and she'll not let anything take it from her. Jack will be her captain aboard the *Rapide*. He can't be anything more to her.

Twenty minutes later she's knocking on Mrs Dowling's door. *Please be in*, she thinks, and mercifully, after another volley of knocks, the door creaks open. 'Good afternoon, Mrs Henley,' says Mrs Dowling. 'Or is it "good evening" already? I was knitting and I've entirely lost track of time.'

'It is evening,' Isabel says. 'And a good one, indeed. I hope you're well, Mrs Dowling. I've come to tell you that I am to go away soon.'

'You are? Oh dear. Not back to Greenwich, already?'

'Oh no, not at all. I shall be visiting relations in ... in Penzance for about a fortnight. I shall take the post from Helston.'

Mrs Dowling tuts. 'That's an awfully long way. I wasn't aware you had any relations in Cornwall, my dear Mrs Henley.'

'They are only distant relations. Second cousins of my father's,' she lies.

'I see. So you have no other Cornish relations, apart from ...' A crease appears between her eyes.

'Apart from who?'

'Oh, I don't know if I should say. It always seems to discomfit you when I mention him – I do hope you don't mind me saying it; I believe we're good enough friends now.'

'Naturally, but of whom do you speak?'

'Why, the Sea Bucca, of course.'

This time it makes her smile, despite the voice in the creek – or maybe, she thinks suddenly, because of it. Everything this evening makes her smile. She says, 'I don't mind you saying it, Mrs Dowling. Sometimes I wonder if there isn't something to it, after all.'

'Oh, child,' Mrs Dowling says, with sudden motherly affection. 'It's the Helford air bringing it out in you, I'm sure.'

The very next afternoon, Mrs Dowling knocks on the door of the old pilchard shed, looking unexpectedly grave under the configuration of curls and hairpins. Isabel wipes her brow; she has been trying, unsuccessfully, to chase a bee out of the kitchen. The outside air is as warm as it was the day before. She can smell the coming summer on it – flowers and the dry scent of grass and always, always, the salty and weedy smell of the inlet.

'Mrs Dowling,' she says, 'What a pleasure. Please, come in.'

The kitchen is as dark and cool as ever – it will take more than a week of unseasonable weather to heat it. Mrs Dowling lowers her bulk onto one of the kitchen chairs. The lines on her face arrange themselves in a pattern of concern. Before Isabel has the chance to ask her if anything has happened,

Mrs Dowling folds her hands together and says, 'I spoke with Mrs Winters at the market this morning.'

Isabel sits down opposite. Mrs Dowling's fingers are long and slender. She wears a thin band of silver, set with three carved coral stones, on her left hand. 'Yes?' she says, apprehensively. 'Was Mrs Winters well?'

Mrs Dowling says, 'She told me her grandson, Joe – you know him, perhaps, he works at Angove's farm – went fishing yesterday out by Frenchman's Creek. Or he meant to, only he saw something in the water that made him go straight back to the village.'

Isabel's hands grow cold. She forces herself to meet Mrs Dowling's eyes. The disappointment in them makes her want to crawl deep into herself. Mrs Dowling says evenly, 'I believe, Mrs Henley, you know what he saw.'

'I … I'm not sure …' She trails off. There's nothing she can say. She has no excuse; she cannot explain why she was in the water with Jack, chest to chest, with only the cloth of her gown and his shirt in-between; why he sat half-naked on the beach with her, and she outlined in wet muslin, every curve visible to anyone who would care to look down from the path. It will be like Greenwich all over again, she thinks, the story spreading, people talking, judging her; she can already hear their whispers: *that loose woman* …

Except this time there's nowhere to escape to. What's more, she doesn't want to leave again, not now that she has a new home.

Mrs Dowling says, 'Joe told Mrs Winters he saw two

people in the river together. He believed the woman was the lady come from London. The one they call the Bucca's daughter, he said.'

She wants to say, it wasn't me. Not this time. Not again. Only it was – and Mrs Dowling knows it. Her throat is dry like the grass outside. She coughs. 'Mrs Dowling, I—'

Mrs Dowling holds up her hand, the one with the coral ring. The lines in her face shift, softening her expression. 'Before you speak, Mrs Henley, I'll tell you what I've told Mrs Winters. I have told her Joe was mistaken. It couldn't have been you he saw with a man in the creek, for you were helping me all afternoon with the canning of the strawberries.' She pauses to let her words sink in and says, 'Weren't you?'

The heat rushes back into her limbs. Greenwich, all of London, recedes. 'I was! Oh, I was! Thank you, Mrs Dowling!'

A thin smile touches Mrs Dowling's papery lips. It's barely visible and vanishes in the space of a breath. 'As widows, we're trusted to keep our virtue because we kept it once before. It gives one a certain freedom, but I fear this could easily lead one to making the wrong choices. Choices which could injure one's reputation.'

The bee from earlier buzzes past Mrs Dowling's head and she swats at it. Isabel says, 'You're perfectly right, Mrs Dowling. I . . . I would never do such a thing.'

'I'm glad, Mrs Henley. You show yourself to be a woman of sense.' A light chuckle. 'The Bucca may protect one from many things, but a damaged reputation isn't one of them.'

The voice she heard in the creek echoes in her mind. *Swim. Come home.* Did she imagine it? Would that there was a Sea Bucca and that he could protect her, she thinks. Quietly she says, 'Thank you, Mrs Dowling. For the . . . canning.'

A full smile appears on Mrs Dowling's face, lighting her eyes. A girlish giggle follows in its wake. 'I shall bring you a pot of strawberry jam next time, shall I?'

'Thank you. I should like that.' She hesitates. 'Do you suppose Mrs Winters has told many people?'

Mrs Dowling rises. 'Knowing her, she'll have told the whole market. Rest assured I shall mention the fine afternoon you and I spent canning together to anyone who wonders.' Mrs Dowling is almost at the door when she turns back. 'Your mother was very fortunate, Mrs Henley. Mr Dowling and I left offerings, hoping for . . . well, you see, the Sea Bucca does not merely lend protection, he may also help when one wishes for a child. Not often, but there are stories, though not one of them is quite like your story. I don't know if your mother knew—'

'She did not,' Isabel says quickly. 'At least, I don't believe she did.' Her voice cracks. 'Did you . . . ?'

Mrs Dowling shakes her head. 'For Mr Dowling and me, it wasn't to be.'

She watches Mrs Dowling make her way up the gravel path. There's something laborious in the older woman's way of walking; some heaviness in her step that wasn't there before. A wild tenderness rises in Isabel so suddenly she takes a step outside and almost calls out, *wait!* But what she would do if Mrs Dowling were to stop and turn, she isn't sure. She can't very well embrace the woman as she would have embraced her mother.

Back in the kitchen, she shuts the door and leans against it, letting her breath out slowly, like the air escaping the pig's bladder the boys in the village play with.

She spends three days packing the small bundle she'll take with her on the voyage. This is not on account of the things she'll take, for there are only ten in total. Rather it is because she keeps unpacking and re-packing them, considering each in light of its usefulness aboard a ship at sea and, of secondary and slightly unwelcome consideration, Jack's opinion. Ever since Mrs Dowling's visit, a sense of disquiet has accompanied her like a loyal pet. She isn't worried about the voyage, but about the difficulty of keeping away from Jack. She came appallingly close to losing everything a second time, thanks to her own indiscretion. She can't risk it happening again.

In the end she carries a spare set of clothing – one to wear and one to wash, as George used to say about his uniform – comprising of a set of stays, chemise, underskirt and a green cotton dress that compliments the colour of her eyes, as well as her cloak and a second pair of gloves. She also packs Jack's book about La Pérouse's voyage, the tinderbox, two candles and, after long consideration, the small, sharp knife she uses to cut bread. All of this she ties into a length of cloth, with a loop under the knot to carry it.

On the day of the sailing, she wanders from the garden,

wet under a dripping sky, to the chair in the sitting room and back again. It's a Sunday, but she cannot imagine sitting still in a church pew that morning. At last, she sets out for Jack's estate. It's only one in the afternoon and Roskorwell is no more than a brisk two hour's walk, but she cannot remain at home any longer. Shouldering the bundle, she starts out on the coastal path. The rain grows fatter and soon she's as wet as when she came out of the water in Frenchman's Creek. The path turns to mud. The cloth of her dress – she has chosen one of a thicker cotton, cream with a pattern of red climbing roses – sticks to her legs, slowing her steps. The bundle drags on her shoulder. Maybe bringing the tinderbox was a bad idea.

After some twenty minutes, she stops and lowers the bundle to give her shoulder a rest. Standing on the shore, she looks out across the river to the spot where the land gives way to the sea. It's hard to see it in the haze of the rain; the water is as grey as the sky. The wind pushes foam onto the waves. On the open ocean, the waves will be much higher. She hopes she won't feel too seasick tonight.

Taking a deep breath, she hoists the bundle onto her other shoulder and begins to walk. The rain cuts through the canopy above and she grows cold despite her dress. The river whirls around the rocks. The path turns and she spots a figure up ahead, a vague smear of colour in the rain. A beat, then the colour solidifies into the red of a Revenue Officer's shirt.

She looks around wildly. Could she climb the cliff and hide among the bushes? But it's too late, the man has seen her. His horse comes trotting down the path and he's calling, 'Hullo there!'

She knows that voice. Her heart sinks. 'Lieutenant Sowerby, good day to you, sir,' she says when he reaches her, as casually as she can while all her bones quiver.

CHAPTER NINE

'Mrs Henley! But what a marvellous coincidence.' Lieutenant Sowerby dismounts and takes his horse by the reins. 'I was just on my way to see you. But what are you doing out in this weather? You'll catch a cold.'

'I . . .' She gropes around for an excuse. 'It wasn't raining when I set out this morning. Not much, I mean. I'm on my way back now.'

Lieutenant Sowerby says, 'I'm afraid you're walking in the wrong direction in that case, but I suspect you're aware of that.' His eyes narrow ever so slightly – or is she imagining it?

She runs her wet glove across her forehead. 'Of course. It's only, I lost my . . . brooch. A . . . a gift from my late husband. I thought I'd walk back to see if I might find it.'

'Oh my dear Mrs Henley, you must be distraught,' Lieutenant Sowerby says, sounding mollified. 'You certainly look it. Pray, what does the brooch look like? I shall help you look.'

'It's …' She doesn't have to close her eyes to see the brooch before her. Her mother wore it often. 'It is shaped like a witch's heart, set with clear stones and an arrow of red garnets. The stones are only paste, but as it was a gift from George …' If she keeps mentioning George, she thinks, Lieutenant Sowerby will soon give up his pursuit.

'Naturally. Let us look together. A witch's heart, you said?'

'It's a good luck token.'

He smiles. 'Surely you don't believe in such things, Mrs Henley? Next you'll tell me you're descended from mermaids, after all.'

Her laugh sounds as hollow as she feels. How in Heaven's name is she going to get herself free of him? Jack is waiting for her; the *Rapide* sails tonight. She pushes her hands into the folds of her dress. 'Such nonsense, isn't it?'

'I should say so. Ah, here it is,' Something glistens on the path – a leaf, she sees at once, with some drops of rain stuck to it that catch the first rays of sunlight digging through the clouds. Lieutenant Sowerby bends down, reaching for it, then veers back up. 'Oh no, I was mistaken. It's only a leaf.'

She looks at him in wonder and suddenly, it clicks. *He's near-sighted,* she thinks, and hiding it. As far as she knows he doesn't carry any spectacles.

They search the muddy path for some time. At last, Isabel says, 'I don't believe we'll find it. Thank you for your help, sir. I'll go home now.'

'I shall accompany you. It's you I came to visit, after all. May I carry your satchel for you?'

She hears the agitation in her voice when she says, 'It's fine, I don't mind carrying it.' She must take care to speak calmly, she thinks.

'Please. What sort of man would let a woman such as yourself carry her own things? I insist.'

He's reaching for the bundle and after a moment, she reluctantly lets go of the looped cloth and begins to retrace her steps. Lieutenant Sowerby follows behind, leading his horse. 'Why did you come to call on me?' she asks. Perhaps the delay can be useful, at least, if she asks the right questions. 'It isn't because of smugglers, is it?'

'Don't fear, my dear lady. Recent intelligence indicates there won't be any smuggling activity in the area for at least a fortnight. Well, at least not from the smuggler that Lieutenant Sullivan managed to wound. He hasn't yet been found, but he's almost certainly still laid up. A gunshot wound will do that to a man.' He straightens up to his full height, self-importance coming off him in waves.

'Have you ever been shot, sir?'

'No, not as such, but I did receive a cut to the arm once. The scar is still visible.' He pushes up his right sleeve and shows her a half-inch line just below the elbow.

'You're very brave, lieutenant,' Isabel says.

He colours with pleasure. 'I'm only doing my duty, madam, as your late husband did his. Now, as this smuggler was likely the captain of the vessel in question, his entire enterprise will have been brought to a temporary halt. Any other criminal activity we expect will be centred around

Coverack or Lizard, far enough it cannot affect you here. So you see, you have nothing to fear.'

He's mistaking her nervousness for timidity, she thinks. Good – let him think it. Making her voice deliberately small, she says, 'I'm ever so pleased to hear it. I positively shake with fright at the thought of these ruffians.'

He appears to study her. 'I am here for you, Mrs Henley, any time you are assailed by such fears. We officers of the Revenue Service have the situation under control, I assure you.'

She almost smiles, hiding her expression in her glove. Then the worry burrows inside her again. She needs to be at Roskorwell by six at the latest. She has time, but Lieutenant Sowerby must leave as soon as possible.

'Why, your bag must weigh ten pounds or more. What do you carry that's so heavy?' Lieutenant Sowerby shifts the bundle from one shoulder to the other.

'Oh, merely some . . . things I've bought at the market and forgot to leave at home when I took my walk.' Her hands clench into fists, hidden by the folds of her dress.

He glances over his shoulder and this time, she could've sworn his eyes narrowed – but then he must have trouble seeing, she thinks, being near-sighted and with the rain a veil between them. They reach her cottage and, seeing no other choice, she invites him in.

Without asking her, he goes into the sitting room and stands looking around for a moment before taking one of the two spindle-back chairs. She takes the other, sitting on the edge of the seat, her hands folded in her lap. Lieutenant Sowerby says, 'I salute you, Mrs Henley, for keeping your cottage so very neat. Why, you remind me of a story I was told when I first arrived in this backwater of a county, concerning a certain Aunt Margaret. Have you heard it?'

She shakes her head and he launches into the story with zest: 'Aunt Margaret came from high society and was disowned because she married a young sailor who turned out to be a pirate. The pirate was killed soon after and from then on, Aunt Margaret lived alone in a tiny cottage on the cliffs. Hers was a simple life, but twice a year, on the anniversary of her marriage and that of her husband's death, she would stand on the cliff in all her finery, her grey hair crowned by a lace cap so fine it looked spun by fairies.'

Lieutenant Sowerby laughs, slapping his thigh. 'Spun by fairies . . . it's so typical of the lack of wit of the people here, isn't it? But there's a warning in the story to women of quality. Don't go marrying pirates.'

He stops laughing so abruptly she feels her heart thump. The story makes her want to weep. It's not the woman's lack of wealth that causes a layer of melancholy to wrap around her senses, it's the woman's loneliness. *Oh, George*, she thinks and then, with a horrible little shock: *Jack*.

She must reach Roskorwell before he leaves. The *Rapide's* anchorage is a secret; she won't be able to find it without him. Flustered, she rises from her chair. 'I shall make tea.' Tea will provide a natural end to the visit. Once they've finished drinking it, Lieutenant Sowerby will have to leave.

In the kitchen, she goes through the by now familiar motions. It's difficult to keep the tray still as she carries it into the sitting room. Her arms feel taut with nerves. As they sip their tea, she converses with the lieutenant as amicably as she can. From time to time she lets a pause fall and waits for the moment he realises he has overstayed his welcome. It doesn't come.

'Pray, what is the time?' she says when she cannot stand it any longer. She has been biting her nail; it's almost down to the quick.

Lieutenant Sowerby consults his pocket watch. 'It's four-forty-five.'

As smoothly as she can, she says, 'As you may imagine, without servants, my jobs never end. I must do the washing before nightfall, as well as ...' She almost says, *cook dinner*, but swallows the words, fearing he'll expect an invitation to dine with her. 'Sweep the floor,' she says. 'I have most enjoyed your company, sir. Perhaps you should like to visit again soon?'

He goes. At last, he goes. Rising from his chair, Lieutenant Sowerby thanks her for the tea. Belatedly, she realises he will likely ride the coastal path back, forcing her to take the longer inland route to Roskorwell. 'Will you be returning to St Keverne directly?' she asks.

'Would that I were. I have business in Manaccan, which shall take up most of the evening. The innkeeper there may turn informer. It'll be a good day for the Revenue Service if he does.'

'I'm pleased to hear it,' she says, carefully trimming the relief from her tone. 'Good day to you, sir.'

'And you, my *dear* Mrs Henley.'

To her dismay, the same feverish colouring she's seen before is back in his round face. He says, 'If only I could convey to you the depth of my admiration.' Before she can stop him, he reaches for her hand and lifts it to his lips as he did on his first visit. Then he lowers it, but doesn't let go. His grip is sweaty. 'My dear, dear Mrs Henley,' Lieutenant Sowerby rasps, pulling her closer. 'If only you'd give into the passion which I'm certain you must be feeling.' She raises both hands to his chest and pushes, half-expecting him to resist. 'Sir! You forget yourself!'

To her relief, he staggers back, the blush intensifying. 'I apologise, Mrs Henley. I did not mean to be so forward; my devotion to you is wholly inspired by your virtue.'

She has barely had time to let out her breath when he pauses on the doorstep and says, 'You do realise today is Sunday?'

'I beg your pardon?' She's thinking of Jack and the ship again. She *must* get to Roskorwell in time.

'The satchel you carried.' He indicates the bundle on the table. 'Things bought at the market, you said.'

'Oh ... I believe I—'

'Please, do not worry. The days blend together sometimes, don't they?'

'Yes,' she says, gratefully. 'They most certainly do.'

The moment the door shuts behind Lieutenant Sowerby's

looming frame she counts to sixty, then opens the door again. It's still raining hard. Her feet pound the path, mud splatters as high as her waist. The bundle bangs into her back with every flying step. She doesn't feel the weight of it now. It's a two-hour walk, but she runs it in one, arriving at Roskorwell minutes after six dripping with rain, her face a furnace, her chest aching with her gasping breath.

Mercifully, the front door is unlocked. She wrenches it open, sprints down the hall and half-steps, half-stumbles into Jack's study. He's still there, together with Dick and a tubby man sporting a prodigious set of grey whiskers. Her legs go slack with relief when Jack looks up from the chart spread across his desk and says, 'Isabel.'

His finger rests on some part of the Atlantic; his tone is one of barely contained irritation. 'I'm sure as the wife of a naval officer, you're aware the tide waits for no one. I'm about to go aboard. Another minute and you would've missed the ship.'

'I'm terribly sorry.' The words come out in a splutter, and she leans with both hands on her hips, catching her breath.

'What in God's name has got you into such a state?' His eyes drop back to the chart as if he's only half-interested in her answer.

'Lieutenant Sowerby,' she gasps, leaning against the windowsill.

Jack straightens up. 'What of him?' He's carrying his pistol in his belt, as well as a sword, sheathed in black leather. The other two men are armed as well, Dick with a single pistol and the grey-haired man with what looks like a cutlass, also sheathed. The sight of the weapons makes her dizzy. The men look like pirates, she thinks.

She says, 'I encountered him on the way here. He said he was coming to call on me. I had no choice but to return home with him. Once he left, I ran as fast as I could.'

'You did well to run. I wouldn't have waited.'

'I know.' More calmly, she says, 'Lieutenant Sowerby told me several things I believe may be of interest to you.'

Jack looks as if he's fighting down a smile. 'Did he now?'

'I may have asked him some questions.'

When the smile appears, it's more of a grin. 'You're thinking like a free trader already. Why don't you tell me everything our friend the lieutenant shared with you whilst we walk to the cove?' Indicating Dick and the whiskered man, he adds, 'You've met Dick Pascoe under less fortuitous circumstances, and this is Harry Tremayne, my first mate on the *Rapide*. Harry, this is Mrs Isabel Henley, whom I've told you about.'

She looks at the men uncertainly – she knows from George and her father that sailors are a superstitious bunch and most consider a woman on board ill luck. But Harry Tremayne smiles genially and Dick Pascoe, too, appears entirely unconcerned.

Jack says, 'She'll make a fine ship's boy, don't you think?'

The three of them laugh. She looks down at her feet to hide the heat rising in her face and sees she has tracked mud into Jack's study. The hem of her dress is covered too.

Jack says, 'Did you not encounter the lieutenant on the

way here a second time? Did he not go to the Customs House?'

'He went to Manaccan to see the innkeeper there. He said the man may turn informer.' Plucking at a thread sticking up from her sleeve, she adds, 'I don't know which inn it is.'

'That'll be the Crown,' Dick says. 'There's only one inn in Manaccan.'

'Aye,' Harry Tremayne concurs.

Jack's expression changes. Where before his face was animated, he looks distant, suddenly. Detached. Darkly, he says, 'I hope there isn't any truth in it. If there is, something needs to be done about him.'

Ice in her skin. She says, quietly, 'Something, such as?'

'We'll have to convince him our side is the more profitable. If he cannot be convinced, we'll be forced to take other measures.'

She takes a step back and almost trips. Fear churns in her stomach. It's a side of Jack she has glimpsed only twice before; when she threatened to betray his identity to the Revenue Service and when he took up the pistol on the bed while waiting for the doctor and aimed it, coolly, at the bedroom door. It's a side of him she has ignored in favour of the picture of the gentleman and seafarer, as well as in favour of how he makes her feel – not like a poor, young widow, but like a woman with a worth of her own.

'What other measures?' Her voice wobbles. Dick coughs, as if he's embarrassed for her.

Jack says, 'You know what measures. You're not a fool,

so don't pretend to be one just to hear me say it.' He says it calmly; conversationally almost. Somehow that makes it worse. She takes another step back and now she's with her back against the window.

Jack drums his fingers on the chart. 'It's a bad business, if it's true.' He turns to Dick and says, 'We'll discuss it when we're underway.'

You think you know him, but you don't. Her head aches with the thought. It dawns on her that her fear about the innkeeper's fate is really a deep fear about what Jack may be capable of.

'Aye, Captain,' Dick says.

Those two words, spoken in Dick's gruff baritone stir something inside her. She could still walk away. She should. These men, underneath their civility and their country-cloaked affability, underneath Jack's talk of fair prices and free trade, they're no better than pirates.

Just as Lieutenant Sowerby wouldn't hesitate to string them up, she's certain none of Jack's crew would hesitate to fire their pistol at a man of the Revenue Service if it meant saving his own hide or his contraband. And Jack is no different.

She should walk away, but this is her one chance to go to sea, the only chance she has had in all these years – or is likely ever to get. She cannot give it up.

The wind is blowing hard enough she can hear the waves crashing on the rocks at the bottom of the cliff, a stone's throw beyond the back of the house. The ocean is calling to her. *What would George think if he saw you now?* The thought hits her so suddenly she almost panics. Is she betraying George's memory by going on a smuggling run to France? Would George have understood? Her hand goes to her throat, clasping the Trafalgar medal. Nelson's face ridged in the silver. *England Expects That Every Man Will Do His Duty.*

She glances at Jack, taking in the way he's half-smiling again already, the way his eyes brighten when he looks at her and the quiet sense of command in him as he addresses Dick and Harry Tremayne, instructing them to go on ahead to the ship. As the two men leave the study, she knows there's another reason she cannot walk away. She's tied to Jack, heart, mind, fate and all, whether she likes it or not.

As if he knows what she's thinking, he gives her a smile that pulls on the rigging inside her and despite the fact that his trade is helping the French and that his work takes him far outside the bounds of the law, the hot rush of feeling holds her and she's smiling back at him.

'That's better,' Jack says. Leaving the desk, he reaches for her and lightly touches her cheek, as if brushing away a stray hair and this infinitesimal touch makes him feel as close as when he held her in the water at Frenchman's Creek, with only his wet shirt and her gown separating them. What's happening to her, that she should feel every little thing so sharply?

With George it wasn't so. She loved George. When he took her to bed, she felt every fumbled touch, every hurried caress before another long goodbye like a small, contained thrill. Yet it wasn't this . . . *fire*. George's eyes on her made her feel cared for, warm, secure. His embrace was like dipping into a calm sea on a hot day. With Jack, it's the opposite. The look in his eyes makes a storm inside her, black clouds, churning water, towering, foaming waves, and all of it heated as if the sun itself lives in them.

She should shrink away from his touch, but instead there's a yearning inside her, a leaning into him. It's dangerous. Jack is dangerous and not just because he lives outside the law and carries a pistol. He has vowed not to wed and even if he *were* inclined to marry, she would not now give up the little freedom her position as a widow has given her. She doesn't want to live in a walled garden like Harriet. For the first time, she's in charge of her own life. Not her father or husband, but she, herself. It's a gift George has given her. She could not give that sort of power to another, not even to Jack. *Especially* not to Jack.

She will have to master her feelings until they fade to nothing. The easiest way to do this would be to avoid Jack, but this is at present impossible. She'll have to try to keep her distance aboard the ship.

Jack says, 'Don't worry about the innkeeper of the Crown. I can be very persuasive – or my purse can be after a good run. I'm sure we'll get him back on our side, if need be.'

'Very well,' she says, so softly it may as well be a whisper. She turns to the window. The clouds have grown tails. A renewed bout of rain hammers the already muddy courtyard.

She isn't sure now if the rushing sound is the sea or the water falling from the sky.

Jack rolls up the chart and sticks it under his arm, covering it with his jacket. 'Let's go.'

The moment they step outside, Jib comes bounding from behind the stables. Isabel stops to stroke the dog's head, then runs to catch up with Jack. She takes three steps for his every two whilst he asks her about the information she got from Lieutenant Sowerby. The wind yanks at her dress, making it flap around her legs as she walks. After the run from Helford, she feels every step pull in her calves.

A lengthy march along the edge of the cliff, made more difficult by the pelting rain, takes them to a point at which the sea cuts into the land, creating a wide cove. Jack leads the way to a path so steep it's hard to imagine the donkeys they use to carry the contraband could make the descent without breaking their legs. The high cliff wraps around the cove and at the centre of it lies the *Rapide,* a brown-hulled mass of rigging and red, furled sails. A rowboat sits on the beach, waiting to carry them to the ship. Even in the shelter of the cove the waves are such that the *Rapide* is swaying at anchor like a colt ready to leap.

Jack stands next to her. 'Isn't she marvellous?'

In spite of her worries about keeping her distance, the sight of the ship thrills her. The innkeeper of the Crown, Jack being a smuggler – none of it matters. Here is a ship to carry her to sea, and *such* a ship. She says, 'She's everything a ship should be.'

Jack grins back at her. 'She is, isn't she? She's a good little ship. Fast, too, with wind like this.' He turns to Oppy, who emerges from the path below. 'Are we fully loaded?'

'Aye, Captain. We're ready to sail when the sun sets. John Spargo sends word, asking whether you want a head-sail set. He worries about breaking the sheer while stowing the anchor.'

Jack looks hard at the ship, gauging the wind. 'I'm inclined to agree, but I'll go aboard directly – I'll speak with him myself.'

'Aye, Captain,' Oppy says. 'Choppy out there.'

Jack nods. 'We'll have to tack out of the cove, but then we can catch the north-easterly. What do you reckon, Oppy, shall we set a record for speed?'

'May make as much as fourteen knots, Captain.'

'Just so,' Jack says happily as Oppy goes ahead of them. She half-expected Oppy to say something about women on ships.

'What cargo do you carry?' Isabel asks Jack, as he crouches at the top of the cliff.

'Tin. They pay a decent penny for it in France.'

'And what will you bring back?'

'All sorts,' Jack says, turning to face the cliff as he climbs down. 'Here, give me your hand. You don't want to misstep on this rock here.'

As they half-walk, half-climb down, Jack says, over his shoulder, 'The bulk of the cargo will be made up of brandy if I can get the price I want. But we'll carry much besides. Cocoa, lace, silks, tea, coffee.'

'So much?' she says.

'We'd take more if we had space for it. I hope to spend a year or two sailing in the *Rapide* and then have a hundred-tonne ship built. Another cutter or maybe a lugger.'

Down on the wet sand, they're sheltered from the wind, but not from the rain. 'Will!' Jack calls to a tall, lanky youth, who comes running over, red, knitted cap in hand. Up close, she sees his breeches have got several patches on them. They're too short as well and too wide at the top, where he has tied them around his waist with a length of rope. Jack says, 'Have you got the fish?' and the boys nods.

'A herring, Captain.' He hands the small, reed basket he carries to Jack, who opens it and whistles appreciatively.

'A fine specimen.'

'Caught only this midday, sir.'

'Well done, Will. It's a shame not to eat it, but I shall make the offering now.'

'The Bucca will enjoy it, sir,' the boy says seriously, and Jack smiles and says he is certain the old merman will.

Will puts his cap back on and looks at Isabel. 'Who are you, then?'

'Mind your manners,' Jack says. 'This is Mrs Isabel Henley, a widow of Trafalgar, and a particular friend of mine. She is to come along on our voyage and help me with the books.' The way he says it almost sounds as if he speaks in jest. Did he mean it when he told her she could be his bookkeeper for the duration of the voyage or was he merely humouring her?

'A widow of Trafalgar?' The boy says, fumbling with his

cap and nearly dropping it. He makes an awkward bow. 'Will Pengelly, madam, at your service.'

Isabel inclines her head. 'I'm pleased to meet you, Will Pengelly.'

Jack says, 'Will here has sailed with us since he lost his father at the age of twelve, four years ago. You won't see a man climb the rigging faster.'

'Dick is faster than me, sir,' says Will, glowing. 'Mrs Henley, would you tell me of your husband? I long to hear about Trafalgar. Pray, what ship was he on?'

'The *Neptune*.'

'Under Captain Fremantle! I wonder if your husband met Lord Nelson?'

'He did,' Isabel says. 'I shall tell you about it on our way to France, if you like.'

Oppy says, 'She's not just a widow of Trafalgar, Will. She's the daughter of the Sea Bucca.'

'*You're* the Sea Bucca's child they're talking about?' Will wrings his cap.

'I'm not really,' she says, stepping away from the others to watch Jack, who has taken the basket with the fish to the bottom of the cliff, where a cave pushes deep into the rock. He places the fish on a stone at the entrance and says something she cannot hear over the wind.

When he returns, she says under her breath, 'You don't really believe the Sea Bucca will take that fish.'

Jack says, 'It's a lucky gull that gets it, most likely. It doesn't matter whether I believe it or not. My crew believes it.'

'That's why you do it? Because your men are superstitious?'

'I wouldn't call it superstitious. Cautious, rather. But yes, that's why I do it – that and the off-chance there may be a way to gain fair winds from the Bucca, after all.'

'You're mad,' she whispers. 'All of you are mad.'

He chuckles. 'And you choose to sail with us.'

The surf washes over her leather slippers as she steps into the rowboat. There's water in the bottom, which Dick bails out with a bucket before they push off from the beach. The sky is dark as if it's already dusk. Rain whips her face, but through the rain curtain, a pale, fuzzy sun is visible, low above the headland, or is it the moon, risen early?

Waves rock the boat. The men pull on their oars, muscles straining under their shirts. 'We'll have to tack out of the cove,' Jack says, 'Before we can get the wind behind us.' The ship is much taller than it looks from the beach. Getting into it from the rowboat will be like climbing to the roof of the cottage with the cottage jerking about like a fish on a line. A Jacob's ladder dangles down the hull, leading up to the deck.

'I'll go behind you,' Jack says, steadying her as she reaches for the ladder.

The gap between the boat and the ship yaws. Her stomach lurches, her hands slip on the rope and then she's across, scrambling up the slick, wet side of the ship. Two pairs of hands grab her under the arms and lift her onto the deck and for a moment, she's on her knees, catching her breath, her hands flat on the deck, searching for something to hold onto.

'Welcome aboard,' Jack says, helping her up. 'You'll want

to clap a hand on there. You'll get your sea legs fast in this weather.'

Her stomach continues to lurch as she stands. If it's this bad in the cove, she cannot imagine what the sea will be like outside the shelter of the cliffs. Maybe this was a mistake.

Jack disappears the moment she's on her feet. She hardly sees him during the next two hours as the men prepare the *Rapide* for departure. Night folds over the cove, stealing away the clouds. As the rain abates, the three-quarter moon casts a silver path on the seething water. Once the anchor is weighed, Jack calls a series of commands, 'Stations for making sail! Lay aloft sail loosers!' followed by, 'lay out and let loose!' once Will and a red-haired man called George Cox are aloft. When everyone's ready, his voice booms across the shriek of the wind: 'Stand by! Let fall sheet!' And, to a boy not much older than Will, 'Look alive there, Betham!'

The wind blows hard into the north part of the cove and it takes the crew a full hour to tack out of it. At last, the *Rapide* clears the arms of the cliff. The ship jerks and then they aren't sailing but flying along the headland, the moon riding high and the waves black around the hull of the ship. Isabel wants more than anything to savour this moment, but the nausea simmering in her rises so sharply into her throat she barely makes it to the edge of the deck in time, gripping the ropes strung there for safety with both hands as she loses the biscuit she had for lunch to the heaving sea.

A cold sweat drips down her face and the nape of her neck, running into her stays. The smell of wood and rope and tar is in her nose, mixing with that of the ocean and the bile in her mouth. The ribbons of her bonnet have come loose and she has not the strength to re-tie them, so she clutches the hat with one hand while gripping the rope with the other.

Spray hits her in the face and she shivers as she retches again, spitting. The wind whips the sea into a frenzy. It goes on for-ever. Eventually, the sickness subsides enough she lays down on the deck, still holding the rope, the pitching sea just beneath her.

After what feels like a small eternity, she crawls back to the centre of the ship and, as suddenly as if someone has snuffed out a candle, the nausea is gone. Wiping her mouth with the sleeve of her cloak, she rises to her feet and, gripping the lines, makes her way along the slippery deck to the rear of the ship, where Jack stands next to Oppy, who holds the wheel.

'How are you holding up?' Jack calls when he spots her. His woollen jacket drips water. He's clutching his hat, a black tall felt affair with a narrow brim, in one hand. His hair whips around his face. 'Fair bit of wind, isn't it? We're making fifteen knots!'

'Is that good?' she asks, pushing the wet hair out of her eyes as she re-ties her bonnet. She must've lost several hair pins.

'Good? It's bloody amazing! I've not seen her go faster. Have you, Oppy?'

'I haven't, Captain.'

Jack says, 'Does your constitution agree with sailing a heavy sea, Isabel? You looked a bit peaky earlier.'

'Losing my lunch seems to have cured me,' she says, hold-ing onto the nearest line with both hands. 'Though the same can't be said for some of your crew. I saw at least three others cling to the rope with their heads over the edge.'

'This wind doesn't make it easy, but they always find their sea legs in the end.' He glances at her and says, 'You do look quite recovered. Remarkable. Well. You had best get down below. It's going to get rougher, still.' He indicates the boiling sky. A low, rolling thunder sounds in the distance. 'It's all hands on deck for the rest of us tonight.'

She says, 'You're three men short on a crew of twelve.'

'I hope for not much longer. What of it?'

'I can help.'

He takes a long look at her, then looks up at the sky again. The ship pitches forward and Isabel grips the line harder. After a moment he says, 'I can't deny I could use the extra pair of hands, but you'd be safer down below.'

She remembers his bemused look when he mentioned the bookkeeping earlier. His comments too about how he'd expect her to work the same as the other men – he was jesting, wasn't he? And she, in her excitement, had taken him at his word. But she can work the same as the men and this is her chance to prove it to him. 'What can I do?' she says.

He looks so torn, she almost wants to take back the words, to tell him of course she'll go below decks, where she'll be safe. But this is her chance. 'Jack,' she says. 'I can help.'

'Keep her steady, Oppy,' Jack says. 'South by south-west.'

'Aye, Captain.'

Turning to Isabel, Jack says, 'I'll take you to Harry. He'll put you to work.'

CHAPTER TEN

Six hours later her hands are raw from hauling on ropes. A fire burns inside every muscle in her arms and back, her mouth is dry with thirst and her mind numb with exhaustion. The wind has laid itself down to rest at last, just in time for the sky to acquire the first pink-grey hint of dawn. The sea still moves like a living, breathing creature, but it's a slower roll now and the ship slides through the waves like a needle through a length of silk.

Jack comes down the two steps that separate the aft of the ship from the bow. His face is so pale it's nearly grey and she remembers with the same shock as before that he was shot in his side only three weeks ago. The worry writhes inside her. *What if this voyage is too much for him?* She has already lost George aboard a ship; she cannot bear to think of losing . . .

She shakes her head. She cannot allow herself to think this

way. Jack can in no way be equated to George. It's simply impossible. *Keep your distance*, she tells herself again. It's easier said than done on the ship, but she must try.

When he's nearly at her side, Jack says something, but the last of the wind blows his words apart and she calls back, 'What did you say?'

Closer still, he says, 'It's calm now. I'm sending most of the crew below so they can get some sleep. You should go and rest for a few hours.'

The thought of a bed is like stumbling upon an oasis after forty days in the desert. She says, 'I should like that. Thank you. Are you well?'

'Fine. Weary to the bone, but we all are. Do you mean on account of my wound?' When she nods, he says, 'I'm pleased to report it has not bothered me in the least, but then I've avoided hauling on any ropes. Unlike yourself. I admit I had my doubts about you coming on the voyage, but you've proved me wrong tonight. Are you hungry? Tom is making some toasted cheese.'

'I'm too tired to eat.'

'I've had Will put your bag in the cabin. Go and rest.'

'Which cabin?'

'It's towards the stern on the lower deck. The door is next to the ladder. You can't miss it – there's only the one.'

Only the one ... his words filter through the numbness. 'What did you say?' she says, to make sure she heard correctly.

'I said, there's only one cabin.' He gives her a quick smile. 'I'm afraid you and I will have to share, unless you prefer the company of the rest of the men. They've got a nice row of hammocks strung along the length of the hold.'

She's staring at him. 'What do you mean, only one cabin? You can't be serious.' When he merely keeps smiling at her, she says, 'Jack, tell me you're not serious.'

'The cabin is on the small side, compared to what your husband will have seen aboard a man-of-war, but I've got a large hammock. One of the perks of being the captain. There's enough space for two, easily, and you'll have it all to yourself for the first couple of hours today. I'm staying on deck with Harry until the first watch is up.'

'But … surely we can't …'

Seeing her consternation, his smile fades. 'I beg your pardon. I thought you were aware of the layout of a ship this size. Where else did you expect to sleep?'

'I didn't … I hadn't …' She's stuttering. The worst is, it's not because she's horrified at the thought of sharing a bed – a hammock – with Jack. It's because she's *not*. 'Why didn't you tell me?'

Sounding exasperated, he says, 'You married a naval of-ficer. Your father was an admiral. I thought you knew about ships – about the lack of space in them. Did you think we'd have a spare cabin set aside just for you?' When she shakes her head, Jack says mildly, 'It's not as if we haven't shared a bed before. The crew won't talk – you have nothing to fear on that account.'

'Couldn't I put up a separate hammock somewhere, at least?'

'I'm not sure where you'd put it, if we had a spare one. There isn't any space. Unless you mean in the hold with the rest of the men.'

The idea of sleeping in the hold of the ship alongside ten strange men is even more disconcerting than that of sharing a hammock with Jack. But how in Heaven's name is she supposed to keep her distance from him if they share sleeping quarters? She was so taken with the idea of going to sea at last, of sailing on a ship across the ocean – 'only the Channel' Jack calls it, but it doesn't signify, because it's the ocean to her – that she never once considered where she might sleep.

She says, 'I'm afraid the sleeping arrangements are wholly unsatisfactory.' She hears how she sounds saying it. Prim and foolish – as if she could fall back on the manners and habits of her upbringing here, aboard a smuggling vessel filled with contraband bound for France.

'Isabel,' Jack says gently. He reaches out and nearly touches her cheek again and, oddly, she thinks she might cry if he touched her now, because she wants to share the hammock with him, she wants to be close to him, but she cannot; she should not want it and, above all, she is so desperately weary, anything could make her cry. 'Go get some sleep. I promise I won't lay a finger on you.'

This is not what she's worried about, but she is too tired to explain, so she merely says, 'Thank you.' Half-stumbling with exhaustion, she makes her way down the ladder and through the door. The room covers the width of the stern but isn't very deep. Besides the hammock it holds a desk and chair; there isn't space for anything else. Early morning light filters in through a pair of rectangular skylights set at a slant in a raised section of the deck above.

The hammock is wide enough for two, though it will be a tight fit, the canvas framed by wooden slats on either end. The sides consist of separate pieces, about a hand's breadth in width, giving the whole an impression of a high-sided, canvas bed suspended from ropes. Since the rain stopped, her dress has largely dried in the wind. She doesn't bother to remove it, nor does she take off her shoes; she's too exhausted. Instead, she drops into the sagging depth of the hammock as if it's her own feathered, velvet-clad and canopied bed in Greenwich and sleeps the moment she shuts her eyes.

When she opens them again she's pressed against George. She feels the warmth of his chest under the side of her face, rising and falling with every breath, and she can hear the beat of his heart, steady and strong. She smells the sea air and sweat on him and knows he has come home to her. A deep, vast happiness surges inside her and she turns her face into his chest, wanting both to laugh and cry as she presses her lips against the cotton of his shirt.

Then she wakes fully and it isn't George's she's pressed against, but Jack. He stirs underneath her, his right arm shifting until it's half-draped across her, holding her in place.

She reels with the discovery. Lying very still, she waits for her heart to resume its natural pace. The cabin bathes in light. The patch of sky visible through the protective wooden grille covering the glass of the skylight is a light, clear blue with a white sun at its zenith. Slowly, careful not to touch the side of Jack's stomach which sports the scar from the gunshot wound, she turns around and glances over the edge of the hammock. Jack's coat hangs over the back of the chair by the desk, together with his neckerchief. How long has she been asleep? She never noticed Jack joining her in the hammock.

The warmth of him against her makes her dizzy with sudden yearning. She wants to wake him and ask him to kiss her. Mad impulse, of course. She cannot; she must not. She's not really longing for Jack to kiss her, she tells herself. She's longing for George. She misses him and she misses how he made her feel. He knew how to kiss a girl and even though their times together were few and far between and the act itself performed with an air of hesitance, she enjoyed being close to him.

She must keep her distance from Jack, despite this absurd situation with the hammock. Besides that, Jack stayed on deck while nearly everyone else slept. He has probably only been asleep for an hour or two at most. All other considerations aside, it would simply be unfair to wake him now.

Carefully, she lifts his arm and hauls herself up on the edge of the hammock. He shifts again, half-turning away from her and mumbling something. *I couldn't* and then what sounds like a name, *Marianne,* she thinks. Or something like that. Slowly, slowly she swings her legs over the edge of the hammock and then her toes touch the deck and she climbs out. Jack stays asleep. She breathes a heavy sigh and is about to turn away from him when she recognises his shirt. It's the shirt that got torn when he was shot, the shirt she mended for him.

Something tightens in her chest. Turning away quickly, she wipes her eyes angrily. What should it matter, that he chose to wear the shirt? She must master these ridiculous feelings.

She takes out the pins from her hair and re-pins it as best she can. There is no looking glass in the small cabin. She imagines the result will be somewhat disastrous. Quietly, she steals out of the cabin and climbs the ladder to the main deck. The hatch is open, sunlight pouring down it. The sea is a mass of sapphire, here and there accented with foam, the horizon a thin, nearly invisible line between heaven and earth. There's not a sail in sight except for the full red mainsail of the *Rapide* as she cuts through the swell.

One hand on the mainmast, she opens her mouth and drinks in the air, her heart soaring even higher than it did when she swam in Frenchman's Creek with Jack; higher, too, than when she first kissed George. This is where she was meant to be all along.

When she came to Helford, she did not think she would ever consider the Sea Bucca story anything other than superstition. Now she thinks maybe there is a Sea Bucca and if there is, maybe she is his daughter. What else could explain this sense of abandon, of utter, delirious freedom she feels being at sea?

Her shoulders and back ache worse now than they did before she slept. She tries to stretch and winces. A sound behind her makes her spin on her heels. Jack is coming up the ladder. 'I thought I heard you getting up,' he says when he reaches the top, as if it's perfectly normal they shared a hammock. 'Good morning, Isabel.'

He hasn't bothered with his jacket or neckerchief this morning, wearing only his shirt, a pair of light buckskin breeches and a one-day stubble along his jaw. Her eyes stray to the top of the shirt, which is partly unlaced. The bit of skin there; she knows how warm it is after waking with her cheek against his chest. The heat of the sun settles into her face. 'Good morning, Jack.'

'It's a fine day for sailing. You haven't eaten yet, have you?' When she shakes her head, he says, 'Will you join me for breakfast? Tom cooks for all of us, but I take my meals in the cabin. I've got to check our course, then we can go down.'

Jack is sitting on top of a barrel, pulled close to his desk, while she has the chair. Tom brings in bread, toasted cheese and beans. At the sight of the food, a sickness rises in her stomach, but it's not from the motion of the ship, it's because she hasn't eaten for so long. The bread is still fresh, the beans well-cooked, the toasted cheese the best she has ever eaten. She tells Jack so and he laughs and says Tom is a fine cook and everything tastes better after a stormy night spent on deck.

Eating at a table with him feels strangely formal after their picnic on the beach by Frenchman's Creek, but Jack talks as freely with her as he did before, and soon the knot in her stomach loosens. After Tom clears away the plates, Jack spreads the chart across the desk and shows her their course, where they are now and where the currents and wind will take them. 'This is where the blockade is,' he says, indicating the sea off the point of Brittany, near a city called Brest. 'It runs down to here, by Quimper, so we'll take the route north of there and avoid the men-of-war of His Majesty's Navy, who I'm sure would give us a welcome a little too warm for our liking if they knew our business. Our destination is Roscoff.'

He points at a town on the north coast. It's only when he says it that it becomes real to her: they are on their way to France. She will set foot in the land of the Revolution, of Bonaparte, of the men who shot and killed George at Trafalgar. She tries to swallow. Jack is looking at her and she manages a whispered, 'France.'

'What of it?'

'They killed George. The French.'

'Isabel.' He reaches for her hand on the chart and she lets him take it. 'War killed George. A war wanted by men in high places.'

'You speak as if you aren't one of them.'

'I'm a smuggler. How could I be one of them?'

'You own land, do you not? You make your fortune trading, whether it's outside the law or not. You cannot in all seriousness pretend you're one of the common men who made the revolution in France.'

He's still holding her hand; now he moves it, gently, so her fingers rest on Paris. 'It wasn't common men who made the

Revolution. Ideas made it. This, here, is a place of ideas, that's why the Revolution happened there. Do you believe Voltaire was a common man? Rousseau? Diderot? Montesquieu?'

'No.'

'How are you getting on with La Pérouse?'

'I've yet to read half of it, but I shall give it back to you soon.' She hesitates, then says, 'If there's time, would you teach me a little about navigation?'

He smiles. 'I'll be glad to. I've tried to teach Will, but he's got no head for trigonometry. Shall I show you the books?'

'You were serious then, about me helping you with them?'

'What made you think I wasn't?'

She laughs and he says, 'You seem to think I jest about a great many things when I don't.'

'I expect it's because some of the things you do are fairly outrageous.'

'Oh, are they? What are these outrageous things?'

Still laughing, she says, 'Going to dinner parties pretending you're not a smuggler, conversing with a man who'd hang you if he knew you were, smuggling contraband from France, involving innocent young widows in your criminal activities.' *And sharing hammocks with them,* she thinks, but she doesn't say it. The way he's smiling at her, she suspects he knows exactly what she's thinking.

'You make me sound a proper villain,' he says, but he's laughing as he rolls up the chart and gets out his ledger. 'If you familiarise yourself with the numbers, you can add to them when we get to France. If you find any discrepancies, please let me know – I'm glad to have a second pair of eyes go over them.'

The rest of the morning she spends learning the value of the contraband Jack smuggles to France and back to England. The nature of the cargo is far more varied than the kegs of spirits she had imagined. Besides many ankers of brandy, Jack and his crew have smuggled everything from raisins, pepper and aniseed to soap, lace shawls and shirt pins.

The difference in prices between the two countries is astounding and she again feels an inkling of understanding for Jack's enterprise that goes beyond mere profits. She cannot deny there is some merit in a trade which allows even the poor to afford small luxuries such as a piece of soap or a bit of salt. Perhaps breaking the law in order to circumvent the tax could in a strange, roundabout way, be considered an act of justice, she thinks. When she tells Jack so, he laughs and says he's pleased she's coming round to his way of thinking. 'Not on everything,' she says. 'Not on the innkeeper.'

His expression darkens. 'I don't expect you to understand, but it's a case of protecting my crew, if it comes to that.'

'Pray it does not,' she says and he nods, saying, 'We're of one mind there.'

During the afternoon she spends many happy hours in the sun on deck, watching the water and the men going about their tasks. When Dick Pascoe offers to show her how to climb the mainmast rigging, she tremblingly agrees. The whole of the crew watches her make her slow, laborious way to the top, where she sways high above the water, feeling as if she'd only have to spread her arms to take to the sky.

On the way down, she steps on the hem of her dress twice and nearly slips. Heart pulsing in her throat, she makes her way back to the deck even more slowly, where, the moment her feet touch the wooden planking, the men applaud. She glows with their approval as well as the touch from the sun. Pushing a finger into the skin on the back of her wrist, she watches it grow first white and then rosy-red again. She hasn't been wearing her gloves. Dick climbs down from the top of the mast in the same amount of time it took her to descend three feet. It's easy for him, she thinks, eyeing his woollen breeches with a pinprick of envy. He doesn't have to worry about a gown.

Dick's bare feet land on the deck with a thud. 'The sun burns you quicker at sea,' he says, watching her press down on the skin of her arm again. White, red, white, red. It doesn't hurt – not yet.

Rolling up his shirt-sleeves, Dick pats his forearm. It's deeply tanned and there are lines inside the skin, black lines under the suntan. She peers at them, trying to make out the shape. A bird, she thinks. 'Is it a swan?'

'Very good,' Dick says. 'The ink has faded some.'

'Why a swan?'

'Eight years ago, I ran into the press gang, who impressed me into His Majesty's Navy, aboard HMS *Leda*, a frigate of thirty-eight guns. She was a new ship, but I didn't much like the captain, nor he me for that matter. After my second encounter with the cat, we called at Gibraltar and I made a run for it. I came home on a fishing boat.'

She shudders at the thought of Dick being flogged with the cat of nine tails. 'You deserted,' she says, thinking of George and what he would have said if he'd known she sailed with deserters.

'I never asked to join the Navy. I got the swan as a reminder to avoid the press gang at all cost.'

'HMS *Leda*, she's named after Leda and the swan, isn't she?'

He nods. 'One of the hands on the *Leda* told me the story. The swan is Zeus, the Greek God, and he … took advantage of Leda. Well, you know the tale better than I do, I'm sure. The captain says you're to help him with the books, so you know arithmetic too, don't you? Anyhow, I thought it fitting, the swan. Though it wasn't the ship's fault that she had a flogging captain.' He pushes his sleeve up further and shows her another ink drawing on his upper arm. 'Have you seen this one?'

It's a mermaid. No, she thinks, studying the blurred, black lines, it's a merman, with hair streaming and a scaly fishtail. 'The Sea Bucca?' she hazards.

He grins. 'Figures you'd recognise him.'

'That's just a story.'

Dick says, 'You know what happened to the *Leda*? She sank off Milford Haven five months ago. Caught in a gale. The crew managed to get off, but the ship was wrecked.' He gives her a meaningful look. 'Something tells me the *Rapide* won't share her fate. Not on this voyage.'

She tilts her head, studying the seaman's face. There are lines of laughter around his dark brown eyes, but he's not laughing now. 'How do you mean?'

'Winds like we had last night and not a single spar lost? They say a woman on board brings ill luck, but not you. With you on board, I'll wager we can weather any storm. I think your father is protecting you.'

'My father, the admiral?' she says, knowing it's not what he means.

He only looks at her, long enough she has to look away, up along the mainmast. She climbed it. She'll do it again, too, she thinks. Maybe if you do it enough you get used to the sting of the rope in your hands, the swaying of the mast, the dizzying height.

Dick follows her gaze. 'You're a born sailor, Mrs Henley,' he says. 'Climbing to the top like that.'

'I was quaking the whole way up,' she says.

'Everyone is their first time.'

She turns to the stern of the ship. Jack is talking to Oppy, shielding his eyes with his hand while he's looking at something — the horizon, she thinks, for there's nothing else to see. The blue of his jacket is only a shade lighter than the uniform jacket George used to wear. Jack's doesn't have the gilt brass buttons, but copper ones, tarnished by the salty sea air. He's taller than George, his hair is darker and he wears it longer, but if she squints, she can almost see George, the way he may have looked on the quarterdeck of the *Neptune*.

Jack would've made a good naval captain, she thinks, if

he wasn't so determined to break the law. The men like him and he seems to handle the ship well – not that she really knows what a well-handled ship looks like. George would have known. He would've been able to explain to her what all the different lines were for.

Jack catches her looking and beckons for her to come over. Behind her, Dick says, 'I'm not the only one who thinks it. About you and the merman.'

'Then I hope it's not put to the test,' she calls over her shoulder. 'Because I'm not who you think I am.' A twinge of doubt – but she couldn't be, could she? Her mind swivels back to that moment in Frenchman's Creek, the words she thought she heard drifting along the current: *come home*. The way she felt she was home, already, in the cool, dark water.

When she reaches the stern of the ship, Jack says, 'Next time you decide to monkey up the rigging, let me know so I can have a net spread.'

'I didn't do too badly,' she says, smoothing down her dress. 'Dick says I'm a born sailor.'

'You slipped on your gown. I couldn't forgive myself if you took a tumble.'

She says, 'I'm not your responsibility, I should think.'

'I've made you it when I let you join the ship.'

'Then let me wear a pair of your breeches next time I climb the rigging. It'd be of more use to me than a net.'

He looks at her in surprise and begins to laugh. 'You hear this, Oppy? Mrs Henley should like to wear a pair of breeches.'

'She'd look very fine in them, Captain,' Oppy says. 'Proper ship's boy and all.'

'She would, wouldn't she?' Jack says, and then to Isabel, 'Very well. You can have my spare pair for the duration of the cruise. It probably is safer.'

They're laughing, but it doesn't matter. She likes the idea of this, of looking like one of the crew and not merely a visitor or passenger, taken on board for one journey only. Tomorrow she'll climb the rigging again and this time she'll do it in breeches.

She eats an early dinner with Jack in his cabin and then goes back on deck until nightfall wraps the *Rapide* in shadows. A million stars come out, more than she has ever seen before. The waning moon rises, huge and bright. She's so comfortable where she's sitting, her back against a massive coil of rope, that she thinks maybe she can sleep up here, under the stars, with the breeze playing with her hair, the rope for a hard mattress. But eventually she rises, stiffly, and goes to the stern of the ship, where Jack has taken the helm from Oppy.

'Are you turning in?' he asks and when she says she is, he calls Oppy and tells him to take over again for a couple of hours.

She goes down the ladder slowly, watching the back of Jack's legs as he follows her. The hammock in the cabin sways as the ship pitches. It's different being here with Jack now. When she went to sleep in the early hours of the morning, she was so tired it hardly mattered that he would join her in the hammock later. But tonight he's in the cabin with her and she's so wide awake it's as if she has slept for a hundred years.

She feels absurdly aware of him, of the space he takes up as he moves about the small cabin, taking off his jacket and draping it across the back of the chair. She remembers what the beating of his heart sounded like when she woke with her cheek to his chest and she turns to the stern of the ship, her face aflame, her skin hot, all of her burning, burning. She places her hand against the smooth, polished wood to cool herself. In a man-of-war such as George sailed on, there'd be windows here, tall ones looking out across the sea, but in the cutter all they have is the skylight.

Jack says, 'Will you not come to bed?' and it sounds so ordinary the way he says it, but it's not, it's the opposite of ordinary and she's afraid to speak lest her mouth runs over with feeling. The deck creaks as he comes to stand behind her. 'You're apprehensive about sharing the bed,' he says and there's a low, almost hoarse quality to his voice, hinting at the hunger she saw in him before, at Roskorwell.

'The hammock. Yes.' She keeps her gaze on the wood, examining the grain in it, which is only just visible by the light of the moon.

'You weren't last night. Or rather, early this morning.'

'This morning I was exhausted. And so were you. It . . . it was different.' She feels his hands on her shoulders. She wants to lean back against him.

'You have nothing to fear. I told you, I won't touch you, Isabel.'

There's something unsaid here, she thinks. *Unless you want me to.* It's there in his tone, in the way his breath touches her hair. He's so close. She could turn around and kiss him.

His hands leave her. She turns and watches him take off his boots and then he climbs into the hammock and lies there, his arms folded behind his head, looking at her. His expression is guarded, as if he's afraid she'll see his true feeling. She wonders if it mirrors her own. She thinks maybe it does.

He smiles and says, 'Come to bed, Bucca's daughter,' and she takes off her shoes before climbing in, wearing her gown, chemise, stays and all. Nerves make her motions awkward and jerky and in response, the hammock sways violently. Jack puts his left arm around her waist to keep her from falling out.

'I asked you to come to bed, not cast us both onto the floor,' he says and she likes the feeling of the laughter in him, the way it rumbles and quivers in his chest. The moment the hammock stops swinging, he removes his arm. She feels the break in contact between them like a rift. Shifting, she manages to create an inch of space between their limbs. It takes effort to maintain it. Jack says, 'There. That's not so bad, is it?' and if there's a slight hitch in his voice, they both ignore it in favour of the pretence that it's entirely regular for the two of them to sleep like this.

'It's not,' she says, though she has no idea how she'll get to sleep. Jack appears to have no such trouble. He bids her goodnight and within a minute, his breathing slows to that of deep sleep. His eyelashes are very long. She didn't notice it before. She wants to run her finger along the lines of laughter by his eyes, down his cheek, to the corner of his mouth. She wants to feel if his lips are as cushioned as they look.

She listens to Jack's breathing, memories of George crowding along the edge of her mind. The way he held her on their wedding night; the way she wept once he slept, knowing he'd leave again in less than forty-eight hours. They fell asleep pressed together like sheets of paper in an envelope, the bed vast around them, but when she woke she found herself on the edge of it and him splayed in the middle. George slept like a starfish when he was ashore, as if he wanted to make up for the lack of space on board his ship.

No risk of that now; the hammock holds Jack and her closely together. Too closely – though she's trying not to, her legs keep touching his. She likes the warmth of him against her. Slowly, her jitteriness abates. It doesn't matter they're sleeping in the same hammock, she thinks. The crew won't talk and no one else knows. She's safe from rumour.

Underneath the hull of the ship, the sea stirs and groans. If she were to hear a voice in it now, telling her to swim, she wouldn't answer. She's far too comfortable lying here, with Jack sleeping beside her. But the sea only whispers, words too quiet for her to make out.

CHAPTER ELEVEN

'Who is Marianne?'

She's standing in the bow of the ship, waiting for her first glimpse of France. The sun beats down on the deck, the sky is a cornflower blue flecked with wisps of cloud. It's not at all warm thanks to the hard south-easterly wind and Isabel has been thinking she should go below to get her cloak, but she doesn't want to miss the moment land is spotted. Jack lowers his spyglass to look at her. She says, 'You were talking about her in your sleep last night. The first night on the ship, too.'

They have shared the hammock the past four nights. The act of climbing in, of the two of them finding their spaces inside the canvas has not become ordinary, but it has become natural to her. She knows it isn't natural, not in the eyes of the world, but shipboard life is so far removed from anything re-sembling her regular existence she feels it hardly matters. She dreads the moment she and Jack will have to sleep apart again.

Jack puts the spyglass back to his eye, then hands it to Oppy. 'Have a look. I can't see it yet, but I know we're close.'

He walks away, motioning for Isabel to follow him. By the gunwale, he says, 'Mary-Anne, not Marianne.' He gazes at the empty horizon. 'She was my fiancée.'

The blow of his words surprises her. She has no claim to Jack, yet she feels as if someone has punched her. 'I didn't realise you were engaged to be married.'

'It was a long time ago.'

'What happened? In the dream, you sounded upset.'

'I must've been. I don't remember. I'm afraid I must beg you to stop speaking of her. I have to concentrate.'

'I can't see it, Captain,' says Oppy when they return to the bow. He passes the spyglass back to Jack.

Another ten or maybe fifteen minutes go by with the spyglass going back and forth between Jack and Oppy and the wind tearing at Isabel's hair, then Jack calls, 'I see it!'

He hands the glass to Oppy and points. 'There. Two points off the starboard bow.'

Oppy looks and cries out triumphantly. 'So it is! Fastest crossing yet, I believe, Captain.'

'You're right. Should you like to do the honours?'

Oppy lowers the spyglass, smiles, then bellows, 'Land ahoy!'

A roar goes up and Isabel is straining to see when Jack hands her the spyglass. His face close to hers, he points. 'Right there. Do you see it, Isabel?'

He's so close to her, the smell of him distracts her: the wool of his jacket, a hint of salt following his seawater bath that morning, and another smell, something undefinably Jack, which she has come to relish.

She has spent the past three days going through Jack's books, checking prices, amounts, sums, as well as climbing the rigging, lounging in the sun on deck and learning the basics of navigation on the few occasions Jack had a moment to teach her.

'Just to the right of the bowsprit,' Jack says, pointing again. 'Do you see it?'

The round lens of the spyglass only shows more ocean, grey, a little choppy, wide. Then she sees something. A strip of brownish grey. 'I think so. I can see a line, hovering just above the horizon. Is that it?'

'It's not hovering. Keep looking. At this speed, you'll soon know what you're looking at.'

She keeps the glass trained on the line, watching as it grows into cliffs, rocky inlets, coves and beaches below a prickly, tree-covered headland. 'But that is Cornwall!' she exclaims, looking at Jack in astonishment.

He and Oppy both laugh. 'It looks the same, doesn't it? I assure you we've been sailing away from Cornwall these past four days. It's Brittany, which is very similar to home. I always did think if I were to make a home in France it'd be there.'

She says, 'But you wouldn't really live in France, would you?'

'Not unless I was forced to flee England. Still, it's a good place. The people – the Bretons – are as kindly disposed to the free trade as the people of Cornwall. I shall take you to dine at the house of my friend Captain Cuvelier and his wife. Cuvelier is my first point of contact when we land. He arranges for the merchants to come offer their goods and take the tin off our hands.' He takes the spyglass back from her and, training it on the growing strip of land, says, 'You had better change back into a dress before we anchor.'

She looks down at her legs, free to move as they like in a pair of Jack's soft buckskin breeches. The breeches are too wide at the top and she has tied Jack's spare neckerchief around them to hold them up. He gave her his extra shirt, too, and declared if one didn't know any better, they'd take her for a youth of fifteen come to join the crew. The first time she wore them, the breeches felt both constraining as well as freeing at the same time. A curious mix, she thought as she walked about the deck for a while to get used to them, to the hilarity of the men. But when she climbed the rigging, she was twice as fast as the day before and never once slipped.

Running her hand over the leather of the breeches now, she says, 'I shall put these back in your seabag for you.'

Jack glances at her before lifting the spyglass. 'Why don't you keep them for the return voyage?'

Thirty minutes later, she steps back on deck in a rustle of cotton. She never before realised how tight the bodice of her dress was. Jack's loose shirt is far more comfortable.

The strip of land has grown. She can see it well without the glass now. 'That there is Roscoff,' Jack says, pointing at a place where the land rises up in the shape of distant buildings, a lighthouse, the pointed spire of a church.

Brown brick houses with blue-painted doors and shutters line the quay. Two boats come out to meet them. One, Jack says, belongs to Captain Cuvelier. It will take them into port, where he will present the ship's papers before they visit the captain and his wife.

A quick exchange between Jack and the boatman follows, something to do with the war, the French customs officers and the weather, she thinks, but she cannot get at the exact meaning of the conversation. Some of it doesn't even sound French, but rather like some of the local dialect she has heard occasionally around Helford.

'I hope my French is good enough,' she whispers to Jack when he helps her down the rope ladder of the ship. Crossing the gap between the ship and the boat proves a lot easier in the calm harbour than it did when she first went aboard the *Rapide* on the eve of the storm.

'You had no trouble with La Pérouse, did you?' he says. 'You'll be fine.'

'I couldn't understand what you and the boatman spoke about.'

'That's because it wasn't all French. I was reared speaking Cornish as well as English. Not many speak it now. It's close enough to the local tongue here that we can understand one another.' He sits down across from her in the boat. 'But not to worry – at Captain Cuvelier's table we shall speak only French.'

'I'm glad,' she says, but her stomach squeezes together at the thought of the dinner. Will the dining customs be at all like the ones she's used to in England? This is her first time dining with any of Jack's friends, not counting the company at Weatherston.

Captain Cuvelier lives in a large, three-storey house overlooking the port, so he tells Isabel when he welcomes her, 'I can see the ships come in from one window and the customs men on horseback from the other.'

Jack introduces her as 'my particular friend, Mrs Isabel Henley, who has always wanted to go to sea'. The latter elicits a gasp from Captain Cuvelier's wife, Madame Lucie Cuvelier, a pretty, dark-haired young woman with a certain earthiness about her, which is soon explained by her declaration that she grew up in the country and shall never fully get used to living in town.

Madame Cuvelier is the same age as her, while the captain is a few years older than Jack, Isabel estimates. He has an animated way of conversing that sees his hands underscoring his every word and the mass of curls tumbling down to his shoulders shake whenever he throws back his head in laughter. The pair have two young children, a boy and a girl, who are brought down and paraded about for a few minutes before they're whisked off to the nursery again.

Dinner is served in a large room with a view of the port. Isabel is glad to sit down: all during the walk to the Cuvelier's house, the ground moved under her feet. When she told Jack, he laughed and said she had grown sea legs.

The sun is beginning to set as they sit down to dinner and Madame Cuvelier calls for the candles to be lit. The glass chandelier above the dining table spits flecks of light on their dishes – a fish stew called *cotriade*, pancakes wrapped around sausages, a dish of chicken and stuffing with an unpronounceable name, artichokes and cauliflower and two different cakes. The food is different from what she is used to – lighter, she thinks, and far better than anything she has had in the past weeks, including the dinner at Weatherston.

As the men fall into the easy conversation of old friends, Madame Cuvelier mentions to Isabel how sad it makes her that their two countries are at war and how glad she is that her husband plays his part in forging connections between England and France in spite of it. It's a different way of looking at the smuggling trade, Isabel thinks, but not an unwelcome one. She says, 'It's very sad indeed. How I wish the war would be over.' Her hand goes to her throat, finding George's medal.

Madame Cuvelier says, 'Is that a medal?'

'It's the Trafalgar medal. My husband died there.'

'Was he in the Navy?' When Isabel nods, Madame Cuvelier says evenly, 'My eldest brother was, too. Auguste.' She gives Isabel a small smile. 'I adored him. He died at the Nile, ten years ago.'

'I'm very sorry to hear it.'

'So am I, about your husband.'

They are both silent, caught in their own reflections. It's strange to be here, Isabel thinks, at a dinner table in France, but Madame Cuvelier is right, it's important that connections are still made. To her own surprise, and despite what happened to George, she finds she's glad to help make them.

'But let us talk of happier things,' says Madame Cuvelier. 'You are quite the adventurer, madame, travelling aboard that ship. How did you convince Captain Carlyon to take you on the voyage? My husband should never allow it.'

Isabel pushes some food around her plate. The gravy from the chicken mixes with the pastry of the butter cake. 'I'm afraid I didn't give him much choice in the matter.'

'That's . . . intriguing,' Madame Cuvelier says, smiling.

With a grimace, she says, 'I threatened to hand him over to the Revenue Service if he didn't take me.'

Madame Cuvelier puts her hand to her mouth. 'And he did not shoot you?'

Isabel nearly spits out her bite of chicken, the laughter hits her that hard. The question is absurd – it's absurd that it's true; the entire situation is bizarre. 'He did not,' she says through the fit of giggles. 'Though I believe he wanted to!'

Jack looks up at her laughter and gives her a smile before he goes back to his conversation with the captain.

'I would have shot you,' says Madame Cuvelier dryly, but she, too, is giggling.

'I think I would have, too,' Isabel says. 'I beg your pardon. It's not really funny. It's only, the situation is so thoroughly bizarre.'

When their laughter fades, Madame Cuvelier beckons for the footman to refill their wine glasses. 'I shall toast your spirit of adventure,' she says, lifting her glass to Isabel. And then, leaning in and lowering her voice, 'So tell me, are you and Captain Carlyon . . . affianced? There is an understanding between you?'

Isabel swallows her sip of wine. 'Oh, no, not at all,' she says.

'I see. But you would be happy to marry again, yes?'

'Captain Carlyon is not inclined to wed,' Isabel says softly, her eyes on the chicken swimming in sauce. 'And neither am I.'

'It's too soon after your husband for you to love another?'

'It's . . . I think it's that, perhaps, but it's also other things. The thing you said, about how your husband would never allow you to go to sea, that's how it has always been for me, first with my father and then with my husband.'

'That's how it is, always, for women,' says Madame Cuvelier.

'Yes, precisely. But for me, you see, it's not like that now. For the first time, I make my own decisions.'

Madame Cuvelier nods. 'While that must be marvellous, to be with one whom one truly loves, it supersedes everything.' Her eyes on her husband, she adds, 'At least, so I feel.'

Isabel glances at Jack. The light of the candles has taken the lines from his face, but she knows where each of them is; the way they appear around his mouth when he laughs, the way his brow creases when he is grave or puzzled. She recognises the mirth in his eyes as if it is her own.

Madame Cuvelier says, 'When the Revolution happened, they declared all men to be equal. The women petitioned for them to recognise all women equal as well – not merely of one another, but the equal of men. Their petition was rejected.'

'I'm not surprised. I don't believe men will ever truly consider us their equals. Not even revolutionaries.'

'But it is my belief that within one's marriage, if it's founded on true love, that equality may exist. Only there, hidden from the world. Hidden, even, from the sight of God, perhaps.'

It's a strange thought. 'Jack – I mean, that is, Captain . . .' she stutters and Madame Cuvelier smiles and says, under her breath, 'You do love him.'

'It's not like that.' Colouring deeply, she presses on, 'Jack says I have singular ideas. I believe the same may be said of you.'

Madame Cuvelier laughs. 'So my husband says, too. We shall be sisters in singularity, then.'

As Madame Cuvelier's laughter subsides, Isabel hears Jack say, 'Nineteen years ago, in Helford.'

'Captain Carlyon,' she says. 'Do I hear you speak of my new hometown?'

'You do indeed. I was just regaling Captain Cuvelier with an account of the mysterious circumstances surrounding your childhood. You see, Captain Cuvelier, Mrs Henley has recently returned to the place in which she was found as a small child.'

'Captain Carlyon tells me you have no memories from before that,' Captain Cuvelier says.

'None, I regret to say.' Isabel dabs her mouth with her napkin. 'Oh, thank you,' she says to the footman refilling her glass with wine.

'But what is this?' Madame Cuvelier says, clapping her hands. 'Mysterious circumstances? Do tell, Mrs Henley.'

'Mrs Henley was orphaned as a young child, my love,' Captain Cuvelier says. 'Captain Carlyon was just telling me the story. Apparently, Mrs Henley was found on the shores of Cornwall, drenched to the bone, at the age of about four, nineteen years ago. The people there thought she must have been pulled from the sea, but there were no reports of a wreck off the coast.'

'But how strange. And this was nineteen years ago, you said?' Madame Cuvelier's gaze is fixed on her husband's. Her voice has grown soft, her eyes wide.

'Nineteen years this September, wasn't it, Mrs Henley?' Jack says, running his finger along the rim of his glass so it rings. 'I remember hearing the story as a boy. A little girl, risen from the sea, they said. It's an odd tale, to be sure, and do you know what's odder still, Madame? People in those parts believe Mrs Henley to be the daughter of the Sea Bucca.'

L'Homme de Bouc, Jack calls the creature in French. To Isabel's surprise, the Cuveliers seem to know what he's talking about. Jack continues, 'She swims like a mermaid, too, and has no recollection of being taught to swim.' He looks up from the glass, meeting the captain's wife's eyes. 'But from the way you looked at your husband just now, I wager the story is not wholly new to you.'

Madame Cuvelier closes her eyes briefly, then, after another glance at her husband, she nods. 'We have a story here, too. Your story reminds me of it. It is about a family of three fleeing Paris at the start of the Revolution. The husband was some high-placed official. The Du Pont family,' she says, as if the name has significance.

Her husband says, 'The family came from these parts, but had lived at their residence in Paris for many years.'

'The mob were after them,' Madame Cuvelier continues. 'They left disguised as peasants. The couple had a little girl, four years of age. They boarded a ship for England, to travel to Falmouth and from there to London. They left Roscoff on the sixth of September in the year 1789, but they never arrived. In fact, they were never heard from again.'

She hesitates, then adds, 'The story went around town. It was such a tragedy, especially with the little girl. There was much speculation about what may have happened. The weather wasn't bad and the captain of the ship was very experienced. He was lost along with the family, as were the rest of the crew, but his widow still lives here.' She turns to Isabel. 'If you like, I could take you to her.'

CHAPTER TWELVE

Madame Cuvelier's voice has grown distant, as if it's coming to Isabel across a vast swathe of ocean. She can hear the sea, too – a rushing in her ears. A ship, lost in the Channel, possibly wrecked off the coast of Cornwall, the month she was found? A family of three . . . could it be? The story fits and yet it's improbable. How could she have made it to shore if she was that girl? She alone, of all of the people on the ship?

She's shaking her head. She doesn't realise it until Jack says, 'Isabel, are you well?'

She stops, looks up. 'Fine, thank you.' In her agitation, she mangles her French.

'Have some wine,' Jack suggests in English. 'It will fortify you.'

She takes a deep breath. 'I'm fine. It's only, I've never heard a tale before that – well, that might fit. It might, don't you think?'

Jack says, 'There would be a great many unanswered questions, but I agree, it just might.'

Switching back to French, Isabel says, 'Would you take me to see the captain's widow, Madame Cuvelier? I should dearly like to meet her and ask if she has any recollections about her husband's voyage.'

'Certainly,' Madame Cuvelier says. 'We shall go tomorrow, first thing in the morning. I believe the family stayed at the captain's house the night before they sailed. Madame Kerjean would have met the girl.'

The floor sways dangerously, as if she's back on the ship. 'She may know me.' The words sway, too.

'We shall go tomorrow,' says Madame Cuvelier again. 'First thing. You will stay the night, yes? I believe our two captains have more to discuss before they can begin the unloading and loading tomorrow.'

'By daylight?' Isabel asks, surprised.

Captain Cuvelier smiles. 'In Roscoff, we don't need to hide the free trade.'

'We're a lawless bunch, aren't we, my love?' says Madame Cuvelier, with such affection it makes both Jack and Isabel smile.

That night, she lies in a large four-poster bed in one of the Cuveliers' four guestrooms, watching the moonlight tiptoe across the ceiling. She misses Jack's warmth, his deep, steady breathing as he sleeps. She wonders if he's thinking about this, too, if he misses her company tonight. And she wonders about Jack's fiancée. Mary-Anne. Why did he not marry her?

Most of all, she thinks about Madame Kerjean, the widow of the captain who sailed to England with the couple and their young daughter. Strangely, it's not the couple's fate that digs the deepest well inside her, nor that of the little girl, awfully sad though the story is. It's the thought of the captain's widow that brings her close to tears. Another sailor's wife left alone, she thinks, another widow of the sea.

The breeze comes in through the open window, playing with the voile bed curtains. The moon is too bright, the blanket too warm, but without it she's cold. She turns and turns again. Soon, the night will lighten and the grey dawn will arrive.

The next morning, she finds Jack in the breakfast room, reading a French newspaper, and halfway through a pot of coffee. They're both up before the Cuveliers. The breakfast room is at the front of the house, overlooking the street and the port, where the *Rapide* lies at anchor between the arms of the seawall. The low morning sun picks out the peonies printed on the cream wallpaper. The room is warm and smells of coffee and bread and, faintly, of ink.

'Good morning,' Jack says, pre-empting the footman by filling her cup. 'You look . . . well.'

Taking the cup from him, she says, 'I look a fright, I'm sure.'

'You do look rather as if you danced the cotillion all night,' he says. 'Dark thoughts?'

'Not dark so much as confusing.' She stirs a spoonful of

sugar into her coffee. She hesitates, then forges ahead: 'I've been wondering about your fiancée.'

With a sigh, he folds the newspaper. 'I don't like to talk of her.'

'What happened?'

'I'll tell you if you promise not to raise the subject again.'

'Very well,' she says, unsure.

'Mary-Anne was seventeen when I was engaged to her. I was only eighteen, but I had my own boat, a small one of which I was ridiculously proud. I took her out in it one day. It was hot and clammy and the sky had an odd colour about it. I knew it wasn't a good day to go sailing, but it had taken me weeks to convince her. She worried someone might find out we'd been alone like that. I told her it didn't matter, that we'd soon be married.'

She's holding her breath, fear churning. After a long pause, he continues, 'The storm took both Mary-Anne and the boat. We foundered less than a mile from shore. I searched for her until my strength gave out. I should've died, too, but somehow, I made it back.'

'Oh, Jack.' It explains so much, she thinks: his insistence it's dangerous to go to sea, his intent not to marry.

Looking down at the newspaper, he adds tonelessly, 'I felt so low after losing her that for several years I didn't care for anything. Least of all the law. The poor harvest the next year gave me a reason for smuggling, but her death had removed the reason *not* to.'

She wants to reach for his hand and try to convey some of

her feeling by touch, for she cannot find the words. Mary-Anne died at sea, like George; her own sorrow is echoed in Jack's.

He says, 'You know how I told you I'd never lost a ship? I lost the boat that day. I didn't leave a fish in the cove – I worried Mary-Anne would scoff at my superstition.' A deep breath, then: 'Make of that what you will. I prefer not to think of the aftermath. Suffice to say I've never forgiven myself.'

'Do you miss her?' she says quietly.

'It was a long time ago.'

She stirs her coffee so vigorously Jack says, 'Are you trying to stir it to death?'

'I beg your pardon?'

He indicates her cup. 'Your coffee.'

She's still stirring. Jack puts his hand over hers. The warmth of it stills her motions and then he takes the spoon, placing it on the saucer. 'It was a long time ago, Isabel,' he says again.

'Yes,' she says, wondering if that's how it'll be with George one day; if she'll be able to look someone in the eyes and say, *it was a long time ago.* She can still feel the warmth of Jack's hand. She keeps looking at it as he picks up the newspaper again. After a while, she drags her gaze away and focuses instead on the port and the grey, rolling sea beyond it. As always, the sight quietens the turmoil inside her – some of it, at least.

*

After breakfast, Jack and Captain Cuvelier go to meet the merchants interested in buying the tin the *Rapide* has carried from England, while Madame Cuvelier takes Isabel to the captain's widow. The house is down a winding street near the church, a plain, neat cottage with stone walls and a slate roof, suggesting Madame Kerjean either never remarried or remarried below her station. Rose trellis climbs the walls and a path of white gravel leads to the front door, which is painted the same vivid blue as those of many of the other houses.

'You'll not want to mention the free trade here,' Madame Cuvelier says, rearranging the cloth covering the basket of pastries she carries. 'Although Madame Kerjean's husband was a smuggling captain, she has since turned away from the free trade and has become very devout. She can be trusted, but she doesn't wish to hear of it.'

'I won't mention it,' Isabel says through the thump of her heart in her throat.

Madame Cuvelier knocks on the door of the cottage. Minutes pass. A blackbird scuttles along the low, stone wall around the front garden.

'Give her time,' Madame Cuvelier mouths when she catches Isabel's nervous glance.

At last, the door opens and a woman dressed in black, with a white, lacey head-covering looks down at them from a statuesque height. She's about as old as Isabel's mother would've been, Isabel thinks, and cuts a fine figure in the austere dress. A large silver cross hangs from a chain around her neck. Despite her mostly white hair, her face is devoid of many of the lines you'd expect of someone her age.

'Madame Cuvelier, to what do I owe the pleasure?' Madame Kerjean's voice is low and clear. Her gaze slides to Isabel. 'I don't believe we've met, madame.'

'This is Mrs Isabel Henley, come from England on the *Rapide*,' Madame Cuvelier says. 'I have brought her to meet you, but before I avail you as to the purpose of our visit, could I offer you these pastries? They've been made fresh this morning.'

'Why, thank you,' Madame Kerjean says. She turns to Isabel. 'I'm pleased to meet you, Madame Henley. Please, do come in.'

She has trouble keeping her hands still. They keep shaking; all of her is shaking as she and Madame Cuvelier follow Madame Kerjean into the house.

The unadorned hall leads to a small sitting room. The space smells of hyacinths: there are two pots, one on a large oak sideboard and another on a low table between a striped silk settee and two brocade armchairs. The room is crammed with furniture in a style that must have been the height of fashion thirty years ago. Madame Kerjean bids them to take a seat on the settee while she rings for tea. 'I know coffee is the thing these days,' she says, 'but I prefer a cup of tea myself. I do hope you both agree. What brings you to see me today, Madame Cuvelier?' Though she addresses Madame Cuvelier, she's looking at Isabel.

'It is this,' Madame Cuvelier says and she begins to tell the story Jack told the evening before. 'So that's how Mrs

Henley was found in a small town in Cornwall, nineteen years ago this September.' She stresses each syllable of the month: *sep-tem-bre,* as if Madame Cuvelier might miss its significance. 'She was soon adopted by her parents, Admiral and Mrs Farnworth of . . . Woodbane House, Mrs Henley?'

'Woodbury House, in Norfolk,' Isabel says. 'But yes, that is my story.' She forces a lightness in her tone she doesn't feel. 'Extraordinary, isn't it?'

Madame Cuvelier says, 'It reminded me of something that happened in our town nineteen years ago.'

Madame Kerjean is now openly staring at Isabel. She's leaning forward in her chair, her elbows planted on a set of bony knees visible under the black cloth of her dress. She lifts the silver cross to her lips and kisses it. *'Mon Dieu, mon enfant,'* she whispers, making the sign of the cross. She draws a lace handkerchief from the folds of her gown and pats her eyes, whispering again, *'Mon Dieu.'*

'Could it be her?' Madame Cuvelier says. 'I don't mean to be insensitive, but you can understand how important it is. The family stayed with you and Captain Kerjean the night before they set sail, did they not? Do you think it's possible?'

'You are twenty-three now?' Madame Kerjean asks Isabel.

'As of last December, as far as I know. My parents chose a birthday for me based on their physician's judgement of my age.'

'And you have no memories? Not of your parents, nor of France? Not of my husband and me?'

'None. I don't recall ever having been here.'

'You have her hair,' Madame Kerjean says. 'The same, what to call it now? Waviness. Not quite curls. But it was a shade lighter.'

'Hair colour can change as we grow older,' says Madame Cuvelier.

Madame Kerjean says, 'She had freckles, like you. And your eyes . . . yes, I believe it could be. Perhaps. Aurélie, her name was. Does it mean anything to you, this name?'

Isabel shakes her head again, her tongue turned to sand in her mouth. Madame Kerjean continues, 'Aurélie Du Pont, she was called. But when they fled Paris, the family took the name Fournier, so they would have taught their daughter to call herself Aurélie Fournier.' She leans in closer and touches Isabel's hair. 'It could be,' she says slowly. 'I can't be sure.'

When the woman draws back, Isabel lets out her breath slowly. 'But how could I — that is to say, how could one little girl have survived when no one else on the ship did? It doesn't make any sense.'

'She could swim,' Madame Kerjean says. 'I remember distinctly her telling me. She was a sweet little thing. *Douce*. She told me she could not wait to go to sea. She dreamt of it, she said, back in Paris. I said to her, 'Are you not afraid of the water? The ocean is very big,' and she said she wasn't, for she could swim.' Madame Kerjean puts the handkerchief to her eyes again. 'I thought she was telling tales. A little thing like that, swim, I thought. My face must've shown my disbelief, for the father told me it was true.

'I taught her myself, as soon as she could walk,' he said

to me, and he explained that he had lost a cousin at a young age, drowned in the pond on the family's land. He'd make sure this would never happen to his child. He said she could swim like a fish. So you see, if any child would've known how to save herself in the water, it would have been this one.' A heavy pause, then Madame Kerjean adds, 'Captain Kerjean was a very good swimmer, too.'

They're all silent. A pigeon coos outside. The sun is high in the sky, already; the smell of the sea blows in through the window, overtaking that of the hyacinths and tea. 'Pastry?' Madame Kerjean says thickly, offering the basket Madame Cuvelier has brought.

Isabel shakes her head. Madame Cuvelier takes a small round cake and nibbles it. Crumbs rain onto the skirt of her yellow gown. The air grows oppressive, despite the half-open window. The ceiling is too low; the beams only an inch above Isabel's head when she stands. There's no space to breathe. She wants to get out of Madame Kerjean's house, the town, the stone sea-wall of the harbour. She wants the open ocean so she can breathe.

She stands up abruptly. 'Thank you, Madame Kerjean,' she says. 'You've been exceedingly helpful. And you, Madame Cuvelier, I thank you kindly for your hospitality and for bringing me here. I'm afraid I must go back to the ship now. Captain Carlyon is expecting me.'

Madame Cuvelier has risen too. She brushes the crumbs from her gown and says, 'Are you quite well, Mrs Henley? You look pale.'

'Some fresh air will help, I'm sure.'

They take their leave of Madame Kerjean in a swarm of platitudes. Yes, Isabel will come see her again if she's ever in Roscoff and yes, it's a marvellous story and thank you, thank you, thank you again.

At last, they're out in the street. As they walk back to the port, Isabel thanks Madame Cuvelier again. 'It's strange to think they may have been my parents,' she says.

'I'll try to find out more about the family,' Madame Cuvelier says. 'I believe there may be an ancestral home somewhere in Brittany. I shall write to you, if you tell me where to direct my letter.'

She gives Madame Cuvelier the name of the cottage and the village. 'I shall look forward to your letter, Madame,' Isabel says and Madame Cuvelier tells her to please call her Lucie.

She declines the offer of another night in the Cuveliers' guestroom. Jack will sleep on board tonight so he can oversee the loading of the cargo until the small hours and she's eager to join him. At the quay, she doesn't have long to wait for a boat to take her back to the *Rapide*. Before the sun reaches its highest point, she's back on board. The top deck is such a hive of activity she flattens herself against the mainmast to get out of the way.

'Isabel.' Jack comes striding over. 'You're back. How was it?'

'Fine,' she says, dragging up the corners of her mouth. 'Shall I tell you about it later? I can see you're busy.' The words are as light as the breeze.

'We sail with the morning tide,' Jack says. 'So yes, it's best if you tell me later. Do tell me, however – do you think they could've been your parents?'

'Who knows?' she says, holding the breeze, keeping it. 'They're gone, in any case.'

Jack says, 'That's one way of looking at it, I suppose. Will you come and take down the numbers for the goods before the men take them down to the hold?'

'Give me a moment to … get something from the cabin. I shall be there directly.'

'Very well.' Jack turns on his heels and marches past the contraband stacked along the gangway to a place near the bow where Harry Tremayne and Dick Pascoe are counting small wooden crates.

She slips down the ladder and into the cabin. The sun falls in at a slant, the skylight is a rectangle of pure blue. It smells of polished wood and of the sea. She leans back against the side of the ship, sinking to a crouch. It is only then that she allows the tears to come, rocking back and forth on the balls of her feet as she weeps for the parents she never knew, whether they were the couple fleeing Paris or whether they were other parents, forever unknown to her. The sea took them, if they were her parents. If they weren't, the sea took them still. Just as she lost George far away at sea, aboard a ship, just as Jack lost Mary-Anne, she lost these parents she cannot even remember. If they were hers.

She nearly chokes on the thought. It's obscene that she should love the sea as she does when all it has done is rob her of her family. *And what of Jack?* she thinks. *Will the sea claim him, too?*

Her eyes move from the skylight to the hull of the ship. Beyond it lies the ocean, vast, unknowable like her parents. Except, she feels she does know it. That moment in the creek, when she felt she had come home, the voice calling to her, the dreams she's had full of shadows in the water – there's a sense of familiarity to it all. Maybe she has always known it, maybe that's why she longs for the sea like she does.

The story Madame Kerjean told her fits, and yet it doesn't. Could she have been on that ship and washed up on the shores of Cornwall? It's possible. Only, the ship left Roscoff on the sixth of September and the crossing shouldn't have taken more than five or six days, yet she wasn't discovered in Helford until September the twenty-fifth. Was the ship blown off course? Had she been in the ocean or somewhere on the Cornish coast, alone, perhaps? But the latter didn't explain why she was dripping seawater when she was found.

Or is she not the girl from the French ship, is she someone else, perhaps even – miraculously – someone whose father could be a spirit of the sea, an invocation against its dangers, a creature of legend, as the people of Helford have been telling her?

She presses the heels of her hands to her eyes. A dull headache pulses behind them. She has never been forced to examine her origins so closely before. Though she wondered, she was content to accept they were unknown. She had her parents, whom she loved, and that was enough. Only now it isn't any longer. The sea calls to her more insistently all the time and she cannot tell if it's because she lives so near it or because of something else.

One thing she does know. When Jack said one couldn't grow up in Cornwall without accepting that there may be some truth in the old stories, he was right. The Helford River, with its hidden coves and trails, with its shadowy creeks and turquoise waters opening to the sea as if to embrace it, is a place in which fairy stories may just be true.

The tears keep coming. She stays down in the cabin too long. The door opens and then Jack is crouching in front of her, saying, 'Don't cry.' He takes her hands from her eyes and pulls her up to standing. She wants to move into his arms, but instead she leans back against the side of the ship. Jack says, 'They were your parents then?'

'I don't know. My father is Admiral Farnworth. My mother was … my mother. Before all else, she was my mother. Those people who fled Paris – I'll never know now.' She wipes her eyes with the cuff of her sleeve. 'I don't know why it makes me so sad. Nothing has changed. They were always either going to be dead or they didn't want me. I knew that from the moment I learned the story of how I was found, but now … I can't stop thinking of how the sea took them, even if they *weren't* my natural parents, just like it took George and …' She trails off.

'And what?'

'What if it takes you, too?'

'Listen,' he says. 'The sea takes, but it also gives.'

'That sounds like blasphemy.'

'Because it's close to scripture? What does it matter when it's true? Besides the practical stuff, does it not also give you great happiness to stand on deck with the wind in your hair and a fast sea below your feet? You've felt it, haven't you?'

'I have.'

'Then if you may not have a merman for your father, perhaps think of the sea as your mother. That way you shall never truly be orphaned.'

'What a strange thought, Jack.'

Looking away, he says, 'I invented it when I was six, when I lost my mother. It helped me, especially at night, when my father had gone to sea, leaving my sisters and me with our governess. I felt terribly alone. I could hear the sea outside my window and I imagined it was my mother, singing me a lullaby.' He's silent for a moment, then says, 'Even what happened with Mary-Anne could not change how I feel about the ocean.'

The image of him as a little boy, alone, makes the tears rise again. The distance between the two of them, however small, is suddenly too much; she closes it in two steps and wraps her arms around his waist. Long seconds pass, then he puts his arms around her shoulders and she leans in, sniffing into his shirt. 'Careful, it's my best one,' he says.

This makes her laugh, in spite of it all. 'It's your most mended one and you've worn it five days without washing.'

'It's my best one because you've mended it and in case you didn't know, it's only wash day once a week at sea. Besides, you've been wearing my other shirt all through the crossing.' He lets go of her and moves to the door. 'Come, why don't you change back into it and play at being a ship's boy some more? I could use your help on deck. We've never carried such a variety of goods in one run before.'

CHAPTER THIRTEEN

The next three days she feels how she imagines a bird might feel when it first learns to fly – as if the world belongs to her. Despondency leaves her; she has decided to stop worrying about the couple from Paris, the voice in the river and old tales about merfolk. It's not even happiness, she thinks, it's a contentedness so deep it's growing roots. They have what Jack calls 'fair winds' – it blows hard, but not too violently in the direction of England. She wishes it would blow the other way, far out into the Atlantic, away from the old pilchard shed and the moment she must leave the ship and her place at Jack's side in the hammock at night.

On her last full day at sea, she cannot stop looking at him. When they go ashore, the closeness between them will fracture. Maybe they'll meet on the coastal path or in the village, or they'll see each other across the dining room at Weatherston. It will never be like this again.

As the day wears on, a terrible restlessness grows inside her. She feels almost delirious with yearning and on the verge of tears at the same time. The yearning is not for the sea, as it normally is. Every night she has resisted the urge to kiss Jack, to ask him to put his arms around her; to beg him to claim something he has not sought.

By the time the sun lowers itself into the ocean she can bear it no longer. They're in the cabin together, as they are every evening, Jack taking off his jacket and draping it across the chair, her turned away, hiding the burning inside her by examining the knots and grains in the wood of the hull. The cabin is full of shadows. It's a new moon and Jack has suspended a lantern from a hook in the deck above, but has not yet lit it, for the sky visible through the skylight is still the bruised purple of dusk.

The longing makes her feel feverish and she thinks if Jack were to touch her now, she'd shiver. She looks up at the twilight, pinpricked with stars, then turns back to the hull when Jack comes to stand behind her. 'A pretty sight,' he says. 'There aren't stars like there are at sea.'

She doesn't care about the stars; not now. 'I should like to . . .' she begins. Her throat is dry, her tongue sticks. She can't say it. It's their last night away from the world, away from its prying eyes and whispering tongues. It's her last chance. She shouldn't think it, let alone say it. She tries again: 'Jack, I want . . .'

His fingers brush the skin of her neck, sweeping away the loose hairs escaping their pins, then his lips touch her skin, just above her fichu neckerchief, so lightly she could almost have imagined it. Her breath catches. Softly, against her skin, he says, 'This?'

'Yes.' A breath, not a word.

He runs his hands along the length of her arms, down to her hands, lifting her left one. His chest is flush against her back the way it was when they rode the horse together and then his mouth is on the back of her hand, touching the soft space between the knuckles as he did the morning after the dinner party at Weatherston and he's saying, 'And this?'

'Yes.' She turns in his arms and before she can think, she's kissing his chest through the cloth of his shirt and then his shoulder, his neck, his jaw, saying, 'And this, and this, and this,' until she reaches his mouth, but she pulls back before she can kiss this, too, because it's madness to be doing this, only it's not – it's the one thing in her life that suddenly does not seem mad. And when he kisses her, it is the only thing that makes sense.

She thought she had come home when she swam in Frenchman's Creek and again when the *Rapide* set sail. Now she knows otherwise.

'We shouldn't . . .' She murmurs against his lips. He smells of the sea – wind and salt – and he tastes of something warm and a little sweet, port, maybe, or honeyed butter.

'Why, Isabel?' He breaks their kiss just long enough to say the words. 'Why shouldn't we?'

She feels his touch everywhere, as if all her nerves are connected by invisible thread, as if by touching one small spot with his lips or hands, he caresses all of her.

He loosens her fichu, letting the neckcloth fall to the floor before making a trail of kisses on her cheek and along the line of her jaw until he's back where he started, his lips brushing her neck.

'Because ...' Her mind has turned sluggish. She casts about for reasons – there were several and they were good ones – but she cannot now find them. All she knows is that she is lifting his shirt, the way she never got to lift George's, for he would remove it himself. There's the line of dark hair, disappearing into the top of Jack's trousers and she wants to see where it goes, she wants to touch it, and there's the red, welted new scar. Her hands move along his skin like butter-flies, searching and finding. His skin tastes of salt, but then he steps back, making her gasp.

'Turn around,' he says and when she does it, he lifts the shirt she's been wearing and begins to undo the laces on her stays and he's kissing her again. Every bit of skin he exposes, he kisses and he's saying, 'I've wanted you since I first saw you.'

'You were bleeding,' she says, and he laughs softly. The shirt falls to the deck, followed by the stays. His fingers work the knot in the neckerchief with which she has tied the breeches. Soon, she will be naked. Standing upright before him, she will be naked. Even with George, she was never fully unclothed except under the sheets, with the candle put out and their hands taking the role of their eyes, fumblingly seeing.

Jack says, 'Even when I was bleeding, I wanted you,' and

this makes her laugh but then he has freed the neckerchief and it drops to the deck, the breeches pooling around her ankles. She almost stumbles as she turns to face him, expecting – what? Shame? Embarrassment? It doesn't come. *What's wrong with me?* she thinks vaguely, *that I can stand before a man so unashamedly naked?*

She blushes, yes, but she blushes easily, always, and the look in his eyes makes her feel unlike she ever has before. Like a siren, calling from the rocks. Beautiful like a merman's daughter. All the things he said to her, teasingly, she sees in his eyes are true. She believes him now when he said he wanted her even when he was wounded. She feels the same wild abandon she felt when she climbed to the upper deck on her first morning on the ship and saw the wide, sky-laden sea. But then he kisses her again and his hands find their way down the soft curve of her belly and they take all her thoughts with them, until she can only sigh.

When they tumble into it, the hammock swings so that despite the high sides, they nearly fall out again. There's a bit of a shuffle and then Jack moves on top of her, the full length of him pressing her into the canvas, causing a low, heavy throbbing. She aches to be touched. His breath hot on her ear, he says, 'We'll have to take it slow or we'll end up on the deck.'

And they do, each touch intent and agonisingly unhurried. Whenever she grows impatient for him, Jack slows her down, saying they have all night, he wants to savour this – savour *her.* She remembers things from before and finds her hands and mouth know other things instinctively. Jack, she discovers, knows her better than she herself. The cabin fades in the heat of his touch; the burning in her deepens until she pulls him to her with a groan. This makes him laugh, softly, against her mouth, and then he gives in. Time sweeps away from her; she's in his arms a moment and always as the stars, previously glimpsed through the skylight, explode inside her.

Later, much later, the hammock is full of arms and legs, sweat and skin pressed together. She has her cheek against his chest, his arm rests in the nook of her waist. Tears are jostling in her throat, making it difficult to speak. Jack is tracing patterns in the sweat on her belly. 'You're very quiet,' he says.

'I didn't know it could be like that,' she whispers. It pains her to think how little she and George really knew each other. Not just physically – the way she talks with Jack is different, too. The way Jack talks with her.

'But you enjoyed it?' he asks, which makes the tightness in her throat worse.

She nods against his chest. 'If I cry, don't think it's because I'm unhappy.' She wants to warn him; she wants nothing to spoil this moment, not a misunderstanding about her threatening tears or anything else. 'I'm not. I'm very happy. It's only . . .'

He brushes the wetness from her cheeks. 'I know. It's your husband. You miss him.'

'Not enough,' she says. 'Since I met you, I've not missed him as much as I should.'

Jack says, 'He was a good husband, was he not?'

'He was. Very good.'

Kissing her hair, he says, 'Then he would want you to be happy, I should think.'

'Yes. I think so.'

'And he wouldn't want you to always be on your own,' Jack continues, running his fingers along the slick skin of her arm.

This is a strange thing for him to say. She blurts, 'You said you wouldn't wed.'

Another kiss. 'I'd reconsider for the right woman. One I could trust to handle the danger that comes with the work.'

She scoffs. She can't help it. Why should he make this pretence? Why promise something he doesn't want? She says, 'Is that what you tell all of us?'

'What do you mean, all of you?'

She has offended him; she can hear it in his voice. Still. 'Don't tell me I'm the only one. The way you know how to . . . how to do all of those things.' George never did.

He half-turns so he can look at her. The hammock wobbles as he shifts his weight. 'Isabel, this is nonsense. Of course we'll marry.'

What? She thinks it and then she says it out loud, 'What?'

'You want to marry, don't you? We're a good fit. Admit it. We're a good fit in every which way — as we have just discovered. And it would mean you'd no longer have to live in a state poorer than the least fortunate of my tenants.'

She pushes herself up on her elbow. The hammock swings

dangerously. 'That's what this is about? You want to save me from being poor?' Her new life may lack many things, but a saviour is not one of them. 'I'm fine as I am.'

'I don't want to *save* you. I'm telling you I want to marry you. Do you not wish to?'

She does. Everything in her screams it: *I do, I do, I do.* But he doesn't, not really. He only feels sorry for her, for her widowhood, her poverty, and now also for the fact that he has bedded her. *England Expects That Every Man Will Do His Duty.* Lord Nelson's words, swimming in her mind. *Is that what this is?* she thinks. Does Jack believe it's his duty to wed her, since he bedded her?

And even if he did truly wish to marry her, would she want to marry again? As a widow, she has her freedom. She isn't sure she could she give it up, even for love. To buy time, she says, 'We've met only, what, four weeks ago?'

Jack says, 'We know each other better than many couples after years of courting. We're well-suited to each other. What more could one hope for in a marriage?' He sounds exasperated. 'Did you think I hadn't considered these things before I took you to bed?'

Seeing her expression, he says, 'I see. You thought I bedded you on impulse, without any consideration for your future, your feelings or your honour.'

So this lies at the heart of it. She's glad of his consideration, but if this is how he feels, then what will he think when he hears of the rumours about her and James? If she were to accept his proposal, she'd have to tell him. And he'd believe her, wouldn't he, if she told him she and James only ever shared the close rapport of friends; he wouldn't hold that proximity against her the way people in Greenwich did. She's sure of it – *almost*. But what if she's wrong?

When she doesn't say anything, he adds bitterly, 'That is what you think of me.'

'Jack ...' She takes a deep breath. 'You break the law for a living. I thought ...'

'This means I must therefore act the villain in all aspects of life, is that it?'

'I suppose I did. I'm sorry.'

He sighs. 'I'm saying this all wrong. Let me try once more to rectify your prejudice against me. I'd like to marry you, Isabel Henley, if you'll have me. I'll go down on my knees to ask you if you want it done properly. I realise both of us lying naked in a hammock is not the traditional way, but I mean every word. I want to marry you, not to save you or because I feel I owe it to you after taking you to bed, but because I believe you'll make a good wife for me and I would try my hardest to make a good husband.'

She nearly begins to weep again. To hide her confusion, she buries her face in his chest. 'I don't know. It's complicated. Since George ...'

'If you need more time, you have it. My proposal stands for as long as you need to come to a decision. But it has been three years since he died, hasn't it?'

'Yes, but ... it's because of George, but it's also because ...' She looks up at him again. 'Jack, I don't expect you to understand, but I'm living my own life for the first time. Independently, with no man ruling my fate, not my father, nor my husband. I don't know that I could give it up.'

'I wouldn't curb your freedom, if that's what you fear.'

'I know, but once I marry again, it's curbed, no matter what your views on it are. Society says it is. The law says it.'

She's glad to see him smile again. 'Have you not realised I hold the law in no great regard?'

She touches the line on his shoulder, the scar from the cutlass. 'Would you let me sail with you if we were married?'

'Of course not. It's far too dangerous.' A chuckle, then, 'So that's what you're after, is it? A ship, not a husband?'

Both, she thinks, *if I could have them. If I could still be free.* But going to sea and being married are two opposing things. One rules out the other. George would never have allowed her to come on this voyage. And neither would Jack if she were his wife.

'Look,' Jack says. 'I'm well aware what I'm asking of you. As long as my identity remains concealed, you'd be marrying John Carlyon, owner of the Roskorwell estate. The doors of society would be open to you, and you would not lack for anything. But the moment my name becomes known as the captain of the *Rapide*, you'd be facing a different future. Those doors would close to you at once. No one would admit you to their houses, their dinner tables—'

'Do you think I care about that? They were closed to me once before,' she says quietly.

'Perhaps not. I expect your recent experiences have

hardened you to this possibility. And there would still be money for a while, but without any more coming in, you'd eventually find yourself poor again.' He pauses. 'Which is another circumstance you have grown somewhat used to these past weeks. It's not what I would wish, but I know if it were to happen, it wouldn't break you. So you see why I believe you're the perfect match for me.'

'But Jack—'

'Shh. Let me finish, if you please. There's one more thing. If I were to be arrested, I'd stand a good chance of being acquitted. Most juries are on our side. But if I were killed in action or that bastard Sowerby got hold of me, you'd lose a husband a second time. And if in time you would grow to care for me as you did for George or even love me as you did him, if I could hope for that, the loss would be all the harder. I understand it's a lot to ask that you would expose yourself to the danger of such heartache once more. I want you to know I'm not asking lightly.'

'But I already do,' she says. 'Care for you like that, I mean.' *And love you*, she thinks, but she cannot say this, not yet. It's too soon, too raw. 'It's only . . . I need time. I need to think.'

'Of course. And you shall have it, but if you won't give me your answer now, then what do you want to do for the time being?'

Quietly she says, 'I'd like to carry on as before.'

'Would that be before I took you to bed or after?'

'After,' she says, reddening. 'If you don't object to the arrangement.'

She feels his laughter in her chest, like a flock of birds. He says, 'I knew you held singular ideas, but I didn't expect they'd be quite this unorthodox. Of course I don't object to the arrangement. What man would? But you will consider my proposal, won't you?'

'Naturally. I will, Jack. And thank you, for . . .'

'Attempting to rescue you from poverty?'

Now she laughs too. 'For being kind to me.'

'Kind is not the word I'd use. Impassioned, rather. Tell me this. May I hope for a favourable response, in time?'

Yes! All of her screams it, but she hears herself say, 'I believe so. I just have to think for a while.'

'Take as long as you need. In the meantime, we'll carry on as before.' His hand slips down as he kisses her again. 'Like this. And like this.'

She sighs into him. Against her lips, he says, 'Are you in need of sleep?'

His fingers make the stars come out in her skin. In kisses, in sighs, she says, 'Not yet.'

On the morning of the last day of the voyage, over another breakfast of beans and bread from France, which has by now grown hard as rock, Jack says, 'We'll have sight of land soon.'

'Yes,' she says, wishing it wasn't so. She can't stop smiling; at him, at the ship, at Tom who brought the breakfast from the galley and who chuckled so knowingly her face grew as hot as the beans on her plate.

'We'll have to stand out until nightfall. Once we're anchored, I'll have one of the crew accompany you home.'

'Couldn't I help with the unloading?'

'It'll take most of the night.'

'I'll stay,' she says.

He laughs, saying, 'You mad thing,' with such affection it makes her heart billow. 'This has been our most successful run yet. Thank you, Tom,' as the steward refills their glasses. Turning back to Isabel, Jack continues, 'I'll pay you as one of the crew. God knows you look it, dressed as you are, and you've pulled your weight in terms of the work. Come to think of it, as we're to avoid Coverack and Lizard after what Sowerby told you, we may have need of your shed. In that case we'll all see you home. We'll have to see what the situation is like tonight.'

'You may use the shed any time.' Her eyes water as she burns her tongue on the coffee.

'That'd be another two percent on top of your fee as a member of the crew,' he says. 'You'll make a pretty penny.'

'It was never about that.'

'I know. But you're not going to be stubborn and refuse payment, are you? You could use the money.'

'Yes,' she says. 'And no, I won't refuse payment.' She watches the steam rise from her coffee. After a moment, she says, 'I wish the journey wasn't coming to an end.'

Jack taps his glass. 'About that. I may as well tell you now.'

'Tell me what?'

'The crew has petitioned me to keep you on for the next

few runs. They reckon you bring the ship good fortune, which is funny as you know what they say about women on board. Ill luck and all that. But not you, they say. Between that first night, when you worked with them on deck while it blew a gale and the general success of the run, not to mention this mightily favourable wind, they're convinced.'

She stares at him over the edge of her glass. Is he saying what she thinks he's saying? She quickly gulps down some more coffee, scalding her tongue and throat this time. 'Convinced of what?'

'You know of what. The story you dislike so – that the Sea Bucca's daughter protects the ship.' A pause, then, 'So what do you say?'

'Do you mean to say you agree with them?'

'Of course not. I don't believe you bring the ship good fortune, nor should you sail with us. It's far too dangerous – I've told you my view many times. But as you may have realised, sailors are a superstitious bunch.'

He takes a small sip and blows on the coffee again. 'Cornish sailors more than most, I reckon. Which means if I *don't* keep you on board, the next time we run afoul of the Revenue Service or we've got a man overboard or a storm blows away the staysail, it won't be because of the wiles of fate or the unpredictability of the weather, it'll be because I chose not to keep you on. I can't have that. The crew and I, we need to be of one mind. So, much as I wish otherwise, I suppose I'm offering you a place aboard the *Rapide* during our next voyage back to Roscoff. I imagine Madame Cuvelier will be glad to see you again. Captain Cuvelier told me you've become fast friends.'

When she doesn't say anything, he adds, 'It'll be a means of securing an income of your own. Considering your views on your independence, that can only be pleasing to you.'

She's silent for so long Jack says, 'Will you give me an answer to *this* proposal, at least?' She's shaking her head in disbelief and then she's laughing. She reaches for his hand, saying, 'I get to go to sea with you again?' Her voice is high and punctuated by laughter. 'You mean it?'

He laughs, too, in spite of himself. 'That's a yes then?'

'I didn't realise you needed an answer. I should like it of all things, Jack. Oh, I can't think of anything more wonderful!'

'Can you honestly not?' he says, more soberly.

It's as if she has swallowed a sharp-edged pebble. Quickly, she says, 'I didn't mean it like that. But if I were to say yes to your other proposal, would you still be inclined to respond favourably to your crew's petition?'

'That remains to be seen.' He drums his fingers on the desk. He's about to say more but is stopped by a shout from the deck: 'Captain! Ship ahoy!'

Jack sets his glass down so hard it sounds as if he meant to break it. He's out the door and up the ladder in seconds. Isabel follows more slowly. By the time she reaches the deck, Harry Tremayne has handed the spyglass to Jack, who trains it on a speck in the distance.

'You see it, Captain?' Harry says and Jack says, 'I see it, all right.' The minutes lengthen as he watches the speck while the crew watches him. After a while, he calls, 'Dick! Come here and have a look.'

Dick takes the spyglass. 'It's her, isn't it, Captain?'

'That's what I thought. Harry?'

'The *Swallow*, isn't she, sir? I thought she was, only my eyes aren't as good as Dick's.'

'Neither are mine,' says Jack. 'But with that bowline, yes, I wager she's the *Swallow* and she's gaining on us.'

'As she's wont to do,' Harry says. 'She's got twice the sail.'

'Twice the weight, too, if we didn't have our cargo,' says Jack. 'Without the cargo, we could outrun her.' He lowers the spyglass and taps his fingers on it, thinking. 'Set all sails!' he calls and then, 'Run a lead line, will you, Betham? And you, Will. Tell me your findings the moment you have them.'

'How long before she's upon us, Captain?' Oppy says, gripping the helm.

'I reckon we've got about half an hour. Let's hope the sea isn't too deep here.'

A few minutes later, Betham calls, 'By the mark seven. Sand and broken shell, sir!'

'Very good. Thank you, Betham,' Jack calls back. And to Harry Tremayne: 'Seven fathoms. Do you think the lines will reach that far?'

'I believe so, Captain.'

Not a minute later, Will Pengelly makes the same observation and Jack calls out, 'Rafts it'll be! Get to it, men! Coffee and brandy only!' His command sets in motion a dance of activity. Men run about carrying ropes, others bring up kegs of brandy and boxes of coffee from the hold and place them side by side on the top deck.

Isabel asks Jack, 'What are you doing? Shouldn't we try to sail away?'

'We will,' he says. 'But we can't outrun the *Swallow* with the cargo we're carrying. We're lashing together the kegs and boxes. Then we'll drop them to the seabed with a marker attached, a small one; the *Swallow* is far enough behind they won't spot it, I hope. They'll have all eyes on us as they try to catch us. Without the weight of those kegs, we should be able to get away.'

'But what of the goods?' she says.

'We're close enough to shore it's not too deep here. We'll retrieve them with a grappling hook in a couple of days.'

'We'll go creeping,' Harry Tremayne says with a grin. He wriggles his fingers. 'Like little mice, across the ocean floor.'

'So we will.' Jack puts the spyglass to his eye again. 'Make haste, there!'

The men sweat under the weight of the kegs as they lift the raft over the bow of the ship, where the crew of the *Swallow* won't be able to see the splash it causes. The moment the kegs and boxes go over the side, the *Rapide* leaps forward. A cheer goes up and Jack points the spyglass at the pursuing revenue cutter again.

'Is it enough, Captain?' says Oppy.

Jack watches the *Swallow* another minute, then lowers the spyglass. 'Let's hope so. If need be, we'll dump some of the cargo.'

'Dump?' Harry says. 'Captain, you'll run a loss.'

'I prefer a lack of profit to another skirmish or the noose,' Jack says. His eyes are on Isabel as he says it. 'With that madman Sowerby about, we're as like to be taken for traitors as we are for free traders. But let's not despair yet. We've just gained ourselves – how many knots, Dick?'

'About three knots, Captain.'

'Good,' Jack says, handing Isabel the spyglass. 'Have a look. Tell me what you think of her.'

It's startling how much closer the spyglass brings the revenue ship. She watches for a moment, then says, quietly, 'It looks like she's still gaining.'

Jack takes another look and swears. 'So she is. Very well. Harry, lose the Swedish iron. We haven't got time to make another raft.'

'Are you certain, Captain?'

'Yes, damn it. And be quick about it.'

More crates go overboard; again the *Rapide* jumps like a startled horse. They're not flying as they did during the storm, but they're fast. Spray flies across the bowsprit and Isabel leans over to watch the hull cut the sea, making a path lined in foam. After a moment, she runs back to the stern of the ship. Every man is on deck, watching the *Swallow*. The revenue cutter is keeping up. Her heart wants to hammer its way through her skin. Is Lieutenant Sowerby on board? Or his friend, Lieutenant Sullivan, who shot Jack a month ago?

If the revenue cutter catches up with them, will the ship open fire? How many guns does the *Swallow* have? The *Rapide* has only six, all carriage guns, nothing like the thirty-two-pounders George had on HMS *Neptune*. As if he guesses her thoughts, Jack says, 'She's got four twelve-pounders on each side, plus guns fore and aft – twelve in total.'

Without thinking, she reaches for his hand and he takes it, squeezing it briefly before putting both hands around the spyglass, steadying the instrument. They watch as the *Swallow* keeps coming on and she's holding her breath, then puffing for air, then holding her breath again, until, after the longest wait, the revenue ship appears to be getting smaller.

'She's falling behind,' Jack says, handing the spyglass to Dick, who agrees. Still nobody speaks until, at last, the revenue cutter drops beyond the horizon. A cheer goes up and Isabel finds herself cheering with the rest of the crew.

'Three hurrahs for the captain!' calls Thomas Moyle, veins popping in his neck, after which another of Jack's tenants, John Spargo, calls, 'And one for the Bucca's daughter!' which makes her want to hide behind Jack. He chuckles, saying, 'You can take a Cornishman out of Cornwall, but you can't take Cornwall out of him. They'll believe it until the Bucca himself comes up from the depths to disown you.'

Peering at the mercifully empty horizon, he adds, 'It's a shame about the iron.' Turning to the men, he calls, 'Once we've landed the cargo, how about we open up one of the kegs and enjoy its contents to celebrate?'

More cheers follow this announcement. 'Take her along the coast, Oppy,' Jack says. 'We'll stand out until nightfall.'

'Where to, Captain?'

'The Helford River.'

CHAPTER FOURTEEN

The only sail they see the rest of the day is a small fishing boat, whose crew of two raises their caps to them as they pass. Just after nightfall, they sail up the wide expanse of river, the wind to their stern. The ship is like a shadow, all lanterns doused as a precaution. It slides past the headland on the southside of the river where Isabel has walked the coastal path. 'Another twenty minutes and we'll drop anchor at Helford, provided Tom Holder gives us the all-clear,' Jack is saying, when Dick suddenly hisses, 'Captain!'

He's a second faster than the rest of the crew, but the moment they see it, a gasp runs through the ship. 'Damn it,' Jack says, under his breath. And then, calling softly, 'Hush! Quiet, there.'

In the mouth of the river lies a three-masted frigate, its two decks punctuated with rows of open gunports. Even at this distance she's a slumbering giant, towering above the water, her masts reaching past the top of the cliff. If anybody on board the frigate were to see them; if the ship were to give chase, the *Rapide* wouldn't stand a chance.

Lights burn on the frigate, but the ship is as quiet as the night. Jack whispers, 'His Majesty's Navy has come to call on us. We'd better pretend we aren't home. Oppy, take us along the north shore, if you please, as close in as you can without running us aground. Do you know the lay of the land there?'

'I grew up in Mawnan, Captain,' Oppy whispers. 'I've been sailing these waters since I was a boy.'

'Good. Take us into . . . Helford's too close. Dick, what do you think? Frenchman's Creek? It's near as well, but it cuts inland far deeper. I reckon they'll be looking in Gweek, too, with the trade in the harbour.'

'Frenchman's Creek is nicely sheltered,' Dick says. 'We can use the cave near the top for storage and it's close enough to Helford Tom will be able to get the boats out to us.'

Somewhere in the bow of the ship, a voice says loudly, 'For God's sake, Moyle!'

Jack says to Harry, 'Make them shut up, will you? Pray they don't spot us.'

Swiftly, silently, the *Rapide* slides closer to the frigate. The river is wide here, far wider than where it snakes further inland. It's not even much of a river, she thinks; at this point it is still the sea, narrowing down to a channel.

Jack has timed their return well. They sailed for France just after the full moon and now the moon is new, the sky a canvas of stars. For the second time in a day, Isabel barely dares to breathe. The entire ship holds its breath. At the stern, Oppy's squeezing the helm so tightly his knuckles have paled. Harry Tremayne looks like he has swallowed his whiskers. Any moment now, a voice will call out, she thinks. Any moment they will be seen. They could not outrun a ship like this. They'll be trapped on the river.

But whether there really is something protecting them or it's simply late enough at night the watch stands dozing, they sail by without a sound from the Navy ship.

This time, no one cheers. The coast is dark and empty, not a lantern moves along the coastal path. Only the wind can be heard, pushing them up the river. It's quiet enough she can hear the splash of a fish that jumped. Shadows cradle the ship as they drop anchor just outside the inlet at Helford. There is the old pilchard shed, the cottage low and dark; there the wall of the paradise garden where she sat with Harriet not three weeks ago.

There's a light in the top left window of the Shipwrights Arms and Jack says, 'That's Tom, giving the all-clear. I sent word to him after you told me about Coverack; he must've been watching for us.' He turns to Harry Tremayne. 'Signal back that we need the boats to come out. I'll tell the boatmen to follow us into the creek. Once the goods are hidden, we'll set a watch and take the *Rapide* back to Nelly's cove.'

'You mean to go past the frigate again?' Isabel asks.

'Without the cargo we're just like any other ship. They can't arrest us if we haven't got any contraband on board.'

Harry signals with the lantern from the larboard side of

the ship. Moments later, a figure comes out of the inn and disappears down the road. Another short wait and the splash of oars can be heard across the water.

'Should you like to go ashore with one of the boats?' Jack says.

She thinks of the cottage, of the bed in which she slept next to Jack when she first met him. She says, 'Could I not go back to Roskorwell with you? Just for the one night?'

'Are you thinking of your empty bed?'

He knows her too well. 'I didn't much like it at Captain Cuvelier's house,' she admits.

'You have but to say the word and Roskorwell will be your home and your bed never empty, not even when I am gone to sea, for it appears you are to come along every time.'

'Jack . . .'

'I'm not trying to rush you. Only, it seems to me that you're fighting something that already exists quite naturally between us. However, this isn't the time to discuss such things – we're both weary and we have a long night ahead of us.' He pauses to call softly to the first of the boats, 'Lanyon, hello!' Turning back to Isabel, he says, 'Fine. Come back to Roskorwell with me tonight.' He gives her a quick smile. 'See if you like it for a home.'

'I already do,' she says, but she speaks so quietly he doesn't hear and then he's calling to the other boatman and Oppy grips the ship's wheel. A gust of wind whistles through the rigging as they sail away from the inlet and tack into the creek.

*

Roskorwell is as they left it. A soft-edged sun rises from behind the house and the grass is wet with dew. They walk side by side, just Jack and her, as if they're returning from an early morning walk and not an eleven-day journey to France smuggling contraband. The only giveaway that all is not ordinary is that she's still wearing Jack's breeches and shirt, as well as over a week's worth of suntan. Jack carries the bundle with her gowns. 'You can change at the house,' he says.

She wishes she wouldn't have to. 'Perhaps I could have my own pair of breeches made for the next voyage.'

'Perhaps you could dress as a boy at all times.'

She looks up at him. 'Truly? You believe I could?'

'I spoke in jest. Isabel, no one wants to see you in a man's garments.'

'Do you object to my wearing them?' she says.

'Dear God, no. You could dress in a bearskin as they do in America or wrap yourself in silk shawls like in India for all I care. Or wear nothing at all — that may be my preference, in fact.'

'Jack!' she says, swatting at his arm, but she's laughing and so is he.

The crew has split up and is returning home from Nelly's cove piecemeal, so as not to arouse suspicion, but there's no need, for at this hour of the day Jack's estate lies deserted. Even Jack's dog, Jib, has not yet roused herself. 'You'll want to watch out for the press gang,' Jack told his men before they left the ship, leaving only Harry Tremayne and Oppy on board. 'The captain of that frigate will be looking to impress new hands into His Majesty's Navy. Beware the king's shilling if you drink at any of the inns along the river.'

Nearer to the house, the smell of salt and seaweed gives way to that of the roses along the white, stone walls, come into bloom thanks to the warm weather. They go up the path as if they live there together and Isabel can see how it will be; the ease of their rapport turned into an every-day thing, their conversation flowing freely, the nights spent in Jack's arms, everything just as it was on board the *Rapide*.

I'm going to tell him, she thinks.

She's going to explain about James and if it is as she hopes, if he understands and he'll still have her, she's going to say yes. *Yes, I should like to marry you. Maybe not at once, but when I am ready I shall, and gladly, for I love you.* 'Jack,' she begins as he opens the door for her. She steps into the dark hall and turns back to him, saying, 'There's something I must tell you. I—'

But she doesn't get any further, because there's a voice outside, a man's voice, calling to Jack. For a fraction of a moment, she thinks, *that odious man, he has the worst sense of timing,* but then she looks across Jack's shoulder and sees Lieutenant Sowerby on the doorstep – and the pistol he's aiming at Jack. The hall sways and she has to put her hand against the wall to keep her balance.

'Why do you look like that? Are you quite—' Jack begins, already turning to the door, but Lieutenant Sowerby barks, 'Mr Carlyon, sir!'

A click as he cocks the pistol, unmistakable in the quiet

morning air. Cold seeps into her veins, circulating until gooseflesh rises on her arms.

Without looking back, Jack motions for her to move deeper into the hall. She draws back in the shadows as he says, 'Lieutenant Sowerby, to what do I owe the—'

Lieutenant Sowerby says, 'Be so good as to lift your shirt, sir.'

'My shirt? What has got into you, Sowerby?'

Lieutenant Sowerby motions with the pistol. 'Lift it or I shall fire.'

Jack takes the hem of his shirt, the one she mended for him, just washed yesterday aboard the ship. He begins to lift it. She's gazing at his back, but she knows what Lieutenant Sowerby is looking for and he will see it: the red, angry welt of a new scar, made by a gunshot wound.

'It *is* you. You're the captain of the *Rapide*,' Lieutenant Sowerby growls. His own shirt is half-unlaced and hangs partly out of his breeches and he hasn't bothered with a neckerchief. A constellation of red spots covers his throat; his tone drips hate. 'How I hoped I was mistaken when Mrs Henley led me here. Perhaps that is the worst of your crimes, Carlyon, corrupting a poor widow into aiding you in your banditry. Did you promise her money, is that it? And she, only wishing to lessen the blow of her heroic husband's death and the state to which it reduced her – she accepted, did she not? Or did you force her, you brute?'

'I did,' Jack says and she doesn't understand, because she's standing right there, not five feet behind him, and Jack didn't force her to do anything; of course he didn't. Does Lieutenant Sowerby not realise it's her? There's a loud rushing in her ears. Through it, she hears Jack say, 'You cannot blame Mrs Henley. She never wanted any part of this. I did force her. I threatened to murder her if she wouldn't comply.'

He speaks reasonably, calmly. He's not only admitting guilt; he is making it worse. She wants to say, *Stop, Jack, none of this is true,* but with his right hand, low by his side, he's motioning for her to stay back.

'Murder and worse, I'm sure,' Lieutenant Sowerby says. 'It's exactly as I thought. How frightened she looked when you dragged her off to your ship! I saw it all from atop the cliffs. It was clever of you to anchor in that cove on your estate, away from the path, I'll give you that. But I saw everything. You couldn't even leave poor Mrs Henley in peace when you sailed! You made good use of her, didn't you, you miserable brute?' There's something lecherous in his tone now, underneath the hatred and anger. It makes Isabel's hair stand on end.

Lieutenant Sowerby is still talking. This is good, she tells herself. As long as he's talking, he isn't going to pull the trigger. 'I wished nothing more than to come to the poor woman's aid, but I could not betray my position. Not when I was about to catch the most notorious smuggler in the county. Mrs Henley's trials and tribulations aboard your ship would have to be her sacrifice to the peace of our nation. A heroic contribution to the war effort, like that of her late husband.'

What is he talking about? she thinks. He's mad. And it's all because of her; this is her doing. She led him here, to Jack. The hallway grows dim, the sight of Jack's shoulders, squared against Lieutenant Sowerby's tirade, fades as the world closes in on her, black spots blocking out everything until she finds the wall again under her hands. She breathes in deeply the smell of wood and the sweaty, bile-filled scent of her own fear.

'Sowerby,' Jack says, but Lieutenant Sowerby doesn't listen. He keeps talking: 'It hasn't been easy to wait for your return these past two weeks, sir. It wouldn't do to arrest you without your cargo – the Revenue Service has a more stringent view of what makes a smuggler than I. However, now that you have returned, we'll soon have our hands on it. Poor Mrs Henley's virtue will be avenged.'

'That's right,' Jack says, still with that measured calmness, as if they're talking about the weather. 'I used her and I used her well. She begged me to leave her be, to let her go home. Mrs Henley isn't to blame in the least.'

No! She's screaming it, inside her mind. She wants to scream it at the top of her lungs, but her tongue won't move. She coughs, but neither of the men turn to her.

Lieutenant Sowerby says, 'I believe you, sir, because I'm well acquainted with Mrs Henley. Such purity of character! How she bears her burden is entirely admirable. The poor woman, she was a bundle of nerves when I called on her last. I realised at once something was amiss. Well, it appears Captain Hamer's arrival in the *Hornet* was not quite so necessary after all. According to the Lieutenant Governor, the Revenue Service is doing such a poor job of stamping out smuggling, we're in need of the Navy's assistance. I say, who's doing a poor job now!' A desperate laugh bursts from him.

'Surely we can talk about this,' Jack says. 'As an officer of the Revenue Service, you see the prices of goods, you see they aren't fair. People can't afford some of the most basic things when they're taxed to such a degree. I'd compensate you well if you were able to find it in yourself to look the other way while I provide a necessary service. Could we not—'

Lieutenant Sowerby cuts him off again, snarling, 'How dare you try to buy me! If I needed more proof, you've just given it. But the scar is all the proof I needed. Lieutenant Sullivan has good aim, doesn't he, Carlyon? As do I.' He moves closer, the pistol aimed at Jack's chest.

Jack takes a step back. 'My men will be here shortly and they won't take kindly to seeing their captain held at gunpoint. Leave while you still can.'

'It'll come to blows then,' Lieutenant Sowerby says. 'For an arresting party is on its way also. They'll be here any moment, but I won't let them have the pleasure of arresting you. The moment the *Swallow* pulled in and Lieutenant Sullivan informed me the *Rapide* had returned, I came for you, Carlyon.' Voice rising, he says, 'It'll be a nice surprise for Captain Hamer when I give him news of the captain of the *Rapide*'s arrest and subsequent death as he tried to escape.'

Bile rises in Isabel's throat; sweat pours down her back.

'I have a right to a trial,' Jack says, tensely.

'I'm sure you believe you do, as a smuggler. It would suit your purpose just fine. You'd be acquitted in a heartbeat, wouldn't you? But you don't get a trial as a traitor, sir. I won't bother with the noose this time. You aid the French in a time of war, you and your friend here.' He indicates the space behind Jack, in the hallway.

He hasn't recognised her, she realises suddenly. His near-sightedness – to him she's only a figure in breeches and a man's shirt. She looks down at her feet, letting her hair drop in front of her face, and shuffles closer, one tiny step at a time.

Jack, meanwhile, moves his hand, slowly, slowly, to the pistol he carries in his belt, but Lieutenant Sowerby shouts, 'Don't move! Lift your hands up!' And then, icily: 'Turn around.'

He raises the pistol to Jack's face now, taking aim, using his left arm to steady the weapon. Jack is still facing him. Lieutenant Sowerby snaps, 'Turn around, Carlyon, damn you!'

Isabel takes a deep breath, swallowing down the bile and then she's running and before Lieutenant Sowerby can pull the trigger, she half-pushes, half-slips past Jack. She flings herself in front of him, arms wide, crying, 'You shall take me before him!'

Shock, frozen, on Lieutenant Sowerby's face. He briefly lowers the pistol before he lifts it again to point at Jack's forehead. 'Mrs Henley? How . . . ? I . . . No it will not do; it won't do at all! You were led astray, surely – you still are. And the way he has clothed you! You devil!' He spits the words at Jack, looking ready to pull the trigger. 'You debauched, deviant rogue!'

'Lieutenant Sowerby,' she says quickly, making her voice soft and pleading. 'Please, do not shoot Ja . . . Mr Carlyon, sir. Please, I beg you. Please, *please*, lower your pistol.'

Lieutenant Sowerby studies her. 'You are not yourself, madam. After everything he's put you through, it's no wonder. Let me assure you, you are perfectly safe now. You don't need to defend this criminal; he cannot hurt you any-more. I have come to save you from his clutches.'

'He's not a criminal or a devil,' she says. 'He's my fiancé.'

'Isabel,' Jack says warningly, but Lieutenant Sowerby cuts him off.

'What!' he gasps, shock morphing into hatred. 'He's . . . you . . . you smuggler's *whore!* And I believed you were . . .'

The muzzle of the pistol moves. Jack shoves her aside, hard. She stumbles and falls, the side of her head hitting the gravel. All motion becomes silent and slow. She watches Lieutenant Sowerby's pistol's trace her fall to the ground, slowly; she watches it slide back in his hand, as if something has kicked it, also slowly. A shot rips the air. Dirt flies up, inches from her face, all of it slowed.

She's looking at the dirt, stunned. He tried to shoot her. How . . . why . . . Lieutenant Sowerby, an officer of the law – tried to *shoot* her. Her mouth forms the word, 'Why?' but all that comes out is a ragged gasp.

'Isabel!' Jack is crouching by her side, pistol in hand.

She wants to say, *I'm fine,* but her tongue moves uselessly in her mouth, because behind Jack, Lieutenant Sowerby is reloading his pistol. He's fast. He has got it done in fifteen, maybe twenty seconds at most and then he's raising the muzzle of the weapon again and she screams, 'Jack, watch out!'

A second shot rends the morning air. This one seems even louder than the first. The sound of it echoes in her head, banging off the bone of her skull. She waits for another spurt of dirt to fly up, but instead Lieutenant Sowerby's face does a funny thing, pulling sideways, almost as if his expression is leaking away. He jerks backwards and there's a noise, like a gurgle, which turns into a terrible choking sound as he falls on his back, tearing at his shirt, which is turning red, far redder than Jack's was when he got shot a month before. Lieutenant Sowerby's legs kick violently, once, twice, and then he is still.

'Isabel.' Jack puts his pistol on the ground and helps her up. She's dazed, too dazed to think, too dazed almost to stand. 'Are you hurt?' He's dabbing at her head with a handkerchief. There are drops of blood on the handkerchief, as red as Lieutenant Sowerby's shirt, but there are only a few. Her mind slowly clears.

'I'm fine. Oh, Jack!' She sounds like a seagull, she thinks, voice shrill, rising and dipping on his name, *Ja-a-ack.*

He picks up the pistol, reloads it and pushes it back into his belt. Then he puts both hands on her shoulders. They smell of something sharp and bitter – gunpowder. 'Isabel, listen to me carefully. You must go home at once. Don't talk to any-body. They don't know about you – about our connection. With some luck, Lieutenant Sowerby won't have mentioned you. And if he has, he believed you innocent. You must use the cut on your head as proof of my violence towards you. Tell them that—'

'No! Jack, no. Never!'

'Tell them I threatened you, that I forced you to aid me with the smuggling and how I hurt you when you didn't comply. Show them that cut. They'll believe you, but they may not even come to you – he may not have said anything about you. Don't go to the ship or try to meet with any of the crew, at least not for some time. They may be watching you as Lieutenant Sowerby did. Go now. They must not find you here.'

'Jack, I can't . . . I couldn't do that.'

'You will do it, for me.'

'But—'

'I have to go.'

'Jack, no. I'm so very sorry. Please, please forgive me. This is my doing – I led him here – God knows I did not mean to, but—'

'I know you didn't. Don't worry on that account. Isabel, I *have* to go. Go home. *Now.*'

'Can't we . . .' Her mind hurtles. 'Can't we hide him? No one needs to know. If we just—'

'There's no time,' Jack says. 'You heard him. An arresting party is on its way.'

'But there aren't any witnesses.'

'The man came to arrest me. He lies dead on my doorstep with a bullet in his chest. Do you think they're going to care there aren't any witnesses?'

'The ship,' she says, brightening slightly. 'We can get away on the *Rapide*.'

'And go where? I put all my funds in the cargo – until I sell it, I've no money. Besides, we haven't time to assemble the crew and get her underway. They'll be here any moment. I must leave now or it'll be too late.'

'Then I'll go with you.'

'You will not,' he says sharply. 'If they find me, they'll hang me. I'm a murderer now. No jury could acquit me, even if they wanted to. Probably, there wouldn't be a jury. And if they find you with me, you may suffer the same fate. I will not have you come. It's out of the question.'

'Jack—'

'*No*. This was a mistake. I should never have involved you.'

'But where will you go? Tell me that, at least, so that I may write to you – so that I may come see you.'

'I can't tell you that. If I told you and they questioned you, they may get it out of you.' Brushing away her tears, he adds, 'It's best if you don't know.'

'No! Jack …'

'Goodbye, Isabel.' He places his hand on the back of her neck and kisses her, hard, and then he turns and strides to the stable.

'Wait!' she calls, running after him, but he's already

strapping the saddle onto Myra. 'Go home!' he calls, hoisting himself up. Pushing his heels into the horse's flanks, he clicks his tongue, urging the horse into a gallop. She watches from inside the stable door as he blurs with her tears and then he's out of sight, away down the road. The smell of horse muck and hay burrows into her nose. She wants to sink down in the straw and weep until there aren't any tears left in her, but she can't. She must go home. *For me*, Jack said. She hopes the men of the Revenue Service don't come to her. If they do, she must pretend, for Jack.

She begins to walk. One foot in front of the other. Lieutenant Sowerby's body lies by the open door to the house. The puddle of blood around him is as red as some of the roses. He hadn't shaved – she only sees that now. A blonde stubble sits on his pale, round jaw. There's blood in this, too, and blood on his lip that has already stopped trickling. She never liked him, but the mix of pity and disgust she feels is such she's going to choke on it. The air smells of him, of his blood. It's stronger than the scent of the flowers. *He was going to kill you,* she reminds herself. *He was going to kill Jack.*

One foot in front of the other. The dew has gone. The road is hazy with dust. Behind her, the sea rushes at the rocks, waves touching and falling back, touching and falling back, a never-ending rushing. The ocean is calling her, but she has no words to answer.

CHAPTER FIFTEEN

She's still walking. This is good, it means there is a destination somewhere, a place to go; it means she's not sitting by the side of the road weeping. She's on the coastal path. The path is dry. The small streams coming from higher up on the cliff have mostly dried up in the warm weather. One foot in front of the other. She needs to think. There must be something she can do to help Jack. She caused this – now she has to fix it.

She was about to tell him, *I love you. I didn't want to tell you before, but I do.* She was going to tell him and now she may never see him again. She thinks of the empty cottage waiting for her in Helford. The cold, empty bed under the rafters. The hollowness of not knowing where he is and whether he is safe.

She has been walking for a while, she's about half-way home. This means it has been an hour since she left

Roskorwell. Sixty minutes, approximately, since she last saw Jack. Seventy-five since he shot Lieutenant Sowerby. She's nearly at the spot where she met the lieutenant two weeks ago, when she was on her way to Roskorwell and he came to call on her. How she hated his intrusion at the time, the delay he caused her; how she feared missing the ship. Now she hates herself for not seeing what Jack saw all along: that Lieutenant Sowerby had a far sharper mind than she thought. He followed her and discovered Jack's identity, because of her, and Lieutenant Sowerby lies dead in a puddle of blood on Jack's doorstep, also because of her.

She has to fix this. There must be something, or some-one . . . *Harriet.* She will go to Harriet and say – she doesn't know what, not yet, but she'll think of something. There has been an accident. Yes, that's what she'll say. There's been a terrible accident. A misunderstanding, too. Lieutenant Sowerby believed Jack to be the captain of the smuggling vessel *Rapide. Can you believe it, Harriet? What delusions the poor man suffered before he turned his pistol on himself?*

It may just work. Lieutenant Sowerby was holding his pistol, after all, and had fired a shot. He's holding the weapon still, unless the revenue men coming to arrest Jack have re-moved it. Harriet's husband, Sir Hugh, is the Deputy Lord Lieutenant of Cornwall. Harriet will tell him the story – Lieutenant Sowerby awfully confused, a terrible tragedy, Mr Carlyon unfairly accused and so on. Sir Hugh will be able to help, won't he, if Isabel can make the story believable?

But Harriet will ask her why she was at Roskorwell. She

must have a reason. She had come to Mr Carlyon for his advice about . . . a reconfiguration of the old pilchard shed into a stable. Yes, that's what she'll say. She must go to Harriet before the real story can spread. She's already turning back when she stops dead in her tracks. Jack's breeches – she's still wearing them. *Damn,* she thinks, the way the men on the ship say it sometimes: *Damn.* She can't knock on Harriet's door in a pair of men's breeches. It'll take another hour, at least, to go home and change.

She sucks the salt-tinged morning air into her lungs and begins to run. Even now, even in this most dreadful of moments, she notices how much easier it is to run in breeches than in a gown. She runs until her breath sears her throat and her sides sting as if someone is pushing the blade of a knife into them. She hurtles into the cottage, pulling the shirt over her head and untying the neckerchief that holds up the breeches, fast as the wind, dropping everything onto the floor. Her hands shake as she ties the back of her striped, cotton dress. Then she's out on the path again, sand and dirt flying as she runs to a rhythm made of his name: *Jack, Jack, Jack!*

The last stretch before she gets to Weatherston she forces herself to slow, walking up the drive instead of running. She pulls some of her hair down to cover the cut on her head and wipes the sweat from her face, her neck; she steadies her breath. If she looks a little ruffled it's fine, she thinks. It's only to be expected; it'll lend credence to her story about Lieutenant Sowerby shooting himself.

At last, she mounts the steps to the entrance and knocks. The doors stay shut. She's about to knock again when a footman opens them and admits her into the black and white sanctity of the entrance hall. 'I'm here to see Lady Darby,' Isabel says and her voice echoes in the space, an octave higher than usual.

The footman leaves her. She expects him to return and tell her Lady Darby will receive her, but instead the door to the green drawing room opens and Harriet herself enters the hall. Her face is paler than usual, her mouth a rosebud, tight and small. Could she have heard the news already; could the story have spread that quickly?

Isabel folds her hands together to hide their shaking. 'Harriet,' she says, masking her anguish with a forced lightness. 'How pleased I am to see you!'

'Mrs Henley,' Harriet says, her voice as small as her mouth. 'I wish so very dearly I could say the same.'

At first, she doesn't catch Harriet's tone. Or maybe she does, but the words don't register. Her mind is racing ahead, following the same rhythm as her feet did earlier: *Jack, Jack, Jack*. 'There's been an accident,' she says. 'Jack – Mr Carlyon is in trouble. He—'

'Jack? *Jack?* Really, Mrs Henley,' Harriet says and now Isabel catches her friend's tone: layers of disappointment and disapproval. Harriet says tightly, 'I wasn't aware you were on such familiar terms with Mr Carlyon. As far as I knew you had only met him the one time, when you both dined here at Weatherston. But I see now that I was mistaken. I suppose . . .' she falters. 'I suppose it shouldn't come as a surprise, given the news I have had from London.'

A wobbling pause, then Harriet bursts out, 'I thought we were friends, Isabel! I thought I had at last made a friend my own age and of my own rank here in the wilderness! How could you not have told me? How you could have let me tarnish my reputation by associating with you, without warning me why it was you left London?'

That is what this is about? She cannot have this, not now. She cannot let the rumours about her and James come between Harriet and herself, endangering her one chance to help Jack. 'Harriet, whatever you've heard—'

'No.' Harriet holds up her hands, palms out, as if to ward off a dangerous creature. She shakes her head again. 'No, Isabel. I feel such a fool. Of course there was a reason you came here. Why would anyone choose to leave town and move to this Godforsaken corner of the world if she wasn't hiding something? I'm such a dolt.'

'Harriet,' she says through the tightness in her throat. 'You're not a dolt. Believe me, there's nothing—'

'And now this with Mr Carlyon,' Harriet says. 'How could you be so – so *loose*, Isabel? So entirely devoid of respect for morality and for God's laws?'

'Oh!' Through the pounding refrain in her head, realisation dawns on her. 'It's not like that, Harriet dear—'

'Don't call me that.'

'Jack – Mr Carlyon, he's my fiancé. I know it's quick, but we both feel a very strong attachment. I couldn't hide my happiness from you, my dear friend, so I called him by his familiar name when perhaps I shouldn't have — not yet. But I'm afraid he's in trouble, which is why I've come to ask for your help.'

'I should say he's in trouble, if he were indeed engaged to *you*,' Harriet says. 'Pray, does he know you carried on with a common sailor in London? One who served under your late husband, no less? Did you tell him before he proposed to you? If he even did, which I highly doubt.'

'Harriet, I . . . no, I mean . . .' She's stuttering, unable to answer her friend's charge. Harriet is right. She did not tell Jack about James. She should've told him when he proposed. But all that matters now is that Jack stays out of the hands of the Revenue Service while she tries to repair the situation. *Please let Harriet see sense and help her.*

Harriet says, 'I thought so. How could you so ill use a friend of mine, Isabel! Well, you may rest assured, he isn't in trouble any longer on that account. Sir Hugh has availed him of the truth.'

'The truth? Whatever do you mean?'

'Mr Carlyon paid us visit not two hours ago.'

Isabel stares, her mouth open. Her breath is coming too fast, it burns in her throat, which still feels raw from when she ran the distance between Helford and Weatherston.

Harriet continues, 'He came to beg a favour of Sir Hugh. He had just had some bad news from family up north and had to travel there at once. He was going away for a long time and was in need of pocket money for the journey. There was no time for his bank to arrange it, so he asked if Sir Hugh would be interested in purchasing any of his horses. Sir Hugh was so good as to buy all three that were to remain; the fourth, Mr Carlyon rode north.' She clicks her tongue as if impatient. 'But if you truly were his fiancée, you would know all of this and not look so thoroughly surprised, Isabel.'

'But I *am* his fiancée! What did you tell him?'

'Me?' Harriet puts her hand to her chest. 'I didn't tell Mr Carlyon anything. But as I had only just heard the news of your shameful conduct in London from my dear friend Violet Hartley, it was at the forefront of both my and Sir Hugh's minds. So when Mr Carlyon mentioned he owed you a debt for the use of your shed and asked Sir Hugh to direct a portion of the payment for the horses to fulfil it, Sir Hugh wasted no time in telling him exactly what sort of woman you are.'

Her breath comes faster. The black and white diamond pattern of the floor whirls under her feet. Jack was here. She wants to speak, but her throat has closed up.

Harriet says coolly, 'Sir Hugh told me Mr Carlyon was scandalised, as anyone would be, but he did not show any particular interest in the news. So you see, I don't believe a word of you being his fiancée, Mrs Henley. He would not have acted as he did if you were. I believe you were after him, the way you went after that sailor, because you are what you are – a hussy. I only hope your husband was spared the knowledge before he was killed.'

'It's not true!' The words free themselves from the cage of her throat. 'None of this is true! I—'

'Of course you'd say that. I should like you to leave now, Mrs Henley. I shall neither receive you in my house, nor call on you again.' When she merely stands there, staring, Harriet adds, 'Goodbye.' Turning to the door of the drawing room, she calls, 'Davis! Mrs Henley is leaving. Do see her out, if you please.'

Harriet is blurring at the edges. Her mouth is a smear of rosebud-pink as she says, 'Sir Hugh will send a man with the money for the lease of your shed. If you had any decency, you'd refuse it. Mr Carlyon won't even be here to use it. But I believe decency is a foreign concept to you.'

Harriet turns and goes through the door of the green drawing room, her back a blur. The tiles in the hall are blending together, too, and the front the steps, the beds full of roses, a few so heavy they droop on their stems and the sky, heavy with the scent of them, and the long winding drive – they are all a blur.

The entire way home, she expects something to happen. Harriet will realise her mistake and come after her. The men of the Revenue Service will charge down the path, ready to question her about the events at Roskorwell. She'll wake up in Jack's arms in the hammock aboard the *Rapide*, crying tears of relief.

At the cottage, her heart jumps: the door stands wide open. Someone is here. But no – she left it open in her hurry to go see Harriet. Inside, it's cool and dark. There's no food except for a bag of dried beans. She can't eat, so it doesn't matter. On the kitchen floor are Jack's breeches, shirt and neckerchief. She folds them before placing them on the table. After that she trails through the sitting room and out the back door into the paradise garden. Nothing has changed here. There's maybe a little more fleabane blooming on the wall, but that's all. The grass is the same, the well, the trees. She sits on the whitewashed bench and pulls up her knees, wrapping her arms around them. She sits very still. If she moves, she'll cry again.

A robin lands on the table, pecking at a crumb or maybe a flake of paint. She watches the bird until it flies away, listening to the lapping of the sea-river at the foot of the wall and hearing the voices in it. *Come home,* they say, but there is no going home, because her home is where Jack is.

She misses him; aching, hollow. It's only been a few hours. She isn't sure how she's going to get through the next day and the one after that.

But the next day she does know how – by keeping busy. The pink-grey dawn has brought new clarity. She doesn't know where Jack is, but he knows where she is. Once the worst of the storm has passed, Jack may send word and she could join him, wherever he is. If he would want her to. The rumours about her and James – surely they won't matter to him after everything that's happened. After they lay together in the hammock, too, skin pressed to naked skin. Maybe they never mattered. He'll send word eventually; she will hold onto that. Keeping busy will make the time pass until then.

First, she must eat. It has been over twenty-four hours and she feels it in her stomach, a slumbering nausea. She soaks the beans and wants to light the fire to boil them but realises she doesn't have her tinderbox. It was in the bundle of things she took to sea, which is sitting in the entrance hall at Roskorwell.

'Damn,' she mutters. The revenue men will have found it by now. Is there any way they might learn it belongs to her? Nothing in it had her name on it, but the gowns are finely made. Not many women around here have gowns like that. She's going to have to tell the revenue men the story she planned to tell Harriet, if they come.

For a sliver of a moment, she wonders if she should go to the Revenue Service instead. She could knock on the door of the Customs House at St Keverne and speak with Lieutenant Sullivan. But no, better not. Her story is full of holes – likely it would take him only a few questions to discover the lie.

Jack's breeches and shirt are still sitting on the table in the kitchen. She holds the shirt to her cheek as she takes the garments up to her bedroom. It doesn't smell like him; the shirt smells like her. Through the small window, she can see the water of the inlet rippling.

The sight calms her and she senses again the strange familiarity of the sea. She wishes she could remember the moment she came out of the water as a child, but her first memories are of her mother's silk skirt, the scent of the garden at Hardwick – a pervasive apple smell – and the way her wet shift chafed at the skin above her knees. And something else – a cool, dark quiet, smooth as silk, comforting like her mother's hands, lifting her. *The sea.* Could she truly have survived a shipwreck at the age of four that killed all others on board?

She shakes her head, shoving the breeches and shirt under her bed. Downstairs, the beans are floating in their cold bath. What day is it? Friday. She won't be able to buy a new tinderbox until the market tomorrow morning.

Mrs Dowling opens the door at her first knock. 'Mrs Henley! You've returned. How is your family?'

Isabel takes in the woman's kind, lined face, the enquiring expression lifting the grey eyebrows. 'My family?' she says, wonderingly. For the briefest of moments she believes Mrs Dowling is talking about the Du Pont family in France. How could she possibly know? Then the lie comes back to her. It seems a thousand years since she told Mrs Dowling she was going away to visit family in Penzance. She says, 'They are well, thank you.'

'Have you only just returned?'

'Late last night,' she lies.

'You must be clean out of food,' Mrs Dowling says, stepping aside. 'Please, come in. I've some bread and cheese to spare.'

'Oh, thank you!' she says, moved. 'I shall pay you back, Mrs Dowling.'

'No need whatsoever, my dear. Why, you must be famished after such a long journey. Do you have anything in the house at all?'

'I've got some beans,' Isabel says, stepping into the large, low-ceilinged kitchen. 'Only I seem to have misplaced my tinderbox.'

Mrs Dowling says. 'My, what sun you've had on the road. Oh, I nearly forgot! I have a treat for you, Mrs Henley. Last week I managed to buy some of the best coffee and at a very good price, indeed. I shall make you a cup directly. Here's some bread, dear.'

The bread is still warm from the oven, the coffee hot and sweetened with more sugar than Isabel can afford herself. 'If you like the coffee, I could get you some at the same price,' Mrs Dowling says. 'I bought it – well, off market, shall we say.' She lowers her voice. 'It was smuggled from France, you see.'

'Oh.' Isabel feigns shock.

'It's simply impossible to buy decent coffee at the regular price,' Mrs Dowling says. 'Do let me know if you'd like me to purchase some for you when the opportunity presents itself.'

'Thank you. It's very good coffee.'

Mrs Dowling smiles so widely Isabel sees she's missing several teeth in the back of her mouth. 'It is, isn't it? Speaking of smugglers, have you heard the news?'

Gooseflesh rises on her arms at the mere mention. 'What news?' she says, blowing on her coffee to hide her interest.

'There was a murder in the early hours yesterday morning, not far from here. A smuggler shot and killed a man of the Revenue Service – an officer he was, too. Can you believe it? I have it from Tom Holder at the inn.'

Mrs Dowling is silent, waiting for Isabel's reaction. After a moment, Isabel says, 'But what a terrible thing.' She says it too tepidly, she thinks, her voice as flat as the surface of her steaming coffee.

Mrs Dowling appears to think so too, for she raises eyebrows again and says, 'Now, I may feel prices aren't fair, but I don't hold with murder. The smuggler has fled, a man by the name of Carlyon. He's a squire, owns an estate down at Roskorwell. The Revenue Service is searching for him, as is the Navy.' She drops another spoonful of sugar in her coffee and stirs.

Isabel is still blowing into her cup. If she keeps doing it, perhaps she won't weep.

Mrs Dowling continues, 'Oh, but you haven't heard that yet either, I'm sure! There's a frigate at the mouth of the river, come to do something about all the smuggling. Well, so they say, but it seems their real business is impressing men into the service. Tom says he's keeping his son indoors as much as he can – the boy's big for his age. I daresay if I had a son, I wouldn't let him out at all.'

Isabel blows little puffs of air onto the coffee, watching the ripples it creates. There's a storm brewing inside her.

'Mrs Henley?' Mrs Dowling says. 'You're awfully pale. Have I frightened you, talking of murder?'

Isabel looks up. 'You haven't.' She squeezes the warm porcelain of her cup. Should she risk it? Mrs Dowling knows everyone for miles around. And she can be trusted, can't she? 'Mrs Dowling, if you happen to hear of the smuggler – that is to say, Mr Carlyon's whereabouts, would you be so good as to tell me?'

'Would I . . . ! Whatever for?' Mrs Dowling gapes at her, her cup suspended a hand's breadth below her mouth. 'You know the man?'

Isabel swallows hard. 'Mrs Dowling, may I rely on your discretion?'

'Of course, Mrs Henley. Always.'

'Mr Carlyon is my fiancé. He shot the officer of the Revenue Service in self-defence. To defend me.' Quietly, she adds, 'He's the man Joe Winters saw me with in the creek that day. It's very important I learn where he is.'

Mrs Dowling closes her mouth, opens it again, and closes it once more, like a fish. When she finally speaks, she surprises Isabel by not asking a single question. She only says, 'I see it's of the utmost importance that you reach Mr Carlyon. Very well. I'll ask around and see what I may learn.'

'Thank you, Mrs Dowling. I'm terribly grateful.'

Mrs Dowling drinks her coffee, then says carefully, 'Do you know what you're doing, my dear? If they find him, he'll hang.'

'I know.' The tears come then, but only a few. She brushes them away with her sleeve. 'I have no choice.'

'You love him, you mean,' says Mrs Dowling, reaching out and giving Isabel's hand a small squeeze. 'Well, I know how that is, though Mr Dowling never had as exciting an occupation as that.'

She smiles again. 'That's a good thing, Mrs Dowling.'
'I know it, my dear.'

She walks home carrying a cloth in which Mrs Dowling has wrapped a chunk of bread, a small, round cheese, a piece of ham and her spare tinderbox with enough tinder to last her a week. As she prepares a simple evening meal of beans, ham and bread, she's feeling slightly more hopeful. Mrs Dowling may find out something or Jack may send word, either in a letter or through one of his crew or maybe Tom Holder. She simply has to wait.

The days lengthen until they push deep into the nights. She waits three weeks, four weeks, five. The cut on her forehead heals, leaving a tiny scar. No word comes. Mrs Dowling hasn't heard anything of Mr Carlyon's whereabouts, she regrets to say. Neither has Tom Holder when Isabel stops at the Shipwrights Arms to ask if he's had any news from his friend from the cove. The Revenue Service never knocks on her door. She doesn't hear from Harriet, either, but she didn't expect to. She considers visiting some of Jack's tenants who are part of the crew of the *Rapide* but worries about attracting unwanted attention.

Every day, she walks the coastal path looking out to sea, wondering where Jack is. Is he thinking of her? Does he miss her the way she misses him, as if some vital part of herself has vanished? It seems impossible that their time together consisted only of weeks and she lived all of her life before without him. It's impossible that it should be so again.

One night, she wakes in a sweat, emitting a thin, almost whistling cry as she wrestles with the sheet. In her dream, they had caught Jack and killed him. Upon waking, she doesn't remember how he died, but the fact of his death was certain and her screaming, which started in the dream, carried over into the confused state in which she opened her eyes to the dark bedroom.

When morning comes, she walks to Frenchman's Creek and climbs down to the water. The tide is halfway out, making the cave at the top of the creek accessible from the beach. The contraband is still there, all the kegs and crates and boxes. Nobody would dare move it now, not with the Revenue Service out in force searching for it.

Something about the quiet of the creek and the overgrown, sparsely used trail leading to it strikes her as eerie. If any voices call to her from below the water, she doesn't hear them. She no longer has a desire to swim, not without Jack. On her way home, she keeps looking over her shoulder, feeling as if someone walks behind her. The tall grass whispers along the hem of her gown. Bumblebees flit among the wildflowers, gulls cry overhead. The water is still – stiller than any water she's seen. If you threw a stone in it, you wouldn't break the surface, she thinks, but shatter a looking glass.

Another week passes. By now it's mid-summer and the heat whips up the clouds until it thunders for three nights. Still she waits. And then one evening when it's still bright out, there's a knock at her door and when she opens it, she finds Tom Holder standing there.

Her heart leaps and the words pour out, '*I'm so very pleased to see you, Mr Holder, please, come in, I hope so very dearly that you may have some news for me.*'

Her words play leapfrog. They put a frown on Tom Holder's face. She steps aside to let him through and he seats himself at the table in the kitchen. Late-evening gold drops in through the window, a soft light that makes everything appear lovelier. Tom Holder's face, too: there's something noble about his tall, lined forehead, the deep-set eyes and the way they move from her to the stone counter and back. But he's looking grave, she sees now.

'Has something happened?' she says, uncertainly. 'Is it Richard; has he been taken by the press gang?'

Tom Holder has his hat in his hands and is turning it slowly. 'I bring word from my friend from the cove.'

'From Jack! I knew it.' She feels like taking Tom Holder's hands and dancing around the kitchen with him.

Tom Holder says, 'They've captured him, Mrs Henley.'

CHAPTER SIXTEEN

Tom Holder is still talking, explaining something, but all she hears is, *they've captured him*. She looks down at her hands. How odd that just a few weeks ago, Jack held them. How odd that he may never hold them again. 'What?' she says after a moment. 'I beg your pardon, I didn't quite hear . . .'

'I said, I regret to be the one to tell it you, Mrs Henley. My friend from the – oh, what the hell – Jack managed to send a note. He paid one of the hands on HMS *Hornet* to deliver it. He didn't want to send it directly to you in case they're keeping an eye on you.'

'Please, could I see this note?'

'He asked me to destroy it and avail you of its contents.' Tom Holder is speaking quickly, as if he's reciting a series of learned facts and worries he'll forget one. 'He's being held on the *Hornet*, where he'll be tried for murder under the laws of the service.'

Black spots congregate before her eyes. 'But he can't be! He isn't even in the Navy!'

'Captain Hamer has impressed him just for the purpose of trying him. He doesn't care the crime was committed before. He has also told Jack he personally guarantees a guilty verdict and that Jack will be hanged from the mainmast yardarm this Friday at three o'clock in the afternoon.'

She turns away from the table just in time and spills her dinner across the floor. Tom Holder offers her a cotton handkerchief. Her eyes sting with tears. 'But that's just three days from now,' she whispers.

'I'm afraid there's more. In the note, Jack mentioned Captain Hamer intends to sail his ship into the river for the hanging, as far as he can go without running her aground. It won't be far; it's a big ship. Captain Hamer wants people from the villages along the river to come out and watch. He wishes to make an example of Jack. He told Jack all of this himself.' Tom Holder wipes the sweat from his brow. 'Jack asks that you don't come, Mrs Henley. He asks you to promise you won't go out and watch.'

She's shaking her head. It can't be true. 'No.' Is that her voice? 'No! No, no, no!' She clutches her head, stomach writhing.

She lost George much too soon. Must she now also lose Jack? What has she done that God has decided to punish her in this way? Was it the familiarity with James? Not loving George enough, perhaps? Was she cursed at birth or when someone – *something* – plucked her from the ocean and set her down, alone, afraid, on the road in Helford?

She remembers it, suddenly. Not much — not her home or her parents or anything like that. But she remembers the fear. The loneliness. The way she stood there, not knowing where to go, whom to ask for help. Knowing she wouldn't ever see those whom she loved most again. The memory is there — a memory made up of feelings.

There's something else as well. A smell. Seaweed, salt, something sharp. Gull droppings, maybe. And apples. She went in through a wooden gate, didn't she? She can see that gate now. Dark green and shiny as if the paint had not yet dried. She remembers her hands, which were tinged green, also. The green of the sea. And her mother's arms, the safety of them, and the voice she didn't yet know, speaking words she couldn't understand but which she now believes were, *oh dear child* . . .

But before that, before her mother's arms, there was the fear. She's feeling it again now at the thought of losing Jack. Her voice has dropped to a whisper. It's still going, *no, no, no.* Over it, a little loudly, Tom Holder says, 'I'm terribly sorry. Will you promise?'

Promise? She has to think. What must she promise? To love Jack? To have and to hold from this day forward?

Tom Holder says gently, 'Promise me you won't go and watch, Mrs Henley. It's a dying man's last wish.'

Black spots, all over the kitchen. They start in the corners of the room and move closer, crowding her vision. She grips the tabletop. 'I promise,' she whispers. 'Did he write anything else?'

'Only this: he asks that you think well of him and says to listen to the sea so you'll never be truly alone. He's something of a poet, isn't he? What else . . . it was a long note, Mrs Henley. Ah, I have it. Dick and Will Pengelly are with him. The press gang took them, but Captain Hamer is unaware of their free trade activities. Other than that there were some instructions on what to do with the contraband. You're to have Jack's share of the profits.'

'I don't want it.'

'Mrs Henley, I don't know the whole of your situation, but I advise you to take it. Jack wants you to have it. It would allow you to live more as you are accustomed to.'

She's still clutching the innkeeper's handkerchief. The tip of the cloth sticks out from her fist like a white flag. 'Are you able to send a note back?'

'No. I'm sorry, Mrs Henley. I'm afraid I must go. There will be customers. I would've sent Richard, but I can't trust that he won't get picked up by the press gang. Besides, the message was too important – he may have got it wrong.'

Through the fog in her mind, she says, 'Will you be all right, Mr Holder?'

'They don't want anyone my age.' He stops turning his hat and looks up at her. 'Will *you* be all right, Mrs Henley?'

'Yes,' she says, feeling the fear bore inside her, making her arms and her legs hollow like the limbs of a bisque doll. The only thing not hollow is her head, which is pounding: *Jack, Jack, Jack.* She rises stiffly. At the door, she says, 'Thank you, Mr Holder.'

He puts on his hat and touches the brim saying, 'That's Tom for you, Mrs Henley. I wish you courage these next three days. It will all be over soon.'

When the door shuts, she gets a bucket of water from the well, flatly, and with hollow motions she cleans the floor. She washes her face and puts on a clean dress and then she steps out the front door. The sun clings to the horizon and the air is scented with summer. Dried seaweed covers the banks of the river and the beaches of the coves she passes as she walks the coastal path.

Night folds over the headland. The open sea shimmers blackly beyond the shadowy bulk of the frigate. The ship moves lightly on the swell, masts poking holes in the sky. A lantern at the stern swings back and forth, casting a golden path on the water. Against the glow, silhouettes walk the quarterdeck – figures without faces. She can hear their voices like a distant murmur across the water. It's a ghost ship, she thinks, fear clawing at the sight of the mainmast from which they will hang Jack.

The path moves gradually down to a shallow cove. She sits in the shadow of a large rock, arms around her legs, chin on her knees, eyes on the frigate. Jack is there. If she could only cross the dark water and haul herself up the side of the ship, right where those wooden steps are set in the hull, she could see him and talk to him; she could touch his hands through whatever bars they're keeping him behind.

She could swim across. It's not far. Even in her gown, she could do it. She could reach for the steps and try to climb up, but they would see her. They'd catch her and they would question her. She'd never see Jack. She might even make things more difficult for him. If only she could swim across and become invisible, making her way through the ship unseen. If only she could find him and tell him, *I love you. I should have told you when I had the chance.*

Until now she has felt too hollow to cry much but watching the ship, the tears run free. Silently, she weeps – for Jack, for the things that will now never be, for the blame that lies on her. If only she hadn't gone to Roskorwell that day, when Lieutenant Sowerby called on her, the day they sailed to France. If only she could take back her demand that Jack take her with him on the voyage.

The guilt presses down on her, making it hard to breathe. A part of her wants to crawl into the water and make a bed under the sea, the surf her blanket, and go to sleep so she won't have to live through the next three days and the rest of her life without him. Another part of her wants to fight. If she could point a sword at Captain Hamer's chest, she wouldn't hesitate to push the blade in.

Then she thinks, *how has it come to this*? How can a man like Captain Hamer, a Royal Navy Captain like her father was before he gained his blue at the mizzen, like George wished to become – how can this man be her enemy? Her hand goes to her throat, feeling for the Trafalgar medal and for an awful second, she believes it's not there. It's as if she has lost George all over again, even as she is losing Jack. But then she feels the ridged silver on the ribbon and her hand closes around the image of Nelson as she continues to sob without a sound.

The voices on the ship continue to murmur. The sea murmurs too, but it doesn't comfort her. After what feels like hours she lies down on her side, her knees pulled up, arms around them, her cheek against the wet sand. Pebbles press into her shoulder and hip. She's still weeping, but now it's a dry sort of weeping; she has run out of tears.

Some hours later she opens her eyes to the first touch of dawn. The tide is close in; most of the beach has vanished. She sits up slowly, sore all over. Brushing pebbles from her dress, she blinks against the sunlight pouring down the mouth of the river. The silhouettes on deck have turned into sailors; she can pick out the colours of shirts and hats, the buckets they carry, the way they gesture as they speak in the same muted tones as the night before. They're less ghostly in the thin morning light. One of them must be Captain Hamer, she thinks, unless he's still in his cabin.

The men on deck will have been a part of the ship's company for some time. They won't desert, unlike the new hands, who have been snatched from the streets and public houses and impressed into the service. George was on recruiting duty once. They could never get enough volunteers, he said. He regretted that the press gang was what he called 'a necessary evil'. The new hands, the ones who didn't volunteer, will be under lock and key until the frigate gets underway. Only when the ship is far from shore will they be let out. When will that be? she wonders. After they've hanged Jack?

The ship is so close. It's less than half a mile from the beach. If she shouted out, Jack might hear her. If she swam across … but no, they'd catch her. If only she could be invisible, she thinks again, a ghost among ghosts. The sea murmurs, whispers, sings. Lullabies in an ancient tongue. If only …

Her hand flies to her mouth and she bites down hard on the skin between her thumb and forefinger to keep from calling out. In her mind, she hears George's complaint and watches the regret flash across his face as he recounted how he led the press gang. *Necessary evil. Never enough volunteers.*

Jack's breeches and shirt – that's it, that's the answer. She will volunteer. She'll wear Jack's breeches and she'll cut her hair so it won't look like a woman's and then she'll volunteer to join the ship's company as …

She remembers Jack, on the day they sailed, saying, *she'll make a fine ship's boy, don't you think?*

If she plays her part well, no one will know, at least for a few hours. As a volunteer, she won't be locked up. And as a ship's boy, she won't be important. Nobody will pay her any attention – so she hopes. Her youth and inexperience will help make her invisible.

If Dick Pascoe had volunteered, she imagines the ship's officers would've been suspicious. Why would a man like that volunteer, a man of an age to have family, a set of skills, a job? Same with any other member of Jack's crew. But if she volunteers it won't be like that. She'll say she's only fifteen. She'll look it, once she has cut her hair to above her shoulders. She'll tighten her stays as much as she can. The cloth of Jack's shirt, which is far too big for her, will hide the swell of her bosom. They'll believe her. They *must* believe her. It's her only chance.

She'll be a boy looking for adventure or perhaps a boy needing to get away from home. Too many mouths to feed — that sort of thing. She looks at the ship bobbing on the swell. She'll swim across. It won't be difficult, especially in Jack's clothes; the buckskin of the breeches is light, the shirt lighter. She'll swim to the ship and say she has come to volunteer. It'd be better to get a boat to take her across, but she worries whoever might row it for her may get impressed into His Majesty's Service just like Dick and Will.

Once she's on board, she should have enough time to find Jack before they discover her deception. He'll be locked up in the brig with someone guarding him, most likely. She'll have to think of a way to get him out, but for now, the main thing is to get on board the ship.

Her mind leaps. What if she manages to free Jack? What if they get off the ship together — *then what*? Escaping the ship is only the first step.

She gets to her feet and scrambles back onto the path. When she came to Helford, she intended to keep to herself. She wasn't going to allow anyone to get close again. That was the plan. What a failure she is. In the span of less than three months, she has managed to acquaint herself with half the village, befriend a crew of smugglers, gain and lose the good opinion of the one woman well placed to be her close friend and fall desperately in love with a smuggling captain condemned to die in two days' time. And how glad she is her plan failed, despite the heartache and the fear; how glad she is to know them all. Especially now, when she's going to need all the help she can get.

Harry Tremayne's house, at the end of the Roskorwell estate, is far bigger than the old pilchard shed, with whitewashed walls and ivy trailing up to the low, slate roof. She had to ask at two different cottages to find the right place. Before she walks up to the front door, she looks around carefully, but there's nobody about. She prays it's early enough in the morning that Harry Tremayne will be in.

After her second knock, the door opens and a slight, grey-haired woman stands looking up at her. 'Yes?'

'My name is Isabel Henley,' Isabel says. 'I'm looking for Harry Tremayne.'

The woman doesn't say anything, she only keeps looking at her. Isabel lifts a hand to her hair – it has come partly undone and there's sand stuck to it. Glancing down at her dress, she discovers more sand and a few dried pieces of sea-weed. Colouring a little, she says, 'Are you Mrs Tremayne?'

'That I am,' the woman says slowly.

'Could I speak with your husband, please? It's rather urgent.'

A bone-dry laugh escapes the woman. 'My husband? That'll be difficult. He's been in the ground for twenty years.'

'But—'

'Harry is my son.'

Harry's voice thunders down the hall. 'Mother! Who is it?'

'A woman for you, come on urgent business.'

Harry is at the door in seconds. He leads her inside, saying, 'I'm so very sorry about Jack. Oppy brought us the news late last night. They're putting the word about – Captain Hamer wants a crowd on Friday.' He looks her up and down and says, 'But what has happened to you, Mrs Henley? You look as if you've drifted in with the tide.'

She brushes the sand from her dress before she sits in the embroidered chair Harry's mother points her into. 'I spent the night on the beach. I came here the moment I woke; I hope to God I wasn't followed.' The words fall from her lips like drizzle. 'May I call you Harry?' At his nod, she says, 'I need your help, Harry.'

He says, 'We haven't yet managed to move the contraband, but once we do I'll make sure you get your share.'

'That's not what I'm here about,' Isabel says, unable to keep the irritation out of her voice.

'Of course,' Harry says. 'And if you think it's the first thing on my mind, you couldn't be more wrong. But it's what Jack would've wanted.'

He speaks as if Jack is already dead. A violent shiver runs through her, not of fear, but of anger – at Captain Hamer, Lieutenant Sullivan aboard the *Swallow*, and the entire Revenue Service. Mrs Tremayne brings two mugs of small beer and a slice of bread each for her and Harry. The bread is dark with a hard crust and a soft, moist centre. She takes a bite but finds she cannot swallow it. Over the edge of his mug, Harry says, 'Why did you spend the night on the beach?'

'I was watching the frigate.' *And weeping,* she thinks, but she doesn't say this. 'I've come up with a plan to save Jack.' The bread has become dough in her mouth. She takes her handkerchief and, pretending to cough, slides it into it.

Harry looks up from his mug of beer. 'You know he's being held aboard the *Hornet,* don't you? The day after to-morrow, they're going to . . .' He trails off.

'I know. I may have a way to get him off the ship. I have to try – and I need your help.'

Harry leans forward, his elbows on his knees, mug between his hands. 'Tell me.' Just that – *tell me* – in a tone that suggests he'll do anything.

Something heavy lifts inside her. She says, 'How quickly can you have the *Rapide* ready to sail, with as small a crew as possible?'

'With a skeleton crew, I expect I'll need six, maybe eight hours. Half of that will be to assemble the crew.'

'Is she still moored in Nelly's cove?'

'She is.'

'And are you able to sail in the next three days? The ship will need to be ready and waiting. I don't know how long it'll take me.' She takes a flea-sized nibble of the breadcrust and chews.

'To do what, exactly?'

'I'm going to volunteer to join the Navy. I'll find a way

to free Jack when I'm on board the ship.' She takes a deep breath. Her words turn to drizzle again. 'I won't let them take him from me – from us. I'm going to get him out or . . . or die in the attempt.'

She thinks, *I'll die anyway without Jack.* She doesn't know if it's true. She continued to live her life after she lost George. Every day she felt the stab of memory, but she didn't give up. This time, she doesn't know if she can do it. Once was enough, maybe. Or maybe there will be too many cuts, between George and Jack. Maybe she'll bleed too much inside. 'It may not work, but I'm going to try,' she says.

Harry is looking at her, his expression a mix of disbelief and admiration. 'When the captain said you were stubborn, he wasn't jesting.'

'Jack said that?'

'I think he meant it as a compliment.'

She smiles. It's a wan, small smile, but it's the first time since Tom Holder brought her the news that she has managed to produce one. 'I wonder.'

Harry leans back in his chair, fingering his beard, his dark eyes resting on her. 'Why don't you ask him yourself when you see him?'

She wants to kiss him for saying it. 'Maybe I will.'

Harry's smile fades. 'There's one problem. Papers. The captain's will have been revoked – they've searched the house – and I haven't got any. We can sail without, but we may be taken for pirates.'

'What sort of papers?' she says.

'A special licence to pull into French ports despite the embargo, as well as proof the ship is on the register. The *Rapide's* port of origin is Penzance.'

She nods. 'I'll try to think of something. But we can sail without?'

Harry says, 'I'd prefer not to, but if it's the only way, we will. I'll have the *Rapide* ready to sail by nightfall.'

Harry stands when she rises. At the door, she turns back to him. 'Thank you, Harry.'

'Good luck to you, Bucca's daughter.'

'Thank you. I shall need it.'

The door to the Shipwrights Arms is locked, but the blinds are open. It's half an hour past noon. She knocks and when nobody answers, she puts her face to the window glass. A shadow moves inside, shaped like a person. Then the door is unlocked and Richard lets her in. 'Please, may I speak to your father?' she says, and Tom Holder comes from the back and says, 'What can I do for you, Mrs Henley?'

She explains that she requires a horse. 'I need it tonight or perhaps tomorrow. Possibly even Friday morning.' She doesn't know how long it will take to free Jack. 'It'll need to be saddled and ready. I promise you'll have it back in a day. I may be able to send someone or you can retrieve it from Nelly's cove.'

Tom Holder scratches his head. 'You may have a horse, sure, if I get her back.'

'You will. I promise.'

'Very well, then. She'll be in the leftmost stable. I'll leave the door unlocked. Her name is Rosie-May, she's the fastest of the two. Are you going to tell me what you need her for?'

'It's better if you don't know,' she says.

'You'll have to be extra careful if it's Friday. We're expecting a lot of guests.' He grimaces. 'I'd like to close the inn as a sign of respect, but it wouldn't do Jack any good, would it?'

The chill settles in her skin again. 'I understand.' A beat, then, 'I hope very much to deprive them of the spectacle, Tom.'

He flashes her a smile so bright it makes him look ten years younger. 'That's good news if there ever was any. I'll be glad not to sell a single mug of ale on Friday.'

Tom shows her the horse, a handsome, stocky farm horse which, he says with some emphasis, can easily carry two. She thanks him and asks if she could borrow one of his or Richard's caps. Tom Holder goes back into the inn; when he returns, he's carrying a blue knitted cap in one hand and a letter in the other. 'I nearly forgot. This came with the post this morning.'

She takes the letter, examining the small, textured envelope, the elegant script.

'It's from France, I believe,' says Tom Holder, pointing at the smudged stamp, which reads: *Roscoff.*

It must be from Madame Cuvelier, she thinks. Half-turning away from the innkeeper, she tucks the letter into the bodice of her dress and then takes the cap from him, gauging its size. 'It's Richard's,' Tom Holder says.

'Thank you, Tom.' She takes her leave and flies down the road to Mrs Dowling's house. The tide is out, the air is filled with the smell of drying seaweed. The soles of her shoes slap the dirt road and she sweats under the already hot sun. Mercifully, the landlady opens the door at her first knock.

'I haven't time to come in, I'm afraid,' Isabel says. 'I only wished to tell you that I am to go away again and, though it shall take me a little while, I'll ensure the lease of the cottage is paid in full.'

Mrs Dowling says, 'I heard the news about Mr Carlyon.'

'Yes,' she says, keeping her voice steady. She lightly touches George's medal. 'It's awfully sad.' Maybe it's the way she says it; maybe the hope shines through or she speaks the words too casually.

'So it is,' Mrs Dowling says, eyes locked on hers, understanding dawning. 'And will you be making this journey alone?'

She chews her lower lip, then says, 'I hope I'll be able to make it with someone very dear to me.'

Mrs Dowling nods. 'I'm awfully pleased to hear that, even if I don't fully understand. Shall you be needing anything for your journey? Any food, drink; any linens, perhaps?'

'Only your good wishes, if you please, Mrs Dowling.'

'You have them, naturally,' the older woman says, her hand against her cheek. 'Oh, dear girl,' she clucks, shaking her head. 'Wait here.'

Mrs Dowling disappears in the gloom of the house.

Moments later, she's back, carrying a bundle of cream wool. 'Take this with you,' she says, thrusting the bundle at Isabel. 'It can be cold on the road. Or at sea.'

The wool is impossibly soft, knitted up into an intricate pattern of lace. Isabel is holding the finest shawl she has ever beheld. She lifts the cloth up to her cheek, feeling its downiness. It smells faintly of lavender. 'I can't take this. It's much too fine.'

'Take it, please.' Mrs Dowling says. 'My mother made it for me. I wore it on my wedding day. I hope . . .' She glances up, across Isabel's shoulder, at the inlet and the river beyond. 'I hope there's a chance you'll wear it on yours.'

Her throat tight, Isabel says, 'Thank you, Mrs Dowling. If . . . if I don't get to take it on my journey, it'll be waiting for you at the cottage. It depends on where my journey leads, you see. It's possible it'll lead somewhere I cannot take this or anything else . . .' she trails off at Mrs Dowling's expression. She did not mean to begin talking like that again, with the words running fast and her hands moving as if they, too, wish to talk. 'I'm sure all will be well,' she says.

Mrs Dowling clucks again. 'Please be careful.'

'I shall. Thank you for everything, all the many things you've taught me these past weeks.'

The lines in Mrs Dowling's face move until she's smiling again. 'Yes, where would you be without me? You couldn't even light a fire.'

Looking at the shawl in her hands, Isabel smiles. 'Or bake bread.'

'Or wash your clothes. These need a wash, don't they — there's sand all over your gown.'

'I must go. Thank you, Mrs Dowling.'

'I wish you well, Mrs Henley. Take care.' She hesitates, then says quickly, 'If at any time you're in need of aid or protection, remember . . .' She waves her hand at the river.

'The Sea Bucca?' She says it without irony. It may be just a story or it may be something more. It doesn't matter now. She needs all the help she can get — even that of mythical creatures. Maybe especially that. 'I shall,' she says, already walking down the path, back to the road, one hand lifted in farewell, holding Richard's cap, the other clutching the shawl. She's walking fast, going through the steps of her plan in her mind. The ship and the horse — they'll be ready. The ship's papers — she's not sure what to do about those. It seems a minor thing. Harry said they could sail without them.

The main thing is getting Jack off the frigate. The horse will be perfect, she thinks. Rosie-May. An elegant name for a ponderous-looking horse. But strong; she looks the strongest horse on the coast.

She's still thinking about the horse when she jogs down the gravel path, which is why she's all the more startled to see a horse standing in front of the cottage. This horse is the opposite of Rosie-May: a gleaming Arabian stallion, looking unhappy tied to the young oak by the door. *Buttons.* She calls, 'Harriet?'

CHAPTER SEVENTEEN

The river swishes against the stone wall, other than that everything is quiet. Even the horse seems to be holding its breath. 'Harriet?' she calls again and now there are footsteps on the narrow path along the side of the house and Harriet emerges looking sun-kissed and smiling. 'I was enjoying your wondrous little garden, Isabel,' she says, as if nothing is amiss, as if Isabel has dreamt their encounter at Weatherston six weeks ago.

She's staring at Harriet and finds herself saying, 'It's particularly lovely in the summertime, don't you think?'

'Why, yes, the flowers are all in bloom. Should you ... should you like some of our roses? I'd be glad to have Campbell bring you some to plant here. Perhaps around your well. Wouldn't that be lovely?'

She's still staring. Why are they standing here, pretending all is well and talking about gardens? Quietly, she says, 'Harriet, why are you here?'

Harriet looks down at her feet, then, as if to seek support, she goes to the horse and pats his neck. 'I heard the news. I came to tell you how sorry I am. If he truly is your fiancé . . . well. No woman should have to experience the loss of the one they love, let alone twice. Even if your character isn't what I hoped it was and Mr Carlyon committed the crime of which he stands accused.' Fixing her eyes on Isabel she says, 'I understand there won't be a trial.'

'He'll be tried for murder on board the frigate,' Isabel says. She wants to scream. 'Captain Hamer guarantees a guilty verdict.'

'Just so,' Harriet says, her hand fluttering across her forehead. 'But he did kill poor Lieutenant Sowerby, did he not? I couldn't stop weeping when I heard.'

Her hands turn to fists, partly hidden by the wool of Mrs Dowling's wedding shawl. '*Poor* Lieutenant Sowerby tried to shoot me.'

Harriet blanches. 'I beg your pardon?'

'Your poor Lieutenant Sowerby was going to shoot Jack in the back. He was going to claim he killed him whilst Jack tried to escape arrest.'

'But how could you know this, Isabel?'

'I was there. And when I stepped in front of Jack, Lieutenant Sowerby shot at me. He missed, by about this much.' She shows Harriet with her thumb and forefinger, three inches, no more. 'That's when Jack shot him. He killed Sowerby to protect me. The only other crime he committed was smuggling contraband. For that he should be tried by his peers, but that's not what Lieutenant Sowerby liked to do, nor Captain Hamer.' She sighs, her hand on the door. 'Now, if you'll excuse me, I have things to do.'

Harriet's fingers trail down her left cheek, smoothing away something Isabel cannot detect. 'Of course. I'm sorry to have bothered you. I . . . if it hadn't been for that news from London . . . we could've been good friends, could we not?'

'What friend lets a friend stand accused without trial?' she spats. 'I ask you, Harriet! What friend does that?'

'You mean Mr Carlyon? But—'

'I meant myself. Whoever gave you the supposed news from London was wrong. Yes, there were rumours about me. Yes, it's why I left, in part. I couldn't stand being talked about like that. But the only thing I did wrong was befriend a man below my station. Should I not have done it?' She shrugs, not caring anymore, at least not for Harriet's opinion. 'Perhaps I shouldn't have. It was outside the bounds of propriety, certainly, and not worth all the trouble it caused. But all I ever did was talk with him and . . . and go on walks, for God's sake! There was never any intimacy beyond that of mere friendship. You've no idea how lonely I felt after I lost George.'

'I think perhaps I do,' Harriet says softly.

She ignores this; her indignance is too hot. 'Yet you chose to believe the first letter you received. You never asked me, you never let me explain. Our friendship was finished for you before it began. Yet here you stand, saying we could've been good friends. What stuff! Friendship is more than chatting about gardens over a cup of tea. I've made some true friends since I came to Cornwall and I regret to say you aren't one of them.'

Harriet turns to the horse, patting it again. In a clipped voice, she says, 'I had better go. Sir Hugh will be expecting me.'

'Goodbye.' She doesn't wait for Harriet to leave. Going into the house, she throws the door shut behind her. She places Mrs Dowling's shawl in a heap of finely spun wool on the table along with Richard's far coarser wool cap and stomps up the stairs to the bedroom. She feels foolish for taking the shawl. Even if everything goes according to plan, there is no chance she'll be able to bring it with her. She can't take it on board the *Hornet* and she won't return to the cottage before the *Rapide* sails. She'll have to leave the shawl here for Mrs Dowling to find. It was such a kind gift; she hopes Mrs Dowling will understand.

The carriage clock in the bedroom points to a quarter past two. She has forty-eight hours and forty-five minutes left. The sight of the bed leaves her momentarily reeling. She bends over, hands on the mattress, taking deep breaths to steady herself, the room. This is where she first saw him. This is where he said, *I think I'm in good hands*, with that smile. Despite the pain he was in he smiled at her like that.

Slowly, the floor stops swaying. She wipes her forehead and kneels down in the narrow space between the wall and the bed. Jack's breeches, neckerchief and shirt are where she left them, folded in a small stack. The clothes smell like her, but Jack wore them. Suddenly, unexpectedly, the tears come rushing into her throat again. She swallows them down – she has no time for crying.

Back in the kitchen she takes the largest of the two knives left in the wooden box on the counter, the one she uses to cut meat, and puts her finger to the blade. She hopes it's sharp enough. She has never had to cut her hair before.

Taking a fistful, she holds the knife, ready to cut through the bunch where it hits her shoulder. No, she thinks – she'll go shorter, she'll cut it to chin-length. Turning the sharp of the blade away from her face, she pushes it into the bunch of hair, but it won't give, slipping from her hand instead. Gripping the strands again, she slowly saws through them. The result is uneven, but it's short. Very, very short. There's an awful lot of hair on the floor. It looks a bit like seaweed. Fine, sand-coloured seaweed.

She takes a second fistful and begins to saw at it when a knock on the door almost makes her drop the knife. Rooted to the floor, she barely dares to breathe. Has the Revenue Service finally come to question her? But why would they, when they've already captured Jack?

Another knock, then Harriet's voice: 'Isabel? Please open the door.'

She lowers the knife. If she stays quiet, Harriet may leave again.

'Isabel?'

There's an itch in her throat. She fights it, but eventually it comes out in the shape of a cough behind her hand.

'Isabel? Please, I must speak with you!'

No, you mustn't, she thinks. Not now.

There's the sound of hands moving against the door and then the latch inside lifts. If only she had put a lock on the door.

Harriet's face is pale in the doorway. Relief washes over it when she spots Isabel. 'Oh, there you are. I knew you were in. I checked the garden.' She opens the door wider, steps through it, catches sight of the hair on the floor, the hair in Isabel's hand, the knife. Both of her hands go to her mouth. 'Oh! Whatever are you *doing*?'

'That's none of your concern,' she says.

'You're cutting your hair!' Harriet says, stepping closer. 'Oh, but you're doing it all wrong.'

'I – what? I beg your pardon?'

'You're taking too big a bunch at a time. That's why it's so uneven,' Harriet says. 'You've been hacking at it, haven't you?'

'Sawing, rather.'

'You'll want to take only a very little and slice through it quickly, if you want it to look a little neater.' Harriet lifts up a strand of hair no thicker than a piece of string. 'No more than this. Here, let me do it. You'll never be able to do the back properly yourself.'

Before Isabel can protest, Harriet takes the knife from her and begins to cut her hair. 'How do you know this?' Isabel says. 'You weren't a barber in a past life, were you?'

Harriet giggles. 'Would that I were! I once cut off rather

a lot of my hair. It was far more difficult than I thought it would be. After the first few minutes of fruitless hacking, I realised cutting it in small sections was the key.'

'Thank you,' Isabel says, as the first strands of hair drift to the floor. 'Why did you cut your hair?'

'Oh, as a sort of protest, when my parents promised me to Sir Hugh. I was fourteen. I thought if I cut my hair, Sir Hugh wouldn't want me anymore.' She giggles again. 'Poor Sir Hugh. I must've looked a fright. I wouldn't know – my parents banned me from using a looking glass for a year, until the wedding. By then it had grown back a bit. Sir Hugh didn't mind in the least.'

'You were very young,' she says.

Harriet half-shrugs. 'Not much younger than you.'

They're both silent. The only sound is the scratching of the knife as it goes through the hair. A small mountain of it covers the stone flags at her feet. She feels strangely unworried about this, as if her fears for Jack blot out all other concerns.

Harriet says, 'I could've done worse. Sir Hugh has always been good to me.'

'You could've married a naval officer who got killed at the age of twenty. Or got engaged to a smuggler.'

Harriet smiles. 'How I hated the thought of marrying him, though. Poor Sir Hugh, I hope he never realised. He was so much older than me and so terribly forbidding and stern. He still is, of course; you've seen him.' She lowers the knife and says, 'So you see, Isabel, I do know a bit about loneliness. I experience it every day in my marriage.'

'I'm sorry,' Isabel says, in spite of herself.

Harriet resumes her cutting. 'Yes, well, so am I. I'm sorry I didn't let you explain after I got that letter. Sir Hugh was terribly angry that I should've befriended someone with such a – I'm sorry to say it now, but such a tarnished reputation. He feared it may reflect on my own. I . . . I thought I agreed with him, but I have missed seeing you these past weeks and I see now I have done you an injustice by not giving you the chance to tell your side of the story.'

'I spoke very harshly to you just now,' Isabel says. 'I apologise, Harriet.'

Harriet says, 'I deserved it. I knocked again just now to tell you that. However, I didn't expect to find you trying to cut your hair! You're lucky I came in. You may have cut yourself if you tried to do the back on your own.'

'Aren't you going to ask me why I'm cutting it?'

Working on some strands at the back, Harriet says, 'I'm sure you have your reasons. I confess you've piqued my curiosity, but I feel rather as if I have forfeited the right to ask. There is one thing I should like to ask you, however, though I don't know if you'll care to answer.'

'Ask,' she says, shifting her weight from one leg to the other. With her hand, she leans on the kitchen table, brushing the wool of Mrs Dowling's shawl.

'Do you love him?' Harriet says.

It's strange how just a few words can make the flood surge inside her again. She struggles to keep still, to not start weeping again. 'Yes,' she says. 'Yes, I do.'

'As you loved your husband?'

'More.' She waits for the slap of guilt, but it doesn't come. She and George were children, she thinks, or very nearly so. They had so little time in which to know each other. It's different with Jack. The way they talk together, it's as if they've managed to fit several years of understanding in the span of weeks.

'And does Mr Carlyon love you?'

'Yes.' So simple – and she's so certain, though he has never said it.

Harriet sighs behind her. 'I envy you, Isabel.'

'You envy me? You must be mad.'

'I don't envy the situation in which you find yourself, naturally. I can only imagine the despair you must feel on account of Mr Carlyon's impending fate. Only . . . I always dreamt of that. Of true love.' Another giggle, this one short and a little flat. 'I'm such a dolt, aren't I? I believed in fairy tales, too, for the longest time. Sometimes I think I haven't done enough growing up yet. That's what Sir Hugh says, that I'm in many ways like a child, still. But you see, I don't have that with Sir Hugh. Love. There is a certain level of affection, but nothing like what you have with Mr Carlyon. I wish . . . I wish there was something I could do to help.'

Isabel sucks in her breath sharply. 'You would help me?'

'If I could.'

'Could . . .' she barely dares to ask. 'Could Sir Hugh not pardon Jack?'

'Oh, Isabel. Sir Hugh doesn't have that sort of power. And I'm afraid he wouldn't want to if he did.'

Her mind races through the different steps, the ship, the horse, Jack's clothes, the story she'll tell them on board the *Hornet*, about how she wants to volunteer . . . 'There is something,' she says. It takes her the remainder of the haircut to explain.

'You'd like me to forge a special licence?' Harriet says, placing the knife on the kitchen table with a clang. 'You want me to break the law to help a smuggler? You don't deny he is a smuggler, do you?'

'I don't,' she says. 'But hanging him without a trial for a murder committed in self-defence also constitutes a breach of the law. It's up to you to judge which crime you consider the more egregious.'

Harriet is silent for a moment. Her cheeks are rosier than usual against the pale canvas of her face; her mouth, rose red, moves as if in prayer. Eventually, she says, 'I'll do it, on one condition. You write to me, once you have got away. Tell me about all your adventures. I shall be living them through your letters, dear Isabel.'

'I'll write. I promise,' she says.

'These documents, they have to be in Mr Carlyon's name?'

'And bear your husband's seal.'

'Very well. Could I bring them to you tomorrow?'

'Could you take them to Mr Harry Tremayne at Roskorwell, please, as soon as you possibly can? He lives in the white thatched cottage at the end of the estate. I won't be here.' She takes up the pile of Jack's clothes and unfolds the pair of breeches.

Harriet is looking at her strangely. 'You plan to wear these garments?'

'Yes,' she says. 'They belong to Jack.'

Harriet starts. 'Do you mean to say you and him – actually, don't tell me.' A small smile, then, 'You may have wondered why Sir Hugh and I are childless. He's too old for that sort of thing, he says.'

'I'm sorry, Harriet.'

'It's just as well, I suppose.'

With her left hand, Isabel touches the ends of her hair. They only reach to her chin. She has never worn her hair this short before, not since she was a child. 'Thank you for cutting my hair. I would've cut off my ear, probably.'

Voice low, Harriet says, 'Isabel, what is it you mean to do?'

She gazes at Harriet, wondering if she can she be trusted or if she'll run straight to her husband and tell. But she needs Harriet's help – she has already involved her by asking her to get the ship's documents. 'I mean to volunteer to join His Majesty's Navy,' she says, deciding.

Harriet shrieks. 'You never! Isabel, do you have any idea what you're doing?'

She explains. By the time she has finished, Harriet's cheeks are like polished red apples, her eyes bright as if she's in a fever. 'Oh, the daring of it!' she says, clapping her hands as if she's just watched the conclusion to an exciting play.

Isabel says, 'I'm going to see in the looking glass if I may pass for a boy.'

'Put the breeches on first,' Harriet instructs. 'And you shall need a weapon.'

Glancing up sharply, she says, 'A weapon?'

'You don't mean to go without, do you? You'll need to be able to defend yourself. I appreciate you can't take a pistol or a sword, but you ought to take this at least.' She lifts the meat knife from the table and holds it out to Isabel.

She takes it, turning it over in her hand, inspecting the blade. 'I suppose you're right. I hadn't thought of it.' She checks Jack's breeches: thank heavens there are pockets. Deep ones, too.

Harriet says, 'What would you do if it weren't for me? Your hair would look an absolute fright. It looks dreadful as it is. But what's this?' Knitted lace spills from her hand as she lifts Mrs Dowling's shawl from the table. 'Oh Isabel, this is exquisite! Wherever did you get it? From London?' She caresses the wool as if it's Button's gleaming neck.

'It was my landlady's wedding shawl,' Isabel says. 'She thought perhaps I might be able to make use of it.' It's the first time she blushes in Harriet's presence. The first time, too, that she grasps the extent of Harriet's confinement in what she calls her walled garden. Suddenly, she understands what her friend meant when she said she envied her.

'It's simply wonderful. Did she make this?'

'Her mother did. I won't be able to take it, however.' She takes the shawl back from Harriet, re-folds it and places it on the table with reverence.

Harriet tries to help her with the ties on the back of her dress, but not having the experience, she's slower than when Isabel does it herself. The dress falls to the floor in a waterfall of cotton. Up in the bedroom, Harriet angles the looking glass in such a way Isabel is able to see most of herself in small, broken images: a length of buckskin-clad thigh here, a swish of chin-length hair there, the blue knitted cap completing the picture.

Everything but the cap is too big: she has rolled up the shirtsleeves and has tied the breeches at the top with the neckerchief. It's strange wearing Jack's clothes again. She spent the happiest time of her life wearing his shirt and breeches aboard the *Rapide* and also the most desperate after Jack shot Lieutenant Sowerby.

'You'll pass,' Harriet says, surveying her. 'You might want to slump a little, with your shoulders like this.' She demonstrates the stance. 'Just to ensure no one sees the shape of you underneath that shirt. It will make you look younger too if you appear uncertain.'

'You have deception down to an art, Harriet,' she says.

Harriet giggles. 'I've had much practise, living with Sir Hugh. Now, when have you last eaten?'

'I couldn't eat. Not now.'

'As I thought. You must eat, Isabel, or you'll be too hungry to rescue Mr Carlyon.' Harriet's hands fly to her cheeks, cradling her face. 'I can't believe I've just said that! I can't believe we're doing this.'

She likes how Harriet says, *we're doing this,* as if she, Isabel, doesn't have to do it alone.

'I shall make you a pot of tea,' Harriet says decisively. 'It can't be difficult, surely.'

'The fire isn't lit. It'll take far too long.'

'Why ever have they not kept the fire lit?' Then, realising: 'Oh! Of course. A biscuit then or perhaps some bread?'

'I have an end of a loaf left. Thank you, Harriet.' She glances at the clock in its walnut case. It's a few minutes before three.

Harriet lifts her skirts. From atop the stairs, she glances back at the bedroom door. 'What an odd little bedroom you have.'

The coastal path is damp; it has rained short but hard while she was inside. The green tunnel drips rain and bright flecks of sunlight. The air is sticky, but she's remarkably cool in the thin leather breeches.

There was something forlorn about Harriet when she left. Isabel didn't wait for her friend to ride off on Buttons before she set out. Now that she has dressed the part, she's eager to go play it, a mix of hope and dread whirling inside her.

When she's nearly at the cove, a terrible thought stops her in her tracks. What if the *Hornet* has moved? She breaks into a run, her breath shallow in the prison of her stays, which she has fastened as tight as she could to flatten her bosom. Two more turns of the path, one, and there she yet lies, thank heavens, guarding the mouth of the river, her sails furled, some of her rigging unexpectedly slack.

Catching her breath, she removes her shoes and leaves

them on the beach before she gets into the water. The flat of the blade in her pocket pushes against her hip as she swims, Jack's shirt billowing around her like a cloud. The sea is cold, but not as cold as it was when she swam in Frenchman's Creek with Jack.

The dance of nerves slows; the sea calms her as it always does. She's far from shore now, the water under her black as night. On board the ship, voices ring out and when she looks up, she sees a small crowd assembling along the gunwale. Shouts and pointed fingers: it's as if they're pointing right through her disguise. She closes her eyes briefly, steadying her resolve as she continues to swim towards the ship. She's a boy, fifteen years of age, hungry like a starved dog, she reminds herself. She isn't Isabel Henley anymore.

Maybe she never was, she thinks suddenly. The way she feels she could keep swimming forever without tiring; the way she revels in the cool embrace of the sea, coming home in its vast arms – maybe she's someone she never believed she was. A child of the sea.

As she approaches the ship, the words come to her again: *Come home. Swim.* Spoken in the voice of the river, of the current, of the wind and the gulls.

She cannot listen to it now. She must concentrate on the frigate. Looking up again, she can see the faces of the men assembled on deck. They're faces smooth with youth and faces heavily lined with age, light and dark faces and one with an eye patch, and they're all turned to her as she closes the last twenty feet between herself and the ship. Up close, the frigate is far bigger than she thought. The hull towers over her, twice the height of the old pilchard shed, all gleaming wood broken up by gunports. Along the waterline, a feast of seaweed and barnacles sticks to the ship. She's close to the open sea now and what she assumed was a gentle bobbing up and down turns out to be a serious roll.

She aims for the wooden steps set into the hull near the bow, but her first attempt to grab the lowest rung sees her dip under the surface. She swallows her breath just in time and when she comes back up, one of the men on deck throws a rope over the side. 'Take it!' he shouts.

The rope twists like an angry snake. She stretches out her hand, treading water, but it slips away. Just as she thinks she'll go under again her fingers close around the rough hemp. She hoists herself up, feet slipping on the rungs of the ladder.

A cheer goes up along the gunwale and she feels it in her chest, an expanding warmth, as if it's the crew of the *Rapide* cheering her on. Again the ship rolls, but this time she's expecting it and she holds still, waiting for the *Hornet* to right herself again. The rope burns her hands as she pulls herself up, feeling the strain in every one of her muscles.

When she reaches the deck, large, calloused hands grab hold of her arms. One set belongs to the eye-patch-wearer who's saying, 'There you are, boy, there you are,' with a mouth full of gums. They pull her up over the gunwale and set her on her feet. The ship rolls and she moves with it, shifting her weight as she finds her balance. The men are craning their necks to take a look at her as she stands, dripping, on the deck. The wind whips at her shirt and she grasps the hem with both hands to keep it in place. When she lifts her head, she's looking at the point of a knife.

CHAPTER EIGHTEEN

The knife is slotted in the hand of a young officer. Judging by his uniform of a blue wool jacket with gilt brass buttons, cream shirt and breeches, he's a midshipman like George was. The knife is like one George used to own, too: a dirk with a curved blade and, she expects, a mother-of-pearl inlaid hilt, though she cannot see it as the midshipman's surprisingly beefy hand is wrapped tightly around it. The young man's hair is darker than George's, but his eyes are similar, grey-green in colour and wide-set. His age, she thinks, is the age George was when he died.

If things had been different, George could have been standing here pointing his dirk at an intruder. The thought cuts. It's the first such cut in some time – she has been too busy worrying about Jack. And the thought is wrong, too, for George would've advanced through the ranks, especially after Trafalgar; he wouldn't have been a midshipman any longer.

'State your purpose, coming aboard a vessel of His Majesty's Navy in this manner,' the midshipman orders.

Water trickles onto the deck as she stares at her bare feet. She wants to push the hair from her face but worries the motion may betray her. She should have practised in front of the looking glass. Which of her gestures mark her as a woman; what habit might give her away? Everything depends on her acting skills. She cannot contemplate what will happen to Jack if she fails.

As the ship rolls, she again moves to keep her balance. Nine days on the *Rapide* have taught her well; she doesn't stumble. The ship smells like the *Rapide*, too: wood scrubbed with sand and seawater, the smell of wet hemp and clothes in need of a wash.

'Well?' The midshipman snaps when she merely stands there, staring at her feet. She must remember to lower her voice. 'State your purpose, lad!'

She says, 'I wish to volunteer, sir.' Not too high, but too uncertain. She lifts her hand to her mouth, chews on the nail of her pinkie finger, then remembers Richard's cap, and pulls it off, holding it against her chest.

'You wish to – what? Speak up!'

'To volunteer, sir. To join the crew.'

Most of the crew has gathered around to watch. Some of them laugh and one calls out, 'More fool you, boy!'

'Quiet!' the midshipman calls and, a little more kindly, he says, 'Look up when you speak to your superiors. You wish to volunteer to join His Majesty's Navy?'

'Yes, sir.' She looks up at last and holds his gaze, everything inside her turned to liquid. *Please believe me.*

The midshipman is very young, just like George was. He's a boy compared to Jack. The thought comes to her, unbidden. It's unfair to George, who never got to grow fully into manhood. And now she stands here deceiving George's fellow officer in order to save a man who doesn't look so very harshly upon the French and their Revolution, who smuggles contraband against the King's laws. Everything is turned upside down, yet her feeling forbids her to do anything but charge ahead with the deception, to try to find Jack, to get him out. She says to the midshipman, 'I should like to join His Majesty's Navy sir, very much.'

'And you couldn't wait for the press gang, could you? You had to come aboard by *swimming* across?' As he speaks, the midshipman slides the dirk back in the leather sheath on his belt.

Letting her shoulders slump like Harriet told her, she says quietly, 'I was hungry, sir. And I feared the officer in charge of the press gang might not want me.'

'What in God's name made you think that? The press gang will take anyone!' shouts one of the men and another calls, 'They'd take your nan if they could get her!'

The midshipman turns and barks, 'Quiet there or I shall take your name!' To Isabel, he says, 'What's your name, lad?'

She had come up with something, hadn't she? She stumbles around the corners of her mind, groping – 'Jack,' she says, too softly.

'Jack what?'

'Jack . . . Dowling, sir. Of Helford, sir.'

'Well, Jack Dowling of Helford, if you are so hungry you couldn't wait a day longer to make your application, I had best take you to see Lieutenant Knighton.'

'Lieutenant Knighton has gone ashore, sir,' says a doleful-looking man in a black and blue striped shirt next to the midshipman.

'Right. So he has, Bryant. In that case, you'll have to face the captain,' the midshipman says to Isabel. With a snicker, he adds, 'Don't look so worried – he's not going to eat you. You may be in luck. The captain might take you on sooner than Lieutenant Knighton, who can't bear the sight of too many landlubbers among the ship's company. How old are you?'

'Fifteen, sir.'

'Follow me.'

It's only now, as she follows the midshipman down the gangway to the quarterdeck, that she feels a small thrill run through her. It's not enough to blot out the nerves, which have started to turn her legs to jelly, but it's there. She has made it this far. She's aboard the ship. Jack is somewhere nearby. It takes all her willpower to follow the midshipman and not run off in search of him. Perhaps he can hear her footsteps on the deck this very moment . . .

The *Hornet* is at least five times bigger than Jack's cutter. A maze of rigging covers her masts, her upper deck gleams and her quarterdeck is raised high above the main deck. Another thrill, this time just to be on board such a ship, the thought of sailing on her roving through her mind. She can see why George loved the Navy – more than he loved her, perhaps.

'This way, lad.' The midshipman breaks in on her thoughts, going before her through a door next to the steps leading up to the quarterdeck. The meat knife, deep in the pocket of Jack's breeches, rubs against her hip with every step. They enter a narrow corridor with doors on each side and another door in the bulkhead in front. The air is stiff with polish; the wooden doors shine like burnished copper and there's the scent of coffee wafting down the passage. The midshipman stops in front of the bulkhead door and knocks. At a gruff call from inside, he sticks his head through the door, saying, 'I bring a volunteer, sir.'

'Can't Lieutenant Knighton do it, Withers?'

'He's gone ashore, sir.'

'I see. In that case, bring him in. I hope you've got a decent seaman-like creature for me.'

'I'm afraid not, sir,' says Withers, stepping aside whilst holding the door open for Isabel.

She steps into the captain's cabin, which is of a gargantuan size compared to Jack's cupboard aboard the *Rapide*. There's no sign of a hammock, only a fine, polished oak dining table with a set of chairs around it, a music stand in one corner and a large mahogany desk, from behind which Captain Hamer studies her, quill poised as if he's about to write a sonnet. He's perhaps ten years older than Jack, with a strong jaw, a benevolent smile at odds with the piratical glint in his eyes, and salt-and-pepper hair tied back in the style popular in the Navy some ten to twenty years ago.

A memory tugs on her mind – just such a cabin, somewhere, with the stern windows looking out across a bay, glittering in the sun, with just such a desk and such a captain, too. Was it her father's ship? She visited one of Admiral Farnworth's ships, HMS *Leander,* only once, when she was eight years old. She doesn't remember what its great cabin looked like; she only remembers the view of the tripping water out of the stern windows and the desire to go to sea. And she remembers the galley, the chef's great steaming pots, the furnace blazing, and the small corner in which she hid, not wanting to leave the ship.

She gradually becomes aware she's staring at the captain and quickly lowers her eyes the way she thinks an impoverished boy of fifteen would.

'What's this then, dripping all over my carpet?' Captain Hamer's voice is deep and resonant. It stirs something inside her, another vague smear of a memory, but it flits away before it can take form.

'My name is Jack Dowling, sir,' she says. 'I should like to join your ship's company.'

'Look up when you speak to me, lad. Why do you look like a drowned cat?'

Withers says, 'He swam across, sir.'

The captain is studying her far more closely than the midshipman did. The tip of his quill rests just below his lower lip and his eyes are hooded as he gazes at her. She has to fight the urge to look down again. After a moment, the captain places the quill in the inkwell. 'Hm. You're very keen. You're aware we don't usually lie at our leisure in a pretty little cove such as this? We go to war, lad. If you join the ship's company, you may fall in the next battle.'

Like George did. She's still holding Richard's cap; her other hand goes to the medal, hidden under Jack's shirt. She could not bear the thought of going without it. Lifting the black ribbon, she wraps her hand around Lord Nelson's silver silhouette. 'Yes, sir,' she says quietly.

'That prospect doesn't faze you?'

She feigns embarrassment, says, 'Not any more than dying of hunger, sir.'

The captain gives a nod. 'So that's why you're so keen.' He narrows his eyes as if to see through the shirt, the skin and sinews covering what lies inside. 'You're hungry, is that it?'

'We've got too many mouths to feed at home. I was sent out to fend for myself, sir.'

'And you couldn't go down the mines or go a–fishing? That's what they do here, isn't it?'

'Yes, sir. No, sir.' A breath, then, 'I ... I should like the adventure, sir.' *Please believe me. Please, please, please.* She must convince the captain. If they send her back to shore ... no, she cannot think of it.

'Should you, indeed?' Captain Hamer says slowly. He doesn't appear to expect an answer. Instead, he continues to look her over, suspicion growing in his eyes. She grips the medal harder, drawing from it the strength to keep calm, to keep standing there as if nothing is amiss. Inside, the fear grows claws. Can the captain tell? Why is he looking at her like that, as if something about her doesn't add up?

At last, Captain Hamer says, 'We don't hold with theft on this ship, lad.'

'Theft?' Bewildered, she takes a step towards the desk. Instantly, Withers draws his dirk again. Pointing it at her, he says, 'Keep still.'

Captain Hamer says, 'Thank you, Withers, but it's hardly necessary. Yes, theft. We don't approve of it in the service. You get to run the gauntlet for it. Do you know what that is, lad? The men line up along the gangway and beat you as you pass through. Very unpleasant. They tend to beat hard. They don't like a thief on board as they've nowhere to safely store their possessions.'

'What . . . why . . . I didn't . . .' she stammers.

'Those breeches are very fine for a boy like yourself. Buckskin, are they? I don't have much of an eye for fashion, I admit, but they're a gentleman's pair I'd say. They're far too big for you.'

The ship pitches heavily and she moves her hips, finding her balance. When she meets Captain Hamer's eyes again, she sees he has noticed. Her mind reaches but finds nothing. What can she say? They belong to Jack? They'd hang her alongside him. 'I . . .'

'You cannot account for your possession of them, can you? And what have you got there?' the captain says, waving his hand. 'That thing you're grasping around your neck.'

She opens her hand and looks down at George's medal. The silver glints in the sun dropping in through the stern windows. The smell of coffee bores into her nose; sharp and bitter. The captain has a silver pot on his desk. She and George used to sit in the garden with a similar pot set on the iron-wrought table, a porcelain cup decorated with forget-me-knots on each side. The coffee pot was one of many wedding gifts.

'The breeches belonged to my father, sir,' she says slowly. 'He died at Trafalgar. My mother can't feed all six of us on her widow's pension.'

The corners of Captain Hamer's mouth lift. He looks almost relieved, as if he wanted her to be better than he believed she was. 'Is that so? And that's his Trafalgar medal, is it?'

'It is, sir. It was given to my mother afterwards. She gave it to me to remember him by.'

'May I see it?'

She fumbles with the ribbon, fingers stiff with nerves. At last, she hands the medal to the captain, who holds it up reverently before handing it back.

'Hm. I admire your spirit, boy, swimming across like that,' Captain Hamer says. 'And your father served with Lord Nelson, did he?'

'Aboard the *Neptune*, sir,' she says, tying the ribbon around her neck again and praying Captain Hamer doesn't know Captain Fremantle who commanded the *Neptune* or any of his fellow officers. 'As second lieutenant, sir,' she adds. It would've been better to be able to say, *as maintopman* or *as bosun's mate* or some other fairly anonymous position aboard a man-of-war, but they would not explain the expensive nature of the breeches she's wearing.

'You seem an enterprising sort. You take after your father, I expect. I suppose it explains your manner of speech, too. I confess you had me confounded for a moment there, lad.'

Inside, she silently swears an oath Dick Pascoe would have been proud of. She hadn't thought to change the way she spoke; she doesn't even know how. She worries there are other things she missed in her hurry to get to Jack. What if her entire plan fails because of it?

Captain Hamer continues, 'You're a strong swimmer, you've shown that, but what else can you do? It's experienced hands we want, not boys barely breeched.'

Isabel says, 'I can sew and . . . and repair things.'

'You know carpentry?'

'A little. I've done jobs for my mother. And my father taught me some navigation, sir.' Another deep breath. 'Please, sir. I'll do anything.'

'He taught you navigation? You shall have to show me sometime what you know of it,' Captain Hamer says. 'We're about to get underway.'

Her voice rises dangerously with shock. 'We are, sir?'

'Only to the next cove. We have some business to conclude here before we truly set sail. We shall sail to Gibraltar and from there to the East India station. How would you like to go to India, lad?'

'I should like it very much, sir,' she says truthfully. Sailing to India — it's the stuff of dreams. With Jack at her side, maybe she could, she thinks. Together with him she could go anywhere.

Perhaps Captain Hamer hears the longing in her voice. He says, 'Well. You do look keen. That's that, then. I shall take you on as a ship's boy for the duration of our next cruise. Prove yourself worthy and you may make an able seaman yet.' He rubs his chin, eyes on her. 'Perhaps in time I could persuade a friend to admit you to his midshipmen's birth. Mine's overfull, but I feel I must do something for the son of a fellow officer who fell at Trafalgar. Hm. We shall see. For the moment, you'll have a hammock, three meals a day and your daily portion of grog. You can send your pay home to your mother.'

Turning to Midshipman Withers, he says, 'Take him to the mizzen topmen, Withers, he'll berth with them. Are you hungry now, lad?'

'Very, sir.'

'You'll have your supper soon, when the watch changes.'

Captain Hamer takes his quill and writes something on the sheet of paper in front of him. Motioning with the quill, his eyes on the sheet, he says, 'Now off with you. You've made a puddle on my carpet.'

She lingers by the door, awash in emotion. Here's the man who has condemned Jack to death without a trial, yet he is offering her three meals a day, a hammock to sleep in, the possibility of advancement. No . . . not her; he's offering these things to a poor boy who lost his father, a boy who's hungry, who needs help supporting his widowed mother.

She opens her mouth to say something, but she worries the conflict between the hatred still balled in her chest and the cloak of warmth around it will spill out, so when the captain says a little irritably, 'Off with you, I said!' she only says, 'Thank you, sir,' and goes.

Midshipman Withers takes her onto the gundeck, where he introduces her to the mizzen topmen not currently on watch. There are six of them squashed together in the space between the stored hammocks and the guns. The hatches of the gunports are open. In the light falling through them, the men regard her warily until Withers mentions her father served with Lord Nelson at Trafalgar and the atmosphere somersaults. They vow they'll teach her the trade as her father would surely have wanted. She may be a ship's boy now, but she can be a topman like them in a year if she works hard.

'You're not afraid of heights, are you?' says a man with the same kind of inked drawings on his arms as Dick Pascoe.

They ask her what ship her father was on. 'The *Neptune*,' she whispers, looking down at her feet. 'You should get a pair of shoes made,' says the inked man. 'Terry Burks, the gunner's mate, makes a great pair if you're willing to pay for it.'

A bright-haired man called Red Will who's whittling a piece of wood into a mermaid says he has a cousin who was at Trafalgar. Soon, he's regaling the berth with stories.

'Captain Hamer is a good one,' Red Will concludes, after a

lengthy epos about the Battle of Copenhagen. 'He's a proper fighting captain, always after a prize. The only reason he hasn't hoisted his blue yet is because they don't know him well enough at the Admiralty.'

'He'd rather go after a Frenchie twice the size of our ship than toast King and Country at some ball in London,' says the man with the inked drawings. 'I ask you, which does more for winning the war?'

Red Will says, 'This business with the smugglers may tip the balance. The Revenue Service has lost control of the situation. If our captain puts a stop to it, the Admiralty will reward him, I tell you.'

'That'll be good for all of us,' says a man with a plait as long as Isabel's was before Harriet cut it. 'Though if he gets a first rate, we'll be on blockade.'

'And if peace breaks out, God forbid, we'll be cutting bricks ashore,' says the inked man.

'Let's hope for neither,' Red Will grunts above his wooden mermaid.

Isabel only half listens to their conversation. She must find a way to slip away. But how? Her hands play with Richard's cap as she thinks, but then the man with the long plait says, 'Tell us more about your father at Trafalgar,' and she looks up to find all of them gazing at her. Quietly, she says she prefers not to speak of him.

The man says, 'Aww, come, give us a tale,' but Red Will shoves him, saying, 'Leave the mouse alone, Paddy. It's no good losing one's da.'

They call her 'mouse' after that, because she's quiet as one. She's glad, for it allows her to think instead of talk. She needs to find Jack. He'll be locked up in the ship's prison, the brig, she thinks – wherever that is. Somewhere on the lower deck or in the hold, maybe.

Slowly, her clothes dry. *Jack's clothes,* she thinks. She's beginning to feel as if they are hers. The men's voices murmur around her; the sea sighs below the gunports. Perhaps when these men go on watch, she'll be able to get away. But what if they notice? If they sound the alarm; if they start searching for her, she'll lose her one chance to save Jack. Her heart, mind and everything in her strains for him.

Suddenly, the *Hornet* shudders. A grinding noise reverberates through the hull. On the top deck, men's voices sound. They're singing. It's impossible to make out the words, but there's a rhythm to it, underscored by a clanging, as if a thousand hammers are banging into the ship.

'That's them turning the capstan and raising the anchor. Means we're off,' says Red Will. 'We're only going up the river, but it's your first sailing, Mouse. Wouldn't you rather be on deck?'

'Could I?' she says, fighting down a shiver at the thought that they're sailing to the place of Jack's execution. This is good, she tells herself. This may be her chance.

'Want me to show you the way up?' Red Will says, looking up from his mermaid. The knife catches the light and reflects it in his face, brightening his ruddy complexion.

'I can find it,' she says. 'But thank you.'

She slips away, taking her new name, Mouse, and making it her own: she must be quiet, small, unseen, like a mouse, like a ghost. This is a ghost ship and she's a ghost moving through it to find her ghostly lover. Her entire plan depends on her finding where Jack is being held prisoner without being discovered. Jack's life depends on it. And possibly her own.

She steals down the length of the lower deck, then climbs to the deck below, past the surgeon's room and sickbay, into the main hold. The smell of wood and sea mixes with the stink of bilge water. The light is so dim she has to wait for her eyes to adjust. The hold is empty but for a loud creaking running from front to aft. Most of the hands are on deck as the ship sails down the river. The only man she encounters coming out of one of the storerooms ignores her. She keeps her head down, her shoulders slumped.

Long minutes pass, ten of them, twenty, maybe more. She has lost all sense of time. It's awfully dark down in the hold; dark and hollow, the way she felt when Tom Holder told her they were going to hang Jack. They won't hang him now. She only has to find him. She's so close.

She presses on, taking care not to step in the bilge water pushing up from below the ship's hull. The smell of it settles in her throat; she can taste it. She wants to call, *Jack, where are you?* She imagines him answering, guiding her as he did when he taught her navigation on the *Rapide* and he positioned her hands as she worked the sextant.

Two more doors open onto storerooms. They're filled

with bags of grain and kegs of something. She moves on past them. She's taking too long. Perhaps she should call out. She's about to do so when she hears a sound further down in the bow of the ship. Voices. Low ones, talking quietly, but the great cavern of the hold carries them over the creaking noise and quiet as a mouse, she approaches the door.

She cannot hear what the voices are saying. She wants to rush at the door and wrench it open, but she doesn't know who's behind it, nor if anybody is guarding what looks like another storeroom. Stomach roiling with nerves, she crouches in the dark behind a massive coil of rope. She watches the door and the hold around it until she is certain: nobody guards the room. There's no one to stop her.

She takes the three steps that separate her from the door so quickly she stumbles over a length of rope. A loud thud: her shoulder aches where it has slammed into the wood. The door doesn't give way. She holds her breath. Every sound down here carries, but nobody comes. Behind the door, the voices have gone silent. Then someone says loudly, 'Give us our dinner, will you, Morley!'

There's an iron ring for a doorhandle. She turns it and she can hear the latch within lift, but the door remains shut. She digs in her shoulder, pushes.

The voices behind the door are silent. They're waiting. There's a crack in the wood as wide as her finger. She puts her eye to it, but the room is so dark she cannot see anything. She puts her mouth to the crack, calling softly, 'Jack?'

There's a shuffling and a groan in a man's voice – another

man, she thinks, not Jack. She calls again, louder, 'Jack?' and now someone is coming to the other side of the door and the hold of the ship starts to spin. She's dizzy with hope and yearning and then his voice is there, less than an inch away, behind the wooden planks of the door: 'Isabel?'

She thought she would never see him again. She thought he would die. She's crying and laughing at the same time, she's soaring – her heart is soaring. It's like swimming, like an effortless floating, the ocean holding her up. 'Jack, it's me,' she says, and he's laughing too, saying, 'I'm dreaming, aren't I? Isabel.' Her name is like a sigh. 'How? How have you managed it?'

Soaring, falling. 'Jack, the things they said about me – about me and the sailor, they aren't true.'

'Did you think I cared about that? All of London could've bedded you and I'd still desire you.'

Legs weak with relief, she leans against the door. 'I've come to get you out,' she says and with those words, the reality of the situation dawns on her again. Jack is here, but she has yet to get him out. Grabbing the doorhandle with both hands she twists and twists, the iron digging into her fingers. Jack says, 'Isabel, listen. It's locked. You won't be able to open it. And there's a guard. He's gone to get our supper, but he'll be back any moment. You must leave at once.'

'What? No! I've come to get you out.'

'If he finds you here; if they learn you were there when I killed Sowerby and that you were on the ship when we carried contraband, they'll put you on trial too. If they hurt you or worse … I couldn't forgive myself. Listen to me, please. I don't know how you did it, coming here, but you must go, Isabel.'

'Don't be absurd. How many of you are in there?'

'Eight besides me, but—'

'Jack! I haven't come all this way to—'

'Listen to me,' Jack cuts in. He speaks quickly. 'We haven't got time. I love you. Do you hear me? I love you; I love you. I should have put it in the note, but it's better to tell you now. It's a miracle you're here and I got to tell you. It makes me trust God exists. I'm ready now, or as ready as a man will ever be, I reckon.'

'Stop, please! I beg you.'

Ignoring her plea, he continues, 'I wish it wasn't like this. It's going to hurt you. I never meant for you to have to go through that again. I'm sorry, Isabel. I just need you to know I love you. I'll love you to the very end. I'm so grateful I got to tell you, but now you *must* go.' A pause; she cannot speak. He says, urgently, 'Promise me you'll go.'

'Stop it! Stop saying those things.' The words burst out of her. 'I'll get the key. Jack, I'm not going … I won't leave you here.' She's weeping again. She swears and this makes him laugh softly against the door.

'Such language. I suppose you learned that on the *Rapide*,' he says. 'Go. I'm prepared now. I only needed to tell you; it was the one thing keeping me. You will be all right.'

'I won't be. Not without you.'

'You're stronger than you think, Bucca's daughter.'

The uselessness of her tears makes her swear again. Her mind rushes on. Then she feels the meat knife between her hip and the door and just like that the plan is there, fully formed in her head. She got confused seeing the prison unguarded, that's all. She always knew it may not be as easy as simply finding the brig. Of course the door would be locked. It's a prison, isn't it, or a storeroom made into a prison – of course there'd be a guard.

Harriet was right to tell her to take a weapon. She'll hide behind the coil of rope and use the knife to force the guard to open the door. Or she'll hurt him and take his keys, if she must. She hopes she can. It's a hard, dark hope.

Words tumbling over each other, she says, 'Jack, I've got a plan. I wasn't thinking – there wasn't anybody here, but I've got a plan. I'll go, but I won't be far. I'll get you out. Trust me. You only have to—'

A sound behind her, something between a clang and a thud.

'Isabel!' Jack cries and then she slams into the door a second time, this time with her right temple. Her head throbs as she turns to face a pistol.

CHAPTER NINETEEN

The man holding the pistol looks like he eats hobnails for breakfast. Only an inch or so taller than her, his muscled arms look ready to tear through the rough-spun linen of his shirt, his roped neck through the tightly laced collar. The man's beard is as red as that of Red Will of the mizzen topmen and despite the lack of light his bald head shines with perspiration. By his feet stands a large, iron pot. The sharp smell of cabbage mixes with the stink of the bilge water.

She expects the man to shout at her, but his voice is unexpectedly soft when he says, 'What are you doing down here with the rats?'

She has to strain to hear him above the creaking of the ship. Her back flush with the door, she places her palms against the wood. Jack is just behind it. He stays silent, so as not to betray the connection between them. She says, 'I'm terribly sorry. I'm new, I've only just come aboard. The captain has taken me on as a ship's boy. I was trying to get up on deck and must have taken a wrong turn somewhere.' Her voice dips and lifts. It's not difficult to sound scared when she says, 'It's awfully dark down here. I'd be grateful if you could tell me how to get back up to the deck. I never meant any harm, I swear.'

The guard lets her finish, then says, 'Horse shit. I saw you talking to the prisoners. So you're the lad who swam aboard, are you? They were talking about you in the galley. If the captain has only just taken you on, he'll be glad to be rid of you when I report you. If he doesn't lock you up with the rats in the brig, that is, when he learns the reason you gave him for coming aboard is false.' He gestures with the pistol, indicating the way back to the ladder. 'This way. Let's see what the bosun has to say about your lies.'

The hold grows dimmer, the noise of the ship louder. It's filling her ears, then her head, making it difficult to think. 'Please . . .' She hates begging. She must beg. 'Please, sir, don't report me. I . . . I lost my father and I have nothing to eat at home and—'

'Enough of that,' says the guard. 'You should've thought of that before you snuck down here. I saw you with my own eyes, didn't I, talking to the landlubbers in there. Did you know there's a murderer as well?' His eyes narrow. 'Were you talking to him, perhaps?'

'I wasn't, I swear. Please—'

'Enough.' Like a twig breaking, the guard's patience runs out. 'I'm taking you to the bosun.'

If they take her off the ship or lock her up, Jack is lost. She got so close. He's right there. She can almost touch him, hold him, kiss him. They're going to hang him and there's nothing she can do. Tears run down her face, into the corners of her mouth, down into her neck. There's such a noise down here, the creaking, sawing noise of the ship as it cuts through the water. She can't think. 'Please,' she says again and now she's no longer trying to make her voice sound lower or act the part of the fifteen-year-old boy, it's just her, Isabel, begging. 'Please, I beg you.' The guard is looking at her intently. 'Please,' she says. 'I shall tell you the truth.'

'You had better, right this minute.'

'I'm not truly a ship's boy. I'm a girl. A … a woman.' Her sobs make the last word bounce up and down, *wo-man*.

The man lowers the pistol as he takes a step closer, peering at her in the dim light. A red flush creeps up his jaw from his neck; the sweat begins to make a trail down his sharp, boned cheeks. 'By God, you are! How the devil did I miss it? It's obvious as day to me now. What in God's name do you think you're doing, coming aboard dressed like that? Did you honestly mean to sail with us?'

She presses ahead. 'I've come aboard to … to see my brother. He was impressed into the service. He's all I have in the world, sir, and he … he may be going away for a whole year. I only wished to sail with him. Please, I beg you, do not report me. I only wish to be with my brother.' She lifts her hand, runs it across her face. 'I can do the work, sir, I promise you, I'll work harder than any of the boys.'

The guard laughs. He shoves the pistol back in his belt. She forces herself not to look at it as he says, 'Who's your brother, then?'

'Will. Will Pengelly.'

'Aye, he's in there. And you're Will Pengelly's sister, are you?'

'Yes. My name is Isabel Pengelly.' She keeps her voice steady, but only just.

'Well, Isabel Pengelly, you make a nice case for yourself. I suppose I could let you both slip away in the dead of night, but it'd be on my head if we lost a newly impressed man. Nor can you stay. Where would you sleep, for one, with the men not half an inch apart in their hammocks? Not to mention, a woman on board brings ill luck. Last thing we need, that is.'

'Please, sir. I beg you—'

'Stop with the begging, will you? I've got no choice but to report you. You'll be taken off the ship, there's no question of that. However, because I have a sister myself and care for her like you care for your brother, I shall let you have a moment to say goodbye to him. If he was impressed, he must've been taken all of a sudden.'

'Yes, sir, it was terribly sudden. I didn't know he had gone until the next day.'

'Look, do not fret for your brother. It's not as bad a life as that. You'll see him again and he'll send his pay to you, I'm sure, so you won't go hungry.' He bangs his fist against the door and calls, 'Will Pengelly there! Do you promise to send your sister your pay for her keep?'

A few seconds pass, then Will's voice rings out loud and clear: 'I will, sir. Pray, is that my sister there? But how can it be?'

'So it appears. What's your sister's name, Will Pengelly?'

A desperate, quiet moment, then: 'Why, it must be Isabel. I have no other sister.'

The guard grins. 'So it is. You'd better appreciate what she's put herself through to come see you, lad.' To Isabel, he says, 'We're about to anchor in the river outside some little cove. I'll give you five minutes with your brother, then I'm taking you to the bosun. He's sending a party ashore shortly, so you won't have to swim again.' Guffawing, he adds, 'It's a good thing they'll see you for themselves! They wouldn't believe it if I told them. And the captain fell for it, did he?'

So did you until I told you, she thinks, but she says, 'Thank you for allowing me to see my brother, sir. I'm ever so grateful.'

'Step aside, Will's sister, so that I may open the door.' Half-turning his back on her, he reaches under his shirt and lifts a key on a leather string. There's a click as he pushes it into the lock. Isabel slides her hand into her pocket, inch by inch, until she can wrap her fingers around the hilt of the meat knife.

The guard pushes the door open a crack, his hand on the pistol in his belt. He calls, 'Will Pengelly there! Step outside to see your sister, though you may not recognise her the way she's dressed.' He laughs again, then adds more soberly,

'You've got five minutes. The rest of you, if there's any trouble, I'll see you all flogged at the grating, you hear me?'

Her heart pounds in her head. The ship groans as it rolls and the door swings open outward with the motion. Stepping back to avoid the door, the guard clasps the hilt of his pistol when instead of Will, Jack emerges from the room. His hair is matted and several days' worth of stubble graces his jaw, but his eyes are sharp as they light on her for the smallest of moments.

The guard begins to say, 'You're not—' and then Jack lunges at him, throwing his full weight into the man. The guard staggers back as Jack's fist slams into the side of his face. The other eight men come spilling from the brig and in the confusion, Isabel watches the guard yank the pistol from his belt; watches his finger wrap around the trigger and the muzzle lift until it's pointing directly at Jack's chest, not ten inches between them. It's as if she's back on the doorstep of Roskorwell, watching Lieutenant Sowerby prepare to shoot. With a ragged cry she pulls the meat knife from her pocket and throws herself at the guard.

There's a dreadful resistance as she pushes all her strength in the blade, then a grunt, followed by a silence so loud all other sounds flee before it.

She's staring down at the blood on her hands. The knife is bloody too. Even in the dim light of the ship's hold it gleams darkly and there's blood on the sleeves of Jack's shirt, which she's wearing, and also on the shirt Jack is wearing. It spurted and there's a spray of drops. The guard is folding into himself like a puppet without stuffing, his hands gripping his stomach, an awful moaning coming from his mouth. His shirt is the bloodiest of all.

'No,' she says, but there's no sound, there's only the silence in her ears, loud as thunder. 'No. No, I didn't mean to,' she says. 'I didn't … I didn't … I …'

'Isabel.' Jack's voice snaps through the noise. 'We've got to go.'

'I … I didn't mean to.' She's staring at the knife. Her hands remember the feeling of it, of the resistance of shirt, flesh and sinew as she pressed it into the man's skin. There was something hard – a rib, maybe. The blade didn't go in as far as she thought it would. She didn't mean for it to go in at all.

Jack's hands fold arounds hers. 'I know you didn't. He'll be all right. It's his side, just like when I got shot, remember? It's the same spot. It hurts like a—' He swallows the word and says, 'Like hell, but the surgeon will be able to help him. We've got to go. Come.'

'He's right, Mrs Henley. We must go.' Dick Pascoe, the inked Sea Bucca on his arm shifting as he tries to steer her away, but she's stuck. Her feet have grown roots reaching deep into the ship. The knife trembles in her hands, both hands clasped together, black with blood, Jack's hands folded around them. The guard is on the floor. He's making puffing noises, as if he's stepped into winter and the cold is taking his breath away.

'Here, give me the knife.' Jack uncurls her hands and takes it from her. Horribly, he wipes it on his breeches before turning to the others. 'I say we go aft. If we're quick, we may be able to slip into the water before anyone realises what's happened.'

One of the men says, 'I can't swim.'

'Then you're out of luck, I'm afraid,' Jack says. 'Follow me or make your own way. It's the same to me.' He turns back to her and, still holding the knife, says with sudden, vehement feeling, 'I shall spend the rest of my life trying to prove deserving of your love.'

The way he's looking at her drives the darkness back, but then she glances at the guard again. He's still puffing, his face grey and sweaty as he lies, doubled over, on the wooden planks.

'Will, you take this,' Jack says, handing Will the knife. Jack kneels by the side of the guard and draws up the man's shirt. The guard looks as if he is going to lose consciousness any moment. Jack unties his neckerchief and, balling it up tight, presses it against the guard's stomach. He takes the pistol from the man's right hand and puts the hand over the wad of cloth. 'Hold this, Morley. Press on it as hard as you can. The surgeon will be down soon.'

'Carlyon, you bastard,' the guard splutters, closing his eyes. 'I hope you rot in hell.'

'Just keep the pressure on it.' Jack pushes the pistol into the top of his breeches. Getting back to his feet, he says, 'Come, Isabel.'

Will puts his hand on her shoulder, looking five years older than he did when they sailed to France together, saying,

'Mrs Henley. Forgive me for saying so – you may not wish to hear it presently, but you did the right thing.'

How can it be right? she thinks, but when Jack says, again, 'Come,' and tugs on her hand, her feet loosen at last, as if Will has cut the chains holding them to the deck. She trips after Jack, Will and two of the other men, Dick Pascoe and the rest following behind.

Her hands are slippery with the guard's blood. She has to wipe them on her breeches or she'll lose her grip on the ladder as they climb to the lower deck. Nausea rises inside her as she wipes first one hand and then the other, but then she looks at Jack, at his back as he climbs the ladder in front of her and she thinks, *he's here.*

She didn't mean to do it, that with the guard. She never meant to hurt the man, but he threatened to shoot Jack. And if he hadn't, they would have hanged him. She thought she had lost him, but he's here, he's alive, and the nausea drops away and she regrets what she did – she will always regret it – but she would not undo it even if she could.

They have a long way to go yet. In her mind, she goes through the steps: the lower deck, then the upper deck, the long plunge down into the water, the swim back to shore and the horse, Rosie-May, waiting in Tom Holder's stable. The ride to Nelly's Cove, the setting sail on the *Rapide.* Any of these steps, they may be discovered. Any step may be their last.

Jack has reached the lower deck and crouches by the edge of the hatch, eyes blinking against the light and holding out his hand to her. She takes it and as he helps her through, she says, 'I love you. I need you to know it, too.'

He smiles at her the way he did when they first met, nearly three months and several lifetimes ago, and says, 'I do know it. But tell it me again when I can respond as I should like.'

'How is that?' she says and he grins, unexpectedly and wonderfully and, pulling her close, he says, 'I think you know.'

He kisses her hard and far too briefly. He smells the same as when she last saw him, of the sea and faintly of sweat, but there's something else this time – the smell of the hold of a ship. His stubble scrapes her chin. Then he releases her and, looking at Dick, says, 'Everyone here? Let's go.'

She follows Jack along the deck, as do Will, Dick and the six other impressed men. They take to Jack's leadership naturally, she thinks; they don't question it, they simply follow him. He would've made a good officer like her father and George if things had been different.

The air has grown close; the frigate feels smaller, as if the wooden hull is trying to squeeze them through. The lower deck is crowded with men. The ten of them pass by, keeping their heads down as Isabel did before. Ghosts among ghosts. No one pays them any mind. Up on deck, the ship's bell rings four times, a resonant *ting-ting* she remembers from visiting her father's ship. The sound causes a commotion, with men running up the ladders while thunderous feet sound above.

'That's four bells in the first dog watch,' Jack says quietly.

'Change of watch and supper time for the men coming below. We're in luck; we couldn't have timed it better.' He takes the guard's pistol from his breeches and holds it close to his chest as they trail the crew to the nearest ladder. Will does the same with the meat knife from the cottage. With one hand Jack motions for the group to follow him to the top deck. When they reach it, a bosun's mate in a blue frock coat screams in their faces: 'To your stations! Make haste there you bunch of filthy landlubbers or the bosun will have your hide!' A drop of the man's spittle lands on Isabel's left cheek. She fights the urge to wipe it away.

'Aye, sir,' Dick Pascoe says as they move past the man, going along the gangway at a trot as if hurrying to their stations. The sun still rides high in a sky flocked with clouds, the sea is a brilliant blue canvas, almost turquoise, stretching from the bow of the ship to the shoreline. The shore is all towering cliffs apart from a cove just visible around the bend in the river. It's not the shallow cove from which she watched the ship before, but a deeper one. They're perhaps a third of a mile away from it. Bosahan cove, she thinks, or some other place along the coastal path she'd recognise if she were looking down at it rather than from across the river.

They're nearly in the stern of the ship when a voice calls, 'There you are, Mouse! We've been looking for you!'

Red Will is beckoning from the mizzen mast. 'Over here!'

She slows a fraction, but Jack grabs her hand again and pulls her along.

'Ho there, Mouse!' Another of the mizzen topmen shouts

and then a third voice calls: 'Halt! You there, halt!' A bosun's mate blocks their path, looking gritty and ready to strike.

'Run!' Jack shouts. Veering to the left, he yanks her along the deck, going straight for the gunwale. They're steps away from the side of the ship. Everybody is running, Jack and her, Dick Pascoe and Will Pengelly, the six other men who were imprisoned with them, the bosun's mate who stopped them and at least ten other members of the ship's company. Some of the topmen who had already gone up to their stations are coming down again.

'Stop them! They're prisoners!' cries somebody – an officer, she thinks, but she's not sure, everything is a blur of shirts and uniforms, and, sticking up above the throng, a sword and two cutlasses, their blades catching the glint of the sun.

Two of the impressed men plunge over the side of the ship. A third, the man who said he couldn't swim, hangs back. The deck is a writhing mass of officers and seamen trying to get to the gunwale. A shot rings out, followed by a cry. Was it hers or someone else's? Jack is pulling on her arm and her feet are stumbling on the tilting deck and there's the gunwale and the safety of the waiting sea, just four steps away, three . . .

A hand claps onto her shoulder and drags her back. Her fingers slip from Jack's. There's ice at her throat. The bosun's mate who tried to stop them keeps her in place, one arm digging into her waist, the other holding the flat of his cutlass against the soft skin of her neck. The man smells of his ration of grog. 'Halt!' he shouts. 'Or I'll run the boy through!'

In the sudden hush, several men grabble for Jack, but he throws himself onto the deck and rolls out of their reach. Getting back to his feet, he says, 'I'm the one you want. You don't need the boy.'

'No!' she cries, but the bosun's mate snarls, 'Quiet!'

Jack steps closer, until he's less than a yard away. His arms hang loosely by his side, the pistol in his right hand points at the deck. From the corner of her eyes, she watches another of the impressed men clamber onto the gunwale. The splash when he hits the water breaks the silence. Several of the crew rush to the side of the ship. A lieutenant and two midshipmen come hurrying down from the quarterdeck. 'What's going on here, Hancox?' the lieutenant calls from some distance.

'These prisoners were trying to escape, sir!' The bosun's mate calls back. He puts more pressure on the blade against Isabel's throat and she can't get at the air, it's right there, but it won't go down.

Without thinking she grabs the cutlass with both hands and wrests it from her throat as she sucks at the air. The sharp of the blade cuts her palms; the sting snatches her breath away again. The bosun's mate pushes the steel into her skin once more. Then a shot rings out and the cutlass slips away. She doubles over and retches. Behind her, the bosun's mate slides down to the deck, his left hand grasping his right shoulder, blood trickling through his fingers.

Unable to reload, Jack throws the pistol onto the deck and picks up the dropped cutlass. 'Come on!' he shouts and she's back on her feet again, her hands dripping blood as she runs, but this time it's Jack who abruptly stops. 'Will!' he shouts.

She whips around. Jack is already halfway across the deck, rushing to Will's aid as he tries to defend himself with the meat knife against an opponent twice his size, who wields a cutlass like it's a sewing needle. Will is bleeding from his right leg and dancing to keep from getting cut again when Jack engages his opponent with the bosun's mate's cutlass. 'Go!' he calls to Will. 'Take Isabel!'

But when Will grabs her bleeding hand and tries to pull her over the side of the ship, she shakes him off, wincing at the pain. 'Not without Jack!'

She barely hears the lowering of the anchor. All of her is focussed on Jack, whose opponent counters every blow. The pair's movements are so quick and light it's like watching the wind play with a leaf. She isn't sure which of them is the wind and which the leaf; they're too well matched. Stiff with nerves, she watches, taking in the concentration on Jack's face while the man with the cutlass grins as if he's enjoying himself.

The men on deck watch with her. No one tries to help either party as they fight just steps from the side of the ship. A sound makes her look away: more officers run down the steps from the quarterdeck, Captain Hamer himself in front.

'Jack, they're coming! We must go!' she calls. Jack looks at her, then in the direction she's pointing. The man with the cutlass strikes and this time, Jack doesn't counter the blow. Flinging his arms out, he staggers back. The tip of the weapon only just misses him.

She gasps, weak with relief, but then he trips over the leg of a man standing behind him. The cutlass hits the deck as his hands search for something to grab onto and then he's falling. She watches as if it's not really happening, as if it's not really Jack who hits his head on the gunwale and drops over the side of the ship like a rock. There's a ringing in her ears, a creaking mixed with a high-pitched noise and she realises it's her, she's screaming, her mouth wide. It lasts perhaps three seconds and then she's flying.

CHAPTER TWENTY

She doesn't know how it happens, whether she jumps or runs or shoves people out of the way or all of these things at once. She only knows she's suddenly at the gunwale herself and then she's going over it, face forward, arms out.

The plunge blinds her. The world is made white, foam and bubbles. Her hands sting where she cut her palms. When the water clears, so does her head. She turns towards the bottom and kicks her legs. Below her is a shape, blurred by the sea and partly shielded from view by the hull of the ship.

She's flying again – only now it's underwater flying. She swims as if her legs have grown fins, as if her throat has gills and she breathes water like air. The river here isn't very deep; the draught of the ship is only some thirteen feet and the bottom is not far below it. She reaches it in less than a minute, but the lowering of the anchor has stirred up the river bed and there's a cloud of sand in the water.

She can no longer see him in the murk. Has he gone under the ship? A flare of panic threatens to numb her, but she kicks harder, shoving it away. Gills and fins, deep, slow water-breathing. She gropes blindly under the hull, feeling her way along the river bed. Rocks, seaweed, plants, a creature, large and slithery. Her fingers brush something soft. Cloth, she thinks, and the water is clearing now, the sand settling on the bottom. Jack's eyes are closed, his face relaxed as if in sleep. His hair forms a halo around his head.

She moves behind him, wrapping her arms around his chest. He's heavy, even under water. Tugging at him, pushing with her knees on the gravelly bed of the sea-river, she manages to haul him into a sitting position. He's so heavy. How is she ever going to carry him back to the surface? Panic creeps up on her again, but the river wafts around her like a cloud, like air, and then she's off, feet kicking hard against the bottom. Or maybe they're not feet, maybe her tail swishes against the riverbed and it's a different kind of kicking – a pushing of fins. The voice of the sea calls, in the swirl of the current: *Come home. Swim.*

She swims, holding Jack. He's dead weight in her arms. The water helps hold him up, like a thousand icy hands. Breaking the surface, she rolls him onto his back. She's gasping, believing, for the most fleeting of seconds, she needs water, not air, to breathe. Then air fills her lungs and she looks at Jack as she swims.

She cannot be sure he's still alive. He must be alive. She cannot contemplate the other. The ship is just above her.

Faces look down from the side. She can't see them clearly; she only sees Jack, the blood running from the side of his head where he hit the wood of the gunwale, into his hair and down the side of his face. It's running awfully fast – because of the water, she tells herself. She thinks he's still breathing, but she cannot be sure.

Her vision clears a little. One of the men on the ship is aiming a pistol at them, but he doesn't shoot. It'd be difficult to aim well from up there, with her in the water. It's quite a distance. She remembers George telling her how difficult it is to aim correctly unless you're right up close to the target. It's why the midshipmen still carry dirks, he said.

It'd be easier to aim with a musket, she thinks. The marines use muskets in battle, but they wouldn't be carrying them while the ship is anchored. The French use muskets, too – George was killed by one. Maybe she's French. Maybe she was on that ship, the one that was wrecked. It doesn't matter now. All that matters is that she gets Jack to safety.

On the frigate, they're lowering one of the boats. Looking over her shoulder, the shore is coming closer. A man stands on the strip of beach in the cove waving his arms. It's Dick Pascoe. He's getting back into the water, wading towards her. She swims faster. With about a third of the distance left, Jack suddenly coughs and, spluttering, opens his eyes.

'Isabel.' His voice is hoarse. How she loves hearing it – the wonder in it, the strength. She wants to weep, but she can't. She needs to keep swimming.

He turns in her arms and for maybe ten seconds they float

together, treading water. Then there's a splash and Jack says, 'They're coming,' and, looking past him, she sees the boat in the water and the men pulling the oars.

He wipes the blood from the side of his head and they swim, keeping pace together. Dick returns to the beach. When they reach the point they can stand, they wade to the shore. Dick grabs hold of Isabel's arm and it's only then that she realises she's stumbling with weariness. In her mind is still the voice she heard in the water. *Swim. Come home.* The water calls to her, blue-soft and cool. The sun dazzles. *Come home . . .*

Dick snaps her out of it. 'Where's Will?' he says.

'I last saw him on deck.' She wipes water, strands of hair, the tug of the sea from her eyes.

'I've got her,' Jack says, wrapping his arms around Isabel. It's not cold, but she shivers.

Dick says in a rush, 'All the others got off, apart from Kimbrel. Couldn't swim, the poor bugger. And Will.'

'Damn,' says Jack, shielding his eyes as he looks at the frigate. 'They'll have got him now if he didn't get off. Thank God they're not aware he's a smuggler.'

'He tried to escape,' she says. 'He was hurt.'

'They've got a surgeon on board. Hopefully they won't punish him for trying to escape – it's what every impressed hand would do and they sorely need men. There's nothing we can do now, in any case; he'll be back in the brig until the ship sails. Come. That boat will be here any minute.' As they hurry up the beach, he looks back at her and calls, 'Are you all in one piece?'

She calls back that she is, closing her hands into fists, trying not to wince. It's difficult to climb back up to the path with the cuts in her hands and in her bare feet. Jack asks if she'll manage without shoes and she nods.

'Where to, Captain?' Dick asks when they reach the top of the cliff.

Before Jack has the chance to answer, she says, 'Harry Tremayne has the *Rapide* ready to sail from Nelly's cove.'

Dick stares at her as if she has just told him Harry Tremayne is ready to take them to the moon.

'Do you mean it?' Jack says.

'Harry said he'd have her ready tonight. There's a horse waiting for us at the Shipwrights Arms. Only one, though.' She looks back at the *Hornet*. The boat that's after them is halfway between the ship and the cove.

Jack folds his arms around her, kissing her wet hair. 'You're a marvel.' Another kiss, then, 'I think we should forego the horse. It won't be able to carry three and we'd be forced to take the road. Let's go through the wood, instead.' He's speaking quickly. The boat is pulling closer. 'What do you think, Isabel?'

The wood receives them as the water did before, sucking them into a sea of green. They crash through the undergrowth. Isabel keeps her hands close to her sides, the cuts in her palms burning, her breath heaving. She wishes she had time to loosen her stays. Twice, she stumbles as a pebble presses into the sole of her foot. Jack keeps looking back at her, as if he cannot believe she's there.

Her hands ache and her muscles scream and her mind keeps turning back to the guard, crumpled in the hold and the knife gleaming red in her hands and the image is making her cold despite the warmth of the summer evening and yet – *and yet*. She doesn't remember having been happier. In spite of it all. Even the first night with George, after their long, blustery wedding day in October, she didn't feel this. Even the day he came back from a year at sea. Not even the last night she spent with Jack in the hammock aboard the *Rapide* did she feel anything approximating the desperate joy coursing through her.

The spaces between the trees grow blue, then grey, then dark as they go, their trunks black silhouettes against the incoming night. They never see their pursuers. Once, they hear voices behind them, but they're distant, like an echo of words spoken long ago.

After two exhausting hours they burst from the wood. Bone-weary, they cross the field to Nelly's cove more slowly, the half-moon lighting their way. As they close in on the edge of the cliff, she sees the ship: a shadow against the sea, sails like old blood furled on the masts; the wooden hull dulled to a deep, ash grey. The moment the three of them appear at the top of the cliff, a rowboat launches from the *Rapide* and thirty minutes later, they clamber onto the deck and there's Harry, embracing each of them in turn, saying, 'Captain, we thought you lost,' and, 'Mrs Henley, it's an honour to sail with you again.'

'Isabel,' she says, smiling. 'It's Isabel, Harry.'

Jack says, 'Will didn't get off the ship. Do we have enough crew to sail?'

'There's eight of us, including the three of you, Captain.'

'Good.' Raising his voice, Jack calls, 'Stations for making sail! Lay aloft sail loosers!', followed by, 'Lay out and let loose!'

'Raise the anchor!' Harry calls in the wake of Jack's commands.

Jack says, 'Is every man aware we sail without papers? They're willing, regardless?'

Harry grins. 'They would be for you, Captain, but there's no need.'

'My papers were revoked. I have none, now.'

Harry exchanges a glance with Isabel. 'I beg to differ, Captain. There's a neat little set of them waiting on your desk.'

Jack has been watching the sails come down, now he looks at Harry. 'How do you mean?'

'Have a look, Captain. I think they'll suit our purpose.'

A shiver runs through the ship as the sails catch the wind. Isabel follows Jack into the cabin. A set of documents sits on top of the desk tied with a yellow silk ribbon and kept in place by the weight of the inkwell. Next to it is a parcel wrapped in cream muslin.

'But this is extraordinary,' says Jack, inspecting the papers by the light of the lantern.

'Is everything in order?' she asks softly, taking care not to get any of the crusted blood from her hands on the parcel.

'How did you get these?'

'Harriet,' she says.

Jack laughs. 'Lady Darby got these for us? With Sir Hugh's seal?'

'She helped me cut my hair, too.' She opens the muslin wrapper. Folded up inside is Mrs Dowling's wedding shawl with a note on top. In flourishes and curls, it reads, 'Dear Isabel, I expect you may have need of this. I wish you both every happiness. That you may always live outside your walled garden. With love from your friend, H.A.

P.S. I found this letter when I folded your dress. As it is unopened, I thought I'd best include it.'

She places the muslin cloth holding the shawl on Jack's desk, careful not to touch the wool, and lifts the note. Underneath is a small envelope, the paper creamy and textured, stamped *Roscoff*. She breaks the wax seal and withdraws the letter. Jack is still examining the ship's licence. She turns away from him and, by the light of the moon falling in through the skylight, reads:

My dear Mrs Henley,

As promised, I write to you regarding your possible family, la famille Du Pont. While I have yet to gain intelligence about any living relatives or the family's estate, I have come across the most curious of stories. Numerous people have told it to me; there are some variations in their telling, but in the main it is this:

Long ago, in the time of Tristan and Iseult, it is said there was a woman who formed a union with a merman. A child sprang from this union and was called Du Pont, for she formed a bridge between our world and that of merfolk. According to the tale, the child's descendants possess the ability to transform into merfolk at will or in times of great need — the stories vary on this point — but if they keep to their aquatic form too long, they find themselves unable to change back. One member of the family, a Jean-Jacques Du Pont, who lived until 1712, is buried in the cathedral of Saint-Pol-de-Léon. I have visited Monsieur Du Pont's grave and found an image of a merman carved in the stone.

I hope you won't think me fanciful in relating this tale to you. It is but a story and in this age of reason appears unlikely to be true. However, as Captain Carlyon mentioned the Sea Bucca in connection to your appearance in Cornwall, I felt it too great a coincidence to ignore.

I hope you will visit Roscoff again soon. I shall be glad to show you the cathedral if you like.

With warmest regards,
your friend, Lucie Cuvelier

She lowers the letter, the phrase, *in times of great need*, revolving in her mind. Outside, the water of the cove laps at the hull of the ship. She has but to think of it to feel it: the sea's cool embrace, the underwater breathing, the swish of a tail. Memories drift closer until she can touch them. They're memories she did not know she possessed.

A raging sea and a fear so deep not even the voice crying out for her can mitigate it. It's a voice she knows well, crying a name she hasn't heard in years. Aurélie. Then the suck of the water, cold and dark around her. Everything is calm. The storm still rages above, but under the surface she's safe. The fear leaves her. Her dress is a sail, a veil. It blooms around her. There's a flash of scales and someone is saying, Aurélie, it is time to swim. Hands push her back up to the surface. She doesn't want to go, but they insist.

Don't leave me, she says in words made of water. The voice flows, ebbs, swirls: I must find your maman. Did her father speak the words or the sea itself? The ocean breathes deeply. It's about to spit her out, back into the place where things are hard and harsh and bright. I want to go home, she says, but the voice of the sea answers: swim, my child.

'What have you got there?' Jack, behind her, a hand on her shoulder.

She folds the letter and shoves it into the pocket of her breeches. She turns to him, smiles. 'Nothing.'

The memories hold her, but Jack is here, holding her too.

Reaching for her hand, he catches sight of the cut. 'My God, Isabel.' He takes both her hands in his and inspects the palms. 'Why didn't you tell me?'

'There wasn't time. And it's fine, the cuts aren't deep. See? The blood has already dried.'

'I wish Rowell was here to take a look at them.'

'It doesn't hurt. Not much, anyway. I could always see a doctor in France, if need be. That's where we're going, isn't it?'

'If you like. We can go anywhere. With these papers, we can pull into any port. Where would you like to go?'

'Anywhere, with you.'

He smiles and kisses her. She says, 'How is your head?'

'Fine, too.' He casts a glance at the skylight. 'I have some money left from the sale of the horses and there are the kegs of brandy we stored on the seabed when the *Swallow* gave chase, which I mean to retrieve. With that I can pay the crew, but I don't know when I'll be able to get hold of the profits from our most recent run.' He kisses her again. 'You don't mind being a bit poor for a while longer, do you? It'll be like starting over from scratch.'

'That's not so bad, is it? It's what I did when I came to Cornwall.'

He laughs. 'And look where it got you. You have a day to make up your mind as to our destination. For now we can ride the northeasterly.'

'You'd truly let me choose?' She thinks of all the places *La Pérouse* described in his book. But perhaps they should go to France before they go anywhere else, she thinks. Perhaps she'll be able to learn more about the Du Pont family and the story Lucie Cuvelier told in her letter. In time, she'll tell it to Jack, she thinks. For now, the memories are hers alone.

'You've more than earned the privilege.' Jack lifts her left hand to his mouth, not touching the cut, and lightly kisses her fingertips. 'Isabel,' he says, in the same wondering tone as when she first found him imprisoned on board the frigate.

The deck rolls under them as the ship pulls out of the cove. 'You should be on deck,' she says. 'And I should like to be, to see us get underway.'

'As long as I get to hold you,' he says.

Back on deck they stand in the stern of the ship, Jack's arms wrapped around her waist, his chin in her hair. 'Do you forgive me?' he says.

'For what happened with Lieutenant Sowerby? Yes.'

'For getting you involved in all of this. You said you didn't want any trouble.'

She smiles. 'I don't mind it so much now.'

'You called me your fiancé to Sowerby. I've been thinking about it a lot. Did you mean it?'

'I did. I should like to marry you, Jack, only let me have my freedom a little longer. Until then, may we not love each other as we are now?'

'As a man and a woman, you mean, rather than a man and his wife?'

'Yes. If you don't find that strange.'

'I don't see why not,' he says, kissing her hair. She hears the smile in his voice. 'Listen. I've told you before, but I'll make it a vow. I won't curb your freedom when we wed.'

'I know you won't.'

'Good. It's important to me that you know it, Isabel.'

She half-turns so she can kiss him, then says, 'I wish Will was with us. I hope he'll be all right.'

'Let's hope Captain Hamer's need for men is more pressing than for setting an example, so Will won't face punishment for the escape attempt. As for him being impressed into the service, it's not what anyone would want—' He stops himself and says, 'Not what most would want, I should say,' and she knows he's thinking of George, who lived for the Navy and died for it. The thought doesn't cut as much as it used to. Her hand reaches for George's Trafalgar medal, but she cannot find it. Her fingers trail along her neck. The black ribbon is missing, too. Her heart skips a beat as Jack says, 'Will's a good sailor. If he keeps his head down, he should be fine. Who knows? He may make a career of it.'

'My medal,' she says, feeling under her shirt. 'George's medal.'

'What of it?'

'It's gone. The ribbon must've broken.' She waits for the hurt, the hollow cutting, but it doesn't come. She continues to feel horribly content.

Jack says, 'I'm sorry, Isabel. I know how much it meant to you.'

'It's fine.' Strangely, it is, more or less, as if with the ribbon breaking, her mooring line has been cut.

Quietly, Jack says, 'When I was in the water, I could've sworn a mermaid came to me. I saw her. She was beautiful like you, with streaming hair and eyes like yours and the same mad little freckles you've got all over you. She had a tail of silver scales and her breath was like an ocean current. I could've sworn she brought me to the surface.'

She feels his breath against her hair. Laughter trickles from her. 'You were unconscious,' she says. 'How could you have seen her?'

'She was a vision, like you,' Jack says, kissing her again. He tightens his arms around her as if he never wants to let go. Laughing softly, he says, 'Did I ever tell you, you're the most stubborn creature I know? I can't believe you came and got me off that ship.'

'What can I say?' she says. 'I am my father's daughter.'

'The admiral?' he says and she smiles and says, 'Perhaps.'

She leans back against him, her hands clasping his arms. She doesn't feel the cuts now. The open sea is dark silver in the light of the moon; the sky is awash with stars. Behind them, Nelly's cove fades from sight, then the cliffs, then all of the land, until there is nothing left but this, a small ship on a boundless ocean, a sharp wind in the sails and his arms, holding her until the night, too, is fading. In the sound of the wind, in the rushing of the waves is a voice calling her. *Come home,* it says and she whispers back, so quietly only she can hear, *I'm coming.*

Acknowledgements

So much of *The Sea Child* is inspired by Cornish culture and the landscape, so first of all I'd like to thank the Cornish people for welcoming our family these many years.

This book would not exist without the following people, whom I cannot thank enough: My unparalleled agent Madeleine Milburn, thank you for believing in Isabel's story. Your encouragement, ideas and guidance have been invaluable.

My brilliant editors, Clare Hey at Simon & Schuster UK and Susanna Porter at Ballantine, it's an absolute joy working with you. Thank you for your inspired vision, wisdom and support. A massive thank you also to Meredith Pal at Penguin Canada.

Thank you to Genevieve Barratt, Jess Barratt, Aneesha Angris, Olivia Allen, Alice Twomey and Pip Watkins at Simon & Schuster UK and to Anusha Khan, Jennifer Hershey,

Kim Hovey, Pam Alders, Cassie Gitkin, Jessie Bright, Katie Horn and Sophie Normil at Ballantine for helping to bring *The Sea Child* into the world. And to Valentina Paulmichl, Hannah Kettles, Hannah Ladds, Meghan Capper, Casey Dexter, Georgia McVeigh, Rachel Leoh, Saskia Arthur and everyone at MMA who have helped make *The Sea Child* a reality.

Liz Fenwick and Bex Hogan, thank you for your friendship, advice and your willingness to share your love of Cornwall with me. Jane Yang, thank you for being my friend and travel companion along the road to debut publication. Writing can be a solitary endeavour, but has been made less so for me thanks to my lovely author friends both online and offline, especially Hannah Gold, Beach, Ellie Sandall and the rest of the Stamford Writers group as well as my fellow 2026 debuts Ellie Levenson and Rebecca Fallon.

Thank you also to my wonderful friends in Cambridgeshire for countless cups of coffee, pub nights, chats and laughs. To my father, who I miss so very much and who loved books as much as I do, and to my mother, thank you for inspiring a lifetime love of reading, and thank you to my brothers and their partners for being there, both for me and our parents.

And last but never least of all, thank you to my family. Brandon – Jack to my Isabel – I couldn't have done it without you. Thank you for believing in me. Best team in the world! Noortje, Emma and Sebastian, you amaze every day with your kindness, sense of humour and imagination. Your love and encouragement kept me going. Thank you. And Luna and Sophie, golden retrievers extraordinaire, thanks for hanging out with me during the writing.

Author's Note

While I enjoy swimming, I'm neither a great swimmer, nor experienced at sailing ships – though, like Isabel, I did marry a Naval officer. Regardless, the sea has always drawn me and it was this love that formed the first ingredient of *The Sea Child*. I wrote the novel in a burst of creativity following a stay in Helford on the Helford River and the Cornish landscape, culture and history, as well as Cornish folklore all inspired the writing. Taking long hikes along the coastal path and exploring the area, including the stunningly secluded Frenchman's Creek immortalized in Daphne du Maurier's novel, I felt completely in awe of the landscape: the sea, the cliffs, the coves and beaches. It's a thoroughly magical and romantic place and I could picture Isabel walking beside me, as well as Cornish smugglers from ages past unloading their contraband under cover of a new moon.

When I read about the sea spirit in Cornish folklore, the

Sea Bucca, I knew I wanted to write about the power of the sea. During that stay in Helford, I came across a book, *Cornwall and its People* by A.K. Hamilton Jenkin, originally published in the 1930s. In it, he writes:

Living as he does within sight and sound of the sea, [the Cornishman] has little in common with the townsman who glorifies it for its beauty or sentimentalizes over its treachery and untameable power. To the Cornishman rather it is a harvest-field from which it is possible to wrest a hard-earned living, sometimes a battle-field upon which he may be called to fight for his very life. In consequence of this he neither dreads nor romantically loves the sea, for he knows it for what it is.

Reading this, I knew I had met Jack, whose practicality in his approach to the sea and smuggling contrasts with Isabel's mystical connection to it and yet inadvertently emphasizes a certain romanticism as well. During my research, one of the things I discovered was that, while smuggling was prevalent in all of England in the early 1800s, in Cornwall, the smuggling trade was so widely supported that it was difficult for the Revenue Service (which later became HM Coastguard) to obtain a conviction when trying smugglers in court. The jury would almost always acquit them regardless of the evidence. This rebellious streak in Cornish culture – born oftentimes from necessity due to poverty – further inspired my writing, as did the Cornish language. I grew up in a part of the Netherlands that has its own regional language, which is at risk of dying out, and have great respect for those working to revive the Cornish language. Where Jack speaks

Cornish in the book, he would've been one of the last people to do so, as by the 1800s the language was rarely spoken. At the time, the magic of folklore formed a part of the everyday for many people. The idea that there was a sea spirit protecting sailors was quite ordinary and leaving a fish in the cove for the Sea Bucca, as Jack does, a common practice.

As the wife of US Navy officer, I've lived in five countries and relate to Isabel's experience of moving to a different place, which I wanted explore in the novel. In terms of research, A.K. Jenkins book was instrumental, as were several other works, particularly Harry Carter's *The Autobiography of a Cornish Smuggler,* which details his experiences and those of his more famous brother, John Carter of Prussia Cove on the Lizard Peninsula in the late 18th century. Much of my understanding of the goods carried on smuggling runs, the culture on board smuggling ships and the runs to Roscoff in Brittany came from Carter's account.

Apart from this, my research consisted of hiking parts of the South West Coast Path, which was created for the Revenue Service to hunt smugglers. The first time I hiked across the cliffs to Nelly's Cove to explore it as a setting, a gale nearly blew my husband and me off the cliffs. While rain pelted down, the sun suddenly broke through the clouds and a rainbow appeared, reaching from the headland down to the sea and ending in Nelly's Cove. It seemed like a sign and I knew the cove had to be the *Rapide's* anchorage. Another interesting thing happened when I first hiked down to Frenchman's Creek. At the time, the path was very overgrown and there was nobody about but my eldest daughter and me. It was terribly quiet, yet I could've sworn we weren't alone—we both felt as if someone walked behind us. This eerie feeling in what is one of the most beautiful places I've ever visited made it even easier to picture the past and Isabel hearing the call of the ocean. Cornwall is such a magical place that the experience didn't surprise me.

While most of the locations are historically accurate, some places have sprung from my imagination, most notably Jack's estate in Roskorwell, as well as Weatherston Hall and Woodbury House. Isabel's cottage is fictional, though there is an 'old pilchard shed' in Helford. The customs house in St Keverne worked for the book, but in 1808 the closer customs house was in Gweek and in 1822 this was moved near to Helford Village. The Shipwrights Arms in Helford has existed for centuries and remains a lovely, cosy pub, but Tom Holder the innkeeper is my own creation, as are all the other characters in the book. There wasn't a Crown Inn in Manaccan; with a possible informer innkeeper I felt couldn't use the real pub there for a setting. There was a Revenue Cutter called *Swallow*, but her part in this story is imagined, and the cutter *Rapide* is entirely fictional—I based her layout on ships' plans from the time. There have been ten Royal Navy ships named *HMS Hornet,* though none were a frigate anchored in the Helford River.

During the writing of the novel, I've consulted maps, moon cycles and depth charts in order to render the smuggling operations and Isabel's experiences as accurate as possible, but it may be that certain coves in the book are deeper or shallower than in reality and the same goes for sections of the river. Lastly, I've tried to strike a balance between Isabel's striving for independence and the struggle women faced, and can only hope I've succeeded. Besides all of the above, I love writing about love, which holds its own kind of magic, both in Isabel's world as well as in our own.